Gary Sinclair is one
only has healed him
also teach us how its ..., body, and spirit. Gary Sinclair
and *Healing Alex* delivers.

—Doug O'Brien, Doug O'Brien and Associates, NY

*Healing Alex* is so timely. There is not a single soul within reach of this book that has not inwardly longed for healing and restoration. The stresses and complications of modern society have battered us all. For some, healing is an *impossible* proposition. The truth is that there are NO impossible situations, only situations that *seem impossible* at a certain level of knowledge and awareness. Elevate your level of awareness just a tiny bit, and some situations will suddenly move from "impossible" to "obvious." This book elevates awareness! And through its reading, many will find the restoration and healing they seek. We have had the blessing of knowing and working with Gary Sinclair, and he is truly a man raised up for such a time as this.

—Waring and Jackie Wong, Real Estate Professionals

Awesome and inspiring, Healing Alex by Gary Sinclair borders on sheer genius that can only come by Divine inspiration. Healing Alex would have helped millions after 9–11. It still will, because you … are feeling the call to read it now.

—Eldon Turner, Lifestyle Editor–Estylo Magazine, Director of Music–Hollywood Lutheran Church, Hollywood, CA.

*Healing Alex* by Gary Sinclair is *not* a book about religion but a compelling investigative teaching of various alternative approaches revealing the real healing system of life. Healing Alex is a *must own* for anyone who pays attention and has a desire to change the patterns their 60,000 complete thoughts a day produces. It will help you to stop seeking love and realize, *you are that,* and thus allow receiving love to become the evidence that you are a giver.

— Mary Newton, Executive Assistant

WOW … an absolutely amazing story … and yet this truth is what I have been seeking for years. I feel like a bright light has just come on in a really dark room of my life. I guess the Universe provides enlightenment when and where you least expect it. You have taken what so many of us have searched for and struggled with for years, and boiled it down to this sweet, easy to swallow substance that if taken, will cure many, many ills. I finally understand "Love you to Life" and now I am learning Love begins in me!

—Tami Voss–Small Business Owner

From the beginning, Gary's words mesmerized me and made me feel as though I was right there experiencing everything that was transpiring. I waited breathlessly to see what would happen next. His characters are real people with human dimensions, and their world is a real world down to the minute sensory details. Through it all, his compassion for people shines as the dominant theme.

—Bonita Lillie, Author *Hands–On Essays*

A story of a young man's journey, *Healing Alex* by Gary Sinclair; a learning experience out of innocence lost. When a special person enters Alex's life and teaches him how to heal himself, love and self–discovery are the primary words that set Alex free onto a new path to teaching others. There's an Alex in all of us waiting for that special person to enter our lives. *This book is that special person.*

—Richard Pascente, Stylist

For *Healing Alex* by Gary Sinclair to be so direct, flowing, and in many ways simple, it is odd to imagine upon reflection how it could have such an impact in my day to day life But it did and still does. From memories as inconsequential as a bad traffic day to lost loved ones, life can start to feel cozy, round, and soft, and smell like spring … well read it, you will understand. Not only can it change your life, but the story itself is beautiful.—Joshua B. Warren, University Student

Spirituality is an important part of our being, and I believe very much in the power of healing. It's not just for those many years ago, but it is here and available for us today. Gary Sinclair's teaching on the paths to healing fit with what I believe to be truth for our lives today. I've had the pleasure of meeting Gary and found his words in day to day life reflect what he writes. As the old saying goes, "practice what you preach" and Gary can be found guilty of doing just that. His writing can direct us all to new life if we will but open our minds and our hearts to receive.

—Rev. Larry Abel

"When the Student is ready, the Teacher will appear!" Life changing is the Teacher that appears in Healing Alex. While most still seek... in the most simple of ways, Gary Sinclair unfolds answers and help we all never stop looking for. To all, and especially my friends... this book is for you!—Lori Donato, Song Stylist

It is absolutely refreshing how much truth is in this work of fiction. *Healing Alex* is a very beautiful example of spirit and energy; two things the people of this world clearly long for.... It really couldn't come at a better time.

—Robert McDonald, Grant Writer

*Healing Alex* is entertaining, inspiring and often deeply moving. Gary Sinclair has used a flowing work of fiction to present life–changing healing techniques effective regardless of the reader's religious background or beliefs. The healing potential of this book is breathtakingly phenomenal. *Healing Alex* is truly one of the greatest divinely inspired books of our time for expanding the reader's perception of their place in the universe and the potential they hold.

—Stan Stevens, Web Administrator, England

The words go deep, so rich in truth, yet so utterly simple. I definitely am not the same person that began reading this book. It has changed my life dramatically and inspired me so deeply. I thank God for Gary Sinclair's integrity and brave expression of what is in his heart. The Light brightly shines through each page of this inspiring and liberating book making crystal clear spiritual and energetic truths. I am now Love Living more completely than ever before. I encourage everyone to try every experiment or experience for yourself. Thank you, Gary, for every powerful word!

—JG, Love Living in Kentucky–Pastor's Wife

A spirited young boy, the love lessons of his grandmother, a stranger that is a deceiver and a stranger that becomes a friend. This is a book of fiction that offers a tangible force of healing and hope. I loved the book, but more importantly, I, like Alex, found a way to use "love to heal." It is life changing and must be experienced by all ages, young and old.

—D. Wilson

*Healing Alex* is a very powerful and riveting story about the power of love and how to use this gift from God. It's very deep and enlightening, yet simple to apply. Gary Sinclair's book has taught me how to use this beautiful gift of love, and changed my life. Thank you!

—M. Hilton, Bookkeeper

An amazing and divinely inspired work, Healing Alex by Gary Sinclair is a book that will reach millions with their ability to unlock the God Given power of love and what love can do in their life and through their life to help them and others reach their highest potential.

—Jon C., National Business Manager

# HEALING ALEX

Gary Sinclair

# HEALING ALEX

Tate Publishing & *Enterprises*

Published by Tate Publishing & Enterprises, LLC
127 E. Trade Center Terrace | Mustang, Oklahoma 73064 USA
1.888.361.9473 | www.tatepublishing.com

Tate Publishing is committed to excellence in the publishing industry. The company reflects the philosophy established by the founders, based on Psalm 68:11,
*"The Lord gave the word and great was the company of those who published it."*


*Cover design by Tyler Evans*
*Interior design by Blake Brasor*
*Edited by Vince Conn*
*Special editing assistance by Barbara Wixen–Prevo*
*Song Lyrics: I Can Only Imagine by Bart Millard used by permission Simpleville Music, Inc.*
*(As sung by Mercy Me)*
*Song Lyrics line from Butterfly Kisses by Bob Carlisle*

Published in the United States of America

ISBN: 978-1-60799-817-4
1. Self-help, General
2. Body, Mind & Spirit, Healing, Prayer & Spiritual
09.08.4

Healing Alex is dedicated to all the people who have gone through my personal Life Clean Out!© Training Program and Celebrate Life© Seminars and learned how to be *Love Living*.

Having taken nearly every form of energetic healing modality training, the list of appreciative names would take pages. To you, be blessed as you read *Healing Alex*, discovering the "Gifts Go On!" To those involved with all the extensive editing, you have helped make this book *a miracle made real* for others.

The real techniques and healing processes explained in this book are dedicated to you the reader. May *Healing Alex* renew your mind so that you understand what your spirit already knows as this work in Cyberphysiology brings you renewed life and a love that knows no measure. Truly, love changes all it touches and pulls whatever it touches toward its highest potential. May it open truths that instill in you the opportunity to reach your highest potential.

—Gary Sinclair, Author
Cyberphysiologist

# Healing Alex:
## The Miracle

Book One

"You live your life as either a warning or an example, and those around you know which way you live."

—Gary Sinclair

# Chapter

It was an awful thing to have happen in the woods, and Alex knew it. You would, too, if you were in his shoes and had been there with them. The faster he ran, the more his heart felt like it was coming out of his chest. He shivered as if cold, not realizing that fear and panic had overtaken him as he sought the quickest route out of the woods. Everything, even the trees, seemed larger than life, and every sound in any direction made his stomach jump.

*Where was Joe?* His brain raced. Having taken off running in total panic, he had no idea, but Alex was not lost. He knew where he was and where he would need to run to reach safety. What should he do now? That was the question.

As a good–looking lad of twelve, he had been raised in what was said to be a model family in his prim and proper community in the upper state of Maine. He had grown accustomed to going out into the woods to smell the pine scent in the air. Spring was his favorite time as everything that added new green gave off a fragrance that he could identify after a little practice. In Maine, the evergreens stayed ever–green, adding new growth each spring.

Often, he would just pull what looked like a lump of leaking sap from a favorite overgrown spruce tree as he began making his way along his preferred trail, deeper into the woods. The favorite tree was at the first split in the main trail. Squirrels seemed to know him, as he had been doing this for years. If deer were near, they would raise their heads majestically, staying motionless until they were assured that the friendly energy they were feeling was only Alex. Were it not, they would bolt out of sight nearly instantly, showing only a white tail flash.

Oh, how Alex loved the woods! Any time he had to write a paper for school, his woods managed to make it into the manuscript in some way. Every child creates a favorite place. For Alex, it was not in his mind; it was in his heart, and it drew him deeply in as often as possible. To him, this was indeed his "Hundred–Acre Wood," although it really was larger than that.

He never expected to encounter a stranger that afternoon as he took his favorite right fork deeper into the woods. He once met a boy, Robert, from the other side of the woods. They became friends, and he would often visit Robert's potato farm. He had to take the left fork at the split and a couple of shortcuts to get to Robert's. He pulled a hunk of "spruce gum," as the locals called it, from his favorite marker tree and was taking practice aim at the tail of a squirrel with some small stones when an uneasy feeling came over him. He looked around, not exactly sure what he should be looking for. There were no deer and no bears, which had been known to roam these woods. Putting his hand to his eyes, he looked up and into the deep green of the Maine pines, cedars, and spruce trees.

A voice spoke out from a direction opposite from where Alex was facing. Although Alex was hesitant, not being accustomed to meeting anyone in the woods, the thought flashed through his mind, *Maybe this is the man who owns these woods.* Alex never had met the man.

Walking toward Alex, the man put out his hand in a friendly gesture and said, "Hi there. I wasn't expecting to meet anyone here. My name is, well … my name is … just call me Joe."

They shook hands. Alex was silent, still surprised at encountering a stranger.

Later, Alex would remember the handshake as being warm and the man as being very friendly when he replayed this day repeatedly, hoping that somehow it would change. However, it never did; it always ended the same way.

Alex, noticing another big spruce tree with a couple of big hunks of spruce sap glistening in the sun, asked, "You chew spruce gum?"

The man in the plain, white tee shirt tucked into blue jean shorts replied, "Can't say I have. I'm not from these parts."

Assumptive as he was, Alex created a mental image of Joe visiting with Robert at the potato farm and never questioned more from that direction.

"Where do you live when you're not visiting the farm?" Alex asked.

"I come from a city called Philadelphia."

Alex had been out of potato country only once in his life, just to the city of Bangor, but he knew that Philadelphia was far, far away.

Alex pulled at the sap discharge dried onto the bark of the tree, radiantly golden as the sunlight passed through it, only to find that it was thoroughly crusted on.

"Here. Use my knife," Joe offered. In one swift motion, a beauty of a carving instrument was properly presented, handle first. It took Joe only a quick moment to produce it from a small backpack he had dropped to the ground. The backpack seemed to have come from out of nowhere, and Alex noticed that the straps were as white as Joe's tee shirt. The small pack itself was made from a hunter's print of multiple brown patches.

It took only a slight wiggle with the side of the blade firmly planted under the drooping sap to free it. Picking off the small fragments of bark that came with it, Alex said, "When you put this in your mouth, just hold it there for a few minutes so it can warm up and turn into gum. If you just chomp on it like a gum ball, you'll end up with splintered pieces everywhere." Alex's mind flashed back to a time when he had done just that and learned his lesson.

"Nice knife!" Alex exclaimed as he handed it back. Joe wiped the edges against his blue jeans, checking to make sure that the unique, German–manufactured design was free from sap.

"I only use it for very special occasions." Joe said at the same time that Alex began to speak.

Alex stopped then began again, saying, "My dad's hunting buddy had a knife that fancy. We used it when we went hunting."

"Yeah, hunting," Joe repeated. "You might say that's how I use it as well. Is this the best path, or do you recommend another, for just getting lost in the woods?" Joe asked.

"Oh, this path goes nowhere." Alex replied, adding, "Everything to the right fork comes out nowhere. But I guess I mean the left fork for you, the one we're on," he said, still believing that Joe was staying at his friend, Robert's, farm.

"How far can you go?" Joe asked, pointing as though they should go on together with their journey deeper into the woods.

"Well," Alex hesitated, his mind working its way through to all of the familiar endings, "you never do come out; you just turn around and come back."

"Do you cross any water, encounter any clearings, or climb any ridges?" Joe asked as if interested in finding a particular location.

"No. Not really. There is this one place. If you stay straight each time, the path offers you a chance to change directions where butterflies hatch this time of year. I know they are hatching because I saw several from my bedroom window this morning and many more earlier. You know the type," Alex said, holding out his hands in a three–dimensional shape. "Big and orange and yellow and black and…"

"Yellow Swallow Tails, I think they're called," Joe said, pointing to a flutter weaving merrily through the trees just above their heads. Without hesitation, Joe was quick to say, "May I come watch with you?"

Alex blamed himself for being so stupid and later realized that this man to whom he had said *yes* didn't even know his name.

"Do you live with both of your parents?" Joe asked as they passed one of the places where they could have chosen another direction.

"My father is in the army. He's the team leader of a bomb squad in the war," Alex said. "And my mother works for a doctor."

"Do they know you're out here?" asked Joe, continuing his line of questioning.

"Oh, no. I come here all the time by myself. Dad has walked every trail with me at some time or another as he talks to me about growing up. He calls it man talk. I miss him when he goes away like this."

"Well, he should be home soon," Joe replied in a somewhat comforting tone.

Having answered Joe's questions, Alex's thoughts returned to butterflies. Eager to see them escape their cocoons again, the two traveled on silently. Their footsteps would occasionally snap a twig. One of them would have to hold a branch out of the way, only to hear the whoosh it made as it returned to the position nature intended.

Alex was so eager to make it to the clearing that he almost forgot he was with someone else. The sight he beheld when he stepped into the field nearly left him breathless. He remembered the stunning beauty of the butterflies from past visits here, but what surrounded him now far exceeded his expectations. The air all around looked like a small whirlwind of orange and yellow flowers, all fluttering in a natural breeze. There seemed to be a pattern in the chaos of activity. Alex had studied butterflies and knew this was where they were trying their wings for the first time.

Without noticing what Joe was doing, Alex headed to the far side of the clearing where he knew the flowers were an attraction to the butterflies. In this location, he found a feeding frenzy among the full–fragrance blooms. He looked everywhere for a chrysalis from which a butterfly would emerge and found several with signs of life about to come forth into the bright sunlight. This was something Alex had done before. It always amazed him that something that looked so helpless could come out of that little case, dry out, unwrap, and stretch its wings to fly.

It was his father who had taught him not to help in the process that the butterfly must go through after seeing Alex stretch the wings on one particular butterfly, only to find that it still could not fly. Dad explained that it had to stretch its own wings so that blood might inflate them to ready them for flight. After that, he left chrysalis creatures alone and just watched in amazement at what God created. They would lay dormant for a period then awaken and come out to unfold their wings and fly. In the back of his mind and with a smile on his face, he could hear his father's voice singing, *Oh I marvel at the wisdom of my God, Oh I marvel at the wisdom of my God. He made …*

Being unaccustomed to having anyone else along when he went into the woods, Alex had forgotten about Joe until movement caught his eye. Toward the opening of the path they had come in on, Joe had taken what looked like a smooth, thin, silver blanket out of his small pack and was spreading it on the ground.

"What's that?" Alex asked, not sure what to make of a blanket that shone brightly in the late morning sun.

"It's a space blanket," the reply came. "It really is a blanket. It's so small you can fold it up to nearly nothing and carry it in a pack. If you were lost, it could keep you warm on a cold night."

Alex drew closer, delighted at learning something new. Touching the surface of the blanket, it came as a surprise to him that it was so thin. In fact, it was hard to look at because the sun's reflection did his eyes no favor.

"Lie down," Joe said patting a spot next to him as he stretched himself out, looking relaxed. "Just look up and see all those butterflies. Man, this is one sight you don't want to miss."

There was no hesitation in Alex as he reclined on the twin–sized blanket next to Joe. It was true. The butterflies seemed to be inches away, and as the two remained motionless and silent, the magnificent new butterflies landed on them repeatedly.

It was quite some time, with Joe watching Alex's amazement, before Alex remembered again that he was not alone. When he did, he said to Joe, "I'll bet you'll come here a lot now."

"No, not really; probably only today," came the reply.

Thinking back, Alex began to wonder out loud, "How did you find that trail?" Pausing, he added, "And why only today?"

Joe responded, “Remember when you crossed in front of the church and went down the dirt road toward the woods?”

“Yes.”

“Well, I wondered where you were going,” Joe said. “There were no houses on that side of the road, and it looked like that short dirt road only went into the woods.”

Suddenly, Alex jumped, startled. A hawk seemed to swoop out of nowhere, grabbing up a field mouse just a few body lengths away. Neither human nor mouse had seen what was coming, and both he and Joe felt their hearts pound as though from an electrical shock. Maybe it was from the shock of the hawk’s dive, but the words had come and gone, and Alex seemed not to have understood the implication of what Joe had said. It was something that Alex should have paid attention to.

When they began to breathe naturally, their hearts slowing to a more rhythmic pace, Joe took out his precious knife and laid it where Alex could see it, as if adding a sense of safety to the environment.

Alex went back to watching the butterflies as they settled back into their mesmerizing patterns. There were no more interruptions until he noticed that Joe’s hand was moving. It was directly over Alex’s waist, as though he were reaching for something on the other side of Alex. Alex also noticed that the knife remained on the blanket where Joe had placed it moments before. Then Joe’s hovering hand came down—right where his father had told him no one should ever …

It all happened so fast. It got ugly, quickly becoming a haunting experience that would be inescapable in his mind. It was over. Running … running … running … Joe was behind him somewhere. At knife point, he had promised to tell no one. Joe had told him that he knew where Alex lived and would kill him if he told. The fear of dying for telling the truth made his heart pump even faster, and he was grateful that he knew all the paths out of the woods.

He ran in the direction of a side trail, knowing that if he chose a path that led straight out of the woods, he might face that man again. There was nothing about this day that he ever wanted to see or feel again. His body would occasionally shiver in revulsion, and he felt a shock even greater than when the hawk had taken the field mouse. This was different; this was Alex's own life or death.

*Which path, which path …* his mind went on, still trying to decide which dirt path was the safest escape route. Then the thought hit him: *Dad won't be home. Dad is over there.* He thought of his mother, and then tears began to fall. Although Alex loved his mother, his bond was strongest with his dad, just as his sister Kaitlyn's was with Mom.

*No, no!* his brain told him. *These are things Dad said I can only talk about with him, and absolutely, positively to no one else. If Dad were here, he would repeat that this is something private for us to deal with. It's personal and private and not to be discussed with anyone else unless I say we need to. I want to protect you from any possibility of danger from talking to the wrong person*—more danger he did not need.

*Okay, okay,* he told himself. *I'll go to Robert's. He can help. It will be a secret.* Then his mind flashed back to the clearing. *No! Joe will kill me. I know he will.*

He remembered the last secret he told Robert. It was about someone in school who kept trying to cheat during exams. *No, I can't go to Robert's; he tells everything. Everyone in school would know that I've been …*

Anyone close enough would have heard the smack as a branch met Alex's forehead. The impact was enough to slow Alex down and cause him to think this through a little more. *There is no one I can talk to since Dad's gone. I need to get home. Yes, I need to get home before Mom does, before she can demand to know where I've been. She always knows when I'm lying. She has that way of looking at me and saying, Honey, I just don't believe you, so why don't we sit down and have a little talk.* Mom didn't seem to mind stepping in for Dad while he was away, but this is one time Alex was going to have to man it up and wait for Dad to come home.

*Oh, my heart,* he thought, putting his hand on his chest and feeling the pounding beat as he took a deep breath. After a few more breaths, he began to think about all the other paths that would lead to the outer edge of the woods. He finally decided that the one farther north would be a good place to see the entrance where he and the stranger had started into the woods.

He slowed as he mumbled a prayer that Joe would be nowhere to be found. His fear was that he might be waiting for him there, just to warn Alex one more time that he would kill him if he told anyone.

As he neared the edge of the woods, the shock of it all was once more made real as his mind's eye flashed back to the hand that hovered over him as he lay watching butterflies in the clearing. Then, like a movie in fast forward, it played all the way through to his escape. Alex might never have realized he could escape. It was at the moment when Joe's attention seemed finally to wane that Alex took it as a clue to run like hell. There was no looking back; there was only the urge to run like his life depended on it. The butterflies were forgotten.

Realizing that he was now at the edge of the woods, thinking of all that he had been through, the tears flowed once again. He needed his father now. Deep breathing helped his energy to return a little; however, in his mind, the drama began to play out once more, getting faster, the clarity more intense, as it played: "Hi there. I wasn't expecting to meet anyone here," Joe in his white tee shirt and jean shorts, the warm handshake, the backpack, the spruce gum, the knife, the walking trail, the butterflies, the silver blanket, the hawk, the hand. Oh, God, the hand. A gut wrenching reaction continued to devour his energy and solidify even deeper into a more painful reaction.

Cautiously, he peered out as he neared the end of the path at the entrance to the field that wrapped around this part of the woods. His hand went over his heart, still racing in panic, while his breathing remained heavy. Moving ever so slowly, hoping that he would not give away his location, he scanned the area until he knew for sure that no one was nearby. *Is it safe to cross the field?* he asked himself as he looked toward the highway he needed to cross. *What if he's there and spots me running?* This thought started the panic again, causing Alex to hear, '*I will kill you!*' reverberating through his mind as though from an echo chamber. Suddenly, he recalled that those were the last words he heard Joe scream at him.

Alex spotted the white cross at the top of the New England–style white clapboard church. "We never lock our doors," Pastor McGregor had told him just last week at the church anniversary dinner. Although the members were mostly young families, the church was celebrating a century and a half this summer. Inside, it had always seemed old and musty to Alex. When sunlight streamed through the stained glass windows, there was always enough dust in the air from the activity within to allow beams of colored light to cross the room. A table in the front of the sanctuary held a big open Bible, a chalice, and a loaf of broken bread that had been varnished to preserve it.

*I can make it,* Alex thought. *All I have to do is run straight to the road, directly across, and through the front door.*

Without looking back toward the first path he had entered earlier, Alex ran at his best lightning speed until he had crossed the road, made it inside the church, and closed the door. Only then did he feel secure enough to look across the road to assure himself that he was not being followed. He had already made plans to exit through the back door in one of two directions, should the case merit.

Just to be on the safe side, Alex locked the door. He knew it wasn't the right thing to do, but no one was ever there during the afternoon. Even Pastor McGregor, who comes in the mornings to practice his sermons, goes to visit someone from the church every afternoon. Assured that Pastor's old, beat–up wreck of a car was not still in the side lot, it seemed okay to lock the door.

His heart quieted a bit as he felt for the first time that he was safe. The worst had to be over. Now he had to find a way to hide all of the feelings and emotions still warring for his attention before he could face his mother. *Oh no. Mother. What can I tell her?* The thought surfaced as though he had spoken it aloud.

His mind would not allow him to dwell there, so he began to scan the inner sanctum of his home church. He walked to the back pew on the left side and sat on the stuffed burgundy velvet seat cushion.

Ignoring his pounding heart, he searched the sun streaks crossing the room for the usual dance of the dust motes he was accustomed to seeing on Sundays. The church felt different today than when it was three–quarters full of friends.

Noticing the loaf of varnished broken bread, he remembered a time when he had stood there reading verses out of the big Bible about how God loves us and cares for us. In his head, he asked, '*Where were you?*' without any expectation of an answer.

With a deep sigh, he began to relax. Without realizing that a numbness of sorts was overtaking his body, he truly did relax in spite of what had happened to him. He soon found that he was able to get up and move about without fear that someone was waiting to pounce on him. He did take a glance out the left window, but expected that he would find nothing out of order. Even at his young age, he knew that someone who commits a crime would want to get out of town. Still, he wanted to remain cautious, so he made his way to the back, planning to exit to his home just a block away. Suddenly, he remembered that he had locked the front door and returned to unlock it before making his escape.

As he passed the altar, he looked at the cross and thought again, *God, where were you? Please, oh please, send my father home!*

Exiting through the back door, Alex felt the need to move quickly again. He picked up speed and quickly completed the distance between the church and his home. Once there, he closed the door and hurriedly peeked out through the windows—checking all directions and hoping he would find nothing to fear.

"What are you looking for?" his sister, Kaitlyn, asked in typical inquisition–style. She had come downstairs, believing that her mother had come home. Mom's job as a nurse often kept her late at the medical clinic.

Thinking quickly, trying not to let on that anything was wrong, he authoritatively replied, "I was making sure the locks work."

"Duh, like they're all broken," Kaitlyn said, heading toward the kitchen. "Grandma sent over a plate of molasses cookies if you want one."

Following her to the kitchen, he realized that it was comforting to see a familiar face, even if it belonged to his little sister. What could he tell her? His inner voice answered, *Nothing!*

Grabbing one of Grandma's famous cookies and a glass of milk, he headed toward the stairs to escape to his bedroom to figure out how to handle Mom.

"What do you have all over you?" his sister asked as he mounted the first step.

"Nothing that I know of," Alex replied.

Kaitlyn, in a proving–herself–right attitude, caught him at about the fifth stair, where he had stopped to take a drink of milk. She began to brush his shoulders and back in her aggressive prove–you–wrong style.

With a shock at being touched, Alex pulled back immediately in a swooping motion, made it to the top of the stairs, and headed to his bedroom.

"My, aren't we touchy today," Kaitlyn called after him as she turned around and headed back down.

By the time Kaitlyn put her foot on the bottom stair, Mom's hand was turning the knob on the front door.

"Hi, love," Mom said as she smiled and headed toward the kitchen, led by her nose. "Oh my, Grandma did it again!" she exclaimed as she picked up one of those flat, six–inch wonders that would melt in her mouth, especially when slightly warmed in the oven. That heat softened them, bringing out the butter flavor.

"Is Alex home?" she asked, beginning to make preparations for supper, despite the fact that they both had molasses cookie crumbs in the corners of their mouths.

"Yes, Mom," Kaitlyn replied. "He's up in his room. I think he's been out running."

"Alex … running?" Mother mused.

"Yes, I think so. He was hot and sweaty, and I had to brush stuff off him. I guess he fell down and didn't think to brush himself off."

"Oh. Okay," Mom replied, accepting Kaitlyn's assessment. After all, Kaitlyn liked to be right and usually did whatever was necessary to prove it.

Mom started fixing supper. It wasn't long before Alex, fresh from scrubbing everything over and over in the shower, yet still feeling dirty, came out of his room. Realizing that Mom was home and that he would have to face the truth, he prayed. *Please God, you know I can't hide anything from Mom and Dad. Oh God, how I wish my father were here so I could talk to him.*

As he headed down the stairs, he mulled over several scenarios that had run through his head in the shower while trying to scrub those horrible feelings out of his skin. Some of the scenarios might possibly work. Clearing the last stair and heading toward the kitchen, he tried to come to a decision on which one to use.

"Kaitlyn said you've been out running and fell down." Mom started. "Sorry about the fall. How far did you run?"

Without hesitating, he responded, "From the farthest side of the backwoods where Dad and I used to go to see the butterflies." He realized that he was actually telling the truth, and that Mom should suspect nothing wrong since it was true. He put his hand over his stomach as, once again, the sickening feeling came over him.

"Good for you," she replied, letting her smile show her approval. "Your Dad would be proud you. Now help me set the table."

It now seemed as though the day's trauma had just been dismissed. To his way of thinking, and to his great relief, the burden of having to tell Mom had been lifted, causing Alex to take a deep, relaxing breath.

Smiling inside, he remembered that Mom had said it was Kaitlyn who had told her that he'd been out running. Again, she was right. He was pleased to take another deep breath and relax even more.

"You're okay, right?" Mom asked.

Alex thought, *Oh no. Here it comes.*

"I mean, your sister said you fell and got covered in debris."

Once again, Kaitlyn saved his hide. He replied, "It was nothing. I did a good ground roll and didn't realize what I had picked up on my back."

Once dinner was over, Alex immediately headed back to his room with another flat, molasses comfort cookie in his hand. This was Kaitlyn's night to clean up, and downstairs was no place he wanted to be unless Dad was there.

He tried his best to stay calm, but the moment it went quiet, his mental movie began to run again. It would begin with hearing the stranger's voice, then it would proceed to seeing the man's image, and continue on through to the trail where Alex had changed directions to make sure he wasn't being followed.

He got up and put on a homemade combo CD of some of his favorite music. It played through the speakers of his stereo, a gift his father had given him before leaving for the war. He had served his first tour overseas when Alex was younger. This time, he was there by special request from the President of the United States because of his special training and skills. Even Dad had to humbly admit that not many people were as good at defusing explosives as he was. "It's one thing to put them together," Dad would say, "but it's quite another to take them apart."

Alex sang out loud to the first song and then the next. It seemed to be helping his mood. The second song was one that his father loved. Together, they had attended a Mercy Me concert, where he heard the song for the first time. Even though Kaitlyn came along, it felt like it was his special night with Dad and Mom. It was his twelfth birthday.

The song, "I Can Only Imagine," made Alex smile as he sang along, remembering how Dad reached over and patted his knee. As he kept singing, he came to the words, "Surrounded by your glory, what will my heart feel?" Instantly, his mind was back in the woods where there were no signs of God anywhere. He pushed the skip button on the CD player, thinking that the next song would be better. After all, this was his favorite music.

As it started to play, he recognized the song by Bob Carlisle about a dad and his little girl. He and his dad had made this song meaningful to themselves as well. It played on to the bridge, where the title and theme rang out, "She gave me butterfly kisses." Back flashed the movie again, only this time it began with him lying on the silver blanket with kiss–landing butterflies coming down from above. He quickly pushed the skip button again, hoping to get to a safe place in his mind. The music became more bearable; however, it never really did what he was hoping it would do.

It wasn't the volume level or the music selections that were bothering him. It was as though someone had pushed the repeat memory–movie button inside of Alex's head, and what was showing on his home screen didn't get any better. His whole body seemed to have felt the effects of it once again. *He knows where I live. I heard him say so. Am I really safe here?* And his mind would show him the beautiful knife, now horribly etched into his painful memories. For Alex, long–term suffering seemed to be settling in, as is often the case for people who suffer traumatic experiences.

Thinking of times past when he'd had a headache, he remembered that two aspirins sometimes helped. Since Kaitlyn had conveniently declared that he had taken a tumble, he headed back downstairs to ask his mom for two aspirins to help relieve his body aches; he easily received the permission he sought.

No one noticed that he added another glass of milk, which really didn't seem to be agreeing with him, and another molasses cookie with the two aspirins he held in his hand as he headed back up the stairs.

After hours of thinking and remembering, and several practice conversations with his dad, Alex finally exhausted himself into a restless sleep.

In one of those conversations, he did extremely well practicing at being a man and sucking it up the way he believed he needed to. It seemed like it would be easy to tell his dad what had really happened that day. He tried to allow his dad to talk in these practice conversations, but it never seemed to help. There were no answers. All attempts ended with believing that it would have been so different if Dad were home right now.

In his restless sleep, the projector of his mind kept running his movie, waking him with a start. In his dreams, someone found out what had happened to him and told his friends at school. In those frightening moments, he was reminded of the high school girl the kids talked about. Bubble was the name he had heard them call her.

She got so sick from something awful that had happened to her that she couldn't even keep her food down at school and was sent away to a special school. Kaitlyn said Mom told her that it was one of those things that should never have happened. Alex had once heard Bubble tell his father, "If only they'd lock up my stepfather and throw away the key." By that afternoon, she was meeting with Pastor McGregor, whom Dad knew would help her.

After remembering that Bubble had been sent away, and not wanting the same fate to befall him, Alex vowed, *I won't tell anyone. I won't even tell my dad.* With his life at stake, he thought his vow was a good one.

With that, he finally slipped deeper into sleep. In the closet of his heart, he was locking up the pain and suffering and vowing for his life's sake never to let it out. At his young age, he was on his way to becoming like many people who experience trauma, who hide the pain deep inside rather than seek healing for the wounds in their hearts.

Whether from exhaustion or from his vow never to tell anyone, Alex finally fell into a restless sleep when his mind's theater stopped playing the movie of his painful experiences.

# Chapter 2

It was early when Alex awoke. Even without a clock to look at, he knew by the daylight that it was morning. At his body's demand, he got up and made his way to the bathroom, being careful to listen for who else might be up. The only sounds he heard were coming from his mother's room.

"Alex, are you up? Can you get our suitcases from the basement?" Mother's voice echoed down the hall.

*Suitcases?* Alex thought. *Why suitcases?*

"Well, Alex? Will you get them, or do I have to do it myself?"

Shuffling sleepily down the hall to Mom, he discovered that she was indeed placing clothes on the bed in preparation to pack a bag. Mom's butterfly print shirt, a favorite of Alex's, was there on top of a stack of blouses. There it goes again—the movie.

"Well, are you or aren't you, Alex?" came the question again.

"Where are you going?" Alex asked vaguely, scenes from the butterfly movie still running.

"I told you," Mom replied. "Don't you remember? This is the week you're staying with Grandma while I take Kaitlyn with me to camp. This is my week to be the nurse at church camp. I know I told you, Alex. And you said that you didn't want to go. You asked if you could stay with Grandma. It's all arranged now. I need suitcases—two, to be exact. Let's make it the two big ones, because we know Kaitlyn will have to take half her room with her," Mom said, chuckling at the truth of what she spoke.

Turning toward the basement where the suitcases were, his thoughts turned once more to his Dad. *Where is help when you need your father?* his inner voice asked.

The morning's activities progressed rather quickly. Included in the schedule were blueberry pancakes with the fresh blueberries Kaitlyn had picked the day before to help Mom. While doing the cleanup, Alex noticed that the baker's dozen, as Grandma always called it, was nearly gone. He smiled inside, knowing that he could convince Grandma to make more of her special cookies.

Maybe it won't be bad going to Grandma's. She doesn't get personal. Going to church camp would just mean having to stay in a bunkhouse with friends, as the nurse's cabin has only one small bed. Kaitlyn would sleep on blankets on the floor. She would do whatever was necessary to impress the others that her mother was the nurse. Alex was just thankful that he wouldn't be going to camp this year.

When it was time to take their suitcases to the car, the phone rang. Alex could tell from his mother's side of the conversation that it was Pastor McGregor, even though Alex wasn't quite able to make sense of it. Something about needing help and of course he can, as she was off to camp.

When Mom hung up, she looked at Alex and smiled. "Pastor McGregor is taking a carload of kids and supplies with him up to camp this morning and needs someone to come stay at the church. He has someone coming to bring him something this morning, and he can't make contact with them to say that he'll be at camp. He asked whether you might be willing to hang around there, at least until someone shows up, and I told him that of course you can."

This would not be a problem, since Grandma's house is only three blocks away. He certainly can wait for the person Pastor McGregor is expecting.

"Alex," Mom called out, "you need to pack something to go to Grandma's. That includes clean underwear, young man. You hear me?"

"Yes, Mom," he replied, mounting the stairs with a little more excitement about his day. He grabbed his backpack, which instantly triggered images of another backpack and a knife that he touched. He shivered, reaching into his dresser drawer. *Oh, thank you, God,* Alex half–prayed, half–thought. *Grandma loves me.*

Soon, they were all in the yard, with Mom reminding Alex that Grandma had promised to bring him up for the Wednesday night camp meeting and that they'd all have dinner together. "It won't be long. I'll see you soon, love." She said, as she hugged him while pointing to Kaitlyn to get into the car. "Hug grandma for me. She is such a dear. You have a good time, but no teasing. And Alex," she said grabbing his face with both hands and looking straight into his eyes, "no hiding Grandma's teeth like last time!"

He laughed, remembering Grandma's reaction.

"Alex," Mother reminded him, "you'd better get on over to the church now. Pastor was nearly ready to leave when he called. He said that Robert Ackers wasn't there yet, but that he had called the farm and learned that he was on his way."

*Robert? Yes, Robert Ackers.* His mind wandered back to the story he vowed never to tell. *I can't tell him anything,* he thought. *I can't tell anyone anything.*

Walking to the church, his backpack casually slung over to one side in his usual fashion statement, he noticed a Ford truck pulling up, with *Ackers Potato Farm* printed on the side.

As Alex stepped onto the grass at the entrance to the church lot, Robert slid out through the passenger door of the truck, gave a half wave, and said, "Where were you yesterday? I went all the way to the butterfly field searching for you, and you were nowhere around." Robert reached into the back of the truck and pulled out his small suitcase.

*Oh my God!* Alex screamed inside his mind. His face registered his fear, and that shiver he had experienced so often since yesterday afternoon, returned. *Robert could have been killed!* his mind shouted. However, no such words could he utter.

Already heading toward the pastor's car, not looking back at Alex; Robert was not waiting for any explanation. Alex was relieved; he could let the matter drop since Robert hadn't seen his reaction.

Pastor McGregor, with his full beard and even fuller belly, came out through the side door of the church office, dressed rather casually for a man of the cloth. "Oh, Alex. Yes. Glad you could come. I just need someone to wait here for about an hour, maybe less. I have someone coming to bring me an envelope. Just put it on the shelf in the back of the pulpit, and I'll get it when I get back from camp. I really appreciate this, Alex." Pastor McGregor said as he slid his hand across Alex's shoulders, reminding Alex of when Kaitlyn brushed off the debris from his back. Without thinking, Alex's hand once again went to his middle to steady *that* feeling in his stomach as he slightly pulled away.

"You okay, Alex?" Pastor asked, sensing something was wrong. "You're staying with Granny, right?" was his next question.

"Yep," was all he could manage, hoping that no further conversation would be necessary.

"Well, tell Granny that the kids will love that bag of molasses cookies she brought over yesterday. They're all packed in the car, ready to go with us. Except one," he chuckled as he patted his belly. "But then," he added, "I guess it's going along with us as well," and he laughed enough to make the boys smile. He was known as one who appreciated invitations for dinner. Because he was a widower, the women of the church did what they could to ensure that he rarely had to cook for himself.

"All in," the pastor called, and soon they were off. Alex was just committed to an hour or so at the church, and then he would be off to Grandma's—or so he thought.

Headed toward the back door from which Pastor McGregor had emerged, Alex's thoughts turned to yesterday's escape. He also remembered the feeling of safety inside the church and thus welcomed the warm glow that greeted him. As always, the sun was streaming in, reflecting various colors in its beams. Trying to keep his mind from thoughts of yesterday, he studied the pattern of one particular stained glass window. It was the one with a shepherd holding a staff and a little lamb. Alex was counting the pieces in the window when he began thinking about a sermon he'd heard that told of the lamb as a sacrifice. While he pondered, the front door opened, and a man walked in.

In a way, the stranger immediately reminded him of his father and caused no fear in Alex as a flashback of another stranger would have. This man and Alex's father were close in both height and weight and were similar in other aspects of appearance. His smile was what really caught Alex's attention. It was like sometimes when Dad looked at him, Alex felt like Dad was looking inside of him instead of just looking at his face. Dad called it heart touching, and this man seemed really good at it.

"You're the Williams boy, aren't you?" the man asked.

"Yes."

"You sure look like your dad. What do they call you?"

"William Alexander Williams, III," Alex replied, his chest sticking out a little, proud to be told he looked like his father. "I'm named after my father, my grandfather, and the whole family line, I guess."

And they both smiled.

"The name William is interpreted to mean 'conqueror' or 'protector,' among other attributes," the man, Mr. Parsons, said.

Telling him that his nickname was Alex, he went on to explain to Mr. Parsons that Pastor McGregor had gone to camp and had asked him to stay.

"Then I guess you're waiting to collect this, son," Mr. Parsons said as he reached out to hand Alex a package he had been holding. "You're staying with your grandma while your mom is camp nurse this week?" came the question from this friendly stranger who seemed so much like Alex's father.

"Yes. How did you know?" Alex asked.

"Oh, I study people all the time, Alex. I sort of make it a way of life to understand people; what they do; where they go; how they do it; and ..." He said more, but it seemed to go right over Alex's head.

The next thing Alex remembered was Mr. Parsons saying, "If you'd like, I'll come by and we can sit on Granny's rockers for a porch chat some morning."

Without hesitating, Alex said, "That would be great." After all, this man reminded him of his father. He thought to himself, *Maybe I can talk to him. He doesn't know me, and I don't have to say a thing about* ... Alex clutched his stomach again.

"Glad you feel that way, son. I'm Mr. Parsons, and I would like it very much. It's hard these days to get people to stop and listen," he said. "Best I disappear now." Mr. Parsons turned and headed out the door.

There had been no handshake and certainly no hug of any kind.

Alex put the package on the shelf in the pulpit right where Pastor McGregor had told him to put the envelope, and then looked back at the stained glass he had been counting. Well, no need to know how many pieces there are now. That would make for a good Sunday during–church project. Grabbing his pack, he followed the same way out that Mr. Parsons had taken. It was a good, safe feeling to go out through the front door this time.

It took a short time to get to Grandma's house. It was only three blocks from the church, straight down on the same side of the road. Like many small towns in northern Maine, blocks in Alex's town often consisted of a single house surrounded by open land. There were no skyscrapers to be seen here. Grandma's house was unusual for Maine. Mainers rarely built houses like this. It looked more like something you might find in the South, maybe in Virginia. But like every other house in the area, it was made of whitewashed clapboard. What made it unique was the deck on the second floor, which came out from Grandma's bedroom and faced the woods. It was built directly above a part of the porch that made an L shape around half of the house. With snow like they would get in the winter time, people didn't want an upstairs deck to clear, let alone a half–house porch. Adding to that, with the first signs of cold weather came ice on the wood deck. It still was perfect for Grandma. She didn't care about the ice. She was smart enough to keep a set of cleated rubber straps by the door, which she would put over her shoes, making it easy for her to traverse the porch, go down the wooden stairs, and out to her detached garage where her car was kept protected from the snow. She had Alex and his dad make an extended rail on the bedroom deck with built–in flower boxes. Every spring, she would start seedlings in her kitchen bay window over the sink and produce the most brilliant shades of bright red geraniums, along with multiple colors of zinnias and asters. When they would grow too thick, a bouquet of precious cut flowers would be seen on the communion table at church, adding more color to what already came through the windows. This year was no exception.

Stepping into the yard, it was easy for Alex to see that he needed to mow again. Grandma was one for everything looking sharp. Alex was making the outside lawn area look great by the time he was seven. His father had tried to teach him how to start the gas mower when Alex was six, making it clear to Alex that Dad would be doing the mowing until Alex was big enough to start the mower himself. That was also the first year Alex had tried out for the newly formed Little League in town. He remembers being embarrassed that he couldn't throw a baseball far enough. To add to that insult, he was unable to start the mower even once that year. So his job at the age of six was to walk around picking up anything that needed to be moved as Dad pushed the smoking mower. But this year things were different. To Alex's delight, a new, green mower with *John Deere* in bright yellow letters had been purchased from Chad's Repair Shop.

Grandma came out the kitchen door with two glasses of what Alex hoped was her fresh–squeezed lemonade. Walking to meet Alex, Grandma said, "I didn't think you would ever get here, Alex. I called the house over an hour ago, and there was no answer. Where have you been?"

Alex just smiled as Grandma set the glasses on the porch rail and gave him his usual hug around the neck and her customary kiss in the middle of his forehead.

"Come. Let's sit down and talk," she said, indicating the white wicker porch swing. "I'm sure you already know what I made for us. This one's yours," she said as she placed a glass of lemonade on a side table.

Alex told his grandma about Pastor McGregor needing him to stay at the church to accept an envelope from Mr. Parsons. Grandma told Alex something that he already knew—that she baked all day yesterday so that she could send molasses cookies to camp this morning. Grinning from ear to ear, Alex wondered whether there just might be more.

Grandma got up quickly and said, "Oh. Speaking of cookies, I nearly forgot! They're on the counter. I'll be right back."

Alex would have been glad to go on this little errand for her, but he knew not to get in Grandma's way when she was on the move. While he waited for her to return, Alex got to spend a brief moment thinking about what he could tell her. When she came through the door with one cookie on her plate and at least three on Alex's, his heart opened wide again as it always had with her. She had a way of making him feel special. Only his father was able to duplicate what Grandma made him feel. Even then, it was not totally the same. After all, if Dad kissed him in the middle of his forehead, he would blush, and they would both end up laughing. Sometimes his dad would say, "I'm going to get you like Grandma does," while holding both of his hands, preventing him from getting away. With Dad, he would immediately rub the remaining mark off, but with Grandma it was different. She never slobbered.

"Grandma, when I was at church," Alex began, "that man who came to bring the package said he would like to come by and have a porch chat with me sometime this week, and I said yes."

"Good for you, Alex. I'm sure you miss your father. Another man to talk to might be a good thing. What did you say his name was?"

"Mr. Parsons," Alex replied.

"Not sure I know anyone by that name," she said. "I thought I knew everyone in these parts."

Alex didn't know anything about where Mr. Parsons had come from. He just knew that the man reminded him of his father.

"If Pastor McGregor knows him," she said, "I guess that's good enough for me. He's welcome on my porch anytime, Alex. I hope he does come so you can have a new friend."

They chatted for some time, with Alex silently wondering what Grandma would say if she knew. Remembering his vow to live by telling no one back in the woods, he knew that he could say nothing of it. Topics such as the weather, the height of the grass, the broken fence across the street in the lot no one seemed to care about anymore, were all safe to talk about. Grandma told Alex that they would leave early Wednesday afternoon for camp because she wanted to help in the kitchen and not just go there to eat. That was just the way Grandma was. If there was something she could do, you'd better not get in her way or try to change her plans. Stillness settled over them as they enjoyed their lemonade.

# Chapter 3

Alex knew there had been a grandpa. His dad had told him a few stories about him, but his grandfather wasn't there when Alex was born. He had died saving the lives of men in another war while Alex's father was still a teenager. He was Alex's dad's hero. That is why Alex was named William Alexander Williams, III.

One of the soldiers he had saved, dad related to Alex, had come to the house in full dress uniform to give Grandma a tin box of things that had belonged to Grandpa. Dad said there wasn't much in it.

One thing that was in the box—and Alex knew that Dad had it with him over there even now—was a small pocket Bible with a copper–colored metal cover. Dad said Grandpa kept it in a pocket over his heart so that if he got shot, the Bible would protect him. Alex remembered checking the cover for signs of wounds, but there were none to be found. It wasn't easy to picture Dad over there with his dad's Bible in his pocket. Although Alex could see Dad's face and remember his touch, picturing him over there just didn't work.

Another thing the soldier returned in the tin box was a picture of Grandma. It was a black and white photo with edges that seemed to fade away. The eyes told Alex that it really was her. He had no idea how young she was in the picture. Mom said Grandma was considered a beauty back then. Alex couldn't imagine Grandma in the fancy prom dress of satin, with a broach, as she called it, on a ribbon around her neck. A hairdresser had done something with her hair that made her look more grown–up, even as young as she was. All of her hair was piled on top of her head in fancy curls of some sort.

The last thing Alex remembered seeing in the box was a lace hanky that his great grandmother had made for Grandma as a wedding present. This made it *really* old. Mom said that the special white lace all around the edges had been made by hand. Although the lace impressed him, never having being good at knots himself, what he liked most was that holding it up to his nose and breathing in the fragrance reminded him of Grandma. Chanel No. 5 was what Mom called it. Grandma just called it "the fragrance of love."

"Grandma," Alex began, breaking their comfortable silence, "did Grandpa like your perfume?"

"Perfume, Alex? Do you mean the fragrance of love?"

"Yes," he said, "I mean the stuff on the hanky Mom showed me in your box from Grandpa."

"Well, Alex, the truth is that I never put that perfume on the hanky. Your grandfather did that when he took it with him overseas. Wait just a minute," she said, and she got up and went through the front screen door again. Minutes later, she appeared with a little golden bottle that said No. 5 Chanel on it. "This is it. This is the actual bottle he sent me," she said, pulling it toward her heart as a warm tear ran down her right cheek. "The fragrance of love." She spoke it in a whisper, as if to someone else.

She didn't need to open the bottle more than just a bit, as just that much allowed the strong floral scent of the fragrance of love to escape into the area around them. It smelled just the way Alex remembered when he took a breath through the hanky for the first time.

Alex moved slowly, hoping that Grandma would catch the hint that he wanted to give her a hug. It wasn't often anyone had seen Grandma cry. The last time Alex witnessed it was when her dog had to be put down. Rex was so old that he was blind and could no longer take care of himself. They held a special service in the backyard after Alex and Dad had dug the hole. Grandma had gone with Dad to the vet to love Rex and hold his head to the end. When she came home she said, "I have always loved him to life; today I have to love him to death."

Grandma finally realized that Alex was nearby and came out of her memories. "Life is for the living," she exclaimed and gave Alex a hug that was welcome and meaningful.

"You know, I'm not sure who cried more that day when the soldier came, Alex, your dad, me, or the soldier. It can't be easy for a man to go see a widow with what remains of her loved one's belongings, especially if that loved one had died in his place."

Grandma looked off into the distance with a detached gaze, and then added, "Nope. That was a rough day on all three of us."

*A rough day,* thought Alex. *That was yesterday,* as flashbacks ran through his head along with the thought, *I can't say a word to Grandma … Not one word ever.*

Hoping to change the subject, Alex turned Grandma's attention to her second favorite subject, food. Feeding her grandkids always took first place in her heart. She had said that at the last church supper in a way that impressed her grandchildren and showed other people one of the ways she chooses to love.

"Any special plans for food while I'm here, Grandma? I mean, can I help you cook?" Alex knew that although his Mom believed cooking was more for girls, his Grandma had a heart for anyone wanting to share her kitchen.

"Well, one thing is for sure," she said. "You're always welcome in my kitchen." And with that she got up, grabbed the two dirty plates, put them on top of each other, and put her fingers down the insides of the two glasses, putting them together with a clinking sound. “You sit and swing a while, Alex. I need to do a few chores inside.”

“I could mow the lawn.”

“No, you’re looking a little peaked today. I think the best thing for you is a day of rest. The lawn will only grow a grasshopper’s whisker higher by tomorrow.”

She cleared the screen door, and he could hear the latch catch behind her.

It wasn’t long before the whir of a vacuum cleaner could be heard and then music, layered over the noise of the vacuum. These were two of the many sounds Alex had become accustomed to hearing when he stayed at Grandma’s. Finally, it grew quieter, but with softer music still floating out from inside the house. It sounded to Alex like one of those orchestras old people listen to so they can feel happy.

By scooting over and tipping his head to the side, he was able to look through the window. He saw Grandma pick up a book with a white library code sticker on the spine.

# Chapter

The next time Alex checked in on Grandma, she was sitting with her head resting against the back of her chair—eyes closed, mouth open, and with her glasses and book in her lap. The last thing he wanted to do was awaken her.

"Hi there, Alex." A man's voice came from somewhere near the street. Alex looked in the direction of the voice and saw Mr. Parsons waving at him. Alex again marveled at how much he resembled his father.

"You up for that porch chat this evening?" He asked the question with no hesitation, as though it were a planned event. Remembering that Grandma had said Mr. Parsons might be a good friend for him to have, Alex waved him up to the porch, and soon they were chatting away. Alex felt comfortable, as though he had always known Mr. Parsons. And this time they shook hands.

"Remember you said you studied people?" Alex asked Mr. Parsons, who was seated in Grandma's rocker. Alex had settled into his favorite place on the porch swing.

"Yes," came the reply.

"You learn anything?" Alex asked.

"Well, yes, I must say I have. People are my life, and they are indeed the most fascinating creation of all."

"What's fascinating about them?" Alex probed.

"Probably the most fascinating thing about people is the way they use thought and memories, son," replied Mr. Parsons.

"Memories?"

"Yes, memories."

Alex's mind flashed back to you–know–what rather quickly, a memory he wished he didn't have and one that he was committed to never tell anyone about.

Mr. Parsons seemed to know that something was flashing through Alex's mind.

"You know, Alex, if you were to think about your best memories ever, I think you could make a long list."

Pondering, Alex smiled and nodded in agreement at Mr. Parsons.

Continuing, Mr. Parsons said, "If you were to choose your number one best memory of all time, I could tell you things about it that you wouldn't think I'd know. I could tell you a thing or two without you even telling me anything about what took place." Mr. Parsons emphasized that last part.

"Really?" Alex questioned. "How can you do that?"

"Well, nearly everyone seems to have a particular process that they use to store their good, light memories and a way to store their bad, dark memories."

At the mention of bad memories, Alex's face darkened, and Mr. Parsons continued cautiously. "We're not going there; we're not talking about the bad memories. I'm just going to tell you about your best memory. You just let me know when you think of the one you would put at the very top of your good list, and I will begin."

Alex paused, thinking only about the best things that had ever happened to him. Many of these memories involved his dad, and now they also hurt a bit because his father wasn't home; Alex missed him so much. Finally, he made a choice. *Oh yes. This would have to be the number one.* "I have it," he said, smiled, and pointed his pointer finger right up in the air in front of the middle of his face as if a signal to start.

Seeming to pause only long enough to gather his thoughts, Mr. Parsons said, "So, Alex, continue to think only about this memory, and don't tell me anything about it, okay?"

"Okay," Alex replied.

"Do you see it in bright and vivid color, like watching a movie on a screen right in front of you, nice and close and very bright?"

"Yes," Alex replied a little surprised at the effect Mr. Parsons' gift seemed to have on him, a gift he said he developed by studying people.

"Do you see the movie sharply focused?"

"Do you see yourself just the right size, the same size you are in real life?"

Alex kept nodding.

"Can you experience it even better by making it a panorama that wraps all the way around you?"

Alex just looked at his memory in amazement as Mr. Parsons got nothing wrong—nothing.

"Take a minute and think about all the sounds you hear, Alex. You're hearing sounds that you would consider to be in harmony, like your favorite music coming from all around you at the most comfortable volume, tempo, and rhythm. If you could, Alex, you would be thrilled to make the sounds last forever."

As Alex showed signs of wanting to make those sounds last forever, Mr. Parsons paused, knowing that Alex needed a moment to catch up. Alex's eyes had become a little glassy as his thoughts had, for the moment, turned totally inward to make the sounds last. Thinking in terms of them lasting forever changed his physiology, or body language and his breathing became very deep and relaxed. Mr. Parsons could have been quiet for some time as Alex would have just remained deeply peaceful from outside appearances. Alex would have to admit that this was more than he could fully comprehend.

"You still with me?" Mr. Parsons spoke again. "Am I getting anything wrong?"

"No. Well, I mean, yes," Alex said. He was a little confused by what he had just experienced. "I mean, you haven't been wrong. It's just that I don't understand how you know all of that about my memory. Do you think you could do this with everyone?"

"For most people, what I am saying will generally prove true. Since it was true for you, the next time we meet, I will bring a written list so that you can check it, going line by line like I have talked to you today. You can see if any of those other good memories hold as true to what I say as this one did. I think a list always makes it easier. You seemed up to the challenge today."

"So that's it? That's all?" Alex questioned, thinking that wasn't much of a challenge. Mr. Parsons got everything right!

"Think back to that memory again. When you're totally there, feel all the feelings associated with this memory; then smile at me again like you did before, and point that finger so that I know you're ready."

Alex had no trouble getting back into it; after all, this memory was number one.

"Do you find these feelings to be warm and soft and flexible, maybe like silk or satin? Better yet, maybe they feel more like that baby blanket it took you forever to let go of."

Once again, Alex smiled, in his own way acknowledging that Mr. Parsons made no mistakes.

"Are those feelings steady, coming straight from your heart so that your breathing is relaxed, as deeply relaxed as every other part of you?"

"Yup," Alex replied, his grin growing broader.

"Do those feelings feel huge, Alex? Do they have a nice, round shape and feel as light as a feather, or maybe they're even weightless?"

"Yes," came the answer. Alex was glad that the questions were coming at a slower pace so that he had more time to experience them.

"As you really think it through, Alex, you will discover that if these memories had a taste and a smell, they would be favorites of yours, maybe from a favorite holiday, just as if they had a color, it would be your favorite one."

"I just don't get it, Mr. Parsons," Alex said, shaking his head a little, although not in disagreement. "Where did you go to college?"

"All of this is life, son, this is about living the real deal. This is the way it's done, the way people store memories."

"Alex," Grandma's voice called from inside the house, "can you come help me find my glasses?" Without hesitating, Alex was up and into the house to look for the missing glasses. After minutes of searching, even moving her favorite chair, Grandma put her hand in her apron pocket only to feel the familiar shape of her small, wire–rimmed frames. With her glasses safely back on her face, Grandma headed to the kitchen, and Alex turned to go back outside to continue his porch chat. Pushing the screen door open, Alex stepped out and looked around, but Mr. Parsons was nowhere in sight.

*He probably needed to stretch,* Alex thought and proceeded to walk to the other end of the L–shaped porch. Mr. Parsons was nowhere to be seen. *Well, it had taken some time to find Grandma's glasses,* Alex thought.

Heading back to the swing, he considered that this had not been as bad a day as he thought it might be. He had just begun swinging a little when Grandma appeared with a fresh glass of lemonade and a peanut butter and marshmallow fluff sandwich on his favorite, seven–grain, whole wheat bread.

"Glad to see you relaxing, son," she said, without even knowing that Alex had had company. Alex thought about telling her, but he hadn't gone in to awaken her to meet his guest, so maybe he shouldn't tell her.

Mr. Parsons was different. He reminded Alex of his father, yet look at how smart Mr. Parsons was in knowing stuff he believed his father did not. He knew everything about a memory and a lot about people. It seemed he was becoming a friend. Maybe it would just be best to wait for another time to tell Grandma about Mr. Parsons. He did say he would bring a list for Alex, so that meant he was planning to come back. *Yes, that would make it easier.* Maybe Mr. Parsons didn't know everything about Alex's memories; maybe he did make a mistake. At least with a list Alex could easily check by running the list line by line against any memory, and try to prove Mr. Parsons wrong.

The sandwich went down easily; that delicious combination of favorite foods always did. Alex and his mother shared a love for peanut butter and marshmallow fluff sandwiches. She would only eat a half, while he would get one and a half.

"Want another?" Grandma asked, half expecting that he would.

With a sly look, he responded like a once–favorite Sesame Street® character, with a long, drawn out, "Cook–kie!" That made her smile, and she quickly moved to take his plate back to the kitchen and to head for the glass cookie jar. Alex followed in hot pursuit.

The rest of the day was not particularly eventful, but it was busy enough to keep Alex's mind off what had happened to him in the woods. It was probably a good thing that Mom and Kaitlyn had gone to camp and that Kaitlyn was not at home to bug anyone. Grandma was Alex's second–best friend, with his dad being in first place. Without Dad at home, there was no one he would rather spend time with than Grandma.

Night came, and with it came much–needed sleep. It might have been the last glass of warm milk just before bed that did the trick, or it might have been due to spending much of the day reliving memories of other favorite times he had had, writing a list to check against the one that Mr. Parsons would bring. A key to getting through his day was that not one of the memories made him feel bad. Whenever he would think of another good memory, it would go on the list, using a key phrase to trigger the memory. It only took a word like Orlando to trigger going to see Mickey and friends. Another one was "Shamo"—what he thought was the spelling for the name of the whale he once saw at another theme park.

Even when nature's call woke him during the night, Alex was not afraid of the darkened room. Without even turning on a light, he did the necessary and returned to his bed. His mind flashed back for a split second to when he saw Robert getting out of the truck that morning, and Alex felt the conviction again that he should say nothing to Robert about his frightening experience. There was no one around now who could bother him. Alex felt that Grandma's house was the safest place to sleep, and he was not awake long.

# Chapter 5

The following day was a busy one, beginning with helping Grandma turn her mattress and then beating the dust out of the quilt she always kept at the foot of her bed. Nights could turn chilly, even at this time of year. Grandma had Alex sweep the spent flower petals off the front part of the porch where they had blown down from the deck above. All of her beauties were in full bloom. For breakfast, Grandma had given Alex Cream of Wheat with a hint of maple syrup, the real kind that comes from trees in Maine. However, Grandma would trek to Canada every so often to get foodstuffs, and the glass bottle of syrup shaped like a Canadian maple leaf used today was less expensive when she bought it in Canada. Although Alex would have liked a cookie, Grandma had broken up the last few and put them on an outside window ledge to feed the birds, as she often did with stale bread. Young, fuzzy yellow birds were already busily fighting each other for the smaller pieces of cookie when a big, black crow came up and nearly scared the life out of them *and* Grandma. She grabbed her broom and smacked the window hard enough to make the crow jump. Then she ran out the side door shouting, "Shoo, you pest, you! Shoo! I'm trying to feed the babies here. Now shoo!"

It reminded Alex of the time Grandma painted her face all green for Halloween. Dressed all in black, she greeted the kids at the door, shaking her broom at them as she cackled, "Hello my precious." She was so convincing that several kids never would come up to the door to get candy.

She swept a little freshly blown debris off a table she had near the window, and when she was fairly certain the crow was not coming back, she went back into the house in time to hear Alex remarking, "You go, witch."

She cackled back, "There you are, my little pretty," tipping her head and popping her eyes wide.

Laughing, Alex half–cackled back, "You're a wicked, scary granny, even without a green face!"

With that, she reminded him of when they all went to New York for the Christmas holiday and saw the Broadway play, *Wicked*. "I sure can't defy gravity yet, my pretty pet," she said, again cocking her head and popping her eyes, "but soon I am going up yonder … without a broom. Moreover, you can bet I'll be wearing the fragrance of love, and Grandpa will smell me coming." As she spoke that last part, she managed to grab the broom she had leaned against the wall by the door, stuck it between her legs, and made a wide circle around the floor. Knowing that this was not atypical behavior for her, Alex laughed, appreciating her sense of humor. Thinking of a broomstick hobbyhorse he once had, he said, "You sure you're not a cowboy, Grandma?"

She just walked over and gently batted him across the top of his head and then pulled him in to give him another of the hugs that glued their lives together. She called it "real loving." When she hugged him, she put her head up near his left shoulder, unlike the way most some people hug to the right side. She had this to say about it: "If God wants me to love you with my heart, then we're putting our hearts together, not our right kidneys and shoulders." Alex knew there was something special about the way she hugged, because it always made him feel warm inside. She just covered all of him with a hug so big that both kidneys could probably feel it. Then she tried not to let go, even though she usually said it was polite to hold a hug only as long as the other person held, and not to move until the other person moved first. She said something once about breathing at the same pace the other person did, however that was more information than Alex wanted, so he just did what felt natural.

There was no question that this was one of those hugs that Grandma didn't want to end, as she did not stop even when he dropped his arms to his sides. Because he had had a growth spurt and because Gramps had been short, maybe Alex was the right size for her to feel like she was hugging Gramps. But the hug finally ended, and when he saw a tear on her face, he couldn't help but think that she had been remembering him. Indeed she had, as she spoke, "Yes, my love," as if into the air around her. "We're all going sometime, but today is not my time," she continued, still speaking off distantly. Then she turned toward Alex and said, "So come on. We need to start the fixings for dinner to take to camp tonight. Did you forget this is Wednesday? We're out of here with plans to make camp by 2:00. That way I can join the night crew staff, and you … well, you can just go tease your sister like you always do!"

Indeed, he had forgotten, the best of plans, and teasing his sister today was not his idea of fun. Kaitlyn was always the one who could tease, just not take it back. Besides, his intention would go to checking the list, if Mr. Parsons showed up in time.

Right about this time, Alex began to have a sickening feeling in his stomach. The reality of seeing most of his friends at camp that afternoon hit home. *Say nothing*, his brain cautioned.

"What if I decided to stay home?" he asked.

"You got chicken pox?" Grandma shot back.

"Nope."

"Well, then you're not contagious. Your mother would beat me with my broom and peel me alive if I let you stay home. Now come on. You helping or not?

Alex, are you okay?" she asked, as she realized that his face showed something was bothering him—a look that came when Alex's thoughts and feelings were deeply internal.

"Can I go sit on the porch and swing for a bit before we go?" he asked.

"Oh, sure. I have a lot to get ready, and the oven has to heat. You take your time, and I'll call you when I just—" She paused and broke into song: "Can't live without you. Can't bake without you. Can't do anything that I wanted to do. My kitchen's a mess, and now I need you." She turned and went off to the kitchen, still singing words she was making up that he could not fully hear.

Once again, he smiled, in part because she had pulled that stinger out of his heart a little bit more, and in part because if he weren't out on the porch, how could he have a porch chat with Mr. Parsons? As he went through the back door from the kitchen, out to the back of the house, he could hear her singing a song he remembered from church camp two years ago. "*My Lord knows the way through the wilderness, all you have to do is follow. My Lord knows the way …*" as Alex thoughts interrupted, *Oh, here comes Mr. Parsons … different direction from yesterday.*

"There you are, my son." Mr. Parsons said, as he came up the rough, unpaved, gray stone walk. "I was afraid I had managed to miss you today. I brought you these notes," and he unfolded a piece of brown paper he had taken out of his pocket.

Alex reached out for the brown paper and saw, as promised, that it was all handwritten. Unmindful of the time it took, he stood reading, making sure that he understood everything. It reminded him of what Mr. Parsons said yesterday while Alex was thinking of his favorite memory, except now it was more like a checklist he could go through, one by one. He thought, *This will be fun, especially with this good a list.*

Mr. Parsons interrupted Alex's thoughts as he started down to the bottom of the steps. "I'm sorry I don't have more time today, Alex, but it's a needy world out there, and I have lots of things I must get done. If my schedule works, I will see you here in the morning around nine. I really do want to talk to you again." He paused, waiting for agreement from Alex, but was also eager to return to his work.

"Alex," Grandma hollered from the back of the house, "we're ready to go in the kitchen!"

"Okay. That will work out, sir. I will be right here," Alex said, pointing at the white wicker swing.

"Sir, am I?" Mr. Parsons questioned with a smile. "Okay, son. Your father loves you." as they parted in opposite directions, Alex through the screen door and Mr. Parsons down the walk. He was pleased that Mr. Parsons had mentioned his father once again.

"Coming! I'm coming!" Alex shouted into the house. The wonderful aroma of something homemade caused him to stop in the doorway and just close his mouth and eyes, tip his head back, and take a deep whiff through his nose.

"Is that molasses I smell?" Alex smiled, a look of eager anticipation now on his face. He was excited at the thought of making Grandma's famous molasses cookies.

"What's that in your hand?" Grandma asked, nearly frowning. She wondered whether he had gotten into some of her personal notes.

"Oh, Mr. Parsons came by and gave me something to save to read later."

"Did he stop?" Grandma asked.

"No he only stayed long enough to give me something to read." Alex replied.

"Good for you." She smiled. "Is he a Bible man?" she asked, while answering her own question with, "Oh, silly me. I guess if Pastor McGregor had you meet him, of course he is—maybe even a man of the cloth."

Alex folded the paper and put it safely into the front pocket of his jeans as he approached the hook where his "Grandmother Made" cooks apron was hanging. Slipping it over his head, he then wrapped the strings around the back, and returned them to the front of his waist, so that he could see to tie it. He had done this many times before as the apron strings were long enough.

"There is something in the pocket for you, Alex." Grandma said.

Reaching in, he found what appeared to be a big, silver coin. Looking at it closer, he saw that it was a dollar coin.

"Do you know how old that is, Alex?"

Looking at the date stamped on the coin, Alex calculated and said, "It's twelve years old!"

Grandma continued. "That means that coin has lived as long as you have, and you can tell by looking at it that it has not had an easy life. See there," she pointed with one finger to the coin in his hand. "It has scars just like you do."

Then he noticed that Grandma was pointing to one of her own scars on her left arm. "Did I ever tell you how I got this?" she asked.

"Momma said it was for taking someone else's place once. She told me you pushed someone out of the way when you saw something falling, and your arm got cut really bad."

"Better me than her," she said. "If the cases of books and shelving hit her as hard as it hit me, she might be dead. I just had this feeling to look up as the building seemed to shake from whatever they were banging around on the second floor, only to realize the shelf was coming off its bracket and would land directly on top of her. Anyone in his or her right mind would have pushed her out of the way. I nearly made it myself, except for this scratch," she said, looking at her wrist. "Well, I guess I had more than a scratch, but she was all right, and that matters."

"Jesus has a scar like that," Alex said, looking closer at her wrist at the scar's detail.

"He took our place," she replied. "Now put that coin in your pants pocket. You're old enough to take it home now, and I think it's time you got something from Grandpa's collection that we all seem to keep adding to. When you're older, it will help you to remember that God loves you no matter how scarred you get. Your value to him stays the same, Alex. His love for you never changes—nope, never. I imagine God is extraordinarily delighted in you."

It felt good to Alex to hear that just now. *God is delighted—delighted in me,* he thought.

While they talked, she noticed that the stove was ready and they'd best get cooking. Turning toward the biggest mixing bowl in the house, Grandma said, "And now we're making gingerbread and molasses for sixty! Don't let me forget that we have to stop at the store and get more fresh whipping cream on the way to camp 'cause warm gingerbread and molasses is no good without whipped cream on top. I need to remember to call out to camp to see if I need to bring anything else." Mumbling to herself now, her hands went into motion, making the recipe she had memorized years ago. The time went by quickly as they cooked, getting splattered with flour and the other ingredients. Grandma, with her usual precautions, cut markings into the tops of each pan to ensure that each piece would be the same size and that there would be plenty to go around. When she was finished, there was part of a small pan that they should be able to call extra. After all, the number, even counting all possible guests, should not go over fifty, and the pans were marked out for sixty.

"What do you say we …" she hinted, as if she needed permission. Opening the refrigerator door, she took out the whipped cream she had whipped up while the last batch was cooking. There was not a chance that he would say no, and he even got a bigger piece than would be served at camp.

The stop at the store took no time, as she only needed the cream after calling and checking with Mabel Kitchen in the camp kitchen. Soon, they were at camp. The mushy hug Alex's mom always gave him was over, and he was thankful that his sister Kaitlyn, with Mom's permission, had made the decision to stay in a cabin that had an empty bunk. Alex was not sure why Mom's hugs always seemed mushy to him. She never put her head on his left side like Grandma did; she always stayed on the right and sort of squeezed too tightly, leaving a lipstick mark somewhere on his face. She always seemed in a hurry as well. Alex guessed that nurses just did that type of thing.

In some ways, it made it easier on Mom for Kaitlyn to stay in a cabin, allowing Mom to be the camp nurse by herself. All treatments took place in the tiny, one–room cabin the size of a bedroom. It certainly was the last place Alex wanted to be. There was a sink;

a medicine cabinet; one old, dilapidated four–drawer dresser that had to be kicked to get the drawer closed; and one overhead light with no shade. Air–conditioning was the open door, which had a screen door with holes large enough to put a fist through, courtesy of some visiting animals. There was one stand–alone light that could be moved around easily. The one window was small, positioned high enough so that anyone looking in had to be standing on a potato barrel or something else that height. That saved some embarrassment. The bathroom was only a toilet with a shower curtain around it for privacy. That curtain was the worst part because when someone sat down, the dirty–looking orange, yellow, and green–striped curtain touched his or her knees. Alex always kept his pants pulled up over his knees. Sometimes though, whenever he felt he could manage it, he went to the strip of woods between the cabin and the potato fields beyond. The sink in the nurse's cabin was outside the plastic circle, closer to the dresser and just under the medicine cabinet. Over the front door, there was a sign which read *Infirmary*.

Alex helped Grandma take the gingerbread and molasses, along with the whipped cream and some other supplies, over to Mabel in the kitchen part of the Cafatorium. It had such a fancy name because all of the larger meetings were held there at night after everything was cleaned up. Each table had a basket in the middle that held the necessary breakfast dishes, napkins, and silverware, along with a sign that read, "Please do not touch or you will get latrine duty or kitchen patrol." The goodies remained safe!

"Oh dear, dear," Mabel said as she waddled toward the precut pans with the deepest appreciation that she did not have to bake another dessert tonight. As much as Alex liked her, she was one he could choose to live without and for not such a good reason. The last time he was actually at camp as a camper, Alex, along with Robert, snuck over to the girl's cabin and put a garter snake in one bunk, a frog in another, and itching powder on top of the metal headboards of every bunk and on every handle in the place. While they suffered KP for their crime, all the dishes they washed got dropped back into the water with a "nope" and a look that said they ought to have known what they were doing while scrubbing Mabel's pans. They never thought about the fact that her only daughter Greta was in that cabin.

All loaded in and done with the formalities before 2:00 p.m., Alex got the next three hours to himself. All he was told was to make sure his face was in line at the door at 5:00 p.m. when the dinner bell rang. Wanting to be alone and not feeling ready to see his friends when they came out of craft class, he headed back toward the fish hatchery at the front entrance to the camp. Because it was a popular picnic spot, there were several picnic tables near the road entrance where the biggest trout tank was located. This area was out of bounds for the campers. Alex had thought in advance that this would be a good place to sit and look at Mr. Parsons' note and use his good memory list to try to prove him wrong. It just didn't seem possible that anyone could be that right about all memories. Picking the farthest table, the one that was blocked most from view of the camp by the big Maine pines, he faced the big fish tank as he reached into his pocket, took out his brown paper, and then sat down. He just held the paper for a bit, wanting to see the big trout in the tank. There they were with the rainbow striping that caught in the sun as they seemed to brush over each other and roll up to the surface, hoping for a black fly.

Remembering his challenge, he opened the brown paper again and started reading it once more, making sure he understood each handwritten line. As he finished the back side of the paper, he couldn't help but think that it was just too simple. Then his mind switched to the memories he had thought of earlier that he could use to try to prove the list wrong. From his other pocket, he took out a stubby pencil with no eraser and hardly any lead in its three full inches of length. He had already decided that he only needed to mark the mistakes and then give the paper back to Mr. Parsons. From the list on his white sheet of paper, it was easy to choose a memory. The trout in the front tank seemed to make his brain scream to recall a memory of his first fishing trip to Lobster Lake with his father. The lake was not easy to get to, and when he thought they were finally there and parked the SUV, they walked, and walked, and then walked some more. It was one of those trips where they had extra time for man talk, appreciating nature, and being eaten alive by black flies. There are no words to describe the fishing. They always had to decide which of the keepers they were taking home. They had to get used to saying no and putting a fish back wondering whether any of them had been caught before. The limit was twelve, but they actually kept fourteen that day. From what he had in his backpack, Dad managed to make a fire on the point of the peninsula that was their favorite fishing spot and cooked two keepers on a long stick. Eating two was how they reached fourteen.

The lake was so beautiful and the air so crisp that Alex wanted to stay until the stars came out. The walk back was part of the joy of being with Dad. There were no cabins on the lake, but they could have brought a tent; however, even without staying overnight, the day was beyond perfect. Alex was remembering it as though it were a movie. To his mind, there was no reason for this not to be the first memory to check against the list.

Looking at the brown list, Alex placed his finger on line one, remembering that Mr. Parsons had said that he was to remain inside the memory the whole time. If the answer to any line of copy on the paper was wrong, he was sure it would shout out at him, "Gotcha!" because it was wrong.

Line one read: It is a movie.

*Yup.*

He kept his finger going down one line at a time … looking for the magic that would tell him that a line he read was not right, that his memory was different from what was written down.

Line two continued:

> The movie is in bright and vivid color.

Line three:

> Rather than flat, it is three–dimensional.

On down the page he went, with his finger remaining on each line.

> It feels as though the picture is right in front of you, straight on, nice and close.
> The brightness of the movie in your mind, on a scale from one to ten, with ten being the brightest, is closer to a ten.
> It is sharp and steady and with a clear focus.
> The movie is the right size to see you clearly.
> Your speed of motion and all other motion is lifelike.
>
> Making the movie a panorama that wraps all the way around you makes it feel better.
>
> Holding his finger in place, Alex took a deep breath and realized how accurate it all was. He even began to wonder whether it would ever *not* work. Returning to his white page list, he put an X beside Lobster Lake. Thinking back into the memory, the notes continued referring to what he heard, switching from what he had seen, so he ran down through more about the sounds in the memory using his finger as he still went line by line.
>
> They are regular sounds that you would consider to be in harmony.
> The sounds come from all around you.
> The volume of the sounds is comfortable.
> The rhythm and speed of the sounds were like favorite music.
> If you had your choice, you would like these sounds to last forever.

Finishing the front side of the list and realizing that the page wasn't going to have a "gotcha," Alex broke out of what almost seemed like a trance and walked over to the trout tank. As he folded the paper back into his pocket, he wondered again how Mr. Parsons could know all of this. Alex thought. *He said he studied people.* Alex considered, *maybe I will do that when I go to college,* still not sure exactly what it meant. Mr. Parsons certainly was good at what he did.

Alex wished he had brought some bread with him for the trout. Just reaching out his hand made the whoppers swarm toward the surface. The men who took care of them would throw a handful of food out to them. Forgetting that the trout would not bite him like some fish Dad had told him about, he did not put his hand in the water. Instead, he started trying to count them. Noticing that the one with the half–torn tail fin had gone by more than once, he realized his count was wrong and stopped at one hundred.

With a deep breath, Alex stretched and stared upward as an unusual sight flew overhead. He knew it was an American Bald Eagle. Only circling twice, it took a dive toward a trout tank at the other end of the farm. As it got within rooftop range of the main building, lights and noises sounded; it was a warning alarm that the fish were off limits. That may work with most of the birds in this area; however, this eagle skimmed half the length of the tank before its talons came out, and it flew off with a prize nearly as large as those in the tank Alex was standing next to. Seeing an American Bald Eagle was a rare occurrence, and seeing it get a fish in Maine was probably a once in a lifetime event. Alex was glad he was there to see it.

His mind returned to the reason he was there, and he headed back to the table. Unfolding his paper again, he turned it over and placed it on the table. *Feelings,* he thought. *I have to really feel what fishing back there with Dad was like.* And he did, so much so that he smiled as he pointed at his head again, as if to say go.

The next line read:

> Your feelings are warm.
> Your feelings are soft and flexible.
> If they had a texture, they would be soft, satiny, or silky—like the baby blanket it took you forever to let go.

Although he agreed about the texture, that blanket was one thing Mr. Parsons should never have known about. His mom still had about two feet of that light brown, fuzzy blanket he had managed to de–fuzz over time. Without taking the time to figure out how Mr. Parsons knew about it, his finger continued moving down the page.

> The feelings are steady and internal.

The feelings move out from your heart.
Your breathing is deep and easy.
Your feelings cause every part of you to just relax deeply.
Your feelings seem large or even huge in size.
Your feelings are light as a feather or even weightless.
If your feelings had a shape, they would be round.
If your feelings had a smell, it would be a favorite.
If your feelings had a taste, they would taste like a favorite food.
If your feelings were a flower, it would be one you would give to others.

He couldn't remember anything about flowers on the list the day before, but he could easily have missed it.

If your feelings had a color, it would be your favorite color.

Then he noticed that more had been added to the list. It said:

If you pay attention to your feelings, Alex, they will give you a sense of connection; completeness; serving; being taken care of; purpose; responsibility; energy; intensity; excitement; life; and, finally, love, my friend. You might even discover your own special words you might like to add.

There was such a complete peace about this memory now. In some way, it changed a little, checking it against the list. The memory wasn't really any different than he remembered it; it just seemed different. It felt different. It actually felt better.

Checking to see if his newfound friend, the eagle, had returned, he found no such luck. Maybe one whopper was all he needed. He looked back at the white sheet and wondered which of his other best memories would prove Mr. Parsons wrong. For a second he thought of Kaitlyn, as she would tell him which one. She always had all the answers for other people. All you had to do was ask. He was still glad she was not sitting beside him as she had been during previous picnics to this "no fishing hole" place, as she called it.

Alex skimmed the list a couple of times, almost disgusted that maybe he had written the wrong list, because no matter what he did, it worked to prove itself right. With some memories, he would check just the movie, while with others, the sounds or the feelings. All produced the same result. As Alex began to move back toward the big fish tank, his mind puzzled over that burning question: *How did he do that?*

Although the sound of the bell ending craft class had rung long ago, he knew from past experience that when the sun reached the mountain rim behind Maple Leaf Mountain, it was time to line up for dinner. Noting the position of the orange to rose–colored rays tonight, the time was verified by the sounding of the dinner bell. The valley location caused the camp to cool quickly after sunset, so Alex went to the car to get the jacket Grandma had insisted he bring along. Seeing that her sweater was still there as well, he decided to take it to her. This might allow him to bypass the dinner line. He would go through the kitchen door and sneak to the table reserved for the nurse and anyone under her care. If Mom objected, he would tell her, "I really don't feel good, Nurse Williams. Will you take my temperature?" and she would smile and tell him to sit.

Everything worked better than planned. As he entered the kitchen door, Mabel spotted him and asked, "Alex, can you help me lift this pan of mashed potatoes? It's too hot for me to pull over there by myself and not burn my belly. My, my, we're almost on schedule tonight." For once, he was more than willing to help. Soon, Grandma's sweater was hanging on a hook because she was hot from bustling around the kitchen.

By the time he found the nurse's table, which had been moved to a different corner, the attending nurse just patted the chair beside her, indicating that it was reserved for only him. Kaitlyn was nowhere in sight yet, even though all the campers seemed to be already in their seats. After grace, food flowed immediately with flavors anyone would recognize. There were carrots, mashed potatoes and gravy, boiled onions, pot roast, and hot yeast rolls lightly treated with cinnamon. Nothing would be missed that could possibly energize and love these kids to life. Then along came dessert. "Am I surprised!" Mom happily exclaimed as the aroma of the gingerbread filled the Cafatorium. Not one complaint could be heard, just the sound of excited acceptance. Grandma had outdone herself on this one. Although dessert was always good, it was usually cold. This dessert was hot, with an aroma that filled the air with a reminder of special holidays, and was topped with whipped cream. Mabel added her touch with maraschino cherries from a gallon jug, adding the look of a Christmas cap.

While they were clearing the tables, Grandma told Alex that they would not be staying for camp meeting because Mabel did not need her anymore tonight. Truth was, she felt plain worn out again tonight and asked if she might go early. With thankful hearts, the two of them headed home after Alex got his customary shoulder hug and kiss on his cheek from Mom. Thinking back, he could remember only seeing Kaitlyn, but never actually exchanging a word. *Nice!* Alex thought happily.

Once home, Grandma didn't notice that she'd left all of her pans at camp. She also made no fuss over Alex, believing that he could fend for himself. She did offer another piece of gingerbread without whipped cream, should he so desire. "Just fend for yourself," she said and slowly started up the stairs to rest. She paused on the third step as if trying to make a decision as to whether to go back down to sit in her rocker or go upstairs to bed. Several deep breathes later, she continued a slow climb to the top where she said, "Night Love!" as she passed the picture of the husband she so longed to be with.

No one had noticed that, back at the Cafatorium, Alex ate two pieces of gingerbread at the table, including the extra piece that had been left in case someone else had sat there. In fact, Mom did not eat but half of hers; however, the plate was empty when the KP crew started clearing tables on their side. It wasn't important what else he ate now; he just knew that he was well taken care of. The hardest choice was between homemade lemonade and milk.

Later, as he lay on top of his bed, he forced his mind to do more checking against the list he had nearly memorized. Although he was still hoping to find something that went, "Gotcha!" it never did happen.

The silence made his mind wander back a few times, back to his own story that he did not want to think about. Thus, music became a necessary extra. As the words to "I Can Only Imagine" passed by, it seemed to be just a favorite melody. It was "Butterfly Kisses" that made him quickly push the forward button down. As soon as the next song began, he forced his mind back to Lobster Lake. Somehow, that day's eagle was flying over the peninsula at the lake without picking up any fish. At that point, Alex realized that he was dreaming; however, he liked seeing it all again. He thought about having Mr. Parsons meet his dad on the walk back out, since it was now an imaginative dream. But as they started out on the trail, his hands were feeling the leaves, and he was beginning to count his steps as he often did, setting a pace that led him right into sleep.

In the morning, he could not wait to get past his Cream of Wheat and maple syrup breakfast to take up his position on the porch. Even though he began before nine, a respectable time in Maine to start mowing lawns, the John Deere was quiet enough to have caused no notice, and the mowing was done in time for Alex to be on the white wicker swing by nine. Actually, it was 8:50 a.m. according to his watch, when Grandma came out and announced that this was Ladies Aid Society day, and that she would be at the church if he needed her. The plate in her hand indicated that, as usual, goodies were going with her. It would be hard to imagine any of her meetings without Grandma's goodies. "I left a snack for you on the kitchen table," she said, without telling him what to expect or what it was she was carrying out. She went in one direction toward the church, while in the distance he could see Mr. Parsons coming from the other direction. He was still far enough away so that he had to walk to the middle pointed corner of the porch to see between the houses. Standing where the stairs were the view was blocked for Alex.

"Wow. You're ready and waiting today," Mr. Parsons said as he passed the last house and came toward the porch.

"Can I tell you something?" Alex quickly asked, before Mr. Parsons had even made the first of the four porch steps.

"Sure." Mr. Parsons replied.

"I did all my good memories," he said, holding up a sheet of white paper on which he had marked every one with an X.

"And?" Mr. Parsons said, almost sounding proud that Alex had completed such an accomplishment.

"You're right. You do know how I store every memory," Alex said, as his guest walked over to the white rocking chair where Grandma usually sat, adjusted a blue and white checkered cushion, and was soon leaning back comfortably. Alex probably could have shaken hands this time, but when his hand went out, it still had the white piece of paper in it. Mr. Parsons was quick to take it from him and look through it, acting surprised. All the way down the front and back of the page, there were words and names on the list that represented memories he had checked off.

"Not bad. Not bad, son," Mr. Parsons said. "Remember when I told you that your father was proud of you? There's a lot of truth in that statement, son." Then, pointing his finger with somewhat a questioning attitude, Mr. Parsons continued. "You said that I know how you store every memory. Truth is, I probably do; however, I should tell you about my day yesterday rather than talk about you today."

Alex's approval was not difficult to get, so Mr. Parsons went on.

"It was not easy seeing the person I most wanted to help yesterday. He was way down in Houlton at the state prison for doing something at a fast food store using a gun. His first regret was getting caught."

The look on Alex's face indicated that he was not comfortable with a weapon story. Mr. Parsons realized he should go on quickly. Alex looked down toward the front boards of the porch where the rail connected, his eyes fixed on some spot as Mr. Parsons continued.

"It was nothing that you would ever do, Alex. I can tell that already, so relax and let me tell you what I told him and how it helped. Just as I told you I could challenge you about your good memory," he paused, "I challenged him about his biggest bad one and quickly proved that I could help. Even without him telling me anything about his side of the story, I knew why he was there. There was no question in my mind that what he did was bothering him, and now that he was asking for forgiveness from the store owner, I knew I could help."

Alex seemed uneasy, remembering that some things, bad things, were to be discussed only with his father. He had been warned that the truth could cause someone to get deeply hurt when confided to others.

Sensing the pressure Alex was feeling, almost as though he understood there was something on Alex's mind that he did not want to talk about, Mr. Parsons said, "I need to tell you how I helped him feel better, Alex. There is a happy ending to this one, my friend. He found out that Jesus loves him just as much as Jesus loves you."

With that, Alex looked back in Mr. Parsons' direction as if to indicate that it was okay to continue.

"Instead of just telling him all about his bad memory, I told him to only think about this memory and stay there in his thinking, just like I told you. Then, no matter what changes I would ask him to make to the memory, he needed to make those changes to the best of his ability, and signal me when he had made each change."

Mr. Parsons added, "I trust you got that, Alex. I told him to keep thinking about the memory at the fast food store with the gun, and rather than telling him all about it, like I did you, I was going to tell him how to change it so that he could heal."

All of a sudden, Alex had gone from anticipating potential pain to curiosity, as it appeared that Mr. Parsons was once again going to teach him more of the stuff he had learned about people and their memories. Just to make sure, he questioned, "This is more stuff that you learned from other people, right?"

"Oh Alex, you're going to love this part. Since you did so well on your homework—if we can call it that—I truly think you're always going to be one to help other people. So let me tell you what I told him that worked not only for him, but it works for nearly all people, unless, of course, their pain in life is their pleasure." He then added,

"Because everything we do in life, we generally do to avoid pain or to gain pleasure."

That statement was one Alex could not totally grasp. However, he did think of a woman from the church who says, "I just can't help it," when she comes to church all scarred up. The word he thought he heard his dad call her came to mind—"mastakistic," or something like that.

Mr. Parsons' smile seemed to tell Alex that truth would prevail. "I won't be saying it exactly the way I said it to him, but I think you're a pretty smart young man, and you will quickly figure out what I did with him."

"Looking right into his eyes, Alex, telling him to just get right inside that memory that bothered him most, I told him to see it as a movie. He said it was still framed and black and white. However, I told him that a movie in bright and vivid color was what he needed right now." Mr. Parsons looked directly at Alex, as if to see whether the clues had begun to hit home yet. "So what do you think I told him next, my friend?" he asked Alex.

Alex thought for a moment, as if searching for an answer that he should know, and then smiled one of his biggest smiles ever, as if a dam were about to break loose. Reaching into his inside pocket, he took out a brown piece of paper, pointed at it, and said, "Is it three–dimensional as you watch your movie?"

"Very good, Alex," Mr. Parsons replied, grinning. "What I did say was, 'Make the movie three–dimensional.' That was the change I needed him to make. Then the man looked right at me and indicated that he had."

Everything that was on Alex's brown paper was repeated with just enough of a twist to make it something he still had to do with the memory he was working on healing, sometimes even changing the sounds and feelings. Mr. Parsons repeated each statement that he told the man in prison, as if Alex was in training. A few times, Alex's mind had begun to ask the haunting question, *What would happen if … ?* However, most of the time he stayed alert to see if everything on his sheet was there. It was all there; he just said it differently.

Mr. Parsons finished the list and kept right on talking again as if the young lad was in training. "What this actually does, son, is change the way a memory is stored so that any time a person thinks about it after that, the last way it was stored comes to mind, and it's like reading a book about something that happened to someone else. They know all the details and have all the learning and benefit of the experience; it's just that the pain is gone. The stingers have all been neutralized or removed."

"Oh, I like that," Alex said out loud. He put his hand over his solar plexus without realizing that he was giving away signs that he had stingers of his own that he would like to have neutralized or removed.

"I'm telling you, Alex, this is good information for you to have, and I know you will be able to use it to help other people. I'm going to have to leave for a bit, but I guarantee I'll catch up with you sometime again before tonight, and I'll print you another list with what I said to him all written out."

Surprised is not the right word for the look on Alex's face; excitement, joy, anticipation, and relief were all written in his expression.

Like Alex's father would do, Mr. Parsons had found a way to help Alex with his fear and hurt without even having to talk about it—now or even at all. The man talks he often had with his father were always loving and kind, although much correction and instruction would often take place without Alex even realizing all of the positive lessons being imparted. There were a lot of mistakes in life that Alex would never make, simply because their man talks had taught him better.

"Are the lists really that different?" asked Alex.

"Well, you heard what I said," came back the reply.

"No, I mean the difference between the good and the bad memories. I mean the horrible memories like … " Alex held his stomach once more, feeling as though a feature film on fast forward was going through his mind. "Like, like anything horrible."

"Well, I won't admit to knowing everything that has ever happened to you, son. However, if I asked you to think of only one not–so–horrible memory in your past, could you think of one so I can show you the answers we seem to always get?"

*Oh no!* The thought exploded inside his head. *Why did you even ask? That was one dumb move, and now you're up!*

Seeing Alex's blank stare and sensing that he was upset, Mr. Parsons spoke reassuringly. "Remember now, I don't have to know anything about it out loud, ever and always … amen." With his head tilted just a bit, his very loving smile seemed to come from deep inside, having the ability to dissolve all fears.

Alex's mind had gone to his terrible experience in the woods, but a vow was a vow, and he was determined to live, so he would not choose that memory.

Signs of thinking flashed from the movement in his eyes. It was when he held his eyes way down and to the right that he frowned a little, looked towards Mr. Parsons, and pointed his finger as if to proceed. Mr. Parsons' thinking was right; he was still not going to tell him anything, even about this one.

"Because I'm going to get a little pressed for time here, and I do want to write you that list I promised, would it be all right if, for now, we only talk about the feelings you get?"

Alex shook his head no, but he said okay because he was expected to.

Mr. Parsons started. "Well then. Those feelings. How would you describe them, Alex?"

"Cold," came out rather quickly.

"And if those feelings had a texture, what texture would they be?"

Everything he could think of was harsh and sharp.

Mr. Parsons did not wait to hear an answer. "Would you consider those feelings rigid or flexible?"

His widening eyes gave a sense of what the answer would be. He replied strongly, "Rigid!"

"And where do you most feel those feelings in your body, Alex?"

His hand indicated a position just above his navel, and he realized he was telling Mr. Parsons his answers, unlike before, when Mr. Parsons gave him all the answers.

"Do these feelings cause you to feel tense or relaxed? And yes, you can tell me your answers, and if they are not what other people say, I will tell you."

Once again, no word needed to be spoken, as the obvious appeared in Alex's physiology.

"How would you describe your breathing with this memory?"

Watching Alex, Mr. Parsons could see that his breathing was shallow and rapid, which showed that he truly was associated into the memory, as is needed for this type of healing. Body language has a way of speaking without words.

"Are those feeling steady or intermittent, internal or external?" he asked, combining what appeared to be two questions for the sake of time.

Alex had no trouble grasping the meanings, and said, "Steady and internal, but external also," once more placing his hand over his middle, where the feelings still hurt.

"What size would you give those feelings?" was the next question.

"Bigger than the Hundred Acre Woods," came amazingly fast from Alex.

"If those feelings had a weight, what weight would they be?"

"Tons!" Alex responded, with an expression in his big brown eyes that said this was very real.

"If these feeling had a shape, what shape would they be?"

A two–man wood saw was the first thing Alex pictured and felt, but that didn't feel quite right. When he finally said it, what came out as words was, "A broken window with sharp pieces sticking out everywhere."

"Only three more for now," Mr. Parsons said. Then he added, "If these feelings had a smell, what would they smell like?"

"Oh, the potatoes at the bottom of Robert's barn, after winter, before planting." Alex wrinkled his nose. "They call them fertilizer."

"Pretty bad, huh?" Mr. Parsons asked. Then he added, "What if they were a food? What would they be?"

"Potatoes," Alex replied matter–of–factly.

"No, no. I mean, what if your feelings had a flavor like a food? What would they taste like?"

"Throw–up!" he quickly replied, and then thought, *Well, but that's not really food.*

Mr. Parsons just as quickly replied, "Well, it starts as food, and that will do."

"Now what if your feelings about this memory had a color?"

"They would be black," was the answer that was so quick to come.

*Phew!* Mr. Parsons breathed. "Nothing like yesterday … right?"

Alex just sat shaking his head no this time. For a couple of seconds, his mind drifted to the first choice that came up for consideration and shook his head no, even bigger.

Mr. Parsons spoke first. "It will probably be afternoon before I can get back; however, I will do my best to make it before supper, son."

Their right hands met, and Mr. Parsons immediately headed for the steps, went down off the porch and was on his way. Alex stared after this man, who seemed to have all the answers, with a different feeling than the one he had had the first time Mr. Parsons left. Alex watched as he turned left, the direction he had come from, and went past the corner of Mrs. Burns' house next door.

How could anybody not be saying to themselves, *What would happen if … ?* after seeing and hearing what just happened. After all, we're human, aren't we? Do we really store good and bad memories that differently? Do they weigh us down, or are they weightless? When we think about them, are they light or dark? Even Pastor McGregor could be heard to say, "That was one of the dark times in my life." When times got tough and things seem to feel heavy around the house, Mom could be heard to say, "Okay, time to lighten it up around here." Maybe we always have had the ability to use words to create change but just don't appreciate the value of what we say and think.

Out of sight, Alex took his folded brown list out of his pocket. *What would happen if … ? Could it be? Was it possible? Mr. Parsons said it is.*

In his mind, Alex reviewed the hour or so that had just passed and found comfort in it. Alex had found the answer he was searching for, the answer to his internal question, *What would happen if… ?*

"By supper," he spoke out loud into the air, confirming a time to himself to get to the list. Once again, he felt a little numb, as those types of memories seem to take a lot out of a person.

Going up to the room that was his when he stayed at Grandma's, he realized that he still had on what he was wearing yesterday. Although Grandma had not said anything about it, she probably just hadn't yet noticed. Not wanting to get caught by Grandma in the same dirty clothes was enough of a reason to change. Heading back out the door, he noticed that more flower petals had fallen to the deck in the gusty wind coming from the back of the house to the front. He swept them off to the side and out under the bottom rail. Adding the debris to the lawn below reminded him of a couple of things that his father would do for Grandma if he were there, so Alex decided to do them. Taking the trash to the curb was one of the things he needed to do, and that reminded him to also go to his house and do the same.

Taking his time, feeling no need to run, the warm sunshine felt like a reward for just being alive. Apparently, Mom had forgotten to stop the mail, as the mailbox looked stuffed. He checked to see whether anything had come from Dad. Nope, not this time. Alex was a little disappointed, but it was all right. Another day was turning out pretty good, and he was handling things well in his mind. When he got back to Grandma's, she was inside putting things together to go out again, it seemed. He put their home mail in the usual away box.

"You're leaving me, Granny?" he chided.

"Oh, I forgot that I promised Mildred I would take her shopping sometime. Wouldn't you know she embarrassed me into taking her today just before the closing prayer! She knew I had the afternoon to myself as we all held hands and formed our circle. As we bowed our heads, she hollered across to me so everyone could hear, 'Can you tell me why you can't take me to the store this afternoon?' And what did you eat for lunch, Alex?" she added without a stop.

"I'm okay," Alex replied. "I'm not hungry, and I feel pretty good right now."

"Well, you can come along with us if you want to, but you'll have to stay with me. I know your mother is not going to want you roaming around the mall alone."

"Can I stay home, please?" he quickly asked, not wanting to miss seeing Mr. Parsons this afternoon. "Please, pretty please with molasses on it, Grandma?" he begged, folding his hands as if in prayer. After no response, he added, "I won't hide your teeth!"

With that, she smiled and said, "Okay, okay, but only if you promise not to get into trouble. I don't want your mother mad at me. Mrs. Burns said this morning that she would be home all afternoon in case I wanted to stop in, so if you need anything, go to see her, William T." Alex headed toward her to give her an appreciative hug, a heart–to–heart hug, and he knew right where to rest his head on Grandma's left shoulder.

"Trouble" was a name she often said was Alex's middle name. She had a way of reminding him of that when she just called him "William T." rather than William A. He can still remember the day when she introduced him to someone, saying, "And this is my William T." She chuckled, and Alex was thankful that she did not explain, because she was only saying it to remind him of what he had done to rile her that day. No details are necessary, except that it had to do with Vaseline.

Grandma went to get ready for her trip to the mall. She changed clothes so as not to appear needy, as she sometimes put it, in the fashion–conscious mall. He thought he heard her saying something about an oil change; however, he was not fully paying attention by then. His thought had taken him deep inside … *What would happen if… ? What if the list would work for me? Oh, God please!*

He sat on the porch swing and just kicked his feet for a while. His intriguing new friend hadn't arrived yet, and his impatience showed a little. Not wanting to be gone when Mr. Parsons arrived, he ran up to his bedroom and brought his CD player down. Finding a way to have electricity outside was a problem because northern

Maine ice storms made having outside electricity dangerous. But soon there was an extension cord coming out an open window, leading to the end table next to the porch swing.

After a while, he decided to check the kitchen for a quick snack. To his delight, there was a peanut butter and marshmallow fluff sandwich with a note that said, "Jesus loves you," in Grandma's fancy script. The glass beside it was empty; however, the refrigerator contained several things to offer, and he settled on apple juice from Mitchell Farms. The chilled juice was fresh, and the taste easily hinted of McIntosh apples.

Settling back onto the porch swing, it took Alex no time to devour the sandwich, even wiping the sides of his sticky mouth with his fingers to ensure that he enjoyed every bit of it. Still seeing no one in sight, he turned the volume up a bit on his CD player. Returning his plate and glass to the kitchen sink, he justified not taking the time to wash them because he could have missed Mr. Parsons if he had. This was important.

Right he was. As though right on cue, as Alex returned to the porch, he spotted Mr. Parsons coming around the corner of the Burns' house. Holding up another sheet of brown paper, he cut straight across the lawn toward Alex, who was coming down the wooden porch steps to meet him. He first explained to Alex that he could only stay a moment. Mr. Parsons assured him that the statements on the paper would all make sense to him since they had worked on it when they were talking about the man at the prison. Accepting the paper and beginning to look it over, Alex could see that it would be as easy to read as the last one had been. Almost without hesitation, Mr. Parsons turned and started back across the lawn, seeming to be in a hurry.

Realizing that he really did not know this man, a question came to Alex. "When you're at home, do the people who know you call you sir or Mr. Parsons?"

Stopping in his tracks, thinking about how best to answer the question, Mr. Parsons turned back to Alex and said, "May I give you a hug?"

Without hesitating, Alex walked to this man who gave him a full–body, heart–to–heart hug, just like Grandma did. They held, neither speaking. Alex could feel his own heart beating and then became aware of the beating of Mr. Parsons' heart. This man was different.

As if in agreement, they released, and Alex said, "You should meet my Grandma!" Grandma did want to meet him, but Alex was also thinking that Mr. Parsons hugged just like Grandma did. His hug was comparable, and Grandma would love it. It had that way–deep–inside feeling, that heart–to–heart feeling.

Smiling, he answered Alex's first question. "Well, son, the people who really know me and love me like you and your grandma do, can call me anything they want. So you tell your grandmother that Mr. Parsons said 'Hi.'" And with that, he turned to leave. It took him no time to round the corner at the Burns' house, and he was gone once more. Alex didn't realize it yet, but they had not set a time to meet again. By now, Alex just expected that they would. They might even meet up at church sometime.

Heading back to the porch, having just watched his friend walk out of sight, Alex turned his attention to the new brown paper list. There was a lot more writing on this one than there had been on the other. He knew what he wanted to do, but felt uncomfortable thinking about doing it out here on the porch. Unplugging his CD player, he put the extension cord back through the open window and pushed the screen into place. Leaving the cord just inside the window, he headed straight to his bedroom and plugged his CD player in but pushed no buttons. Sitting on the edge of his bed, he allowed himself to begin to think about the thing that he vowed he would never tell anyone about. The memory did not come without pain.

Picking up the brown sheet of paper he had placed on his pillow, he decided he would do what he did before and allow his finger to serve as a guide when he was ready. As it had before, his breathing changed, and his heart began to race as soon as he unleashed his horror. But this time it was in black and white, like snapshots.

Mr. Parsons had been very specific in his instructions to stay totally in the memory while checking through the list. Although

Alex still felt like this was something he did not want to do, in the back of his mind, there still was that … *what would happen if … ? If the list had helped that man in prison, then …*

Alex proceeded. Being careful to stay fully in the memory now, he placed his finger next to the first instruction:

> See it as a movie.

Being careful to follow every line of direction very specifically, he slowly moved his finger down and read on.

> Make your memory a movie in bright and vivid color.
> Move your movie to the center and middle of your screen.
> Make the brightness on a scale from one to ten; if ten were the brightest, at least an eight or brighter.
> Make the size of the picture large and allow it to be very close—like two to three feet away.
> Allow the movie speed to run like normal life.

With each line, Alex found it easier to make the application.

> Always allow your pictures to be clearly in focus.
> See yourself in the movie.
> Allow the edges of your screen to disappear as you allow the memory to become a panorama that wraps all the way around you.

That one did something to Alex, and he took a deep breath, reacting to the shifting energy. What had started out as only pictures a few minutes before, had now shifted to a movie and become "lifelike," so that he felt he was living in it all around in every possible direction. Because of that, the next thing was already happening.

> Make your movie three–dimensional.
> Allow your favorite colors to permeate the background.
> As you see this movie straight on, Alexander, listen to all the sounds you hear, all the words you hear, all the sounds you make, and all the words you say.

Mr. Parsons had made it personal by using his real name, just the way it was given him at birth.

True to the request, Alex got right into what he remembered hearing and moved his finger down the page as he read on.

> The volume of the sounds you hear on a one to ten, with ten being the loudest, is perfect.
> The tones you hear are soft and mellow.
>
> The tempo, rhythm, and speed of the sounds were comfortable, like life's music.
>
> Hear all those sounds now as sounds in harmony with who you are and where you are.
> Yes, there will be inflections, as those sounds will go up and down in pitch and volume.
> Allowing those sounds to become soothing, peaceful, and loving makes a big difference.

Alex nodded his head as if approving.

> Now take all of those sounds and words, and just, well, just allow those sounds to simply last forever.

With that, he paused and just listened with his mind. He seemed to space out a little again, sort of like he did the first time, but this was different—as this produced precious, much–needed relief.

The numbness this memory always brought to the point of exhaustion, was now different. He still felt slightly numb, but it felt like a release.

His finger stayed on the page, and his eyes drifted to where Mr. Parsons had instructed him to really pay attention to all of his feelings about this memory before proceeding. Alex did just that. By now, he had no trouble feeling comfortable with what he was doing.

With his finger on the next line, he proceeded.

Allow your cold feelings, now, to become warm, even body temperature or slightly warmer.
Give those feelings the texture of soft, smooth, flexible silk or satin, like the feeling of that baby blanket it took you so long to give up.

There it was again.

A tear coursed down Alex's cheek, but much of the horror already seemed different. Truly there had been comfort in that blanket.

*I can do this,* he thought to himself. *I can finish this.* He continued down the list.

Make those feelings flexible—in fact, very, very flexible.
Whatever vibration there is, make sure it is a good vibration, like when you walk into a room where all the right people are. You're in the right place at the right time.
When you stop thinking about this memory in a bit, all the feelings that were once there will only decrease—that's right, decrease.

*Nice,* his mind responded, anticipating nothing less.

You should move all the feelings that you have from this memory directly to your heart. If you need to, just place your hand where those feelings are located and move them home to where your heart is.
Those feelings should now allow you to feel relaxed—very, very, very deeply relaxed.
Your breathing will go deep and relaxed as you feel that sense of letting go.
Make those feelings steady and internal, without interruption.
As you think about the size of these feelings, notice how huge they seem to be. Feel their size.
Allow these feelings to become as light as a feather, or, better yet, weightless.
Like most people, you will find allowing these feelings to become a nice, round shape is perfect. That makes them all–encompassing, totally smooth, no rough edges. In addition, some people like to envision a heart inside the perfectly round ball.

> If these feelings had a smell, you would want them to remind you of a favorite holiday time when all your best friends and family were around.
> If these feelings had a taste, you could easily find something from that holiday you truly enjoyed delighting your taste buds with.
> The color these feelings would become, well, that could only be your favorite color.
> Even now, you discover that as you think about this memory, it gives you a deep sense of fulfillment, peace, calm, joy, yet excitement, and finally that you are love, loved, and loving.

Numb. Yup, numb is how Alex was by this time. This was to have become his worst nightmare, the horror story of all time. Yet here it was, the stingers removed. *Only a memory like something that happened to someone else,* he spoke inside, just like Mr. Parsons had said. As he looked around his room, even the colors seemed brighter. Everything had lightened up. For Alex, this was indeed a miracle. He had not felt this light in days. Laying his head back on his pillow, the piece of paper falling to the floor, he felt like he could drift or even lift up off his bed and just float. This was the most marvelous feeling he had ever remembered having.

Without understanding all the implications, he got close to vowing he would learn how to do this and even more. This would become a feeling he would want everyone to own. For now, he at least intended to learn more from Mr. Parsons and help other people in the same way.

Alex was still on his bed, his eyes closed, absolutely relaxed and sleeping when Grandma open the door the rest of the way and walked in, surprised to find him asleep. She quietly closed the door as not to disturb him and headed back downstairs to prepare supper. She had already taken longer at the mall than she had planned, and thus picked up something easy to fix on the way home. She did not have a microwave. Her pacemaker would not allow for such a convenience. Besides that, she always said, "They are nuclear bombing good food out of God's intended perfection."

Putting the oven on preheat, she uncovered the supper she thought would simply delight her grandson. It would not be the first time; however, it could be the last they would share. What the doctors had told her last week was something she had vowed to keep completely private. After all, she was still here, and for now that was all that mattered. Maybe that was why she was delighted to get out of all the extras after dinner at camp the previous night.

Alex was not sure what woke him; he just remembered something had happened, and whatever happened had seemed to change everything. Then he remembered. He thought back to the movie he was sure would just blow his socks off, and his socks never moved. In fact, his stomach gurgled almost as if he were hungry, with no possible reaction to what he had gone through before. He could remember all the details; however, it had become like a story he knew about somebody else when it came to how it currently felt. He ran one more check, as he made his nature call, to make sure nothing was really bothering him—even checked his face in the mirror as he washed his hands, realizing everything was lighter.

Now having the ability to think ahead, having lost the pull of thinking back, he thought of when his father would be home again. *Dad is going to love this one,* he spoke inside to himself as he went back by his bed and found the piece of paper. Folding it up tightly, he placed it in his other pocket from where his white page list of good memories had managed to escape. He remembered showing the list to Mr. Parsons; however, he couldn't remember getting it back.

Like a light turned on, he recognized the smell of ham and pineapple pizza and headed quickly out of his room toward the stairs. "Grandma, you home?" he asked, knowing already that of course she was.

"Alex, I'm in the kitchen. You up for Hawaiian pizza tonight?" she spoke out before he cleared the bottom step.

"Am I?" he responded.

"Glad to see you ate your sandwich. I got all the way to the mall before I realized I couldn't remember if I told you or not." Alex just rubbed his belly and licked his upper lip as a sign of approval.

Supper was just that—easy. Usually Grandma had a way of making sure he ate more than his share; however, tonight he seemed full for some reason. Life itself seemed different. Only Grandma seemed tired and completely worn out at this point. With things changed, it wasn't his nap that made all the difference. He already had made plans to do another memory that bothered him that night. There was no rush; he had the tool in his pocket, and he would do it before he went to sleep.

He offered to do the dishes, such as they were, and Grandma had no problem allowing that. Like his parents had told him before, Grandma was getting older. She went to her favorite chair and started to pick up her book as she put her wire frames back on. No one would question whether Grandma was tired tonight. The church women can wear each other out just being together. Mildred was one to have to see every possible option before buying anything, and today she needed shoes, a two–piece dress that had to have long sleeves and be way below the knees in length, and she also thought she needed a hat that she never did decide on. Poor Grandma was pooped! Alex could hear her talking to herself—"I think I'm too tired to read"—take a deep breath, and relax with a sigh. Putting her book back down on the side table, she got back up and went over to the opposite wall, where she started more of that old people music.

"Come on in here, Alex. Come talk to me. I haven't heard about your day yet at all. Actually, I'm not sure what you did yesterday. Come on. Come sit down in here and talk to me," she said as he cleared the hallway coming from the back kitchen.

Beginning to talk, he said, "Mr. Parsons came by, and we did have a porch chat. I meant yesterday and today. You were sleeping yesterday, and today it was women, women, and more women." He chuckled at her.

"Nice," she responded, smiling at his response. "So he's a nice man?"

"Oh Grandma," he started, "he knows everything about people. I mean all about people. He even taught me how to help people."

The look on her face definitely indicated a question.

"He taught me how everyone stores their good memories. He said I have a gift for helping people, and he wants me to learn so that I can help people like he does. He went to Houlton prison yesterday and helped a man who did something wrong with a gun, and it worked!"

A quick thought triggered in Alex's mind as he remembered seeing the tear when he and Grandma talked about the man coming with Grandpa's things in the tin box. He remembered her getting the bottle of the fragrance of love to show him what Grandpa had sent, and another tear had come. His confidence in what Mr. Parsons had taught him made him quickly say, "I can teach you, Grandma … if you'll let me." Just past twelve years of age and with family around, he had just reached the age where kids begin to make judgment decisions on their own. They begin to study the role models in their life, and Alex had no problem feeling like he could pretend to be Mr. Parsons. Now how could anyone not say *yes* to a child who has learned all about people at such an early age and wants to teach you? And thus, she did.

It took him a while to find the right brown paper, as he now had one in each pocket. He took the first brown paper out from his right inside pocket. His first thought was that he would teach this to her. However, the haunting question, *What would happen if … ?* in his head made him change his mind. He reached into the other pocket to retrieve the other brown page. This time he was sure he knew where the white one was. Mr. Parsons never gave it back. He had no trouble planning to go right to the problem she had recently talked about, believing that in his hand was a solution. Alex said, "Remember when the soldier came with the tin box?" knowing she would definitely remember.

She gave him a tired look like, "Not that now, Alex." However, he insisted on telling her that she would not have to say a thing. He said that he would tell her what to think, and she would just have to think whatever he told her.

"It won't hurt anymore, Grandma. I promise," he coached.

Intrigued, she reluctantly agreed to what this grandson, her pride and joy, was asking.

"Now you have to really remember what it was like from the beginning, like when he rang the doorbell and everything, just like it was a movie happening right now. You just keep thinking right there, and I will tell you what to think, okay?"

Now even more confused than ever and almost too tired to do this, she did at least think back to opening the door and seeing that soldier there in full dress uniform, a little tin box in his hand. "Evening Mama," he said as he took off his hat. She quickly was getting so lost in a memory that touched her life, yet gave her such pain again.

Sitting not far from her, she almost didn't hear Alex's voice saying, "Make it a movie, Grandma, and you just nod your head when you have."

Finally, she responded. "Oh, it is, Alex, one happy, sad movie."

"Make your movie in bright and vivid color in the center and middle of your screen," he said, combining lines already, as though he knew what to say.

He did not notice that she moved her head ever so slightly, and her eyes shifted from down and right to straight ahead, a tear forming again.

"Make the size of the picture large, allowing it to be very close, like two to three feet away."

For Grandma, talking to the soldier made the distance perfect.

"Allow the speed of motion to run like normal life speed." Alex added.

Grandma realized she had slowed it up without knowing it.

Time passed, and Alex wonderfully followed his finger down the page, talking out loud with each line.

Soon was heard, "Now take all those sounds and words and just, well, just allow those sounds to simply last forever."

A good while later, the stored and now active feelings of her memory were "light as a feather, or, better yet, weightless."

All the way to the very end Alex went, only to realize that just repeating all those words had done something in him again as well. He did not really know what Grandma was going to say, and he said nothing, as he just sat looking at her, waiting. It took her time to look straight at him. However, when she did, she said, "Praise God, Alex. He was right; you have a gift." She paused and kept staring right at him as though in disbelief. "Do you have any idea what you just did?" she asked as a near waterfall of tears began flowing rapidly from both eyes. She was rapidly coming out of the numbness and into the pure joy of freedom's release.

"Come over here, Hon. Let me hug you." Like always, it was the heart–to–heart side, even with him bending down as far as necessary. The hug did not last long, and as he backed up, she started talking again, pausing between each hard–pressed thought.

"God bless you, Alex. I can't believe what you just told me to do. Oh my word." She paused again before saying, "I just can't believe what that did. I mean... I mean... The hurt is gone... it's... it's... it's like it's... okay now. I can remember it all... it just doesn't hurt anymore."

Silence fell for a few moments as she tried to regain her composure while placing her hand over her mouth. Alex thought about telling her about his memory. However, he could still hear his vow in his head and made the smart decision not to. He realized he could have told her now, as truly the stingers were all gone just like Mr. Parsons said; however, when his father came home, he now knew he would tell him. For now, he once again made his decision not to tell Grandma, or anyone else, until his dad came home.

"Mr. Parsons taught you all that?" she asked, in part not believing how the memory truly felt. "How could this be possible? You just read that paper to me, and it changed." Strangely, Grandma was sitting there shaking her head no, validating the truth of what took place absolutely, positively, totally, and completely, with a yes.

Once again, more silence, as he did not think she was really asking a question, but instead making a statement. "I wonder what he's taught Pastor?" was her next remark.

"He just put it all down here on my paper," Alex said, not really showing her as he put the brown page back in his pocket for safekeeping.

Grandma's eyes wandered around as if lost for a few more minutes before he came to the conclusion that she probably was through talking for tonight. What he did not realize was that Grandma was seeing a different room based on the lightness she was now feeling.

Somehow sensing it was best to leave her alone, he picked up her right hand, looked right into what now looked like love, glowing on her face, and just smiled. They never said a word as Grandma did indeed seem to be in some type of afterglow. The magic of that moment was a memory Alex would never ever let go of.

As he headed toward the stairs, a haunting thought crossed his mind again, especially after what just happened to Grandma, after what he knew had happened to him. You probably recognize that thought yourself. *What would happen if … ?* There is only one way to know for sure.

# Chapter 6

Alex was anything but sleepy. He had, in the back of his mind, the question, *What would happen if … what would happen if what his newfound friend had taught him worked for Grandma?* Now he knew it did, just like it apparently was supposed to. He changed his clothes and prepared for bed. However, the air of excitement remained.

The CD player began to play, and "I Can Only Imagine" soon came up.

> I can only imagine what it will be like
> When I walk by Your side
> I can only imagine what my eyes will see
> When Your face is before me
> I can only imagine
> I can only imagine
> Surrounded by Your glory
> What will my heart feel?
> Will I dance for You Jesus?

Or in awe of You be still?
Will I stand in Your presence?
Or to my knees will I fall?
Will I sing hallelujah?
Will I be able to speak at all?
I can only imagine
I can only imagine
I can only imagine when that day comes
And I find myself standing in the Son
I can only imagine when all I will do
Is forever, forever worship You
I can only imagine
I can only imagine
Surrounds by Your glory
What will my heart feel?
Will I dance for You Jesus?…

By the time the song got to this place in the chorus again, he had a strange feeling over take him, a feeling that something was still not finished with his miraculous emotional healing. *Surrounded by your glory, what will my heart feel?* It was definitely feelings that were coming up, pent–up feelings, only this time they were totally directed at Joe. He began to realize what those feelings were as he looked over and caught his own face in the mirror.

His mind drifted to an image of Pastor McGregor and the sermon where he spoke about seeing people as if they were in a mirror. "When you see them in the mirror, it is only a reflection of the real person inside. What we do as humans, is we don't like the real person inside because of things we have seen, heard, or felt ourselves do outside," he preached. "God looks upon the intent of the heart just like he looks at the intent in yours. He is always asking you to love the person inside and forgive them no matter what. You may not like or even love what they make you feel, what you saw them do, or maybe what they did to you. However, I am not telling you to be the one to forgive them; God is." The image came and went quickly, and the message it contained was full of impact. It was certainly nothing Alex could have conceived of doing not so long ago, however, now it felt different. The memory was different. Still, it did happen, and it happened to him.

Although it was the right tune, the words he heard as it played were once again, "I can only imagine what my eyes will see when your face is before me … I can only imagine." *What would Jesus do?* he quickly thought. Without a hesitation, he sat down on his bed and began to mumble out softly. "God, you know it wasn't right. Dad told me it wasn't right. If Mr. Parsons hadn't come along, I couldn't take this right now." He paused a good long time, as if replaying a memory to make sure he was all right now. "I have to, God," he said, shaking his head no until it finally turned into a yes. A tear came down the right cheek first and then the left, the fastest escape route the body has for clearing emotional baggage. Somewhere inside, there was a reminder from a voice that sounded so much like Mr. Parsons. *Alex, God is not asking you to forget what happened. God is asking you to forgive the one who made it happen to you. As you retain the memory, he will give you the gift of being able to help others, because you will always remember the memory with all the learning and benefits of the experience—with all the pain removed. That's right, Alex, all.* It wasn't his words after that which mattered; it was the results that mattered. Alex finally found himself free of Joe as he made Joe God's responsibility, wherever he was.

When he got up and started to wash his face for bed, he realized again something had changed. Nearly finished brushing his teeth, he smiled and checked a glance into his eyes again as he thought *I can teach this to Mr. Parsons. He may not know this about everyone.*

With that, his mind crossed to Grandma as he thought about her and the soldier. This made Alex realize her pain had not been like his. Maybe not everything needed forgiveness like his did.

*Click!* The light went off, as a mind still wandering started to bed. He had remembered to turn the CD player off. However, in his head, he continued picking up the lyrics where they had left off on the last song. Out loud, you could hear him softly singing in the darkness of his room, "Oh, with all that I've done wrong, I must have done something right. To deserve a hug every morning and butter-fly kisses at night." His thoughts turned to Dad coming home, and going to sleep was not an issue tonight.

# Chapter 7

Friday came, and Alex realized his days of extra freedom were nearly over. With all his newfound knowledge, he was sort of hoping Mr. Parsons would come by. He sure wanted to tell him about forgiveness and how that made a difference. The more he thought about it, the more he realized maybe he didn't. After all, to tell him about forgiveness, he would have to tell him about what happened in the woods, and he had definitely decided that this memory could not be shared with anyone before he told his father.

Grandma turned breakfast into a celebration of sorts. He heard her singing something from his bedroom and knew the smell of Canadian maple syrup in the air. What he did not know until he went through the kitchen door was that it was flapjacks, as they called them in northern Maine. She was leaving nothing to chance.

Grinning at him, she cocked her head a little, popped her eyes, and said, "There you are, my little pretty. I am going to fatten you up with flapjacks, warm butter, and fresh, warm maple syrup." She dashed straight at him as if to give him a hug, but instead poked her fingers straight into his gut, saying, "Then I am going to love you to life!" With that, she gave him one of the best heart–to–heart hugs she had ever given. "Oh, I love you, Alex, Alex, Alex." The words came out as she squeezed and rocked him from side to side.

He determined that they were having so much fun he would never let go. Knowing Grandma's rule about holding until the other person let go almost made it fun. The truth is, he could feel her heartbeat, and there was no question from inside they both felt love, loved, and loving. That was always the gift they gave each other and even others if they had the opportunity to hug them right. She finally spoke and began to let go, saying, "You wait until I tell your father what you did for me last night. He is going to be so surprised." Pausing, she added, "I don't think I am going to tell your mother. This is really something you have to stop and think through, and she is just too busy for that; having taken a week off and next getting back to work would be her priority." Alex had about decided the same thing. Rumor had it that Dad would be home soon, and he could not wait to have a man talk first. After both washed the dishes, with Alex doing the toweling dry part, they both went to the front porch.

"You need to change your shirt, Alex," the words came. "You have maple syrup straight down the front of you, and the ants are going to eat you alive."

They sat and made the swing go in perfect rhythm for a bit, talking about their tasks in the kitchen at camp, and Alex saying how he saw the eagle at the fish hatchery. The mailman came by and handed him the mail for Grandma only, and added that there was a post from his father in their mailbox back at home.

"Come on, Grandma." You could hear him plead as he held out his hand, begging her to come with him to get the mail. He started toward the steps, his hand still out in a begging position, with Grandma not moving an inch.

"You go get the mail, Alex, and just bring it back here. Whatever it is from your father, if it feels right, I will open it and share it with you. Otherwise, it's your mother's mail, not yours."

Speed was what he used to make the short distance between the houses. Only noticing that there was an official–looking foreign–stamped envelope, he grabbed all the mail and hightailed it back for the check of approval. It was more than relief as Grandma scanned the mail and found that official–looking envelope with the foreign stamps. "Alex, there is a letter here from William for your mom." She kept scanning the pieces, and then, holding something way up in the air, she remarked, "There is also this envelope that says it is from William Williams the Second for Mr. William Williams the Third!"

Everything inside him began jumping for joy. He had to stand on his tiptoes to reach the extension of her fingers. As he grabbed the envelope, he didn't hear anything about another envelope for Kaitlyn. There was no going to a private place to read this letter. Nothing could keep him from tearing the side wide open. He almost tore the sheet the handwritten letter was on. His eyes stared at the words. Inside, his excitement only grew.

> My Dearest Alex,
> Nothing pleases me more than to be able to tell you I am coming home.

He stopped immediately and told Grandma the good news, and then continued reading, as both wanted to know when.

> They said there is only one task left that I need to participate in, and my job here will be finished. I count the days, Alex, and I don't even know how many.
> I have told so many true stories here about you and how proud I am of the man you have become. Everyone wants to go fishing with us at Lobster Lake because those times are probably my favorite, so I talk about them the most. Maybe we need to see if we can buy a lot nearby and build a cabin. I know they do not permit them at the lake. Maybe we just get a big tent and become "The Lobster Lake Bed and Breakfast Tent" for soldiers only. Right now, that sounds like fun. I have missed you so.
> Please, plan to go fishing for one whole day sometime after I have been home three full days. It is a must. You decide where.

Clean the poles, and start collecting night crawlers. Wet the lawn liked I showed you; then just go out with the flashlight at night and "neek up on 'em" like I showed you. Load us up a good fifty or more. I am coming soon.

Yesterday was Monday for you, and you just never left my mind. I felt concerned that you were okay; however, I just knew you were. From Mom's note I figured you were probably up at camp with her as nurse. I have to still write Kaitlyn. I wrote to Mom and told her already. I will send all three notes soon.

I love you.

Dad

"I just don't know, Grandma," Alex said as if to answer a question she had yet to ask. "He has one task left, and then he is coming home!"

With that, he jumped down the stairs, ran out onto the lawn, looked up to the sky, and acted like someone was swinging him around.

Grandma departed from the porch and soon reappeared with a candle sticking out of a cake of some sort. She said, "It is still a little frozen, Alex. However, this calls for a party! Oh, thank you, Jesus!" Then she hit the swinging screen door again with, "Oh, I forgot, a match, and—oh yes—I will make lemonade." When she returned, she had them both in hand.

By then, Alex had about memorized his letter. "When, when, when?" he said out loud as if Grandma knew it all.

"Just be patient there, William T. God's timing is always perfect."

With that, she lit the candle and began to sing, expecting Alex to join her on a new rendition of, "For he's a jolly good fellow; for he's a jolly good fellow; for he's a jolly good fellow; and soon he's coming home!" That was the part he could understand.

A big–bladed knife cut right through the cake, and a piece bigger than anyone should ever take was put on each of their plates.

As they both began to freeze their jaws—the cake really did come right out of the freezer—Alex remembered something. "Did Kaitlyn get a letter?"

"Yup. Sure did," she replied.

"Can we go to see Momma tonight?" he begged.

"She will be home by noon tomorrow, Alex. I think we best wait."

The excitement was too much. He just got more restless. His brain still asking, "When, when, when?"

"Go ride your bike, Alex," Grandma said, deciding that it would cool some of his excitement down.

"It will be dark before I would get to camp," the inquisitive reply came back, not seeming to question that she was not telling him to bike there.

"No, no, Alex. We will wait for your mom and Kaitlyn to come home tomorrow. It will keep. I promise. We don't even know when he is coming."

He raced off to his house, his feet almost not touching the ground. He unlocked his bike off the back gas pipe meter. Grandma saw him make several passes round both the front and back corners of the street. She had already made the decision that it was time she started baking the cookies all Williams loved the best. Flour, sugar, and molasses—in essence, all of the things she needed in the most proper of proportions. The oven had clicked ready, and the first two trays went in. The first two batches were to be baker's dozens for Alex and Kaitlyn to share with their mom, as well as a batch for Pastor McGregor. It was when the third and fourth cookie pans came out of the oven that she went and stood on the porch to watch for and call Alex in, her hair a little fallen out of her usual, pinned–up style. As she wiped the flour once more off her hands on the round–the–neck cook's apron she usually wore, he came past the front. Noticing her, he came right up and bumped against the stairs.

"Got a good reason to not have a fresh, hot, molasses cookie right now?" she said as if teasing him and already knowing the answer. "Put your bike in the garage, and meet me right back here," she said, pointing to the swing. In two minutes, he was all smiles and ready, his breathing still labored from a straight, hard–time ride.

"He's coming home, Alex." Grandma smiled. "And you're going fishing. I know your father."

"He said we had to wait three full days."

"Right. I figured," she replied. "For that reason, I made extra cookies!"

She tried everything she could think of to calm his excitement a little that night. It had been months since his father left. She tried checkers while some of that old people music played. Even a well–worn deck of "Crazy Eight" and "Old Maid" cards didn't seem to do it. Her last resort was warm milk and a cookie. This had been some day. When she thought of what she really had fed him, his mother was probably going to skin her alive.

"Considering we started with flapjacks; had cake earlier, Alex; and your mother is coming home tomorrow with Kaitlyn, maybe we better not tell her exactly what we both ate today." And with that, she chuckled, realizing he was not the only one to sweeten his teeth all day.

Alex was still too excited to go to bed when she picked up her book, put her wire frames on, and reclined in her favorite rocker. What he did realize was that after each night of sleep, he was one day closer to his dad's coming home. With that in mind, he headed toward the stairs.

"You mean I don't get a hug?" Grandma called out.

Alex dropped his head as he turned around, looking at Grandma, and said, "Nope!"

With that, she got up and said, "William T, you come right back here. You will love me to life until the day I die," reaching out in his direction until the necessary heart–to–heart hug was completed.

He then rushed up the stairs and out of sight.

In her mind, she remembered what the doctor had told her and was, for that reason, longing for her son William's return. If things went the way they told her, she would not share Christmas with the family this year. Just as Alex still kept his secret, she had vowed to keep hers.

At one point, as she passed Alex's bedroom this morning, she had looked to see if she could find the list Alex had used with her, because the differences it made were so substantial. She would have asked, except that this was like saying you have something in your life you need help with.

Grandma couldn't expect Alex, or anyone for that matter, to

understand the secret she had hidden all these years. She thought back to the butcher who had caught her off guard less than a year after her husband had died, and at knifepoint did unspeakable things to her. No, no one would ever know. She couldn't talk to her pastor at the time. One woman who had done so was made to feel at fault. No, she was not going there. He had taken her totally by surprise, just as he had the other woman. She would take that horror to her grave, unless she could find and use Alex's lessons from Mr. Parsons. Last night's miracle made her think of Mildred. Everyone knew the secret Mildred hid about her addicted husband. Everyone pretended not to notice the black and blue marks. Everyone knew that the long sleeves and long skirts hid scars. Grandma thought, *What would happen if … ?* while a tear formed on the edges of her eyes. There were others. First, she had to find his lessons and make sure it worked a second time like it did the first.

Picking up her book, she began to read. The story triggered too many memories she did not care to digest tonight. Wonder of wonder, miracle of miracles, William was coming home.

Her mind drifted to some of the good memories she had of her son William as a child. He was like Alex, a good, well–liked boy who stayed out of trouble. She laughed aloud, thinking of one Christmas when she did the best job of setting up a model train set, and had it running when he came downstairs to see the tree. The first thing he did was head straight for the plate they had left for Santa, picked up the flat molasses cookie, and sat on the floor eating it with a grin that said he had gotten the prize. She had to make him turn around to see the train. But now was the time to think, *party, party, party*. Tomorrow she and Alex would go to the grocery store, and she would fix some casseroles and other easy dishes for Mary. That way, William and Mary would have more quality time together in those first few days.

Heading to the kitchen, she already had a good idea of what she would prepare. She just needed to check the panty and start a list. It wasn't long before she was passing Alex's door on her way to take a rest. The sound coming out of his throat made her glad there was a door to close, and that she did. He had the generational curse—he could make a joyful *noise*, but it could hardly be called joyful *singing*.

# Chapter 8

It was just before 8:00 a.m. when the doorbell rang. Grandma had been downstairs already; however, she had gone back up to take a hot bath before they were to share oatmeal, raisins, and brown sugar mixed with warm milk. Alex heard Grandma holler out. "Can you see who that is, Alex? There is someone knocking at the door."

Without question, he obeyed the request and headed to the door, just having changed out of his pajamas. About one–third of the way down the stairs … he knew. The outline of the person at the door was unmistakable.

Seeing Alex coming down the stairs, the voice hollered, "The door's locked, Alex!" tapping on the glass as if to hurry him, while rumbling the door handle with his hand. It should have been easy to open, but it seemed to take an eternity. His father was home!

Dad was smart and moved back just a little, spreading his arms out. Had he walked forward, there would have been a traffic jam in the doorway. Alex charged right at him and grabbed on with all his might, his face turned out from his father's right shoulder. Dad let it last a few seconds, then pushed him back enough to rearrange the fit so that it became heart–to–heart, with both their heads on the other person's left side.

*Thump, thump, thump.* They could both feel heartbeats. The connection was made. Those two hearts knew the loving bond they shared.

"I have missed you so. I am never going away again," Dad said as they continued to hold each other. It didn't matter that the letter had only arrived yesterday.

Remembering where he was, Dad was the next to speak. While half–releasing his son, he shouted, "Mom, are you home?"

"William, it is you!" she said as she rounded the ledge near the top stair, still a little wet from her bath and wrapped in her housecoat. Releasing Alex as if it were okay now, he cleared the stairs before Grandma even started down. It was then that the reality of his father being home really sank in. William and Grandma never missed a smooth transition into a heart–to–heart hug. They had practiced this one until there was never a mistake.

Alex called up the stairwell, "Momma's not home," trusting he was telling his father something he did not already know. "They're at church camp. Mom's the nurse," Alex informed.

"Let me look at you," Grandma said, backing up and pushing her wet, just–below–the–shoulder–length, hair back. There he stood in Marine–dress green. He had to wear the uniform in order to get the right–priced air connections. "Oh my … my hair got you all wet, William," she said as she attempted to brush the water off. "I will go start some coffee. You can rest on the front porch and chat with Alex. Mary and Kaitlyn will be home by noon, and … " Remembering a secret she held inside, she said, "I have missed you more than they have." That was an unusual statement for her to make, with a hidden meaning she would not divulge. She almost regretted saying it the way she had. However, truth slipped out in words, and there was no taking them back. They hugged lightly, a tear falling down her right cheek. News, both good and bad, filled her mind, but stalwart Grandma would not be discussing her current medical condition nor her experience with Alex's list.

They came down the wide staircase side by side as William acknowledged to his son that he knew Mom was the nurse at camp from her letters. He also told him that his duffel bag was already in the house and a load of wash was started.

"Your letters came yesterday," Grandma hollered, as she was nearly to the kitchen. "Alex is the only one who opened his."

They both did as Grandma had suggested and headed toward the porch swing they had hung for her two years before.

"The lawn looks good, son," Dad said as they both hit the hanging swing about the same time.

"So what have you been up to?" Dad asked.

"What was it like over there?" Alex replied.

Dad paused, staring toward the ends of the boards at the edge of the porch. It wouldn't be easy deciding what he would and wouldn't tell Alex. A hint of the smell of coffee somehow made its way out to their noses. Dad took a deep breath in appreciation of a remembered smell that says, *"Home at last."*

"Well, I guess the best thing to say about being over there is that I'm home," he said, pausing again. Then he continued. "One of the things about wars and explosives is that you get to see, hear, and feel things you wished had never happened. I mean, it's hard to believe what people will do to themselves and others. Anything you see on TV is nothing compared to really being there. I just pray you never have to go." And with that, he pulled at Alex's side to make him come closer so that he could put his arm around him. You would have thought that would have triggered what had happened earlier in the week for his son. However, for now, that was resolved in a way that did not need discussion at the moment.

Grandma rounded the corner, coming through the screen door with a tray that for sure held more than fresh, hot coffee. Alex was allowed a cup that was more milk than coffee. As she set the tray down on the side table, William said, "Now that's worth flying half a day and all night for."

Grandma grinned, knowing the hidden meaning in his value of her cooking. "I have oatmeal about to start. I can make flapjacks if you prefer."

"I think one of these cookies will do just fine for starters," William said as he picked up a fresh molasses cookie for each person on the swing.

"So what will it be?" Grandma asked, looking at the two of them. After all, she did expect an answer. Spoiling them with cookies was not her idea of breakfast.

Alex just shook his head as if to tell her he was not making any decisions; Dad was home, and now he could decide.

"I don't have any fresh fruit. However, there are raisins and brown sugar for the oatmeal?" She spoke as if still questioning whether the food she was about to start would be right, or if something needed to be changed.

"We can go pick blueberries," Alex quickly replied, a smile on his face, indicating that was something the two of them had done before.

Knowing it was just to the field in the vacant lot next to the house behind hers, she went quickly to fetch one–cup measuring cups for each of them. Coming back out, she told them they were small containers because they were to pick only enough for breakfast. She would start the flapjack batter and be ready to pour by the time they returned. She also thought to bring a travel mug for her son, William, so that his morning coffee would not be interrupted by going after berries. Off they went as she returned to preparing the meal, her favorite of all activities.

Alex was already acting as though his Dad had never left. It seemed only natural to be picking berries and talking like best of friends almost about anything and nothing. Dad happened to ask if anything exciting had happened while he was away, and Alex started to tell him rather excitedly about Mr. Parsons and the lessons. Like Grandma, Dad was not able to immediately comprehend what Alex was saying: good memories, bad memories, changing memories, prison, Grandma. He finally came to the conclusion that all this stuff was written down on lists that he could read firsthand another time, so he got Alex to agree to wait until they had the papers so Alex could tell him what they said, that way his mind would be clearer and more able to understand. The excitement of just coming home and all that travel had already been a little much. In addition to that, he was never one to sleep on anything in motion, even an airplane.

The story of the American Bald Eagle at the trout hatchery seemed to excite his father, as Alex presented a vivid picture of the talons scraping across the top of the tank and then snatching a prize. "I will show it to you when I see him again," he said as if it would fly over any time just for his dad.

William II reminded his son, "As long as Mom says okay, we really will go fishing all day long, and soon."

"In three full days," Alex replied, as if to set the time limit mentioned in the letter. "Can we go to Lobster Lake?"

"You really want to go way out there?" his Dad said, over exaggerating by nodding his head yes.

The biggest of blueberries in hand, to the point where the containers could not hold anymore, they headed to the house only to find Grandma on the porch waiting with a mixing bowl full of flapjack batter in her hand. If it were up to Alex, they would have been dumped right in. However, Grandma insisted that they be washed first. She had often said, "Cows fly at night therefore everything must get washed in the morning."

It wasn't long before William was on the next cup of coffee, having finished what he was willing to eat. Alex proclaimed he could eat no more, with flapjacks still sitting untouched. Grandma didn't mind. What food remained would feed her birds at the window. They would celebrate today as well, because her son was safely home from war.

William asked if Grandma had the church camp phone number. It was now thirty minutes past 0900h, and he grew anxious to have the whole family together.

"I know that I don't, son," she replied. "They only have that one phone in the director's office," she said as she heard hers ringing in the other room.

"Hello.… You're kidding. Okay. Let me see if I can get someone to come right out. You're sure it's your belt?" pausing again. "Just loose. Ah ha. Threads hanging off; not safe." She continued shaking her head no. "Okay. Wait right there. I just thought of someone I know who might be able to run out and tighten it up, and I am sure he won't mind following you home. If he can't do it, I will find someone. Just let me call around. Ah, you know, the new man from church," Grandma replied trying not to give it away. "I am going to send Alex with him. He knows the way, and will know where you are and how to find you." She quickly hung up, trusting that she had made it clear that all would be handled.

Coming back out onto the porch, she said, "Mary's car needs help. Some kid said her belt is loose, and the belt has hanging threads. She still has about two hours to cover as nurse. However, if she needs a battery, you will have time to swing by the mall on the other end of Mapleton as well." Pointing to Alex, she said, "Go open the garage door and move the mower over. You left it right behind my jalopy. I think there are enough tools in my trunk to fix Fort Knox." Young Alex nodded in agreement, remembering the last time he had used them. Even if half of them sprouted legs and walked away, the remainder would serve just fine. It was one of the safest places to store things of value when you did not lock your garage up every night.

Excitement built fast for Dad as he realized that not only would this be a surprise, but the whole family would be there. It took twenty–four minutes when it should have been closer to thirty by the time they could see the infirmary with the Ford parked beside it, hood still up. He tried ever so carefully to get as close as possible without giving away their presence yet. He wanted to be able to see the whites of her eyes when he first saw her, but that was not to happen.

"Daddy! Daddy! Daddy!" The shouts of joy came from the crest of the knoll to their left. In response to the sound, the car stopped instantly. Without closing the door, Daddy went running to his little ten–year–old baby girl, who jumped up to catch his neck, wrapped her legs in customary fashion around his waist, and chanted, "You're home! You're home!" nestling her head right in under his chin as tight as she could. Although it was as thrilling to her father to see her as it was for him to see Alex and Momma, he still had not seen his prize. He needed a nurse, and he needed her now. Five and a half months was a long time to be away.

"We have to be really quiet," he said, putting Kaitlyn back down and putting his finger to her lips. He motioned for Alex, just now getting out of the car, not to say a word. "Stay right here," he said, pointing at the car as he started stalking his way toward the small cabin with the white sign: *Infirmary*. Kaitlyn crunched down, holding her finger over her mouth to warn Alex to say nothing. When he got to the screen door, he stood up tall as a Marine should and knocked, as if making a house call. Nothing moved. There was not one sign of life coming from that building.

"Hey, soldier," a voice called out from the most gorgeous woman he had ever remembered, coming through the doorway of the Cafatorium directly across the way. "You looking for a nurse?" Obviously, she had seen him first and had a chance to compose herself and prepare a proper entrance. She moved quickly after that. However, he cut her travel time down to a third as he ran and grabbed her pulling her up off her feet. It was the strangest thing to see her white nurse's shoes pointed down as she went limp in his protective arms. The kids waited as long as they could. Both seemed to have started running at about the same time. It soon looked like a football huddle.

Mabel had caught sight of them out the kitchen window and had hollered across to the other end of the room to Pastor McGregor, "William is home! Mary's William is home. He's out there on the grass." After that, the door swung open forcefully enough to make a bang that could be heard by all. Pastor hurried right behind Mabel to join the group now assembled. It was a happy group that came together. Everyone was just glad he was home.

Then, all of a sudden, Mary began to back up slightly, her mouth dropping wide open with an expression of surprise. "You're the one

Grandma sent to fix my car?" she asked, beginning to put the pieces together. "Oh yes. Alex is with you. Of course you are," she said, putting her hand up to the middle of her forehead. "Grandma knows you're here already." She paused only a few seconds before smiling and looking right at her son, saying, "I sure hope you hid her false teeth, Alex," and they all laughed.

More general conversation took place about how the weekdays at camp had gone, before Mabel said, "Your mother came out to help us Wednesday night," directing her statement to William. Then she added, "She's not feeling herself these days. I told her to go home early, and you know her; she's always the last one to leave. However, she was glad I told her to go, and that's not normal for her. You best be watching after her."

"She is getting older," he responded, with Mary nodding her head and looking down toward the ground, remembering back to Wednesday.

Mary added, "And she did make molasses gingerbread and whipped cream for the whole camp before she came out."

"I helped her, Momma," Alex added.

"Of course you did," she responded, putting her arm around his neck. "That grandmother of yours believes she is going to turn you into a cook before she half–teaches anything to Kaitlyn."

William decided it was time and made the decision to end this social gathering. "I have a Ford to fix!" he declared.

Mary said she still had packing to do. Plus, she also had one child with poison oak in one of the cabins who would need one more coating of ointment before being released to go home. "I can be ready in about an hour."

As they all started walking back in the right direction, William looked at Mary, held her hand, and spoke the words that in private moments, drove her nearly crazy. "Hi, toots!" he said, his left eye twitching.

Soon, Alex was in hog heaven and getting dirty in places like all boys do as he assisted his father with tightening the belt. It did indeed need changing. The big question now was will it start? Then, would it make it all the way home?

William checked to make sure it was in P for park, the emergency brake was set, and the battery showed signs of a charge before he told Alex to get the key from his mother and turn it on. Alex's face lit up like he had just been called grown–up. He had never sat in the driver's seat and been privileged to turn a car on before. He clearly heard his father's instructions. "Put your foot on the gas pedal and push it down only once before turning the key." The engine started with a roar, full–throttle and full–volume.

"Take your foot off the gas, Alex," his Dad said, realizing now that he had told him to push the pedal down, but not to release it. Alex did not hear, and Dad had to move around the car to make sure the instructions were heard.

"No trouble with that battery." he said, while thinking, *No trouble with that engine either. Just needs a new belt.*

Mary came out as the car started and went straight to her husband, hugging him once more. She needed the blessing of a man around the house. Things like this were just not for a woman to handle. Even earlier today, when she made the call, her thoughts went to why William had to be over there when she needed him right here. The kids just watched the hug in progress. Alex noticed that he was trying to give her a Grandma hug but she was not in the right position. She held him so tightly that he could not move his heart closer to hers. Soon, she headed back in order to finish packing.

The hood went down as William spoke next. "Turn it off, Alex, and give the keys back to your mother."

"Can't I take Kaitlyn for a ride?" came back the typical, "I am ready to drive now" response.

That look from both of them was all he needed, and the engine ceased. Kaitlyn, already in the other seat as though she were assisting, got out about the same time he did. She couldn't understand why they were not going for a ride as well.

"Go get your things," Momma told her. "I think we have the best excuse ever for being out of here soon." She reached into her apron and took out a bottle of some type of brown ointment and told Will what she needed to do, that she would be right back, and then they were going home.

As Mary passed the director's office, a petite, little grandmother named Agnes came out, giving her the good word. "Your mother–in–law just called and said she is expecting you for lunch, with no excuses accepted. She said it would be ready when you get there and not to call because she was walking down to Rich's Grocery Store. Just come as soon as you are ready." Turning her head a little to the side, and using that "go ahead, make my day" look, Mary said, "Thanks. That's typical of Grandma."

Then she continued down the well–worn path to the fourth cabin on the girls' side, also known as Maple. All the cabins had names from local trees. When they first opened the camp, the cabins were named after the town of the local church that provided the funds and workmen to help build them. That certainly seemed like an appropriate way to say thanks. The very first year, the first group of kids had one child who was traumatized by having to stay in a cabin named after their school rival in the next town. A very wise camp director reacted quickly. Before all was said and done, the kids held a drawing to give their cabins names. By the time it was over, the traumatized child was in Birch.

At Maple, Mary found a very itchy young lady of ten, the same age as Kaitlyn. Although it was in no way as bad as it could have been, she did remind her that scratching was not permitted, and gave her a small container of the soothing brown stuff to take home with her. Mary had already called and talked with her father, assuring him that she was okay, should stay at camp, and that this was all part of the camp experience. He, like most parents, was ready to come immediately. It was just late afternoon yesterday that the rash had started.

William had managed to make a list of some obvious things that could be done to the infirmary before next month's camp week came again. Camp was held during two weeks in June, July, and August, and one freezing cold and generally wet weekend in September. He knew his wife would again be the nurse for the next week, and he would see to it that things were different. The screen door did nothing to keep the mosquitoes, better known as Maine black birds, out. Talk about making you itch. A shade for the ceiling light would help, and being handy, he found much more to add to his list.

"Mary, you think it would be all right if we changed the curtain around the toilet to something a little more colorful?" he questioned.

"Be my guest. Unless someone like you does it, it will never happen around here. Just make it vanilla scented. I hate the smell of fresh plastic." He knew what that was like so he planned in his head to lay it out on the clothesline for some good sun before installation.

It was not long before Kaitlyn came back up over the knoll with one of Grandma's big old suitcases still covered with all those travel stickers. Alex recognized it as one he had retrieved for his mother earlier that week. They put everything extra in Mary's car, since Grandma's would go back into her garage. For now, with the camp director's permission, Mary would take all of the infirmary supplies with her for safekeeping.

"Hey, wait! Don't go yet!" Mabel called out as they were all getting into the cars. She was coming as fast as she could, carrying a box of what looked like Grandma's cake pans under her left arm, and holding something that looked like a jar in her right. "Give this to your Mother," she said, handing a bottle of homemade blackberry preserves to William through the window. "These are her pans she didn't wait for on Wednesday night. I just don't think she is feeling that good lately."

Mary drove in front of William. Alex, not Kaitlyn, as she would have liked, sat in the front seat with Dad. Soon, both cars were parked in Grandma's yard. Mary got nearly as good a hug from Grandma as William did when he first came in this morning. Mary just let go sooner, so Grandma followed suit.

Lunch would border on spectacular. Hardly ever had Grandma fed them all as a family without it being a feast she could have bragging rights about. Everyone there was offered some type of beef, mashed potatoes with meat gravy, two different vegetables, fresh biscuits; and there was only one word for dessert, cookies. Grandma apologized for not having all the salad fixings; however, the air of excitement made anything else unnecessary. Besides, she had walked to Rich's Grocery Store because her son had her car. She was just pleased that she had meat in the freezer, which she had started preparing the instant her boys left for camp. It seemed like a holiday there for a bit. As the day rolled into the late afternoon, William remembered that his clothes were in the washing machine, and used that as a proper excuse to escape, intending to take all the family with him.

Grandma told Kaitlyn that she could stay and help with some of the cleanup. However, with no one insisting, that was the last thing she was going to do. When Mom prodded a little at Kaitlyn, Alex was the one to agree to stay. Most of the cleanup was already done. Grandma looked worn out, and in the back of his mind he remembered that there were still fresh cookies in the jar. His backpack was still up where he had stayed and he knew a couple of other things he could do to make Grandma smile. Would he hide her false teeth? Not this time. A heart–to–heart hug? Yup, he felt so good he wanted to share that feeling with Grandma and just hold on to see what she would do this time. His mother could help Dad with the wash.

By the time Alex reached home, riding his bike back from Grandma's garage, there was a silence to the house activities. Kaitlyn was in her room doing her toenails, of all things. Dad and Mom, he was told by his sister, were having a nap with the radio a little louder than house standards allow.

In his bedroom, he pulled out his two brown note pages, noticing that they had both become well–worn with crease lines showing through in a couple of areas. He went to his desk table, took out some lined paper, and meticulously copied each statement or sentence as he read them, so that he knew he could comfortably read them to anyone. When he finished, he checked one more good memory and then also did the reversal paper on something that had happened at school. Amazed, he noticed it worked just like it was supposed too. He remembered the other night with Grandma, and that it also worked completely. A couple of times while copying the pages, he had thought of his dad. Now he wondered what memory Dad could use to understand how all this worked. He decided his best time to talk him through it would be on their trip to Lobster Lake, if Mom let them go. *Three days to fishing and only one partial day down,* he thought.

At some point that evening, Mom came out of the bedroom, the radio now off, and announced, "I don't think your dad is going to be getting back up tonight. He flew forever to get here, and he is just worn out. She bent down to kiss each kid's forehead and told them, "I'm so tired. I am going back to sleep as well," and disappeared into the inner sanctum, another name the kids had heard their parents' bedroom called. They knew that when the inner sanctum doors were closed, they were never to walk right in. They were required to be polite and knock.

# Chapter 9

The family had breakfast as one complete unit that Saturday morning. Mom was delighted that she didn't have to go into work. She started routine things like washing, adding in the remainder of her hubby's laundry that didn't get finished yesterday, as getting him the sleep and rest he needed was the priority. When William had sat and finished a bonus cup of coffee, he talked through the things he needed to get done that day. He was glad the bank was open, as his funny money had to be exchanged. There were things he needed to change in and out of the safe deposit box, and groceries were a necessity, as Mary had already made clear. Had Mom not borrowed milk from Grandma, there would have been no breakfast.

Kaitlyn asked to go to her best friend Susan's and was given permission with strict orders to be home for supper, and to not ask permission to stay longer. "You do, young lady, and you're grounded," Mother said, remembering a couple of weeks back when she went into panic because Kaitlyn did not come home on time. Alex, on his bike, found her at Susan's eating dinner, without even having called home. Tonight was to be a full family dinner, and this time it was Mary's turn to cook.

With Alex help, Dad wanted to get a new belt for the car and change the oil and the fluids himself; that was right up Alex's alley. They volunteered to go shopping at the grocery store, and they could cross the lot to the automotive store while they were there. Plans were made to do that first so that, as Mom put it, "Your ice cream will not melt in your seat!"

Mom had Alex get the infirmary supplies out of the trunk so she could inventory them and start on a list of what was needed for next month's camp. She was hoping to get all of her supplies at the pharmacy while the men shopped for groceries and car fixings.

"What about stopping at Angela's Donuts?" William asked, realizing that since they had just had breakfast that was probably not the best way to have complimented his wife's cooking. Mom did not say a word; the look and the head going side to side was all the answer any of them needed.

The day seemed to go by faster than usual. Mom decided that Alex must mow their lawn today, tomorrow being Sunday. Even though she enjoyed the task of having Pastor McGregor for lunch after church, she wished, in a way, that she did not have her pre–assigned day to feed him tomorrow. She and Pastor had talked about it during breakfast at camp. Having her husband back home shouldn't change anything; he was going nowhere. The kids always enjoyed pulling stories out of Pastor, and William could certainly ask some deep questions about philosophical things. Picking up the phone, Mary remembered that she had totally forgotten to invite Grandma, and she should be there, without a doubt. Grandma answered as though awakened from a nap and agreed to come. The hardest part was convincing her that she was to bake nothing and to bring nothing, period. Mary claimed she would send her home if she did, and that seemed to be enough to make her agree.

Church turned into fun for them all. It was like a reunion for William. Pastor even made him stand up so that everyone could clap.

William thought of all the men who would not have the opportunity to stand up in their churches back home, and fought to hold back his tears. He pointed up to Heaven, thanking God for bringing him home. Despite the applause, his memories of his tour of duty still hurt. Some memories have a way of doing that to all of us.

As soon as he sat back down Mary took his hand, squeezing hard, one of his flashbacks began. He was back there in his mind, holding another hand. She had jet black hair, was a little older than Kaitlyn, and appeared taller and thinner. The land mine she had stepped on left her with just one hand for him to hold. Looking down and to his right, he remembered repeating over and over, "Jesus loves you," and could do nothing else to ease her pain. He watched her move from panic to surrender, until finally the light left her eyes. He had seen it this way with soldiers, but never before with a child. His only comfort was in knowing the truth: Absent from the body, present with the Lord. What he felt then he felt now, and those feelings washed over and through him. Had his team been on schedule, that little girl would not have died. As captain of the explosives removal team, he felt fully responsible. Sitting here, he thought of Kaitlyn and nearly lost it in front of everyone in church.

Looking at Mary, he leaned over and whispered, "I need to step outdoors for a few minutes," and squeezed her hand, knowing it was a signal she would understand. Mary knew the look that went with the squeeze, as William had experienced flashbacks before. He would tell her later, should he so decide. He usually just kept those memories inside, not wanting to share with others the pain they produced in him. As he walked down the church's center aisle, she silently prayed, *God. Oh God, no more please. Get him through this one. I know you love him. Take it all away.*

Outside, William could no longer man up on this one. A fresh, white handkerchief held to his eyes caught his tears of pain. His experience with the little victim of war had scarred him deeply. He thought of his own son and daughter. He didn't know the little girl's parents, but some locals came to take her remains. He had seen lifeless children before, but never before had he attended one through the finality of departure from this life.

William was finally able to return to church and take his place beside his wife, but his thoughts could not focus on the church service. He was remembering the children of war who would press in for the candy the soldiers shared with them. What he did over there was done to keep them alive, both the children and his men. He constantly reminded himself of this, and that their decisions were made according to the best possible options. Mary, too, had lost attention with the words being preached by Pastor McGregor. Her thoughts went to last night when William woke her at 2:00 a.m. with one of his shivering sweats. When she reached out to comfort him, he sat right up straight and shouted, "Halt," loud enough to wake the house. Now she wondered whether that had any connection to the reason he had to slip out of the church service.

Soon they were standing with the rest of the people and singing out one of those old–time songs that went way back. "On a hill far away, stood an old rugged cross, the emblem of suffering and shame." The song was known by heart by most, all five verses. The board at the front of the sanctuary displayed the page numbers for the hymns found in the red hymnals, and many people held the books open before them, but most never looked at the words. More handshaking and pats on the back for meritorious service came immediately after church. William was polite and stayed as long as he could stand it. He soon reminded his wife, "We need to get going. We have company coming," as he saw Grandma headed across the back lawn carrying some type of pan in her hand. She had already walked home and back.

The lunch went well. To their complete surprise, what Grandma brought in the pan was blueberry gelatin, claiming it was supposed to have gone to church for the young kids and she had completely forgotten it. She had used frozen blueberries and a box of gelatin mix to make up this wonder of wonders. She didn't need to walk back home to get it when she remembered she had left it, because one of the ladies from the aid society announced that they had cookies already there. All those at the table had to admit blueberry gelatin was a first for them. In Grandma's mind, she had done what she had agreed to, as this pan of love was really now from church and not from home.

With both kids out of the room and in the kitchen cleaning up, Pastor said something about being sorry that the woman who was supposed to come on Monday never did meet Alex. However, it made no sense to Dad. His mind was focused on the philosophical question he was waiting to ask. It was one that had been burning in his mind for some time. Soon he was able to ask, "If God says He forgives us our sins and says that He remembers them no more, how does He do that when I know how many times I have asked for forgiveness for things, and yet I still remember them? I mean like they keep coming up for me, why not for God?"

"I guess you missed a good sermon while you were away, William, when I did another one better than today's on forgiveness. I guess the best and easiest way to explain it is to realize that when you ask forgiveness, God rewrites your history. Now that is one beautiful statement to memorize. Asking for true forgiveness allows God to rewrite your history. In that way, it is no longer available to be remembered. When He says, 'I remember it no more,' it just makes good common sense that He does just that. Our problem is that we have never learned a way to take the sting out of our darkest and most painful memories so that we can justify remembering them no more. If we did, we would have a way to make forgiveness have greater meaning. However, even when we have asked forgiveness, sometimes something will trigger a reaction that makes it seem real and right there all over again. We are so marvelously made that I am sure God intended a way of escape from remembering them, as we all seem to do. You just stay tuned in on Sundays, and I am sure I will have more to add."

Pastor McGregor was not known for being the easiest to get rid of when he comes on Sundays, and that when he gets talking, the conversation becomes more like a sermon. Grandma was the first to excuse herself, saying, "Time for my nap." She was tired and admitted, "This has not been an easy week. I just seem really tired these days."

Mary was taken a little aback by the comment, and wondered if maybe next time she was away no one should stay at Grandma's, allowing her to get her rest.

"Oh, don't you worry about the kids," she spoke out, almost as though realizing it may have come across as a complaint. "Having Alex is like having a jewel around, and Kaitlyn always helps me in so many ways. I would miss those kids terribly if you did not let me tend to them at my house. I just haven't been feeling that great lately and probably need to slow down. At my age, 70 is too fast. Have to cut down to 68!" Laughter was heard all around as she and her son exited the house. William intended to walk her home, and used that as his excuse to help end this luncheon.

Alex must have finally accepted the fact that he was not going to lose his father again, since he did not volunteer to go along. He had wanted to leave the church earlier when his father did not return fast enough for his comfort. He did look around more than usual, checking to see if Mr. Parsons was present. His Mom thought he was just checking for Dad, still knowing nothing about his new friend. Alex would tell her about Mr. Parsons, but it just hadn't come up yet.

"Grandma, are you okay?" her son asked.

What flashed through her mind was nothing she was willing to discuss now, or possibly ever. When a man in a white coat gives you advice like her doctor had, you listen and do whatever you want for whatever time you have left. *Live like there's no tomorrow.* Those were his exact words. A well–thought–out sign on the wall read, "Out of the Heart Flows the Issues of Life." Soon, her life would have no issues to deal with.

"Yes, son. Honestly, I am more tired these days, and slowing down a couple of miles an hour might truly help." Reaching over, she grabbed his hand just like she had many times in his younger years. "It is so good to see your smile again." The walk got slower as some thought inside his mom slowed her down. Thinking back over last week a little, especially after the comment about the kids, she remembered the reading thing Alex had done with her earlier in the week and said, "You take time for that Alex. Pastor McGregor had him meet a new friend at church who is really teaching him about people and memories. He helped me a lot, and he's going to make you proud."

He responded with, "He said something to me when we were picking blueberries. However, it did not make sense to me. He said he had it all written down as a lesson. I figure when he is ready we can talk about it."

He grinned as she told him to just get back to his family as she entered the house, pulling the screen door behind her. A hug was not in the offing. She went straight toward her favorite chair, and her son turned and headed down the porch stairs and to the right, back down the well–worn path between the two homes. Indeed, Grandma did not seem like herself.

William was pleased that Pastor McGregor had taken his leave while he was gone. The only one waiting for him at the door was Alex. In a voice loud enough for all to hear, Alex asked, "Can we go fishing tomorrow, Dad?" William was not yet ready to answer that question.

"Oh, go, you two. It will be good for both of you," came Mother's voice from the other room. "I have to go in to work early and am expecting to have to cover for someone who covered for me last week. I think you can pretty much count on me pulling a double. Perhaps some of the effects of war might be shaken off by the lake and the woods—and fishing with Alex might help the most."

Looking directly at Alex, Dad responded, "And you have what for worms?"

They both smiled as if to say, "I know what," and headed out the door. "You'll be glad you cut the grass, son," Dad said, starting to pull the water hose out of the storage bin with Alex.

"Is all our gear still there?" he asked, not really expecting an answer.

Alex only nodded. It would be surprising if Alex had gone fishing with someone else. In fact, it would be a first. He had gone hunting with Dad's friend a few times, but not fishing.

The ground got a good soak in the places already known for

producing the longest and fattest worms. Together, they headed to the attic and retrieved all they would need. They always packed the trunk of the car at night, as Dad figured out what extras would still be needed. They would stop and get snacks and such en route. They could stop and get worms if they had to; however, it is much better getting up before dawn and using a flashlight to pluck them from the moist ground. They would always leave by the first shades of light for a trip like this. Alex was excited enough to want to go to bed early. To his parents' surprise, he was asleep when they passed his partially open door about an hour later. No music, as he often had, and lights out. As William headed on to the bedroom, Mary stopped to see if he had done anything to be ready for the morning. She could not help but notice two well–worn pieces of brown paper neatly folded up on his desk. She opened them both and thought it strange that he had folded up totally blank pages like that. She quietly closed the door and went to prepare for bed.

"Cuddle, cuddle, here comes trouble" she said like she was sneaking up on William with a couple of possibilities in mind and he would know by her familiar words.

# Chapter 10

Dad, all dressed and ready to go, had to wake Alex to ensure they were up early enough to get the best worms. He had even gone outside to make sure they were there and waiting before heading to Alex's room. He only checked from the porch so as not to make any sounds that would trigger the night crawlers to pull back into the ground. There was no way he would allow Alex to miss the thrill of grabbing the biggest and fattest of worms and holding onto them until they could no longer hold themselves in their holes. That was part of the thrill, like angling one onto a hook. He warned him not to pull too hard, as dead worms were only good for worm soup. That would be the last thing poor Alex would want to eat. Now Kaitlyn and catching worms, that was one event that was never going to happen.

The first rays of awakening started to spread across the sky, coming in from the direction of Canada as they reached the edge of town. The car came to a full and complete stop right in front of Angela's Donuts. There was no question; it would be two each, and only maple frosted. Dad broke the house rule—after all, they were not at home—and ordered two large coffees. "Make one of those with about half coffee and half hot milk and at least three small ice cubes," he told the clerk. She was an older lady from church who always sat in the right corner in the choir loft. He knew her by her face, but usually only saw her dressed in the graduation–looking gown that the choir members wore.

"Good to see ya home, William. We all missed you 'round heah," she politely spoke out in what many would call her Maine accent. "From the looks of that thar vest, I would say you two's going fishing!"

"Lobster Lake," Alex spoke out, not waiting for Dad to reply.

"Oh my. Way out thar. Well, you should have a lot less mosquitoes this year because of that spraying deal to prevent West Nile virus. My sister up in Madawaska says their gitten eaten alive when I talked to her last week."

"You have a good one," Dad said as he turned to cross to the cream and sugar station, telling Alex, "I will fix yours, and you know we have plenty of bug spray." Alex just grinned. He had maple frosted donuts and real coffee—a big man's cup at that. He had his dad.

As they got into the car, William realized his son was wearing the same pants he had on two days before, with a couple of grease stains on the front from helping with the car. "I think you slept in your britches," he spoke.

Realizing he might have made a mistake, and thinking of a way to justify his action, Alex said, "You wouldn't want me to wear good clothes fishing."

And Dad said not another word on that subject. He had done the same thing many times as a child. From what he could remember, his father let him.

Making the left turn at the T onto the Kankamongus Highway, an inside family joke, Alex was not comfortable waiting any longer and was anxious to talk to him again about Mr. Parsons' lessons. The timing seemed perfect. They were both two donuts down, and although William had not finished his, Alex had finished his own man–sized coffee. From his pocket, he produced his two new, white sheets of paper and announced, "This is what I told you Mr. Parsons taught me," holding up both pages in only a "see them" style, not handing them to him. "This is my lesson."

"Okay, so what does it all say?"

"Well, it's like this. I am going to read to you, but before I do, you go ahead and think of your best number one memory ever, of all time, and when you are ready, you raise your finger, and I will tell you everything about it without you telling me one thing. You just don't say anything out loud."

Thinking to himself, *Too good to be true,* he proceeded to a secret memory which was his and Alex's first fishing trip to Lobster Lake.

Neither Alex nor his father had realized this might not be the best thing to do while driving. Had Mr. Parsons been there in person, he would have had them wait for sure.

"Okay. Now what do I do?" he said, raising his finger and looking strangely at Alex, who was now checking which page he would be reading.

"You just think about it, and I am going to read, and that way you will know that I know everything about what you're thinking."

"So this is a game?" Dad responded.

"No, no. I really am going to tell you everything about your memory just like Mr. Parsons told me. That's why it is all on this paper," he said, waving it around like the gospel truth that it was.

With that, Dad raised his finger again and said, "You're go."

"It is a movie," Alex began reading his list.

"Yup … One right."

"You see it in bright and vivid color."

"Okay. That makes two." His dad replied.

"Your movie is in the center and middle of your screen."

"Three down, and you're not out!" his Dad laughed back.

And so the "reading session" with Alex continued through many more lines.

When he finished the sounds, without starting the feelings, Dad had to ask, "How did you meet this Mr. Parsons?"

"He brought a package to Pastor McGregor at the church, and

I was there. He asked if he could come to visit me at Grandma's and have a porch chat, and Grandma said yes." Alex figured he didn't have to tell him he had said yes before even asking Grandma.

It all seemed proper and natural enough to both of them now.

"Go on," he spoke, and Alex knew he meant the list because he also pointed toward the paper.

"Now just feel all of your feelings about this memory, and as you do, notice that they are warm …"

Alex continued down the list, describing things his dad would find he could easily change as "light as a feather, or even weightless" were spoken.

Dad especially liked it when Alex got to the smell and taste part.

When the last line was read, rather than waiting, Alex was quick to question, "Did I get any wrong?" In a way, he was still hoping that he did, with a belief that he would see Mr. Parsons again soon and could prove it to him.

"I think that is about as awe–inspiring as I have ever heard. I keep trying to think where you could have gone wrong. However, you weren't really ever wrong at all. I am amazed. Grandma told me you had a gift. I do think Mr. Parsons gave you a gift, son. In all my life, I have never read such a thing."

"He said I do have a gift, and he believes I will always be one to help other people."

They were entering the last bumpy dirt road turnout where the parking area was, when Dad asked, "What is on the other paper?"

Without hesitation, rather matter–of–fact, Alex said, "It is the list that makes bad memories good."

*Nice thought,* William thought, then added out loud, "Well, I guess we have to save that one for later because we are going fishing *now*!"

Alex could wait; so could Dad. This day was not about a session of reading with his son; this was about Lobster Lake fishing and getting back home with stories about the one that got away.

As they got out of the car, a second vehicle drove up. It was a jeep that looked very official. It was Warden Sinclair from the State Department of Fish and Game, who William was on very friendly terms with. "Hate to remind you, Will, he said, using the nickname many had given him, "there have been some black bear up near the north end of the lake lately. Just don't get yourself cornered in there somewhere, and if you see them, you two run like—" he paused as if to realize what he was about to say was not for all who were within earshot. "Oh my word Will, this is Alex," he said, half questioning, half knowing. "When I saw you last," he said, holding his hand below his shoulder, indicating height. "You must be feeding that kid trout." He laughed.

Looking back at William, he said, "You know this is only formality, Will, but I have to check your license."

"Not a problem," he spoke as he reached in his upper vest pocket for the plastic sleeve it was sealed in.

"Get a bakers dozen," the Warden said as he checked the date and seal. "Just remember to eat one." Turning to Alex, he did a Grandma–looking eye pop and said, "Raw!" They both laughed with him.

Another Jeep drove up, and two older men with beards and well–developed bellies hopped out, only to have Warden Sinclair check them as well. One of the men was paying him money, last Alex looked, he noticed that it was the fisherman in the red plaid jacket. The other man had a fisherman's vest like his dad's.

The gear was never heavy, except for when Alex put too much dirt in with the worms. On one trip to a different lake, he had a gallon tin pail filled with dirt to over three–quarters. They stayed in the parking lot until they had only what was needed to take with them after Dad gave Alex the task of carrying the bucket. Today they each had a little, silver, ventilated tin for worms, as well as the best–fitting wicker backpacks. After all, carrying twelve rainbows in a basket was the best a fisherman could hope for in these woods.

They knew every turn in the path to the lake. Dad asked a lot of questions about things Alex had done while he was gone, without bringing up the subject of memories. At one point, the blackberries were so thick they just had to stop and load a sandwich bag full, along with loading their bellies. After all, if you want to avoid the bears, eat their berries before they come to get them. Dad did warn Alex of the direction they would be running in if a furry black mass came grunting from the lake direction. He also told him to drop his backpack and pole immediately, as his life was more precious. Especially when loaded with fish, the backpack had been known to stop many an angry Maine black bear, thus saving a fisherman's life. Yes, being chased by a bear would not have been a new experience to Alex's dad. Being chased by a bull moose would not be new to either of them. In fact, in this area, being chased by wasps was common. It was, as was often the case, his dad who taught him how to plaster those stings with mud. Today, he had a pair of small tubes of something in the side pocket of his wicker pack basket for added protection.

It was a good thirty–five minutes after they stopped for the big, fat blackberries that they could see the lake, and another ten before the poles were all assembled and the first wigglers were being carefully pierced with the barbs on the ends of the hooks. These two weren't squeamish about putting a worm on the hook. They both looked for a perfect spot from which to drop their first line. Then, after ten minutes or so of fishing from the farthest rock section on the peninsula, Alex was the first one to get a good bite. If he had not slipped and nearly gone swimming from the yank on his line, he might have reeled him in; thankfully, all he lost this time was the worm. Many times, the hook, as well as the line, would snap from the immediate getaway speed added to the initial yank on the line. The key was to feel the nibble and pull enough to set the hook without breaking the line.

Dad was next screaming out, "I got one. I got one. I had one. I had one," and they both laughed.

"Really good, Dad," Alex chided.

"Like your action better?" he sent back.

For some reason, it went like this for awhile, like both had truly lost their touch. The two bearded fishermen had by now come up to see how many they had caught, and decided they'd best head north. "The wind's coming out of the east today, so the bears won't bother us," the burliest man in the red plaid jacket told them.

"We're safe, Alex. There goes the bear food," Dad noted as Alex watched one of the most perfect butterflies land close to him, almost as though it were a friend. His mind went back to the field, and he quickly got a review of more than he wanted to process right now; however, it really was okay now. That made it very comforting. He would tell his Dad; however, this was certainly not the time to bring up such news.

*Kaplop!* was the sound that came only feet from him, as something with a rainbow on its side not only broke water, it jumped part of the way out in a wonderful arch, grabbing something flying near the surface. *Pay attention. It's your turn,* came the message from inside his head. Chuckling, Alex thought it sure sounded a lot like Mr. Parsons' voice.

He didn't have to jerk hard to catch what came next. The zipping sound of line being yanked out of his spool told him that this one would be a keeper as long as it came out of the water as a trout. His fingers hurt as he managed to gain control of the line. As hard as the fish pulled, inch by inch he brought it in, only losing major amounts of line once.

Dad seeing that Alex had a fish, reeled in his line while calling out to Alex, "Slow and steady now. I'm coming with the net." It appeared form the pull on the line that this one would not be lifted out without a net. Carefully reaching out with the net, reminding himself that the water is deep here, he waited for Alex's catch to appear above the surface. When the fish at last came into view, both fishermen were in awe of its beauty. Of all the fish they'd ever caught, never had they seen such a beauty. Ever so carefully, Alex continued to reel in his catch that would barely be fitting into the net. "This booger knows how to swim," Dad said reaching out as far and as deep as his arm would allow. "You will remember this fish for the rest of your life," he said as he lifted it up out of the net into the air with two fingers in the gills.

Alex was just beaming. A pair of butterflies came near, almost as though making an examination; however, dad and son had their focus on this mammoth trout still slapping its tail with disapproval. A fisherman's ruler for approving keepers, lest you get fined by the

Warden, was carefully used as Alex took his turn trying to hold his catch. Dad measured as Alex put one hand into the gills, and the other hand helped hold his hand with the fish up. "Twenty–nine inches or more," his dad announced, shaking his head in disbelief that Alex was holding probably the largest fish in the lake. Eleven more of these and they would need a wheelbarrow to get them out.

Although they often put lots of keepers back, there was not a chance he would spoil this dream catch in any way. He managed to thread the fish rope through the mouth and gills, and soon it was back in the lake, the rope securely tied to a tree at the water's edge. Dad's only disappointment was in not having remembered a camera. It had totally slipped his mind. However, there was no question that there would be more than one picture taken when they got home. He wanted one of the two of them in the picture with him holding the fish. After all, he netted it. Now how many more fish would they take home?

It did not take long to have the answer to that question, as a message seemed to have gone out to the other trout—worms at the peninsula. They had fun playing keep or not. Knowing the weight they already had to carry, Dad was being careful to keep it manageable. The walk back to the parking lot was far and not easy. Twelve fish around twelve inches was a norm for them. One at twenty–nine inches and several more also of great length would be both a fisherman's dream and a pain in the back by the time they would get home.

When the sun seemed to be standing still, directly overhead, he could stand it no more and William took his vest off, only to show that he was soaked through and through. He told Alex he would start a small cook's fire in the rock base they had used before, and removed his shirt, hoping for it to blow dry quickly so that it would not attract mosquitoes when the wind went down.

Alex could not resist. "Grrrrr," he shouted at his dad. Alex thought his dad's black–haired, furry chest held a bear of a man inside, waiting to break free. That was the excuse for all the hair that Alex's Dad would give to family and friends when seen in a swimsuit. Dad put his arms straight up over his head, his hands dangling down in a "coming at you" bear fashion, and growled his approval, like that lion that started certain movies. This was not the first time Alex had seen this pose.

"You leave my fish alone!" he hollered back, realizing his whopper was on the storage line and his dad was about to remove one for roasting. The zinging sound of the fishing line made both realize that Alex was probably about to catch the Lobster Lake luncheon special. They both worked on this one again. Dad stayed down on his knees, his arm extended with the net over the water, until they both saw the totally gray sides and sucker looking face that came to the surface. "Nope," they both seemed to say at the same time as it tugged once more in the right direction and managed to dive someplace that lodged the line in rocks. A good tug brought the fishing line out of the water with no hook left.

"Yuck. Worms," Alex said as he remembered the first time he and Robert had cut a sucker fish open after taking a few home for fertilizing a patio garden his mother decided she had to have. Inside they found mostly worms of some type. Pickerel, another good for fertilizer fish, was one of those boney, "watch out, they bite with sharp teeth" fish. They had taken a few of them home for the garden as well.

Dad told him not to worry; they had plenty of hooks. He put his pole down and started assisting in finding twigs, birch bark, and any other sparking material, because the little silver tube he brought with him today was found empty of matches. Today he would use two pieces of rock as flint. The skill level of a Marine made fire sparking easy. While Alex found additional wood to get a good fire going, Dad used his knife to cut the right Y pieces and the green wood cross stick to ensure perfect cooking. Soon, their remembered taste of trout was refreshed, as well as the feeling of the almost acceptable bone or two in the mouth. They were in no hurry to get back to fishing. This had become a day of catching larger fish, and one or two more would have to be it. Dad leaned back, taking a deep sigh, realizing he smelled a little sweatier than he wanted to.

"Anyone up for a swim?" he asked as if a question with a statement in it. Discretionary underwear was what they both wore swimming. No one said if they made a nature call, however the chill of the water was enough to force one. The wind, thankfully to them, dried them off quickly. Dad had swished his shirt around in the water long enough to dilute the sweaty smell that had been there before. It was nearly dry when he asked Alex whether he had left the other list he had in the car or brought it with him. Reaching into his pocket, Alex was sure he knew where it was. He held it high, pleased that Dad was asking about it.

"Will I need another good memory for this one?" he asked, expecting that this would be the case.

"No. I want you to think of only one bad memory that you want to make good."

*Interesting expression from a twelve–year–old,* William thought. He wouldn't expect his son to have bad memories like he did. He would give anything to be rid of his own bad memories, or to change them to acceptable memories.

"You just let me know when you have one, and I will read to you," Alex spoke out.

Choosing which one was not easy, as even remembering them was more than he wanted to do. There was no way what he choose would be one of his worst, like the one in church, nor would he choose one that he would never tell his wife. What he finally chose, only half believing his son's reading could do anything to help, had to do with a conflict at work before being called to active reserve duty once more. It was no big thing; however, if he had it to do over, the event would never have been allowed to repeat itself that way.

"Okay. I think I have what you're looking for," he said, still not sure this would do any good. "Now you're just going to tell me everything about it like you did the good memory?"

"No, no. I am going to just read you what to do. I talk. You listen to me read, and you make the changes I tell you. I mean, if it is not what I read, then you change it to make it what I read. You just change it so it is like my sheet when we finish."

Alex stared at his sheet, getting his finger ready to go down the page, when motion from the corner of his eye caught his attention. Startled, he pointed so that his dad would look, but he said not a word. Dad looked in the direction Alex pointed, up toward the northern end of the lake. His heart pounded in response to what he thought might be a bear. The gift of nature he saw made him thankful. An American Bald Eagle, without a doubt one of the most beautiful sights anyone could ever see, was fishing. Alex got his wish for his dad to see what he believed was his personal friend from his time at the fish hatchery. It circled and circled, occasionally making a slight drop toward the lake, only to soar back, sometimes even higher up. The head would seem to jump from side to side. Finally, it not only descended, but when it got closer to the water, it put its wings out almost as if landing, so that they were able to see the talon–laden claws stretch to grab a keeper–sized trout.

"Now that's fishing," Dad whispered, rejoicing that he had seen something very few would ever behold. "Did you see that?" he spoke to Alex, only half–remembering that it was he who had seen it first. The bird immediately headed north, staying a good, even distance above the water, and disappeared into the tree–lined horizon.

"Can we go find him?" Alex asked, as if that were even possible.

Dad remembered the memory he was to work on again. That, along with the fire they would need to put out, equipment to pack up, and so on, made it more sensible to just stay right there. "I think you were about to read me something," he said, resting his back on the rock he had turned away from to see the beauty of nature in the motion of flight. In agreement with this plan, Alex gave no more instructions, picking up right where they left off.

"Make your memory a movie, Dad, and just nod your head when you have."

The nod came, and Alex continued, line by line.

"Make the size of the picture large, allowing it to be very close, like two to three feet away."

"Allow the speed of motion to run like normal ..." And so it went, all the way to the end of the paper. This time, Alex said nothing. After a short time had passed, he became the first to speak, not realizing that his father was lost in the beauty of the change that just took place and was still trying to figure out how it became something different.

"Okay. Back to fishing," Alex said rather matter–of–factly, because it was what he expected, and now it was time to get on with fishing. He hopped up and crossed the rocks to where his pole with no hook was waiting. Realizing his need, he headed back to his dad's vest and got the perfect hook to weave through the body of another worm. He was good at a fisherman's knot and managed to tie it so that there was near perfection in his work. As he got to where he was searching the perfect worm, he heard his dad's voice.

"Alex, come talk to me again for a few minutes."

Alex had no problem going back to the rock he had been perched on before, expecting the conversation to center around the eagle. Instead, Dad asked many questions about Mr. Parsons and those pieces of paper. When an agreement was made to make sure Dad met him when he came again, or maybe at church, they both went back to fishing.

William, now feeling exhilaratingly numb, couldn't care less whether he caught any more fish for now. It was in many ways Alex's day. His mind had gone numb. In there, it was as if he realized that the possibility existed for him to end some of the pain he continued to carry in his life. He put his line in the water and just stood there staring out over the up and down motion of the tranquil magic of the lake. He didn't even remember putting a worm on his hook, but it didn't matter. Now it was Alex's Father who was thinking, *What would happen if … ?*

Within the next two hours, Alex caught many more trout, two of which were declared keepers. That would bring their total of keepers to ten if they all stayed on the rope. There had been occasions when one managed to tear the side of its mouth and make it back into deeper water.

The sun was coming from another angle before either of them spoke again. The time, judging by the angle of the sun, would be a little after four. Dad had all dry clothes on by now, even his vest. He had given *what would happen if …* some serious thought by now, and because of what had happened in church yesterday, and the sickening feeling it still gave him in his stomach, he asked Alex if he would read his list again. This would be the acid test.

Although he had already read it once and really would rather just fish now, he reeled in his line and came back down to where his Dad was now in a reclining position on the rock where he was before.

"You just read it, son. I am ready when you are." Dad spoke with his finger already up and his mind logged onto holding a hand. The one thing he did not want to do is talk about this to Alex at all. He had vowed he would never say a word of it to anyone.

"Make your memory a movie, Dad, and just nod your head when you have."

It was not an instant reaction; however, the nod came, and Alex continued, line by line.

"Make the size of the picture large, allowing it to be …"

It seemed like everything was making a difference this time. Hearing her voice in a foreign language and spreading the sounds out to last forever almost seemed to keep her alive. Making the feelings weightless—priceless!

By the time they passed the shape and headed into the taste and smell, William Williams II knew his son had been given a gift that could only be called a gift of love, a gift that was, in a way, re-writing his personal history. Maybe now, forgiving himself, he could truly be free. Even though he again felt numb, it was different this time when Alex stopped talking. He looked around, wanting to find answers anywhere as to how, why, and what was really going on here. The trees were brighter green, and the water had a sparkling sheen he had not noticed before. As he turned to face Alex again, he was just sitting there smiling with a "what did you expect" look. Dad was the first to speak. "Do you have any idea what you just did?"

Alex responded, "That's what Grandma said."

"What do you mean Grandma?"

"I had Grandma thinking about the memory when Grandpa

came home in the tin box," he said, not quite saying it right. "And I read her my lesson. She said the same thing."

"And I bet she gave you a hug you still remember," he said, beginning to crawl to his knees, intending to stand up and do the same. They both held on longer than usual. Alex actually remembered what happened to him for an instant while hugging. Should he tell his father? His father did not tell him about his bad memory. As they ended their heart–to–heart session of pure, loving connection, Dad spoke first. "How many do we have?" he asked, pointing to the rope in the lake.

"I don't know," said Alex, starting to walk to the rope in the water. "Ten!"

Dad weighed the height of the sun for time, not wanting to walk out in bear country in the dark, and just having seen the other two men already headed back out, looking disappointed.

"We saw an American Bald Eagle up the way," one of them had called out.

"Yes. We saw it catch a fish right out in front of us," his dad hollered back.

"Can't say we've seen anything like that 'round these parts," the other one responded, and they continued on their way.

"Okay. Your big one counts as three, so that brings us to twelve for weight. I think one more is enough," he said as he picked up the rope to judge the weight. With that, he changed his mind. "Here. You heft this, son. I think we may be through with keepers for today, but you can still fish for a bit if you want to." Not wanting to disappoint his dad, who seemed to have decided that his fishing was over, Alex walked to the point, picked up his pole and wicker backpack, and came back to where Dad was already loading rainbow stripes into his plastic–lined basket.

"You are next," he said, reaching for Alex's pack. Since he had caught the biggest fish, according to fisherman's bragging rights, he had to be the one to carry it home.

"At this rate, we might have time to pick two more bags of blackberries for muffins, and that way we can rest our backs a bit and still make it home in time to have daylight for your picture."

Dad didn't say another thing about changing his memory during the walk to the berries. It was obvious something had happened, something good. To Alex, it was all that was expected, and nothing more needed to be said. Alex's mind focused more on his bragging rights in his backpack. When they rounded the curve where they would be able to see the thickets of blackberries once more, they found a surprise they were definitely not expecting. There were two furry, grizzly looking fishermen filling their well worn and now over–half–full wicker backpacks with blackberries. They were not surprised to see us. They exchanged fishing stories, and Alex got to display his prize. Neither of them had ever seen a fish that size from Lobster Lake. Dad was extremely kind in offering them each any one of our other fish; however, they felt uncomfortable accepting. They said they had gone all the way to the old, run–down logging building and fished off the dock there. Alex and his dad knew it well. They got few nibbles, and what they did pull up were not keepers. "Us men just need a day away from women." one chuckled as if fishing were the answer to putting life back in balance.

When father and son had finished filling their gallon zip lock bags and were putting them on top of what already seemed like too much weight in their packs, Dad offered to take Alex's. However, they were another prize he would carry on his own, just like every other man. When the other men offered to carry their bags of blackberries for only one fish, it became a deal. They were all going to the same place, and they could choose the fish when they got into the parking lot and found another bag to put it in. The one fish they would not be permitted to choose was Alex's prize catch.

Alex began to think that he should have stayed and caught another fish; however, the weight was very real, and he knew giving up one fish was fine for today. They would be back as soon as he could make it happen, Dad willing. The rest of the walk went easily with nice smooth paths to walk on because people had driven Jeeps farther up the road to where the fallen trees made it impossible to go any farther. Dad remarked, "I hope they have learned to drive backward as well as they do front." There was no possible way of turning around before reaching the parking lot. The evergreen trees did not allow such a space in woods that had not yet been torn apart by logging.

Once at the lot, giving up a fish seemed much easier. They actually took the first one they held up as though there wasn't a reason to see the rest. They made some joke about telling the women that they'd already eaten, and then giving them the one fish. Having full backpacks of fresh blackberries should indicate something to the wives, and the absence of fish smell in the packs as they clean the berries should be another giveaway that they did not have the most productive fishing day.

The trip home, as usual, went much faster than the trip up. Neither one brought up the lesson papers, nor anything related to them until they pulled into town. That was when Dad asked if Mr. Parsons knew where Alex lived, thinking that he had met him at Grandma's, not at home.

"He talked about you being away, so he knows who you are, Dad," Alex responded.

"Did you see him at church yesterday?" his dad asked.

"No, and I did look lots." Alex said.

"I do have to talk to him when you see him again," his dad said, and Alex nodded his head in agreement.

Dad honked when they pulled into the driveway, expecting that Mary and Kaitlyn would come out to see the prize of prizes that Alex had brought home. Mother came out; however, Kaitlyn seemed to be nowhere around. Alex, grinning ear to ear, had already made an agreement with his dad to put newspapers on the grass and only lay them out one at a time like they did when they were going to take pictures. Dad made it in and out of the house rather quickly. He did manage to find a camera and some old newspapers that he put down on the grass.

"Where's Kaitlyn?" he asked, realizing that when he called into the house that she did not answer.

"She's out somewhere; should be home any time," was the reply. "I ended up only doing a single shift, and she thinks I am doing a double. Why, do we need her? Remember, she hates this whole worms and fishing thing,"

Grandma came walking around the far edge of the grass, having heard the horn of victory. She would be told to pick one for her freezer, like usual.

"One, two, three," Alex spoke out as he carefully laid them in photo–op position.

"Four, five, six," he said as Dad allowed him to do the whole show with a grin that was almost giving it away.

"Seven, eight, Tadaaa," he said as he had to use both hands to pull Goliath out of his basket. It had been nearly impossible to wrap him in.

"Oh, Alex, you caught that?" Voices of questions and exclamations came simultaneously from Mother and Grandma. William told them they would have brought more, but the weight alone, along with the long hike told them this was enough for this trip.

There was more than one picture taken, and even Grandma got her fingers in the gills in hopes of telling a few fish stories of her own at the Ladies Aid Society. Mother was not concerned about being in any picture; however, with Grandma there and able to shoot, aim, and push, Alex insisted that all three smile for the camera, and he got his wish. Had Kaitlyn been there, she would have been in it.

"Here comes Kaitlyn! Grandma, quick! Take another picture for the family album," William requested.

Kaitlyn's only word was, "Yuck," looking at and smelling the fish. Although she was in the picture, her expression said it was the last place she wanted to be. As soon as she heard the click of the shutter, Kaitlyn asked, "Can I go in now?" already on her way to the front door. "Hi, Grandma," she said as she cleared the top porch step, not even looking back.

"We'd best get these cleaned up and into the freezer before we lose our light," Dad spoke as he began to roll the paper, planning to get the whole thing to the backyard and away from the house before the heads went flying. Once there, he went into the house and brought out two of Mom's knives, one for each fisherman. For Alex, even the thought of handling the knife did not trigger a memory like it would have a week ago. The cleaning took no time.

"We are having fish for supper, right?" Mom hollered, lifting a house window to get her head down to hollering range.

Dad and Alex made the decision that the Lobster Lake prize should go into the freezer to save for any special occasion coming up where there would be more than the four of them present.

Grandma, having gone in the house with Mary, now came out the back door only to be told, "Pick any two, Grandma." Those were Alex's words, and William was not dismissing them for any reason. He knew Alex loved his grandmother. William told his mom that he and Alex had talked about his lessons with Mr. Parsons today and how absolutely amazing it all was. She responded, making sure that he knew what memory she had used when he had done it with her. He indicated that he knew.

"I sure hope Mr. Parsons is in church on Sunday. I want to meet anyone this smart," he told his mother. "I think he has a lot he can teach Pastor McGregor about forgiveness and memories as well."

"I honestly don't know who he is, and I have lived here forever. However, he is a friend of Pastor McGregor and certainly went out of his way to be extremely kind in teaching the lessons to Alex, even writing them down."

She picked the two smallest fish, and William wrapped them in waxed freezer paper, then extra newspaper so that they would stay fresh in her refrigerator freezer.

"Perhaps Alex can come over and teach me some more after he sees Mr. Parsons again. Then we can have a fish dinner."

"Wicked good, Granny," Alex spoke out without seeking any signs of approval.

Mary came back out the door with some muffins that had just come out of the oven for Grandma.

"Oh," Alex exclaimed and headed to the back of the car to produce two gallon bags nearly filled with the biggest of blackberries.

"Forty–five minutes too late," his Mom said. "Muffins all done for tonight."

Still, he handed one bag to her and one to Grandma, just as they had planned to do when they picked them.

"It's never too late with me, son. You come to me in the morning. We've got blackberry buckle a brewing."

It was hard for Mary not to say, "Here. Take them all." However, flapjacks, muffins, and other quick–fixings can always use a blackberry or two.

They all parted company as the balance of the cleaning got finished and the gear was packed away. The dropping sun caused the sky to radiate with the last appearances of purple tinges of light.

Alex knew it was not a matter of asking his father, so he didn't hesitate to ask, "Mom, when can we go fishing again?" as they came through the back door for the last time that night.

"Have to ask your father," she replied.

Alex looked to see him standing there with a finger over his lips in that "don't talk" sign. "You need a bath, son. You smell like fish. Now go," he said, pointing to the stairs with a command that could not be argued with. In a home their size, one big, complete bathroom was what they had upstairs. There were partials elsewhere in the house, but there were no others with showers or tubs. By the time Dad got his turn, the whole house smelled of trout. Cooking fish has a way of doing that. Tonight, they would enjoy pan–fried pieces. Whether she liked it or not, Kaitlyn would touch fish.

Night crawled over the town with a magic cover of twinkling lights. William and Mary decided they should go over and check on Grandma and ask one more time if she was all right. Alex tagged along. Mary took more of her muffins, a bowl with blackberries, along with a container of unwhipped half–and–half, in case anyone wanted to dump a blend over her muffins tonight. Of course, they all did.

After getting serious with Grandma, all sitting on the porch, she had them convinced she was only tired from overdoing again. She admitted age was creeping up on her; however, that was only a state of mind. Sure that nothing was wrong, Mary excused herself because she still had things at the house she really needed to get done. A week away just has a way of making things that are routine fall out of line. Besides, she had two things she knew she needed to talk to Kaitlyn about. Rumors had told her it was time to make a few things clear to every girl around about a certain boy in town. She had waited until they got back from camp and through the weekend, as this would be a heavy conversation. Dad knew what she was doing and why. He stayed behind to admire the twinkles from up above. They had to sit in the yard at their house to enjoy such a wonder. Grandma's porch created a blissful state for such evening affairs.

The partial moon went to blackout from a cloud big enough and thick enough to block out the light, only leaving a white, lacy–looking edge. This change made all the stars seem to pop out even more as if saying, "Ah, here we are." Thinking back to a night more like the beginning of when Dad went away, Alex told him about the northern lights that were all green several nights in a row. Then one night they did the most amazing thing. The whole sky everywhere looked like someone had opened a reddish–colored umbrella with a canopy that covered the whole sky. Grandma remembered that night. It made her think of when Moses was trying to get the people out of Egypt and the water turned to blood. Pastor McGregor's sermon that week was called, "The Night the Sky Turned Red." It was all about God being in charge of creation and how marvelous it all is.

Everyone was silent for a good while, staring into the depths of space without knowing what the other was thinking. Each of them was running a refresher course on a memory that once bothered them, realizing it was a man named Mr. Parsons that had come to make the difference. Out from the silence, Dad reminded them that he had debriefing meetings to go to for the next three days. Mary was aware of them, as she was told the usual time schedule for his meetings his first night home. He would be home all day Friday and then he and Mary were making some type of plans to take the kids away for the weekend. What they had not finalized yet was where.

He just wanted to make sure Grandma knew, and realized it really was okay for Alex to hear.

Grandma got the message, and it went in one ear and out the other for Alex until Grandma replied. "If I see Mr. Parsons on Sunday, I will tell him you would like to talk to him and that you are away with your family." Then she added, "Come to think of it, I still don't know what he even looks like."

"Then he will be the only stranger," Dad was quick to reply.

Alex then made it easy. "Look for a man who looks at you like Dad does, even looks like Dad. Just ask him, 'Are you Mr. Parsons?' and smile."

Alex scratched his head as if searching for more description; then the thought passed that Dad said something about going away. Looking at Dad, who realized Alex had finally gotten it, he had his finger up to his mouth already. Eyes popping, he spoke softly and slowly, tipping his head forward. "No telling."

Alex looked puzzled, realizing he apparently had missed something.

"Come on, son. Time to go home," Dad stood up, stretched, and walked over to Grandma, putting his hand out to pull her up. Their hugs this time were brief by comparison; still heart–to–heart and still contained the words, "I love you. Good night."

Alex did manage to prod his father just a little as they passed the neighbor's corner. He got no satisfaction from his request. What he knew was that Dad was going away, that was okay, and they were all going away for the weekend. Those plans made peace with his mind for tonight.

Back at the house, Grandma happened to notice what looked like a white slip of paper folded up showing a couple pointed corners sticking out just past the back edge of her rocker. Upon further examination, it seemed like she was holding a dream. Remembering the memories she knew she would love to have healed, the value to what she had in her hand was obvious. Knowing that it was not right to just take someone else's lesson, she looked upon it as only borrowing something for the night. After all, she would like to have asked Alex for a copy of the lesson; now she could write one.

At first, the list reminded her of what she had done personally, one–on–one with him. Just that alone now, with his list, made it a necessity to copy it line by line and save it as a most precious piece of memorabilia, standing for what Alex had shared with her as a gift, as well as the gift he would be to other people. Looking at the piece of paper, she was impressed that Alex's handwriting was as superb as it had become. The feeling of never having to ask him to help her like this felt good. After all, the last one to have problems with in your life should be your parents, and more so grandparents. This way Alex will never have to know, and probably no one would ever have to know what had happened to her.

Thinking of the incident when she met that butcher, she slowly took her time and did every change on the list line by line, until she knew that she succeeded again. It couldn't have been a better changing response. Something truly happened again, and the sting vanished. She had forgiven him already after hearing that he had been accused by several other women willing to put him in jail. The knifepoint made a big difference to the judge, she was told. She also learned that at the trial that his testimony of his own personal abuse showed that he followed a pattern of things in his own life that were never healed. Grandma realized you are what you think about, and if his thoughts remained in his past, it would help explain why he did what he did. Life certainly is a mirror reflection of what is on the inside. For her, it was not what happened that mattered; it was what she did with what happened that mattered, thus forgiveness was a necessity.

Next, she grabbed sheets of her best, personal, embossed stationary with the fancy W in the upper left corner, the type she wrote love letters to her husband with and sprinkled on the fragrance of love before she enclosed them in an envelope. Line by line, she copied Alex's lessons, just the way she now assured herself it would work to help anyone, although, for now, that was not her intent.

Stay totally focused in your memory so that as you read each line Alex, it will allow you to just make the changes. Do not go down to the next line until you can be certain, inside, that you have made that change.
Make your memory into a movie in color.
Move your movie to the center and middle of your screen.
The brightness on a one to ten—if ten were the brightest, make it at least an eight or brighter.
Make the size of the picture large, allowing it to be very close, like two or three feet away.
Allow the movie speed of motion to run like normal life.
Always allow your pictures to be very in–focus.
See yourself in the movie.
Allow the edges to disappear as you allow the memory to become a panorama that wraps all the way around you.
Be sure your movie, without being flat, is three–dimensional.
Allow your favorite colors to permeate the background.
Make sure you're viewing your movie straight ahead.

As she saw the space on the page, she felt it had been put there for a pause, and thus she put a space on her page as well. She would not regret a hint of a pause in there, as the energy from those changes would already begin shifting before anyone continued with the rest of the lesson lines.

As you see this movie straight on, begin to listen for all the sounds you hear, all the words you hear, all the sounds you make, and all the words you say.
The volume of what you hear on a one to ten scale, with ten being the loudest, is perfect at about a three or four.
The tones you hear yourself, make sound soft and mellow.
If there was such a thing, the tempo, rhythm, and speed is comfortable, like life's music.
Hear all those sounds now as regular sounds in harmony with whom you are and where you are at.
Yes, there will be inflections of some type as those sounds go up and down in pitch and slight volume.
Allowing those sounds to become soothing, peaceful, and loving makes a big difference.

> Now take all those sounds and words, and just, well, just allow those sounds to simply last forever.

Before the next section, on the back of the page, it looked again like an intended break, so she put an extra blank line in her now third page of copy.

> Alex, you make sure you stay right inside this memory, my son, and just feel everything you can about this memory. Just be right there in the feelings themselves, and then make these changes.
> Allow your cold feelings to now become warm, even body temperature or slightly warmer.
> Give those feelings the texture of soft, smooth, flexible silk, satin, or like the feeling of that baby blanket it took you so long to give up.
> Make those feelings flexible, in fact, very, very flexible.
> Whatever vibration there is, make sure it is a good vibration like when you go into a room where all the right people are, the right place, and the right time.
> Know that when you stop thinking about this memory in a bit, all the feelings that were once there will only decrease, that's right, decrease.
> All the feelings that you have from this memory you should move directly to your heart, no matter where they are. If you need to use your hand, just place it right over those feelings and move them home where your heart is.
> All those feelings should now allow you to be relaxed. As a matter of fact, very, very, very deeply relaxed.
> Your breathing should be allowed to go deep and relaxed—as you feel that … that sense of letting go.
> Make those feelings internal, steady feelings, without interruption.
> As you think about the size of these feelings, notice how huge they seem to be. Feel what you can about their size. Then allow those feelings to become light as a feather, or, better yet, weightless.
> Like most people, you will find allowing these feelings to become a nice, round shape is perfect. That makes them all–encompassing, totally smooth, no rough edges. In addition,

some people like to envision a heart inside the perfectly round ball.

If these feelings had a smell, you would want them to remind you of a favorite holiday time when all of your best friends and family were around.

If these feelings had a taste, you could easily find something from a holiday you could enjoy delighting your taste buds with.

The color these feelings would become—well, that could only be your favorite color.

Even now, you discover that as you think about this memory, it gives you a deep sense of fulfillment, peace, calm, security, joy, yet excitement, and finally that you are love, loved, and loving.

When Grandma finished the copy, she had no problem figuring out what to do to preserve her stationary. She had a special place for special papers. Only one thing had to be done before the four pages of notes were set securely in place for safekeeping. Like the most important letters she had sent abroad, the fragrance of love got dashed between each of the pages in a way that permeated the room, and did not smear any of the lines of copy. Just what time did Grandma go to bed that night? No one knows; no one was up to find out.

She would use these papers often in the next few days, as she felt there were things in her history that just needed changing before she went home to see her William I. She believed this would happen soon. After all, she got her belief she was going to soon die from the doctor in a white coat, a Whoseth of the Highest Magnitude. Everyone knows that he, the doctor, like the Wizard of Oz, has the power to convince people of anything, including how soon you will be better, or how soon you might plan to die. Any "who so ever" to whom you allow authority over you becomes a Whoseth of the Highest Magnitude because you allow them that controlling permission and take what they say as truth about you. That night in her dreams, Grandpa told her once again how much he loved her, appreciated her, and was caring for her even now. "Alex's lessons were no accident. There is a lot God is doing, my love." He promised her that soon people would also begin to understand the power *in* and *of* love to heal. Although he made the statement, right now she did not want to heal; she wanted to join him forever.

# Chapter 11

Kaitlyn, carrying a small suitcase, passed Alex on the stairs when he was headed down for what he hoped would be a blackberry flapjack breakfast. She was proud to announce that she was going to a sleepover at Susan's for the night, and that Dad had just left for a three–day meeting of some type. They each continued in their respective directions with Alex arriving in the kitchen, still expecting Mom to be there with what he had firmly planted in his mind. Well, she was there; however, oatmeal was in a pan waiting for him to scoop out, and there were two muffins left from last night's batch she was expecting him to eat. Next to his plate, she had already poured a glass of orange juice, as if expecting him earlier.

"What about the blackberries?" he asked, trying to get an answer as to why there were no flapjacks.

"You're going to take what I have left over to Grandma's. I called and talked to her already. With Harriet not even coming in, I'm committed to be working all open hours, plus today. I won't be home until late. Grandma liked the idea, as she said you two would be making blackberry buckle and muffins, and I told her she could add mine in. She asked if Kaitlyn could come, but I told her she had a sleepover."

"Do I have to stay there all day?" he questioned.

"Just take your bike and go riding every now and then. Besides, I think Grandma needs someone with her right now. She is very tired, and having someone around to help is good for her. Dad thinks she might be coming down with something."

"I'm not staying overnight, right?"

"No. When it comes to nighttime, I need you right here with me. You know Dad left for debriefing, and you're my man, buddy, when he's gone."

He managed to eat the oatmeal, now a little thicker than usual because Mom had been up early with Dad, doing what was necessary to have his uniform ready and making sure he had breakfast. She knew if she did not, he would be stopping at Angela's Donuts. Actually, he still might stop. He liked maple–frosted donuts as much as both the kids did. For Mom, it was chocolate–frosted logs. Besides, they ground fresh coffee and had whole cream.

Mom reappeared, having changed into her white uniform, as Kaitlyn left out through the door, headed to Susan's.

"Love you. See you tonight. Don't forget to take the berries with you to Grandma's," rolled off her lips, still trying to put all the pieces of another change in life back together again responsibly. With that, she was out the door. It was now just Alex, with no pressure to do much of anything at the moment. He knew it was Kaitlyn's day to do dishes, so plunk into the sink they went. The last thing he was going to do was cover for her without either parent home forgetting she just left for a sleepover. Since he wanted to go biking, he changed into his favorite racing pants so as not to tear another cuff on the chain.

Taking almost half a gallon bag of remaining blackberries with him, it took him a little longer than usual to get to Grandma's, even with his bike. He thought going the longest route, a few blocks away from the church and then back around, would give Grandma the time she needed to have things ready for cooking. When he did arrive, he heard a familiar voice with a familiar saying, "Where you been there, boy? I called your house, and no one answered. I'm losing precious time with you." Almost without hesitating, she continued, "And your speeding around town had better not have crushed those pretty berries." She spoke as she came down the front porch stairs with her pretending witch's fingers reaching for the zip lock bag.

Turning away, the bag in hand, she chanted, "Buckle, buckle heals toil and trouble. In the making we are baking."

*How could anyone* not *want to stay with Grandma?* he thought as he gave his bike full attention all the way into the garage. However, tonight he was definitely going home. Dad and Kaitlyn were gone.

Once in the house with his cook's apron securely double–wrapped and tied around his waist, he could not help but notice Grandma had a new, bright, floral–print apron. He was about to say something when Grandma spoke.

"Buckle, buckle, you're in trouble. You've not washed your hands."

Off he went to the back sink.

"Trust you like my flowers," she said as she spread the base of her apron wide for approval. "I figure if I don't get to wearing it, I might not. Your mom gave this one to me. And, oh, you dropped one of your lesson papers on the porch last night. I put it in your apron pocket."

Alex reached into his pocket and, upon inspection, felt blessed that Grandma had found it. This was the one list he would never want to lose.

Her hands went back into cooking motion. "Okay. Almost ready here," she said as she handed a bowl to Alex with what looked like sugar and spice. "You need to mix the buckle topping, as I am about to add the blackberries to the mix. Then use a piece of wax paper and butter, and grease both muffin tins like I showed you. If I still have more batter, you can get out the small, round cake pan and grease that up." A lot took place in a hurry as the mixes flowed in all different directions.

"Here. Let me put the buckle topping on, and you pour this

batter into the muffin tins. Now remember the rules." All went well, with the last–mentioned, small cake pan being put to use for a smaller, buckle–topped surprise. The smell of any dessert called homemade is always a treat, but when Grandma made it known that they would be sitting on the porch eating a six–inch blackberry buckle all by them selves, Alex grinned from ear to ear. Grandma didn't care for homemade lemonade and blackberries at the same time, so they would drink coffee for Grandma and very watered down coffee milk for her favorite chef.

This type of dessert cooked up fast, and Grandma stuck toothpicks in, declaring them done one pan at a time. Alex did not mind washing anything that needed cleaning because the reward at the end would make it worth it. The way she made the buckle topping was like having candy on top of his favorite cake. It was like Christmas when it touched his mouth. Alex showed no regret that the berries they picked for home came here. In no time they were on the porch, with the extra blackberry buckle nearly gone.

The phone in the house rang, and Alex rushed to grab it for Grandma, answering the polite way he had been taught: "Williams residence."

"Someone for you," he said as she stood waiting to take the phone.

When she finished the call, he thought she seemed a little alarmed. She told him she had to go stay with Mabel from the Cafatorium for a bit because she had fallen down at home and just needed someone there. Alex had no problem with that. She was just biking distance away, Grandma would take her car, as it was not a short walk. He thought of chasing her as she drove away; however, he decided to pedal his bike in a different direction and end up checking in with her later. He was not surprised that a few muffins had managed to find their way into a bag to go to Mabel. She loved sweets no matter who made them. He pedaled as fast as he could down the part of the main street he was allowed to, then turned to go up to the far back cross street. Making a left near the school, he headed straight up to Mabel's area without needing to go onto the main road again at all. He rounded the turn by her house and could see no one in sight, but he recognized Grandma's car. It was the only car in their area of town with a Purple Heart license plate. Stopping was not on his mind at this point, so he made the last turn that would head him back homeward. By now, the muscles in his legs were showing signs they were starting to get tired, so he slowed just a little. When he passed the backside of the church parking lot and neared Grandma's house, he saw a surprise he had been waiting for. They both seemed to see each other at the same time. Alex coasted until he brought his bike to a near stop, dropping it on Grandma's lawn and running toward the house.

Mr. Parsons spoke first. "How's it been going?"

Alex answered, "Well, I can read everything like you said, and it works like you said. I just don't know how to explain how it does it."

"Must be time for a porch chat, son. You got time now?"

Alex scurried toward the porch, taking out the two white pages of notes, showing Mr. Parsons that he had written them in his own handwriting.

"I told you you're going to help people, Alex. You're one of those we think of as *called*."

They settled themselves on the porch, and Mr. Parsons began to speak of how the process works. "As humans, son, we record every event that ever happens to us as a memory. We record our feelings, the sounds, the pictures, and our reactions to them. Truth is, it is never about the content of what we have stored; it's always about the process. We store good memories one way, as we did on that list. We store bad memories another, like the man in prison. Because you can make distinctions between one memory and the other, then you obviously must have a way to do it."

Alex nodded, indicating that he understood.

"One problem is how humans measure time. How do you know what is past, future, or even now? We all have some process that separates each event as we store them. Do you know how you knew to be you this morning?" Without waiting for an answer, he said, "It is all a process of storage and retrieval. The brain stores time using a distance and location process. Sometimes we're looking forward to something, while other times we're looking back. Then with the memories, it uses pictures, sounds, and feelings just as we wrote them down. I added in taste and smell because, as senses, they too can play a roll in the process of storage and retrieval."

Again, Alex seemed to be tuned in.

"Now here is a key. Words create, Alex. There is real power in words. Because words have meaning, we can use them to accurately describe a stored memory and thus the process we use to store them. The words 'I hate you,' create a memory, like a scared feeling, or an intentional knife cut reaction. 'I love you,' with the right feeling and intent, can not only heal the scar, it can also remove all the pain from a memory."

He continued. "Scripture says, 'As a man thinketh in his heart so is he.' Thoughts are turned into words, memories are processed and stored. As you learned the meanings to specific words, you, like everyone else, attached the meanings to the process of what you create as good and bad memories. Think of the process like this. You have a good memory. Do you think in your words it would feel freezing cold, harsh, heavy as can be, and weigh you down?"

Alex was shaking his head.

"Well, that is really it, son. We create a way to perceive time, and then we use the meanings we give to words to create a process to store memories. Each word is a process of perception that seems to work for most people. For most people, they are stored as light or dark."

"What happened when you read your list to Grandma?" Mr. Parsons asked.

"It made her cry and very happy at the same time," he replied without realizing Mr. Parsons had not been there when he read the paper.

"Well, keep doing that, Alex; you teach people, when it seems the right thing to do, how they store their good memories, and wait until they ask if you know how they store their bad ones. You'll help them without them having to say a thing to you about that bad memory. Just know that a stored memory, once changed by a new process, will never regain its original content."

That made Alex grin. He was being taught again, and he already knew he could do it.

"God says, 'I am the way, the truth, and the light.' What I have been doing with you, son, is teaching you how to bring light to people's darkness, trusting that they ask for and seek forgiveness. Any more questions … we done here?"

Alex thought for a moment, then said, "Grandma is going to look for you in church on Sunday. I won't be there because my dad came home, and we're going away."

"Not going to find me in your church this Sunday, not with all the people I need to help."

"Dad wants to meet you, too," Alex stated as if not hearing Mr. Parsons now at all.

"I know, son. Your dad liked it when his bad memory changed as well. He will understand when you tell him the rest of what I told you."

Alex was pleased that he now had answers for his dad.

Mr. Parsons rose, motioning his intent to give Alex a hug again.

Dad's and Grandma's were good hugs, but there was something about Mr. Parsons' that was truly different. There weren't words you could use to describe it. It was like feeling the presence of love.

"My grandma is down at Mabel's because she fell. I'll be happy to show you where she lives if you want to meet her now. Dad is away again."

"I know, son. They will have to wait. Just remember to tell them you've been with Mr. Parsons." Pausing, he added, "You can tell your grandmother I promise she will see me very soon."

Turning and starting down the stairs, he looked back with that loving smile again. He had thought about teaching Alex the infinite power *in* and *of* love to heal, as that is one of the best lessons to learn and so much fun to teach. It could not be taught quickly and would have to wait for now. As he neared the corner of the lot, anyone close would have been able to hear him shout, "God is extraordinarily delighted in you, Alex!" With that, he pointed one finger straight up in the air while doing a two–footed dancing kick jump to one side. Alex couldn't help but notice the scar like Grandma's near his wrist.

"Jesus loves you!" a voice came echoing from somewhere.

# Healing Alex:
## The Miracle Continues

Book Two

"People are like stained glass windows; they sparkle and shine when the sun is out, but when the darkness sets in, their true beauty is revealed only if there is a light from within!"

—Grandma Williams

# Chapter 7

Winter was once again passing in northern Maine. No one would forget the sting of the cold this year, as record snowfall and bitter cold temperatures up to minus fifty degrees had caused many to curtail activities they would normally have ventured to do. When it hurts to breathe just by going out, favorite pastimes like snowmobiling and skiing are reduced. Even Christmas spending was down overall, with an increase in the cost of home heating fuels cutting into the family budget. The winter carnival was in no way what it normally was, as it started one day after the peak of an ice storm. Since the storm seemingly would not let up, it got to the point where the festivities were nearly cancelled. Inches of ice that covered the ground still caused them to cancel many of the kid's favorite activities. Spectators coming from great distances found roads closed due to unsafe conditions caused by the ice. Trees not willing to bear the weight of that much ice cracked and split as the ice pulled limbs down in all directions. Many branches brought down power lines already drooping heavy with ice. Normally, the compounds of salt and sand put on the roads would clear the ice away; however, the buildup came so fast that layers of water ran between the last layer of salt melt and the new fresh ice, making the surface even worse. It was two days after the carnival before true blue, crisp skies appeared from that nor'easter storm.

There was no disappointment a little later in the year at seeing the first signs of the many shades of green that northern Maine would display. The first actual flowers to appear got a reminder that winter was not over as Mother Nature once again gave them a clear coat of slick, shiny ice so that they looked as though they had been varnished. As the next fresh day's rays of sunshine melted the gleam of shiny glass, it was like watching death appear as each flower struggled to sustain itself coming out of cryonic suspension. As had happened many times before, most blooms would not make it.

School had gone well for both Alex and his sister, Kaitlyn. Their grades showed a respect for the educational challenge they were being given. Any parent would be proud of their accomplishments.

Alex celebrated his thirteenth birthday before the friend he considered most dear, Mr. Parsons, came to visit again. He had met Mr. Parsons when asked by Pastor McGregor to stay at the church to accept delivery of a letter that was coming, while he was off to church camp to be the camp pastor for five days. He never did realize that the man had handed him a package and not a letter. Therefore Mr. Parsons was not the woman Pastor had expected him to meet. Then again, he had never been told it would be a woman, just that somebody was coming with something for Pastor McGregor, and he was to put the envelope on the shelf under the altar. He did what he was told and was the better for it, considering how everything worked out.

Alex's history included a painful experience when he was crudely violated by a stranger in the woods the day before meeting Mr. Parsons. This new friend, Mr. Parsons came along at just the right time to be able to help Alex through the trauma of the memory he was struggling with, without Alex ever having to relate what had happened to him in the woods. Alex had learned to place his trust and confidence in his dad, who was in Iraq, and had an agreement with him never to talk about anything traumatic, anything that was disturbing to Alex, until he talked to his dad first. To Alex, it was the lessons Mr. Parsons taught him that provided all the help he needed, lessons that he meticulously copied onto white sheets of paper. One page in particular he considered the best. That was the one that Mr. Parsons taught him would allow people to bring light into their darkness. It not only worked for Alex, but he had used his lesson notes to help several other people. He was sure glad he used them to help his Grandma, because it was not long after that when she passed away and went to be with her husband, whom she knew was waiting for her in Heaven. He also used the lessons with his parents. Those were the first people he helped. He was comfortable working with people he knew. Strangers might not be as easy. All that would change with time, because Alex was "called" to help others, and he was beginning to realize this truth. Mr. Parsons had told him he had a gift, and that he would grow up to help others. The name of William and Williams, he told him, can be interpreted to mean "conqueror" and "protector," among other attributes. William, or Alex as he was called, was growing into both of those attributes rather well. His full name, William Alexander Williams, III, would pretty much guarantee that he would grow up to be a protector and conqueror; after all, that was a double punch for a name. Even historically, an Alexander was known to be a conqueror.

It was a month and a half after Alex last saw Mr. Parsons that his grandmother made her transition. Everybody realized she was not feeling well, even though she tried not to let on. When Dad confronted her with what he and Mom believed to be true about her health, she told him, "William, everyone has a time appointed unto them to die. Furthermore, do you know how long your father and I have been waiting to be together again? Well, son, nothing's going to stop us now; no fussing, no medicine, and for God's sake, no miracle. You and Mary are right; there is something wrong, and I am not going to talk about it. I know all I need to know, and you two don't need to know anything else or even worry anymore." Dad said that he could not disagree with her and said nothing more because truth speaks volumes, and it is often better to just keep silent.

"You've got a family that loves you," she continued. "You and Mary and the kids will be just fine without me." She seemed to struggle for what to say as Dad listened silently. "I know already you're going to turn this old house into the computer business you've always been dreaming about. You should do just that. Thinking about all you have will make letting me go in peace easier. If you had asked me, I would have told you that I never expected to live this long after your father died. Going home to be with your dad is the right thing for me to desire, Will."

After another pause, Dad still not able to say a word, she said, "We can talk more about this later, if you insist. For now we need a hug." Dad talks about standing there for what seemed like an eternity just holding Grandma. He said she seemed to just relax, like the word was finally out and it would all be okay. It has to hurt to keep that type of thing inside. No one knew how long she had been carrying her message alone. While in her arms, he thought back to the night he returned home from Iraq, the time Grandma's wet hair got water on his uniform shoulder as they lovingly hugged heart–to–heart. This time, he was getting her shoulder wet, and neither one cared about water damage.

Grandma had a way of describing that hug so that people knew just what to do. She told everyone that what most people do is hug so that they keep their heart as far away from the other person as possible. They put their head on the other person's right shoulder and hold their body out to the side almost as far away from the person as they can. With heart–to–heart, Grandma's head always went to the other person's left shoulder so that the two hearts had only inches between them. Then she held the person as hard as they held her, for as long as they held her. No patting each other on the back or beating each other up as so many people do. She doesn't let go until they do. Most often, a delicious, warm feeling came over people who hugged this way. She actually felt her own heart at first, then she felt the other person's heart as well, in a connection that can only be described as love. Grandma just did it to people naturally. She never told them why or even how, unless some comment was made. It was then that she taught them a lesson about love, and the healing power of love in a hug.

The porch to the house was a marvelous L shape, wrapping around two full sides of the house. Although Grandma did have a favorite rocker on the porch, and a wonderful wicker porch swing, it must have taken too much energy for her to get there. She didn't go out there in her last weeks. She stayed inside and slept a lot in her favorite book–reading chair in the front room. She didn't read much anymore, other than her Bible.

In her last two weeks, it became obvious to all that something serious was taking place. She was in pain and not able to do things she always took for granted. Her favorite hunk of a doctor came to see her at home in the early part of her last week and gave her special new pain medicine. When her close friends, like Mrs. Burns in the house next door, or her best cooking friend, Mabel Kitchen, the church camp cook, brought her food, she did not touch it. That was the real sign of how sick she had become. Mom and Dad knew long before Alex and Kaitlyn did.

The last thing Alex got to bake for her was a batch of her favorite cookies, and although she tasted the molasses and butter blend, she didn't eat them like they had shared so many times before. With the nearly untouched plate of cookies by her bed, she lay resting, eyes closed. As he was holding her hand, Dad looked at Mom, Kaitlyn, and Alex and said, "She won't be opening them again." Alex couldn't help it; he cried first, and that broke a dam loose in everyone there in the room. Alex didn't remember anything much after that except that it hurt. It hurt really badly. It was the first time he ever remembered hurting that bad. He had spent so much time with her that in some ways she was a parent to him and not just someone he might see one or two holidays a year. He stared in disbelief that she would not open her eyes. She should at least smile that smile once more, the one that always told him how much she loved him. She just lay there, absent in some way. It was no longer her; she would have smiled. So in an instant, what remained was only a shell that had been built to house her love, a love that would never end; a love that would keep on giving.

At her funeral, people were allowed to stand up and talk about what Grandma's life had meant to them. We think the whole town came. So many people came that some had to stand outside. Pastor opened the side bottom stained glass window panels so they could hear. It could not have been a more perfect sunny day, with only the slightest of breezes, and with partial clouds keeping the temperature perfect.

Every time someone got up and spoke about Grandma, people thought, "Just like with me," because she did not show partiality. Grandma believed in teaching everyone real love.

One of the most touching speakers was the college student who said, "I was standing in line to buy a Christmas present for my parents six years ago, without realizing that she"—pointing to the open casket—"was right behind me. I had been babysitting and doing anything else possible to earn what I knew the present would cost. When the clerk told me the total price, I realized that not only did I need a couple of dollars more for the tax, but I had also somehow managed to lose a ten–dollar bill. Not noticing what was going on around me, your Grandma had bent down toward the floor, bumping me from behind just a little, and said, 'I'm sorry, sweetheart. This fell on the floor from your coin purse.' 'Mine?' I knew it was *not* mine because it was a twenty–dollar bill. I had none of those to begin with. But the look in her face told me I was not to ask any questions or say one word to anyone. I cried all the way home. At that time, I didn't even know who she was, and I am sure she did not know me. There wasn't any question in my mind where that money came from. I told myself she had to be an angel because real people did not do things like that." The response in the church made it obvious that she was not the only one who had had those thoughts before. She continued, "Two years later, we changed churches, and I knew for sure when I saw her here, she was the one. How did I know? It was that look she had. She had a loving way of recognizing you that one did not easily forget. Then, even on my first day here in church, I saw her slide money into a lady's pocketbook that was sitting on the pew when the woman wasn't looking, and she probably would have no idea where it came from. Out of the corner of her eye she caught me looking, and with a big smile held her finger up to her lips while shaking her head no. It became our second secret, and I am not sure whether she knew that I was the one who held the first. With the first, I learned the lesson of giving while you're living; however, I learned it well that second time. I can't tell you how many college friends have been blessed because of her lessons to me." With that, she broke into tears. Holding her hand over her mouth, she headed toward her seat. Many of those seated in that service began to realize for the first time that Grandma probably was the secret Santa who deposited the money many of them found during a time of greatest need. If she were asked, Grandma would have said that she had no idea who it might have been.

Many, you would never have thought would say anything, kept lining up, promising to keep it short as the day rolled into the afternoon. Those in attendance heard from a banker, an auto mechanic, a librarian, a policeman, a potato farmer or two, a street crossing guard the children all loved, and so many more. They heard about jackets, scarves, shoes, and food, food, food.

Grandma seemed to do the things people never really thought about, as though it was natural to her. Whatever she did, it changed people's lives with love. It didn't have to be a big thing. It was just her way; service as love, without any expectation of reward. "Love never changes!" she would often say. Sometimes she would add, "But … love changes everything it touches."

An older, semi–retired man who digs graves at the cemetery talked about Grandma bringing gorgeous bouquets of flowers regularly to place beside William the First's gravestone. He said that she would often give some to him because they were fresh, alive, and she wanted his family to know they were loved. He said she would look at him and say, "He knows, and it's sure okay with him!" pointing upward.

One man stood up and took out a well–worn piece of paper,

saying, “I would like to just read you a short quote she wrote and handed to me along with a plate of cookies. It was probably nine years ago, when I was holding out at the Salvation Army Shelter.” Then he read, “God don’t make junk. Moreover, since he only made one of you, he obviously thought he needed you, so live your life like God depends on you. In the end, you will find out that he did. Signed Jesus. That piece of paper changed my life. Obviously, I still have it, worn as it is.” He choked up a little more before continuing. “To this day I look at it often. God depended upon me. Oh my, did that change my life. Today, I am a chaplain, fully aware that I depend upon God because he only made one of me.”

Kaitlyn, Alex’s eleven–year–old sister, got up to speak, only to discover that nothing would come out of her mouth. Mom and Dad just stood and held her hand as Mom spoke for her about precious times she had been describing to them over the last few days. Her one regret was not learning more about cooking, as Grandma had left Kaitlyn her recipe box. She did like to cook, but what she did not like was getting dirty and having to clean up the mess. Alex had done more cooking with Grandma than Kaitlyn had. He could even make many of their favorite goodies without looking at Grandma’s notes.

Finally, Alex stood up and spoke. He just opened his mouth and spoke from his heart, knowing that it made Grandma proud up there. He said that his best times were when it was just the two of them alone, often baking. Her loving squeeze seemed better after cooking. Feeling Grandma and actually feeling her heart was a treat he wished everybody had gotten to have. Then again, maybe they had, as so many were there to celebrate her life, just like he was. Alex felt that Grandma heard them all that day. She always heard everything, even when he thought she hadn’t. Her service left a mark on everyone’s heart. At the end, Pastor McGregor asked everyone to please stand and give a praise offering to God by clapping in appreciation for Grandma. Now that was the start of an exception in their church. Alex had never ever heard the sound of a clap in the sanctuary. Although unexpected, people started to holler, and some even danced a bit. It seemed as though the church was even full of angels clapping their wings. He had to smile, laugh, and cry all at the same time. Pastor may not have expected such a reaction; the noise outside seemed at least equal to what came from within. And it seemed right and appropriate. Someone in the middle section of the right side threw a handful of dollar bills up into the air. When they landed on people, they threw them again. It was wonderful. Everyone was all caught up in those moments of praise and celebration of life. Alex would have bet that Grandma was crying tears of joy.

When the service was over, a stranger walked up to Alex's family in the outside receiving line and said that he brought a fistful of dollars to give to the kids after the service because it would give him a personal way to honor Grandma's love and service to his family and himself. He said that he just couldn't help but throw them when they all started clapping and hollering. He then apologized, feeling that he might have been out of order doing that. Dad told him that no apology was needed, and that Grandma was probably dancing right along with everyone else. The man then told a true story about the night he and his wife were on their knees praying for food for their family of five, when Grandma came to the door with a food basket she and the Ladies Aid had put together. He told us she had no idea how they had gotten his name, as they did not go to that church, but that the gift was not returnable, as it was designated to their family only. The little gift card in the bottom of the basket read, "God is exceedingly proud of you and your family," with a handwritten signature—Jesus—along with the name of the church. "I can't tell you how many more gift baskets we have passed on since then. God is so good," he said, shaking each of their hands and giving Mom a genuine, loving hug.

People had been asked to bring light refreshment for serving in the basement meeting room after the service. For many, it came as a surprise when 60 percent of what people brought were six–inch, round, flat, rolled molasses cookies. Grandma used molasses cookies as a gift to other people so often over the years that it should have been expected. By the time the service was over, so many people had talked about those cookies, that they were the snack everyone craved.

Homemade lemonade was chosen as the cold beverage. They all knew she would absolutely insist lemonade be served. There was hot coffee and tea, but it seemed as though they all drank lemonade.

The church sanctuary smelled like Grandma's garden. If all of the floral arrangements were laid out flat, they would have made a field of beauty that only God could create. After years of supplying the pulpit area with vase after vase of bright–colored cut flowers, mostly from her gardens at home and the fields behind, it looked as though they had all returned to bid her farewell and honor her generosity and greatness in service to others. When people started going home, it was pre–arranged for several of them to take flowers to facilities where they would be appreciated. Only two bouquets went home with the family, made up of zinnias, Shasta daisies, and dwarf dahlias, reminding them of the balcony gardens she lovingly tended. It took Mom two weeks to send out all the thank you notes for the flowers and all the other things people did to help and serve.

Her passing made Alex long to see Mr. Parsons again. It was on Grandma's porch they most often met, and now he wondered if they would ever meet again.

# Chapter 2

Alex had indeed found ways to use his favorite lesson paper from Mr. Parsons to help more people. His relatives were easy to work with, but he was not as daring and forthcoming with more casual acquaintances. Within a day of Mr. Parson's last visit, time worked out so that Alex could teach his mother, Mary, his lesson page. William, his father, had already told her enough so that she knew Alex would be asking her to think of a memory that bothered her from the past and that she would not have to say a thing to Alex about it. She would only make the changes to the memory as Alex would read the changes from his lesson page. That certainly seemed simple enough to do.

As he took out his list, he read the changes to make, knowing full well that Mom was always one to quickly grant forgiveness. He was so comfortable doing his part, knowing that no words about what she was "cleaning out" would ever need to be spoken. What he was asking her to do now would take the stingers out of whatever bothered her most regarding this dark–energy memory. When he ended, they both felt good, as she had followed the directions perfectly. The smile on her face said it all. She looked right into his eyes, as she so often did, and said "Do you have any idea how much I love you?" He did.

The lesson he had shared was given to him when he was only twelve. That was when Mr. Parsons came the first time. Since then, Alex had longed again and again for Mr. Parsons to return. When six months had passed, he had mostly stopped looking. However, in his mind, he was constantly seeking ways to change things that seemed bad or hurtful into good. Alex was beginning to see things as the energy they are, as opposed to their physical components. He also began to understand much through the process by which something was created energetically and spiritually, more so than what that thing is. Life is all about energy and the processes we used to experience life's flow.

Now there was one thing new. Alex was beginning to have a memory process for which he hoped Mr. Parsons had an answer that would help him once again. Many a night, Alex discovered that his dreams woke him with a violent sensation of falling. The dreams would often begin with him doing something he liked to do. Then, instantaneously, something would happen that would cause his stomach to jump with the feelings and sensations of falling. Although he was not aware of it, his first adventure in life was a fall. Alex had never been told of it, nor would he have remembered back to his birth. He birthed so fast that he actually fell out and started screaming immediately, perhaps from pain, but probably from fear. The doctors did not call it a traumatic birth, just fast. His mother's labor had been induced, but they did not expect things to move so quickly. His mother said it was not until they put him into a warm bath that any sense of quieting came. Even then, his hands would jump as if he felt that he was falling again, showing signs that a lifelong trauma may be settling in. There was no way he could relate this deeply repressed incident with what was now taking place in his dreams. If Alex were in therapy, the potential of such an event at birth, or in the first few years thereafter, would have been explored. Often, these experiences are discovered to be the triggering energy to the shifting trauma in such dreams. We are all born with the natural fear of falling; it is given to us for protection. In some of his recurring dreams, he would be in a car that would go over a cliff. In others, he would go over a bridge, the car actually going up and over the guardrail. What he knew for sure was that he was falling and would always wake up in a cold sweat, much like his dad often did after coming home from Iraq, where he was the team leader of a bomb removal squadron. It was strange that one night the dream changed for Alex into something more. It was as though he had such a desire to get beyond the effects of these dreams, that he did stop falling. He stopped when he allowed the dream to continue. In this dream, he fell and landed in water. Then he was pulled down and under into a darkness from which he would surely suffocate and die. It did not matter whether he slipped off a cliff while out walking, or was in a car that went off a bridge; if the dream did not wake him up in time, down and under the water he would go. He would wake up soaked to the bone and gasping for air as though he had been holding his breath, praying he would survive. However, what he remembered was that he never did make it to safety. He always awoke with the realization that he was not going to make it, yet never dying.

When he talked to his mom about the repeating dreams, she told him that she could think of no cause for those particular scenarios unless it was from something imprinted he had seen on television. His dad, who had been over in the war zone and had experienced many difficult things while there, was not one who was able to help with Alex's nightmares. He had enough of his own. They called it "post traumatic stress disorder," or PTSD for short. Mom said that the pills they give him never work. At least Alex did not sit straight up in bed screaming like he knew his father sometimes did.

Alex purposed that he would outlive his dreams sooner or later. After all, he had grown into a very smart and handsome young lad. He was now nearly as tall as his dad and could almost see the top of his mother's head after this past year's growth. Were his grandmother still alive, he would have enjoyed kissing her on her forehead like she always did to him.

His biking skills had improved to such a degree that he was now allowed to make the triangle–shaped road trip between two neighboring cities by himself, and could do it easily, with convenient rest stops, in half of the sunshine hours of a day. The only thing his parents required was that they know when he left and the direction of his travel. In one direction, he had steeper uphill sections in two places; the other way, he had significant slow climbs that landed him at a steep downhill section.

There was one roadside stop picnic–type area called Creek Bed that became a favorite of Alex's because it was 55 percent of the way in one direction and 45 percent in the other. The site was cut into the pine tree forests that covered the area. A slow–flowing stream with wonderful, big, flat gray slate rocks that a person could walk around on came close to the edge of the road. Passersby might see Alex dangling his feet in what most would consider extremely cold water. It seemed it never got warm enough to wet more than feet in that water. Maine's geography and climate had a way of ensuring that cold, spring–fed streams remained cold. If his parents ever drove the roadway looking for him—and they had—they would know in what direction he started, and that this would be his place to stop to catch his breath and enjoy the snack and water he carried in his backpack. Otherwise, he would be pedaling somewhere along his planned route. Peanut butter and marshmallow fluff was his sandwich of choice, no matter who made it. He preferred a chunky peanut butter, but Alex was generally not fussy. Today was no exception.

Right in the middle of the second half of his sandwich, he nearly choked upon seeing a reflection in the slow–moving water of the stream. There was no question in his mind. He knew exactly what the image was and what it meant. He only hoped that when he looked up, it would be real, not be a figment of his imagination.

"Glad to see you too, Alex," the long–lost voice of his friend, Mr. Parsons, spoke out as he continued walking out of the woods on a well–worn path Alex had never traveled.

"Where have you been, sir?" Alex spoke. "I haven't seen you in church or anywhere. I've looked and looked, and, honest, I need to talk to you."

Smiling, and giving Alex that relaxed feeling that comes from a look starting deep within, Mr. Parsons replied, "I know, Alex. That's why I am here. Just as it was in your past, I do not have long. However, you tell me the way you believe I can help you with your need, and I will give you the best advice God's given me. The two of us are never apart these days."

With that, Alex started telling nearly every version of his horrifying dreams, babbling on faster than the stream and hardly pausing to breathe. Before he finished, Mr. Parsons held up his hands and made a T sign, indicating that he had heard enough, and that Alex should take a pause and allow him to speak. "Remember when I taught you how people stored their memories as a process and gave you a way to bring light into their darkness, Alex?"

"Oh yes," he responded, nodding his head.

"Is there any chance you've used the words in that lesson, Alex, to think through any of these memories while you're awake?"

"Well, no," he replied. "Would that have worked?"

"Well, it is all about how you store memories, Alex. It's about the process you use and how you use it with the memories when they resurface. I realize that part of the problem for you is that they're resurfacing during the night. It can be harder to put all the pieces back together to reprocess again when it is daylight." He stopped to think again, like Alex remembered him doing before, with one finger pressed into his cheek. "You know how when you're working on a computer you start to do something, and then some other process happens seemingly by mistake, and it just keeps doing that mistake repeatedly until you change the program or restart the computer?"

"Yup. Dad says, 'It is all about the process,' just like you do."

"Alex, what you're running as dreams is a process of energy you have stored and are retrieving. Somewhere along the route of the process, there has been a short circuit that plugs into another repressed energy source. That is what is happening. Your processes are being connected, one for the start and then a link into a new ending. So, how does your dad fix the computer?"

Alex was quick to respond, "He rewrites the program, I think."

"You mean he changes the process to give it a different ending?" Mr. Parsons smiled at Alex, as if for him to see the prospects of adding light into his darkness once again.

"But this is a dream," Alex responded. "You don't control your dreams; they control you! You don't even know they are coming until you're already asleep and can't do anything about them."

"Remember, Alex, this is all about a process you are running, just like a computer program with a bad overwrite. Nothing has changed; it is still a process, Alex, no matter when the thoughts or dreams come. The story you start dreaming now has a glitch that needs repairing. Remember, your dad would do something to change the ending of the process by rewriting it. Alex, you have the ability to do the same thing. Those changes are only a few thoughts away. You can create a link in your dream process for something else to happen."

Alex liked hearing what was being said.

"The very next time you are aware in any way of being near the edge of anything that needs to be controlled in your dreams, put up a higher guardrail so that it allows you to keep going on to a new location of your choice." After thinking a moment, Mr. Parsons continued. "On the other hand, a bulletproof glass wall can be added so that you can look through at the cliff's edge, knowing that you are undeniably safe—like on that clear walkway out over the Grand Canyon. Add a higher guard rail to the bridge so that it is impossible for you to go over."

He paused and started thinking again before continuing. "If you discover in your dream that you are falling, tell me what you can do to change the ending. Come on, Alex. Show me how creative you are in there. Name some new links you can create to attach a new process."

Alex responded. "Put on a parachute and enjoy seeing the mountain scenery on the way down to the field I would land in. I have a special field I like where butterflies hatch." Alex closed his eyes, mentally seeing the re–enactment happening as though it were real. That was what it would take to make it happen. First, you had to make it seem real inside, where the energy processes of memories are stored.

"Or?" Mr. Parsons requested. "What about when you're in the car?"

"I could land in a net like the man from the canon in a circus. Or I could be in a movie as a stunt man and hit those big, blue, air–filled mats they use for action scenes."

Mr. Parsons responded. "With a car no less … Nice! Creative potential! Okay, but what about if you hit the water? Could you take out the hidden safety air tanks, strap them on, and swim to shore where you would be completely safe?"

He paused and extended one of his big smiles as he said, "On the other hand, pull the plug that makes the car float to the surface like a magic floating boat in a *Chitty Chitty Bang Bang*–style extravaganza, taking you to the nearest safe shore."

"Well, I could, but I haven't."

"Glad to hear you say you could, Alex, because you are right. That's what most people do—they could, but they haven't. Unless you change the process in your programming, the program continues to run as it was. It doesn't know any better. Just as I taught you to use words as the power of creation to change bad memories, now I am showing you how to use imagination to control the outcome, so that when the memory plays again, it takes you where you predetermine it will go from then on. You create a new computer program inside when you make the change. You rewrite a specific dream system file. Remember again, it is all about the process. You, my friend, are always in control of the process that determines what and how you remember." he said as he pointed behind Alex as if pointing out old memories, "and what you imagine as the desire of your heart out there," pointing away from the front of Alex, indicating most people store future memories towards the front and out.

Alex started, "So this is similar to the lesson you wrote down for me before, because we were actually changing the computer program of how we store a memory as a process, partially with pictures?"

"Yes, my son, but this time, the process you are using creates an acceptable ending which interrupts the loop you have been playing, and then it creates a different link that you're willing to run. Humans really are funny, Alex. Most humans, maybe 90% of them, would rather think what they thought yesterday and be satisfied that today is only a replica of yesterday in their time frame. Then they blame God because they believe they have no future, when God has already promised them the desires of their hearts if they will delight themselves in Him. The real problem is that they don't recognize, as God does, that what they are thinking *becomes* the energy of creation as the desires of their hearts. What one thinks about generally comes about simply because thinking energetically creates and attracts like energy. In the field of energy, like energy attracts like energy. This also applies to creation where like energy attracts like energy. We join forces with the powers of creation just by thinking. Now, how marvelous is that? Without going into it more deeply here, Alex, this is called the gift of free will. Maybe we need to talk about that one, the power contained in our thoughts and words, in greater depth sometime."

Mr. Parsons continued, "No, let's not wait. Let's just touch the surface of that subject a bit more now. When people think the same thing every day, they feel like they're going nowhere in life. What they are thinking gets taken as the desire of their hearts and will continue to take them nowhere, simply because it attracts whatever it is they have been thinking. Think of all the thoughts you have every day as being a maze that you so desperately want to be out of. The more you follow the same pattern in your thinking, the more you repeat the same directions in the maze. Yet at some point, one change in thought can take you to a totally different path, because it creates in you a changing link that attracts something different than what has always been. Most humans live on treadmill thinking, getting nowhere and going nowhere because of it. It would help if they realized they are here in *now*, and they will always and only live in *now*. Remember, nowhere comes together in spelling and energy as "now here." The fact they believe they are going *nowhere* is still happening in *now here* time and becoming their creative reality. Life truly is a reflection of what's there on the inside. The problem is, as I said, that people keep bringing what *has been* into daily thought, causing it to happen again in *now*."

There were some deep thoughts in there that Alex didn't completely grasp; however, he did have a rebuttal of sorts which came so quickly that it seemed to take both of them by surprise. "So why did Grandma have to die?"

"Hold that thought, Alex. Apparently, you didn't talk to your grandmother about this. She had talked to me often, expressing her desire to go and be with her husband and her Father God. I think you need to know that her going to heaven was also her choice. It was her way to come out of the maze a winner! Rather than talking about death and dying, Alex, how about you consider life, living, and healing? There is a lot that I can teach you about life, living, and healing that really centers on someone's ability to get into the heart of love and what love is really all about. Most people know nothing about what love really is. They also fail to understand the power it holds. I know you have heard the expression God is love, right?"

"Right," Alex answered.

"If you can be patient and wait a bit, I promise to return again and not be so long this time. I know I can teach you the power *in* and *of* love, especially to help people heal. I would really like to do that. For now, you change those dreams just like I told you, and they won't bother you anymore."

"Tomorrow?" Alex interjected, believing that it should be like before when he came three days in a row for a "porch chat" when Alex was staying with his grandmother while his mother was the nurse at church camp.

"If you're planning on biking this way again, Alex, can we meet a week from today right here at Creek Bed, right here at the same spot? I am going to ask you to do a few things for now that are important. I need you to not say anything to anyone about this lesson I'm teaching you, or even that I'm around. There are so many people wanting to see me face–to–face that we will not have one–on–one time here privately if they have any idea that I'm around. I told you before, it's a very needy world. Most of the time I find people waiting for me to tell them what God can do to help, with them never realizing that they need to participate."

"One more thing I need you to do: when you pedal this way, see if you can bring a can of your favorite fruit–flavored carbonated beverage and a cup to hold at least half of it. You think you can do all that? I know I can keep my end of the bargain if you're able to keep yours. Shall we say high noon?"

"You bet!" Alex said, realizing that Mr. Parsons not only would not disappear, he would continue his lessons again. He had never failed in doing anything he promised.

With that, they shook hands, with Mr. Parsons holding on a little longer than Alex was accustomed. It was fine; it felt right. It just gave him that feeling that one of his dearest friends was back in his life and adding new meaning. When it came to understanding people, Alex wanted all the teaching he could get. So far, everything he had taught him had been of significant value.

Mr. Parsons turned and headed back on the well–worn path into the woods. Had it been before Alex met Mr. Parsons for the first time, the image of the path might have caused Alex to shudder at the memory of what happened to him at the end of a different path in the woods. But Mr. Parsons taught him what to do with bad memories—not only what to do, but how to help others with that understanding as well. Now that trauma was like something that happened to someone else. He had the learning and the benefits of the experience to grow from; however, all the stingers had been removed. Alex thought about walking down that path to see where Mr. Parsons lived, but he decided that since he really did not know the area, and had made an agreement with his parents to stay in sight of the road, he'd head toward home. Although he had seen the path many times before, he had assumed that it was only used by animals, just like the paths he would see when he and his dad went fishing. Besides, there were no houses around, as far as he could tell.

All the way home, Alex practiced thinking of additional endings he could apply to his nightmares. He ran every possible scenario, each one many times. In fact, he was so ready for bad dreams to come, that he was in bed close to an hour ahead of his normal schedule without even meaning to be. He had no idea what time his body signaled that he was once again in the backseat of a car heading toward the mountain curve; then it happened. He had it all planned out just prior to sleep. He would put up a bigger retaining wall. However, he had not counted on the curve becoming a bridge and the car going over the opposite side. As he found himself falling, panicking, he tried to remember what to do, but he couldn't remember fast enough where the plug had been placed to make the car fly, or whatever it was supposed to do. All of a sudden, he was in the water and going down into the dark like before. It was then that he remembered that the plug had nothing to do with flying; it had to do with floating, and he found it right there in the middle of the dash. A *whoosh* sound filled the vivid dream as the air quickly lifted the car right up to the surface, into the light of one of the most beautiful places he could remember: Lobster Lake. Once he made it to his choice point, he had no problem climbing onto the shore. This was the location where he and his dad had often enjoyed a meal of fresh trout. Once safe, he never noticed what happened to the phantasmagorical car. He forced himself to wake up and answer a nature call, with the awareness that the dream was over. While in the bathroom, he checked his face in the mirror and thought, "God is exceedingly proud of you, Alex," just as he had heard both Mr. Parsons and his grandmother say. His smile to himself said it all; he felt the satisfaction of having had another lesson that worked, and that he was not sweat soaked like he always had been after a nightmare.

As he lay back down, he wondered how many nights he had kept his mother up as a child, not knowing how to end his repeating nightmares. Many of them were about falling; however, there were some that centered on scary things from Halloween events. It would have helped his mother to know that she could have done something as silly as creating a magic stick that he could take to bed to use in the theater of his mind, forcing the creatures away forever.

He seemed to outgrow most of them, but the ones he had been having lately were worse. Alex would continue to use his new skill as imagination director of dreams to change many an ending to a safer outcome. In fact, Alex would discover that during his waking hours, he would think things that caused a sense of fear to come over him, and he would be able to do the same type of rerouting process, thus creating a successful ending. He found solutions to his fears while still awake, and then could be done with that particular fear. The key was in going beyond the event, and creating a successful and acceptable conclusion. The more he analyzed this process, the more he recognized the power of words to create change. His mind started creating ways to talk to children that would lead them to create a future before it was even there. He pondered that the way parents talked to their children stored an energy that projected into their future and created change. If parents paid attention to the words they used, and knew that the energy of attraction from those words carried all the way into the child's adult life, they would want to change what they said and how they said it. If people understood this, they would change the way they think about themselves as well. After all, everyone is the accumulation of the thoughts they have had—it might even be said that they are also their own solution. It's all a reflection from within.

Having once again seen his long–lost friend Mr. Parsons, Alex took out his favorite lesson page in hopes that someone he could help would cross his path. Just seeing Mr. Parsons again made Alex's mind search to understand the power in words and how to use words in new processes more effectively. One of the scriptures Pastor McGregor had read not long ago said, "In the beginning was the Word and the Word was with God and the Word was God." Today, Mr. Parsons said that he would teach him more about the power in words soon. For now, this gave Alex something to look forward to, as the next lesson was to be on the fascinating power *in* and *of* love to heal.

# Chapter 3

At fourteen, Alex was now a freshman in high school. He had tried out for the junior varsity basketball team and was as proud as his dad was that he made it. Although he was not a starter, the experience of team play was good for him. His friend Robert, from Ackers Potato Farm, had tried out as well, and was totally crushed when he was told that he was overweight and too short. The way they told him could have been handled better. It was more like they made a joke out of him for even trying out. Some of last year's team members added to the frivolity and were not stopped from making cruel side comments typical of competitive students of high school age. Two days after the rosters were posted, Alex realized that Robert was not getting over the humiliation, and offered to use his lesson list to help him. Because of this meeting, Robert never again mentioned the humiliation he suffered, and went on to be an outstanding guard on the winter hockey team. Robert may not have even tried out for the hockey team had it not been for Alex and his lesson list taking the stingers out of the memory. That paper always seemed to change bad memories into memories that would no longer hold people back.

Alex was able to use his lesson list with Mimi, who was wrongfully accused of being the one who reported some kids who were caught cheating in class. Alex knew she had nothing to do with it, but he did not know who turned the students in to Mrs. Marston. Mimi didn't even know there was a problem until the other kids starting pointing her out as the scapegoat. Alex knew just what to do to help her. Like all the others he had been able to help, working with the list made Mimi feel much better immediately. They could say what they wanted because she knew the truth and did not have to feel the pain of being the accused. It was the initial impact of being accused that hurt the most, and that stinger was removed with words that changed her feelings. A week later, when another test was given, the person who had been supplying the answers for the tests became frustrated when he was bugged for the answers again and refused to give them up. "You always gave us the answers before," Andrew, another classmate, said, believing that they still had the same deal. Mrs. Marston never heard the statement; however, Mimi and Alex did, and they understood what it all meant. As before, Mimi never said a word about it.

The more Alex used his lesson sheet with others, the more he wanted to know how memories worked and how to help others learn to handle the way they processed and reprocessed things that happened in their lives. When he felt the timing was right, Mr. Parsons had appeared again and taught him something new that he could share with others.

His mind drifted to his dad because he knew that Dad had dreams that made him sit right up in bed at night and shout. Maybe if he told him how to use his capacity as imagination director, things would change. Dad could change his dreams or rewrite his programs as he did for his more specialized programming clients who came to WCSS, Williams Computer Sales and Service. Thanks to Grandma's will, Dad now had his dream business just a block from home in the house she left her only child.

Two days after meeting Mr. Parsons at the stream's edge, Alex entered his father's shop. His dad was always pleased to see him in hopes of teaching Alex a thing or two. Alex asked him, "If one of your programming customers comes to you with a program that has a glitch in it, something that makes it start doing one thing and then ends up doing another, how can you correct the problem?"

Dad started by saying, "Well, the first thing you have to do is know what the program is that your working on, so I have them describe it in detail. If it is a systems file, I reload the system."

Alex quickly asked, "What if it's something they put in there special because they needed to remember a certain thing, but now it only did something else. I mean, every time they start it doing what they need it to do, like a memory, they discover that it goes into something they don't want it to, and they can't seem to stop the process."

"It's not easy, son. That's when I have to break the program down and find out all the processes it is meant to do. When I know exactly where it changes the process in the data, I jump in and rewrite the code so that the process does what they need it to."

Alex added, "Would that be anything like when you tell a story to a child and, because you have told it so many times, you change the ending so that it takes them totally by surprise?"

"In many ways, yes. It is all about the process. Thinking along those same lines, children create a process where they have an expected ending to the story that the process should always follow. When you change it, it's like rewriting the code, and when you tell it again, the new ending is what they expect to hear. Unless you repeat the change, they would hear the old ending and give you a look like, 'That's not right.'"

Alex still prodded, "So is it easy to rewrite the process? I mean, that would be like me having a nightmare at night. If I had a way to just change the ending process then my nightmares would be over, right?"

"Well, yes," his dad responded, looking off just a little into the distance, making Alex think that he may have said all that he needed to say. He gave away nothing, and yet felt that he had said enough to enable his dad to help himself.

Alex changed the subject back to computer repair. "What program in computers goes bad the most?"

"The human mind," his dad responded, without even stopping to think. His statement told Alex that perhaps he was still thinking about changing personal memories.

Alex cut in, "I would imagine human error will always be a problem with computers," seeking to change the thinking back to computers.

Dad still was looking off into the distance, showing that somewhere in the conversation the connection between what we have the capacity to do with our minds really was like computers and that, at times, we did have to rewrite a process or program just like Mr. Parsons told Alex.

Just then, Dad spoke. "You gave me an idea, Alex. Let me ask you something. "If you were having a problem sleeping because the dream you were having woke you up, and when you went back to sleep it repeated itself, then why would it not work if you changed the process the dream was headed in? I mean, you know already where it's going. When you woke up, you could imagine changing the dream so that you made it go all the way to a conclusion you would like and approve of. Why would it not then change the way you remember it and the way it comes back up? You know, sort of like, but not the same as that lesson page you read every now and then. You tell us how to change something, and then when we think of it again later, the process stays changed the way we last thought about it, making all the changes."

Dad continued, "I think if I were doing this with a child, I would make him create three different endings. That way he becomes comfortable with the possibilities, and his brain has a choice when he goes back to sleep. I found out early in life that even offering you, Alex, three good choices about anything allowed you to feel responsible for the outcome and you would not get so mad at me. It also helped teach you responsibility, just like it does here with dreams."

Alex replied, "Oh, I know that works. I've done that—created different possible endings." Alex thought it best not to tell his dad any more, as he only wanted to leak enough to not give away that he was getting lessons again. After all, he had made an agreement not to tell anyone that his friend was back.

About that time, his dad said, "Watch this," and hit the switch on one of the computers someone had brought in for him to repair. "See this," he said as a screen came on, flickered, and rolled repeatedly back to just after where it had started, much like a broken television with the horizontal hold not working. "This antique is doing the same thing again and again, and the only way to stop the glitch is to turn it off. Problem is, that won't fix it with this particular computer. I can't stick another program over this hiccup, so what I've been working on is a rewrite that will make it skip the nightmare part, if we can call it that, and make it go into a new process that should fix it. I am about to install the rewrite if you want to watch me put the new process in."

This excited Alex. He believed that his father understood his lesson on rewriting nightmares. He watched intently as the rewrite was uploaded into the computer, and then as the whole system was shut down. When Dad brought it back up, it came up to the point where the glitch was last time, and then the process went on to a completely new screen without any repeating flickering.

Alex had no idea whose computer his dad was working on, but Alex's astonishment showed when he saw that the opening screen read, "Pastor McGregor's Sermon Notes."

"You would have never seen that, Alex, had I not rewritten the process. It would have come up with some other screen. Pastor actually called it his nightmare. He told me, 'No matter what I do, something always sends my church mouse to another church!' Now his computer will behave the way he wants it to. Let me run the process a few more times to make sure it always goes to his notes page, and then you can help me take it back to his office. I know I should learn to trust the process to always work, but it never hurts to run a check."

They walked the three blocks down Main Street to the church and knocked on Pastor McGregor's door. "Knock, knock. Your new mouse is back in the church," Dad said as they stood at the slightly opened door to his office.

"Come in, come in, and come in," Pastor said. "Put that antique right here," he said, pointing to the right side of his big desk, moving a few papers at the same time.

Dad did, indeed, bring a new optical mouse after earlier noting the worn–out, antique mouse that Pastor had been using. It was so old that it only had one click button, no wheel, and a frayed cord.

"How much do I owe you?" Pastor said, pointing to the computer screen. He was delighted to see his sermon notes screen coming nearly instantly into view. Dad responded, "I'll take a donation receipt, please, if you don't mind."

"Name your price," Pastor said, and Dad wrote down what it really would have cost for the repair work, counting the new optical mouse as a gift.

"The church needs a new mouse," Dad said, "so this is a gift to the church." Dad took it out of the package, and turning it over, he showed Pastor it had a name on the other side. In bold, white letters written with correction fluid was the word *Church*. Then Dad rolled it around a little like it was inquisitively searching for cheese hidden somewhere on the desk.

Pastor laughed and said, "I trust it will be okay if I bring this into my sermon on Sunday. My sermon title already will be, "What the Church Mouse Learned." You'll have to wait to know more. I'm not telling Church Mouse's secret until Sunday."

Dad smiled and nodded his head, while Alex examined the lettering on the bottom of the new church mouse, amazed that Dad had done the lettering the way he had.

"Actually," Pastor started, "I wish I had a plate of Grandma's molasses cookies to give you instead of a receipt. Man, do I miss those cookies. I think that was the biggest funeral we've ever had in this town. She was greatly appreciated and is missed."

Dad thought about the cookies and put his hand on Alex's shoulder, saying, "Alex, I think there's an invitation for a cooking lesson here. I think Pastor wants you to teach him how to make some famous rolled molasses cookies."

"Oh no, that's not it! I just wish I had a plateful to give you for the mouse. Oh goodness, I want a plateful for me. Let's be honest here," Pastor said, smiling and rubbing his belly. "If you decide you want to teach me how to make cookies, Alex, you just tell me the ingredients in advance so I can get everything we need first. I have cookie sheets, a rolling pin, and so on. I think I'd only need the ingredients. And if you can, any chance I can get Grandma's peanut butter cookie recipe? You know, the one that she pressed with a fork on the top to make those little ridges that taste like peanuts? Oh my, I think we all miss her cookies."

Alex was a little taken aback, as teaching anyone else Grandma's cookie secrets had never entered his mind. He would need to ask Kaitlyn if he could give Pastor the recipes; however, how could she not agree? Thus, Alex said he would, and for now it all worked out without making any commitment for a specific day or time.

Walking back toward WCSS, Alex told his dad he needed to get his biking done to keep his legs in shape for basketball. Dad was so proud of Alex for making the team. His goal was for Alex to play on the varsity team that he had played on.

After his biking, Alex had homework assignments that he had to get done. Those projects would definitely take Alex all his remaining waking hours. His history project would require research online. Plus, he still had a book report coming up and sixty–five pages yet to read. Then there was algebra, a subject that I think he could do in his sleep and probably enjoyed the most.

# Chapter

After learning much from Dad about computers, Alex was always eager to put more thought into the memories, or programs, we all store, with a curiosity toward the potential of healing, using change work. Paying attention to what his dad knew and could teach him would only help.

Not long after school one afternoon, Alex was sitting on his favorite white wicker swing, the one he and his dad had hung for Grandma when she still lived in the house. Dad said that he would never take the swing down, and would replace it if it rotted, because it was a symbol of love that created comfortable feelings to anyone coming to his store. The swing became a symbol of goodwill. Alex had greeted his dad, who was busy with wires connected from one computer to several others, when he first arrived at the store. He asked his dad what he was doing, hoping that it might lead into conversation like it had before. Dad seemed very intent, though, like his work required his complete attention. He could tell that his dad was under some pressure, so Alex had gone out to the porch swing.

His mind wandered because he had a headache that didn't want to let go since his history exam that morning. He had wondered whether he was coming down with something, but he dismissed that thought because tomorrow night he had a big game. Thinking about his headache and staring off at the bird sitting on top of the telephone pole across the street directly in front, he thought he would actually like to give that bird his headache, as funny as that sounded. Curiosity set in quickly for Alex. Trying to make a game out of the activity of staring, he discovered he could intently stare at the bird and still allow his eyes to see whatever else was all around him. He could see the overhead deck where Dad's new store sign was hanging down from where flower boxes once stood. Then, still staring with his focus only on the bird, he noticed the houses to the left and right, the car driving past, and a yellow weed near the curb. He wondered whether, if he paid a little more attention, he could use all of his senses to sense what the outside world was like, while still only staring at the small, brown bird just sitting there like a statue. Once, when he stopped and shook his head, Alex checked to see if he got that strange feeling again, that feeling that everything seemed to just spread out and dissipate into the area of his full view while he was still staring *only* at the little, brown bird sitting on an electrical insulator. Then he remembered that his intent was to give his headache to the bird. As a process, he tried to feel everything he could about his headache. He then slowly repeated the process, still paying attention to both the headache and his visual focus on the bird. He just felt the pain and did exactly what he did before, slowly allowing his focus, and finally his other senses, to expand.

Little time passed, and then it hit him—his headache was gone, completely gone. He had been focused only on his headache and holding it as his feeling of focus when he first started looking at the bird. He remembered the feeling as though something were taking it and spreading it all over everything he was seeing outside of his focal point. When he added in his other senses, something had happened; change took place using a new process. Of that he was sure. He'd had the headache since before school lunch. It was there when he looked up toward the bird. Now it was gone. Trying to put together all the pieces of what just took place brought a look of sheer puzzlement to his face. Deep in thought, his dad came out to join him for a few minutes. It was stuffy in the shop today, and what he had been working on took a lot of heavy concentration.

"I need a break," Dad spoke, heading over to join Alex on the swing. "My head is pounding from exhaustion. I'm frying my circuits trying to make that puzzle in that computer fit when it sure doesn't want to. I just wish people would accept standard programming or total custom work, rather than asking me to take something someone else created and change it to meet their needs. If they only understood how complicated it is," he chuckled, "I might be out of business." He took a deep breath and began to release some of the pressure that was building up inside. Breathing deeply always seemed to help him feel better, regardless of the source of the pressure.

Alex considered what his dad had said to be a divine appointment to put his newly created thinking process to a test.

"Is your pounding gone yet?" he asked his dad, hoping that it was not.

"Not a chance, but it will be. I'm going to go see what I have in the medicine drawer," his dad said, and began to get up.

"Wait a minute, Dad. I need you to try something I think I just figured out."

His dad answered, "Is it going to stop my head from pounding?"

"I don't know," Alex responded. "I think so. It's a process, I think, like a computer program. It just made my headache go away. I think it changes something in your pain as you move it … out there," Alex said, making a wide sweep of his hand.

With his Dad looking at him inquisitively, Alex began. "Just feel the pounding, Dad, like you said you felt it when you were coming out the door. Be right inside your head so that you're feeling the pounding, and then signal me when you're ready."

It did not take long for a signal to come. The pounding had only begun to let up a little from his deep breathing, so it was easy for him to locate that internal pain.

"Keep staying right inside that feeling, Dad, and look right over there where you see ..." Alex looked in the direction of the pole, expecting to see the bird, but it was gone. Alex had to get creative. Pointing out toward the road, he started again. "Look, do you see that insulator at the top of that telephone pole? Stare intently at that insulator while you're feeling the pain. Just keep feeling the pounding while doing everything you can to only see with your eyes all the details of the insulator and nothing else around for right now."

There was a good pause as Alex tried to make sure that he was not making a fool of himself, that whatever he did before was replicated exactly, except with an insulator. He wondered whether the bird was gone because it had a headache. This certainly would be the test to find out whether it was the process or just a fluke. Alex was beginning to believe that he was learning to understand life as energy. If it was that simple, why didn't everyone know it already? Was it because they were stuck in their physical humanness and didn't perceive life as energy, even spirit energy? If Alex were correct, that would make us spirit beings having a human experience, learning to live a life as a spirit being first and human second. Although human is what we think of ourselves, the actuality is, we are first spirit.

"As you continue to feel the pounding in your head, allow your eyes to stay totally focused on the insulator. Now begin to slowly relax your eye muscles so that you see everything out there in all directions, still staring only at the insulator. Don't turn to see everything around you; just keep looking at the insulator, and notice that you can also see out to the sides; your store sign up overhead in your vision of awareness. Add in Mrs. Burns' house and the dandelion on the edge of the lawn. I think you can begin now to hear sounds, if you can, and feel what you feel outside your head as well."

With that, Dad broke his stare and looked directly at Alex. "Who taught you that?" he asked, a rather stern look on his face.

"No one, Dad. I was just sitting here, wishing the headache I'd had most of the day would go away. I saw a bird where that insulator is, started staring at it while still feeling my headache, and before I knew it, my pain was gone. Just like that, it just let up. I jokingly was trying to see if I could give the bird my headache just by staring at it, and then it was gone. Is your pounding gone?"

Dad said that his pounding was certainly lessened as he took another deep breath, and told Alex to say the process all over again. Alex said it as best he could, repeating the process as closely as possible to what he had done for himself, except without a bird to look at. His dad had to agree that his pounding had about ceased that time.

They both sat staring again, repeating what happened as though to memorize this process that created change. Finally, Dad was the first to speak. "I think Mr. Parsons is right, Alex; you're going to have a true gift of helping other people. You need to try to write down what we just did. I know I would never have thought of it in a million years. You made me stare in one location, thinking about my problem, and then when you added in the process of including the surroundings, it changed. I could hear the sounds around me and even feel my feet swinging here on the swing. While my energy really felt like I was out there, the pain changed as though it were spreading out. It was like from your paper, when you said to take the sounds and allow them to last forever. My pounding spread out and just vanished."

Alex, searching for anything he understood that he could use to describe what he thought took place, said, "I guess out there," as he waved his hand toward the area in front of them, "is like putting a single drop of light blue ink into a bowl of warm water; it just spreads out until it is so diluted you don't notice it anymore. What we moved was the energy of the pain from being contained in us to the whole space out there outside of us."

"That will work," his dad responded. "Add enough water and the color is gone. But, son, when you added in all of space as sight, sound, feelings, and even taste and smell, a miracle took place. That is like a whole new program that takes the energy in the pain and blows out the edges, or boundaries, of the container, and … wow! Talk about thinking outside the box. You're sure doing a lot of that, Alex."

Dad thought of an incident from a couple of days before that still bothered him. Had he the opportunity to experience this incident all over, it would come out differently, as he would never have responded as he had then. He stared at the insulator again and felt that memory and the feelings attached to it that had been bothering him. Just like before, something happened. Something shifted inside and seemed to go outside in the process, spreading those feelings out beyond the borders of the memory, so that they no longer belonged to it at all. Truly, it made him feel better, and he knew that he would not respond the same way in similar circumstances again. He could easily forgive his folly and move on. Saying only that it involved an incident that had been bothering him, Dad shared with Alex what he had just done, as well as the resultant release from his negative feelings. Naturally, Alex had to try it with one of his own. It was interesting that they had no need to tell each other the specifics of the incidents each had dealt with. They used what now appeared to be another way to shift energy, and it also worked.

With a smile as big as his face could contain, William II looked at his son and said, "I think you may have to open Alex's Human Computer Shop; you keep creating program processes that work!"

Indeed, it was all about the process of shifting energy. What they were doing was similar to putting a new program into a computer, a process that created change. Their job was to remember it, practice it, and use it. There was nothing here new that noting it would just run on its own, but each of them was the switch to enact the change they were seeking.

They both sat comfortably, the pressures of the day now deflated. They were relaxed, just pondering their discovery that one can actually diminish the pressures of any day by thinking about them and staring at a bird or an insulator or whatever is in the distance up above eye level, allowing their eyes and all of their senses to just relax and spread the energy out. While staying focused on what had been bothering them and shifting their focus externally, they allowed the world around them to absorb the energy, thus taking it away from inside of them. The world is full of energy that is able to bring balance into people's lives. A person's energy is contained in the box that is the human body, and, as Alex and his dad discovered, there is a way to send that energy outside the boundaries of the box. Thinking about this fact would make Alex turn even more creative.

This day ended on a perfect note. Mom was already cooking supper when Alex and Dad locked up and walked home. Kaitlyn was up in her room working on her scrapbook. Alex had no homework other than a quick ten pages to read in his book for English, *A Tale of Two Cities*. Mom suggested that they go to the movies and see a special theater rerun of the last episode of *Lord of the Rings*. They had run one movie of the trilogy each night in succession. There were a lot of people there. Appropriately, tonight Mom and Dad broke from their conventional pattern—acting outside the box—Mom and Dad bought popcorn and individual drinks. Usually, Mom would dole out pieces of a big candy bar she would buy, or maybe from a package of something like M&Ms. Tonight was, for some reason, different, and seeing the movie again was spectacular.

# Chapter 5

Friday finally came and steadily slid into a night of basketball, where the best of the rival schools' teams would face off against each other again. The junior varsity game came first, and from what the audience saw, both teams had so much to learn. It was like watching a foul–shooting contest. Throughout the whole game, none of the members on either team really broke out in a sweat. When the game ended, Alex showered and changed into his school colors just in time to join his entire family sitting in the third row of the home team bleachers for the start of the varsity game.

"Good game, son," his dad said as Alex walked up the bleacher stairs. Alex wondered whether Dad had really seen the game. Knowing that complaining was a privilege one should only use when hurt or when something really needed to be corrected, Alex remained silent and sat watching the start of the varsity game.

Alex did not have many guys that he would call friends on the varsity team, as they tended to be a clique of very girl–crazy guys who kept to their own. When they were out and around town, all the girls in school would be drooling all over them, and they would treat the girls as though they were trophies they had earned for sporting shorts and a tee shirt and throwing a ball. Jon Campo was the closest Alex had been to having a varsity member as a friend, and that happened very much by accident.

Jon was out walking his dog, Jarman, one day after school when a service truck driven by someone believed to have drunk a little too much alcohol crossed the marked, solid white line on the edge of the road where there was no bike lane. Jarman yelped as his back leg was clipped by the truck. Alex was a little over a block away when he saw and heard what happened. He knew the sound of a bone break from when a boy fell awkwardly during soccer practice. There was no one else nearby. There was no other traffic on the street, and the driver did not even stop, seeming not to notice that he'd hit anything or anyone. Jon was helpless to do anything for Jarman, and looked to be in shock. The weight of a full–grown and much–loved Rottweiler was too much for him to just pick up and carry home. That's when Alex and a varsity team player began a friendship. Together, they carried Jarman nearly one–third of a mile up the back street, uphill, to the corner lot on Norstar Lane, where the veterinary clinic of Dr. Emaleigh was located. Alex stayed with Jon until Jarman's leg was cast and he was able to take him home. Jon was the only child of a now–single mother who worked in the State Potato Federation Office, a twenty–minute drive away. Rebecca, his mom, had bought Jarman as a friend for Jon and a form of protection for the home when they were both away at school and work.

When they first arrived at the clinic, Dr. Emaleigh showed no concerns about getting the necessary paperwork signed, and went right to work on Jarman, just as she was trained to do. It was not the first time he had been to her clinic. She did mention that her Pet Mobile, as it was known, was in for transmission overhaul. If Jon was willing to wait a few hours, she would see to it that he and Jarman got home safely. What she wanted Jarman to do was walk on that cast as little as possible for seventy–two hours. She actually sedated him, causing him to become even more of a dead weight to carry than before. It was looking like Jon would have to stay there with Jarman until the vet was off work. Seizing the opportunity to be of further assistance, Alex told him that he would go get his dad, and that they would be right back with the service truck. Indeed, Alex kept his promise of assistance. Meanwhile, Jon called his mom to tell her about the accident. Dr. Emaleigh talked to her and told her not to be concerned, that Jarman and Jon would both be just fine.

Willy, as Emaleigh called Alex's dad when he came through the door, was more than thrilled to be of special assistance. He was hoping in the back of his mind that, with the right persuasion, he could convince Jon to coach Alex a bit in free throws, especially since a three–pointer, or even a shot from the foul line, was often the difference that won a game. It always bothered Will that his team had lost the state championships by one point. Alex's dad had been a starter on his team in the same high school and did know a good bit about throwing a ball. With the sedated Rottweiler resting comfortably on the quilts Dad usually reserved for tightly packing computers into the back of his truck, the three of them headed toward the Campo's apartment. Jarman was not out of the stupor from the medicines yet as they hefted him into the house. Jon had already made the decision that Jarman should be placed on the braided rug right beside Jon's bed. While Alex and his Dad watched, he lovingly made arrangements so that Jarman would not need to move much to have water and food available.

Dad was the first one to bring up basketball. Jon liked feeling the recognition of being seen as a first–string varsity player. Alex's Dad was nicknamed Pops that day, when Jon agreed to play a few games the next week. It was fun for Alex to hear, "Okay Pops, if you two think you're good enough to beat me!" like there was not a chance they could. From there grew a friendship and bond that would continue to grow until they were the best of friends. At first, they just met to play some practice games, with no indication that there was much friendship there yet. After all, Alex only made junior varsity while Jon was first–string varsity. When the varsity team was around, Alex was not included as one of them, as so often happens in cliques. Jon had no problem occasionally accepting invitations to come to dinner at Alex's home. Alex's folks knew Jon and his mother from church.

The whistle blew, and tonight's game would be one of those where the three–point outside shot would make the difference. Jon was the one who attempted the shot, and the local crowd went screaming crazy. When it hit the rim of the basket, it was as if a tornado had caught hold of it. Everything seemed to go into slow motion as the ball rolled around the edge of the rim a few times, and then slowly, ever so slowly, it went over the farther side and fell bouncing all by itself on the floor below. Alex would forever remember the sight of Jon's face. The instantaneous feeling of defeat that flooded Alex's side of the gym stopped the screaming abruptly, while the other side picked up screaming at the pitch where the others left off. From the middle of Alex's section, someone yelled out, "Jon, you stupid idiot, can't you even get the ball in the hole!" Dad walked up to the man and shook his fist in his face, saying something Alex couldn't hear. When Dad turned back around, his face was bright red. The man was outraged, calling Dad a name, continuing his tirade against Dad even in the parking lot.

"Leave it alone," Mom said as she reached over and patted Dad's arm. "If it had been his son who shot the ball, it would have been totally different," she said, hoping to make him feel better and cool it a little. It was possible that the man's son could have been the shooter; however, his points per game were so far below Jon's that Dad could think of no reason why anyone would have passed the final ball off to him.

Seeing Jon at school the next day hurt, even for Alex. Jon waved a downward swinging arm sign of disgust as some of the team members passed by him, not even stopping to talk. They turned their heads the moment they saw him, and Alex felt the sting right along with Jon. They acted as though Jon were contagious and incurable, and there was no reason to give him the time of day. It made him wonder how victory or defeat could make such an impact that within seconds, relationships could be ruined. He certainly had done his best; the ball was almost through the net. Maybe it wasn't the victory or defeat; it was people and their personal, unfulfilled expectations. It was people trying to live their dreams through others. Alex wanted to take the whole team to the gym and give them each a one–ball shot for a three–pointer on the basis that it would win or lose a game, knowing that type of pressure would probably make each of them fail. Rejecting Jon was something Alex would not do. In fact, Alex could not help but ask him if they could talk soon after school, so that Alex could share his lesson paper with him, promising that he had learned something from a man named Mr. Parsons that helped with things like this. Jon had no reason not to talk to Alex. Certainly no one on the team was going to be waiting to meet and do something with him after school, as was often the case.

Jon and Alex did meet that day after school. Jon never expected the results Alex's therapeutic lesson gave him. Because of the quality of this time well spent, they both learned that having and being a friend had a lot more to do with life than basketball did. That was the day they forged a friendship. Jon would start looking out for Alex, two years his junior, a role that would become obvious even to the other varsity players.

Jarman would also become one of Alex's best friends, as dogs are known to do. Jarman was allowed to stay at Alex's house, right upstairs in his bedroom, when the varsity team went out of town overnight and the junior varsity team did not go. He would sleep on a rag rug braided and sewn by hand by Alex's great grandmother, also known for doing lace and other fancy finger work. Alex loved having Jarman there, and Jarman seemed to love it just as much because he always got a cookie. Jarman knew Pops liked him being there as well, because seeing Pops often meant another doggie cookie for Jarman!

One of the memories Jon and Alex will always think back on was when Alex took Jon to the back field in the woods, where the butterflies hatched in season. Alex had many memories there. This time, they lay on the grass in the middle of the clearing and watched the whirlwind of yellow and orange swirl overhead. Jon had to admit that he had never seen anything that beautiful. All things considered, Alex was totally comfortable being there. It had been nearly three years since his horrifying experience there, and he was over that now—healed.

# Chapter 6

Alex was eager for Saturday to dawn. It was the day he'd been awaiting for a week, the day he would take his bike around the loop. He had a high noon appointment he had no intention of missing. Telling his folks he might just start out a few minutes earlier than usual, he made his favorite peanut butter and marshmallow fluff sandwich, then put it, along with two of his favorite energy bars and two bottles of water, into his backpack. He took his pack upstairs to his room. From his closet, he took one of a six–pack of organic carbonated raspberry beverages and placed it in his pack, along with a plastic cup he had brought home from church last Sunday. With that, he felt he was as prepared as he could be to meet Mr. Parsons at Creek Bed. His excitement would not allow him to go right to sleep, so he got up and started his favorite CD playing. Mouthing the words to songs he had known and loved for years set his breathing to a pace that slowed him up and did the trick. Tomorrow would be a day of new lessons and a deeper understanding of the one thing Mr. Parsons said he studied the most: humans.

Morning came as glorious as any for northern Maine. There was a slight hint of rain in the air. Alex kept close watch of his timing, planning to make the longest part of his trip around the triangle first. That way he would only have 45 percent of his biking journey left after his lessons. It did make for the steepest hills to climb, but today he was up for any task.

He was about to reach the apex of the second largest hill when he realized his tire was low on air. Appreciating that gas stations still had free air pumps where he lived, he stopped on the outskirts of town at Jake's Gas and Repair and started adding air to his tire. As he did, something popped, and then *poof*, the tire went flat. Whatever it was that made the pop sound had been wedged into the tire like a plug, holding in the air. With it gone, Alex heard the sound any bike rider dreaded hearing—the sound of air whooshing out instead of in.

Noticing the lad against the side of the building, a mechanic came around and asked if there was anything he could do.

"Not unless you have a new bicycle tire," Alex responded.

"I can do about as well as that," he said as he walked back into his garage and came out with a little red box that said "20 tube" on the side. "Where you headed, boy?" he asked.

"I'm supposed to meet a friend at high noon at the Creek Bed Rest Area," Alex said, looking at his watch and realizing he had thirty minutes left and now would definitely not make it. His face must have shown his disappointment, because the mechanic said, "Well, I can even fix that," and he pointed to his tow truck parked on the curb at the end of the driveway. "I have to go pick up Mr. Thompson's tractor and bring it in so Jake can put in a new drive tram. I pass right by Creek Bed, if you want a lift."

Alex signed an IOU for the mechanic, embarrassed that he did not have cash with him. He hadn't made plans to stop anywhere on this trip. The way Alex figured it, he would be pedaling past here again in a week and would make good his IOU. It was $4.50 for the tube and $5.00 for the installation. With the mowing money earned with his John Deere tractor, he already had it at home. The mechanic was nice and said that he need not pay the money back, just donate it someplace where it would do good to help others. Alex accepted the offer of a ride with the mechanic, who picked up speed faster than most people consider moving in Maine. Even so, by the time they would reach the picnic area, it would be two minutes past high noon. Alex knew he would be late as it takes time to change a tube.

As the tow truck pulled out of the lot, after leaving him at Creek Bed, Alex immediately began to look for Mr. Parsons. Seeing him nowhere in sight, he took out a bottle of water and his peanut butter and marshmallow fluff sandwich. When he finished eating, he worried that he might have misunderstood the day or even gotten the time wrong, or worse, missed Mr. Parsons entirely. He was so excited when last they met that he could have just missed something in their communication. He took his shoes off and did what he normally did from his favorite rock. His feet had been dangling in the extremely cold water for about a minute when Alex heard a voice coming from the direction of the road.

"Nice day for a walk there, Alex. Glad to see you're here. I saw you and my friend pass me in his tow truck awhile back, so I knew you were here already. Couldn't help but notice your bike in the back as well. Are you too worn out to bike today?"

"Oh, no. I had a flat tire, and he fixed it for me. For a bit, I thought I was going to be late," Alex responded.

"Angels do that." Mr. Parsons responded. "You probably won't see him again."

Alex knew he would, because he had an IOU in his pocket that reminded him of his $9.50 obligation.

Mr. Parsons spoke again. "You give any more thought to what I taught you about dreams? I mean, you did make the changes, right?"

"Oh yes, and they worked. I think I am beginning to know a lot more about memories and rewriting programs and processes, and I am starting to teach others things like that."

"And teach today is what I shall do, Alex. Here. Let me take my shoes off and soak my feet while I sit here with you."

Mr. Parsons made himself as comfortable as he could as he dangled his feet in one of the deeper spots in the cold water, nearly up to his knees. "Wow! This is cold!" Mr. Parsons said. "Maybe we need to love this stream and warm the water up. Love. I think that's what we said we would talk about today."

"That is it!" Alex said as though everything he needed to know could be taught in one simple lesson.

"I may seem to ramble on at times, son; however, you just stay with me as best you can. You see, love is a strange thing and so is the way humans look at it, or even use it. I'm sure you have heard the expression, 'Love never changes?'"

"Yup."

"Well, if you had to think of only one word that you could use to put in place of the word *love*, what do you think that one word would be?"

Alex shook his head, showing that he lacked a word.

"The only thing that I know that never changes is God, Alex. That's the reason you hear that other saying—'God is love.' People really do think of God as being love; they just fail to recognize that when they love, have loved, or are loving, they are using the very energy or presence of God as the process or flow of what they are doing. I am not saying that God is a process, Alex. I am saying that love is what God is. To use love in any way, you are applying what God is to whatever you are doing."

"Let's think of this another way. Let me ask a question that relates to how you feel this as energy. When you say you feel loved, do you feel cold or warm?"

"Warm," Alex said softly, intently listening to what was being taught.

"What you are actually feeling when you really intently feel love is the very presence of God. Now think of the opposite, a time when you are not feeling love."

Alex quickly responded, "That would be like bad memories where they are cold and harsh, and they hurt, right?"

"Right. That is because they lack the energy of love or the greater presence of God. It is not that God is not there. While God is not something that is weak or strong, God is always God. It is humans who allow or block the perfection of God as they allow or restrict the flow of love's energy. People do not automatically think of bringing love into any memory. In fact, if you asked them, they will tell you it is totally missing. Just know, Alex, God is always there."

"Let me tell you another expression you may have heard. Actually, let me back up and say a group of them here. Just notice how one builds on the other, son. God is love. Love never changes. Since love never changes, whatever love touches, love changes."

"Grandma always said that, and I know my mom and dad teach that in Sunday school," Alex spoke.

"Well, someone has to teach it, and people still don't seem to be getting it like I know you will."

"Why don't they?" Alex questioned.

"I think because they refuse to allow themselves to really put God to the test. You, however, you're ready to see what love can change. So let me remind you what we just stated: God is love. Love never changes. What love touches, love changes. That's the secret to healing, Alex, the application of love, not the belief that love works."

"Secret?" Alex again questioned.

"Yes, the secret, and for most people, it is a well–kept, hidden secret. Love heals all wounds. Whoops! That one just slipped out," Mr. Parsons said as he put his hand over his mouth like it was funny. "I need to say that for you again, Alex. God is love. Love never changes. What love touches, love changes, and love heals all wounds. Think of it, Alex. If people understood what they turn loose, and the healing that can be accomplished in using love as the energy of power in the process, the whole world would change."

"Imagine, Alex, God has made all this power and authority available for people to use by being love, loved, and loving, and I do mean actually becoming love, living it and not merely doing it.

Instead, billions keep crying out with their voices and actions for Him to be the one responsible to make them feel loved, and to create all the changes they believe they desire."

"Alex, here is a question that will cut to the real crux of the matter. If today you had to choose, and you knew that you were only able to have one friend, what would happen if you had to choose between one who loved you and one who hated you? Which one would you choose?"

Alex found that as easy to answer as anyone would. "I would choose the one who loved me."

"If only people understood that we all seek love first and foremost. That's the problem, Alex. All human beings need to be loved, with every cell of their being, while they create disease in their thinking and actions, causing disease in their bodies. When you ask them, they will tell you openly that they hate whatever disease is developing inside themselves, yet they fail to recognize that they are the ones causing and/or creating the "dis–ease" or disease. If they truly understood the power *in* and *of* love to heal, they would never hate any cell in their body for any reason. If they were love living, they would even love what others hated most. I think Mother Teresa was the last well–known living example of love living."

"Energetically, as long as a person hates what is, they supply the opposite energy, while at the same time, without participating in the process, they expect God to perform a miracle. In this manner, they are fighting the potential to heal 100 percent. I am not saying that complete healing miracles do not take place, Alex. They are a part of God's love and do happen. What I am saying is that God has given us the ability to participate for ourselves, and even for others in the healing process, and we humans totally miss it."

After a lengthy pause, Mr. Parsons continued, "Someday and definitely another time, I need to teach you another mega lesson. Just know Alex, you are an infinite being and only subject to what you hold in mind. You remember that statement. Dwell on it for some time, and when we meet for that discussion, I know you will be more ready to understand the implications I can show you about you and all people. For right now, I need to show you the power in love to create change. Do you think you're ready for a real off–the–wall scientific experiment?"

Alex nodded his head enthusiastically. He was being offered something off–the–wall. Little did he know he had packed the experiment in his backpack the night before, and had five more potential experiments still in his closet.

"Did you bring that can of soda I asked you to bring?" Mr. Parsons asked.

Alex quickly hopped up, splashing water from his feet as he walked over to the nearest picnic table where his backpack was lying. He took out the can of raspberry soda and the plastic cup.

Coming back to his favorite seat, wet from his feet when he jumped up, the water on the rock made no difference to him as he sat back down. He handed his can and cup to Mr. Parsons, thinking that he was to do the experiment, and Alex would watch and learn from observation.

"You hold it, Alex, and I'm glad to see that you chose raspberry. You'll love what will happen next. What I want you to do is simply open the can of soda and pour about half of the can into your clear cup there."

Alex did as he was told.

"Now taste the beverage in each container," Mr. Parsons said. He was smiling, knowing that most people had to convince themselves to believe the change that would soon take place.

"Go ahead and place your can over there," he said, pointing to a rock off to the side, "and then hold your glass with the delicious reddish pink stuff between your hands in a way that will allow you to look right into the middle of the beverage."

Alex followed the directions implicitly and looked directly down into the cup.

"Now think of someone, or even something, that you really love. I don't need to know who they are or what it is, only that you love whatever. Just think about whatever it is so that you can fully focus on it. Let me know when you're ready. I will make whatever it is, your decision."

Alex had no trouble with that one.

"Here's where the fun begins. This is where you begin to experience the proof that love changes everything, and that love is one of the best healing powers ever. Look right into the middle of your raspberry drink there, son, and just picture, right there in the middle of the beverage, whoever it is , or whatever it is that you chose to love. I am serious when I say to see them, see it right in the middle of your glass. Focus your attention as though you are seeing whatever it is right there. This way the love that you apply as energy, goes to where you focus. I want you to just feel that feeling in your heart, the feeling that you call love. Allow that feeling to be focused right into that glass, right into whatever it is that you are seeing there."

Alex found that it didn't feel strange at all to love like this and could easily hold his focus directly on what he was imagining in the beverage.

"While you 'love it to life' there, my friend, go ahead and think about what it would be like if you made it your intention to heal the carbonation out of the beverage. Imagine the feeling you would get with all the carbonation gone. That's right. That's it. Just you stay focused in the middle of the beverage, and imagine what it will be like healed. One more time, I want to make sure that you have indeed loved it to life, so stay focused right inside and love whatever is once more."

It wasn't long before Mr. Parsons said, "Taste the beverage in your can again so that you can be reminded what it tasted like before you began this healing love experiment."

Alex tasted it, noting that it was the same as when he tasted it before. There was no question that it was carbonated, and it still had a nice raspberry flavor.

With a big smile from Mr. Parsons, Alex was told to taste the beverage in his glass and note whether there were any differences.

At first Alex rolled his eyes as if searching for the flavor that was once there, but his face looked puzzled. "This isn't the same beverage. This tastes like … vanilla cream soda."

"Yes," Mr. Parsons responded, "and … ?"

"It's really flat. I mean," Alex pointed at the can, "it's nothing like what's in the can." His eyes grew large, and his head swung from side to side as if in disbelief. He used love and the intention to heal the carbonation out of the beverage. He was the one who made it happen. This was real, and he was glad he had saved the other half as proof. Otherwise, his mind would have told him he was playing a trick on himself. Nope. This was very real; the beverage was not the same. Mr. Parsons gave him time to take a few more sips of each, making comparison after comparison until there was no question. Alex knew that love had changed that beverage. He even noted that the darker red color of the original raspberry beverage was now a much lighter pink. Quickly, his mind changed to a totally new thought, *What would happen if … we just loved our bodies?* He thought about how much water we have in our bodies. Now his mind began to run wild with loving ideas as well as their possible consequences.

Without going into what actually happened scientifically, Mr. Parsons began. "God is love, and you just used love to heal that beverage. Let me say it again, Alex, so that you can take it all in. Love never changes, Alex. Love never, never, never changes. So, that beverage had no choice; it had to change and become more of what love is, because love applied to anything makes it change to become more of what love is. Think for a second of adding hot water into cold. You know it changes. Well, love does the same thing and changes what it comes in contact with to become more of what love is. Does that make sense, son?"

Mr. Parsons stared off for a second, thinking about how great it would be if parents truly understood the lesson Alex seemed to be so easily able to grasp.

"Yes and no?" Alex questioned, with a look of deep thought on his face. He put both hands up to the top sides of his head as he said, "Does this mean that if I had just loved my grandmother more she would not have died?"

"No, Alex. It was her time, and she was ready to go. You remember all that you heard about her making her transition. Let's talk about the people much younger than Grandma who really could use a touch of love to heal. What most people have when it comes to disease is similar to a computer program. They have a dis ease in their process of life. When they refuse to take care of whatever it is, the dis eased energy creates disease energy. Then what they do is allow their life energy to go even lower while they plead with God to take away whatever they are creating. For one thing, you don't find people talking about how they created their disease. They go so far as to tell everyone around them that they hate what's wrong while professing that they love themselves. Because of that, everyone around them participates in hating what's wrong and begins to plead with God, right along with them, to take it away. Well, God is not in the take–away business, Alex. Why would God be interested in only having what other people hate? What would he do with it anyway? God does not want to take something *out*; God wants to work with what is already there. And what is inside there is that which is in need of changing, in need of the transitional energy of healing. Taking it out resolves the problem; however, it does not provide a complete healing solution. We want to look at full recovery, and that comes from the heart. And remember, God is still there in whatever is, because God is omnipresent. God is *love,* and don't you forget it. God is interested in the intent of the human heart. While humans look upon the outside, and some on the inside, to find what is wrong, God looks upon the heart where love lives and is waiting for them to find it there. When love vacates your heart, Alex, they will call you dead!

"When you changed that beverage by thinking of someone you loved, and I know that is what you used, that energy came from inside of you. People need to become aware of the existence of the presence of God as love inside their hearts, and remember that every cell in their bodies is there because they created it out of the elements of the earth by bending their elbows and putting in food. Just like themselves, every cell in their bodies wants love as a best friend. After all, they are what they created. We know love heals. You proved it with that drink. Love heals all wounds: physical, emotional, and spiritual. What would happen if people understood that everything love touches changes whatever it touches, because love never changes? Imagine what would happen if they decide to not hate what is wrong with cells in their body, and especially if they decided to not make love only God's responsibility. I mean, what would happen if they chose to participate by loving what is instead of saying to God, 'If you loved me, you would take this from me'? As I said, God is not in the take–away business. God designed humans to participate, Alex. Love is what we are, foundationally, on the inside, for as long as our hearts are beating in there."

Alex grinned from ear to ear. He knew what happened to the beverage. How could it not happen to everything else love comes in contact with? Love changes everything because it is love, and love never changes. Now he could prove it as a fact to people.

Mr. Parsons added, "Remember what I said about other people participating in helping? People become more diseased because others help them to hate what is wrong by their very focus of attention. They add their intent for things to get worse by adding their hate energy directed into the other person's body. It goes there, just like yours went into the beverage. After all, water is a basic human component. It is a messenger molecule, much like a computer chip, that science will understand and use to help people heal."

"Yes."

"Well, just as I wanted you to see how whatever it was you loved turned more into what love is, I want to teach you how using your thoughts and intentions in one place can actually use love to help someone else heal in another place."

Not yet sure how Mr. Parsons was going to do it, Alex's mind immediately started searching for who Mr. Parsons was going to have him heal.

"Just follow along with me on this one, Alex. I think you will find it rather amusing and as challenging as changing that beverage. Now, let's have some fun!"

"Healing, amusing, and fun?" Now that is a unique statement. Alex couldn't think of anyone he had ever known who would have called healing fun.

Smiling a smile as big as possible, Mr. Parsons exclaimed, "I am going to teach you how to heal a cloud, metaphorically, way out there," pointing toward the white puffs floating overhead. Alex looked up, shaking his head in disbelief that he would ever be able to metaphorically heal a cloud, let alone hold it between his hands. The beverage was easy. He couldn't possibly touch a cloud.

"I'm sure you're thinking it can't be done, son. However, that is just what the power *in* and *of* love will do. You just follow my directions, and I think you will be amazed while you learn a valuable lesson in life. I want you to look at just that one puff of cloud right over there," Mr. Parsons spoke, pointing to one particular smaller cloud about one–fifth the size of the one traveling beside it. "The small one there just after the tip of that big one."

"Okay."

"Now I want you to once again feel that feeling you get when you intend to just love from your heart. Feel it, and stare intently at the cloud like you would at a bird on a telephone line."

Alex had certainly learned to do something like that already, so the first instructions were easy.

"You just keep intently staring right at that cloud, allowing your warm feelings of love to attach to those dust particles inside that have formed water droplets around them, which formed that cloud. That is nature at work. You just keep focusing all your attention right on that cloud, and I'm going to stop talking while you get to experience love's healing change."

It was not long, just two or three minutes, before Alex noticed that the cloud had turned gray all over and was actually disappearing in places.

Knowing full well that he was about to get too excited to focus long enough for the entire cloud to completely disappear, Mr. Parsons said, "Now just keep your focus. Yes, it is disappearing as you are making it miraculously change; however, it is not over, and you must stay focused so that the dust particles won't turn cold again."

Finally, Alex looked at Mr. Parsons with that look of someone who accomplished the impossible. "Wow!" and just kept looking back up at where the cloud had been, reviewing in his mind the truth that it was there and now it is not! "Wow!" he said again. "Can I only do that with you? Did I really do that, or did you?"

Mr. Parsons laughed right out loud. "My friend, you can do that any time you want, but be sure to remember the reason you are doing it. You are only doing it so you'll remember how to send love to others, even to anything wrong in others to help them heal. And it's you who are doing it, not me. It's all about your intention and attention."

Alex seemed totally lost. He'd just learned how to melt a cloud right in front of his own eyes, and now he is being told he can do it whenever he wants, and to help others heal. He was thinking, *Wait until Robert and Jon see me melt a cloud! I can't wait to show Dad and Mom and Kaitlyn!*

"You need to remember what we're doing here, Alex. I'm teaching you how anybody—not just you—but how anybody can use love to help heal themselves or other people. Changing the beverage is more like you healing something more closely related to you, while healing a cloud relates more closely to working with others to help them heal."

Thinking back to having five more cans of raspberry soda in his closet, Alex asked for clarity. "And I can teach them? I mean, other people *can* do this?"

"You bet you can, Alex. And yes, all people *can* do this as long as they are doing it out of, and with, love. Remember that you should always make sure they understand that you are not teaching them how to change a beverage or melt a cloud; you are teaching them how to use ... well, let me say this the long way again and see if you get it:

"God is love. Love is all there is. Everything is either a lot of love or a little of love, like dis–ease that produces disease in the body needs more love. That disease is calling out to return to love. Now remember, love never changes; however, whatever love touches, changes. So what I'm teaching you is to feel the greatest love of all, the gift of God in you, Alex, and to use that feeling, that love, to change everything you make love come in contact with. When you are teaching others what I've taught you, do it by being love living, and make sure they understand that it is not a trick you do for money on a stage; it is what we are all capable of being and doing when we make that decision to be love living instead of love seeking. Life is what you give away, and what you give away returns. That is why you hear people say, 'If you want love, give it away.' It is that simple, and yet for many people it's complicated. They make it complicated because they spend their lives, looking outside for validation and, specifically, for love. Someone even wrote a song about looking for love in all the wrong places."

Alex thought aloud, "So people who are really sick can heal—God willing?"

"Yes, Alex, they can heal faster than they ever thought possible when they, and those around them, choose to participate in living as love. In addition, they need to choose to stop hating that which is only asking to return to its basic nature and be loved to life instead of loved to death, a statement I so often hear people say."

"I told you your name means 'conqueror' and 'protector.' Alex, you should also know that at home we speak of you as "called."

Alex's mind was beginning to wander again to thoughts of what it would be like to teach all of this to others. This meeting had become so exciting that nothing could thrill Alex more. Mr. Parsons could see his excitement and knew that it needed some calming. It was true, though, the secrets he was laying out would make the deaf to hear and the blind to see; however, Alex was not ready for that step yet.

"I'm going to ask one more thing of you, Alex. I want you to practice what I've taught you today, but don't tell anyone yet that you've seen me again. I'm a good judge of timing and know how long it will take before you can do this without having to think much about it. So what I'm asking you to do is to practice healing beverages, and to pay attention to what you feel and do when you flood each beverage with love. Do the same thing with clouds; pay attention to what you feel and do when you flood each cloud with love.

Really focus on what you do inside when you are sending that love across the distance. For now, just don't say anything to anyone else yet. We will plan on another lesson sometime in the future, if that's okay with you."

"Sure, yes, but what about my folks?" Alex asked.

"I think you can count on them seeing a change in you, my son. But they don't need to know yet that we met today. You just keep practicing, and trust me when I say that I will find you again."

Alex didn't like how it felt to not have a date, time, or even a place all set up for another meeting, but he did agree not to say anything to anyone yet. He certainly would be looking forward to the next time he saw Mr. Parsons. Looking at his watch, Alex realized that he needed to start biking if he was going to be on his usual schedule. He thought he had lost some time at the garage, but he hadn't factored in the time saved by getting a lift from the repairman. Mr. Parsons was already putting on his shoes and socks when Alex began to focus his attention again on the present. Alex picked up the can of soda and tasted it again. *Still raspberry,* his inner voice told him. He drank the rest of the soda, put the can and the cup back into his pack, and adjusted the Velcro on his favorite biking shoes. Mr. Parsons shook hands with him and said, "Alex, you truly are an infinite being, and only subject to what you hold in mind. Always remember Jesus loves you." and then carefully stepped his way back across the creek on the stones, heading toward the wooded path again.

The trip home was mind–boggling to Alex. He kept reviewing what he had done, thinking about how clearly it all happened because of his ability to not only feel love, but, as Mr. Parsons had put it, to be love living. He fully understood that what others should see and feel coming out of him was love. That way, what they really were seeing and feeling was the presence of God, because God is love. Looking upward, Alex spotted another small puff of white that he could not help but focus on even while pedaling his bike. With the right amount of time and focus, just like before, it went away. He realized it was all about energy going where he focused his attention, as well as the type of energy he had to send. Love was the key. Love was the key to healing anything, including life.

Nearing the edge of town, he tried to remember all those expressions about love that Mr. Parsons had used, trusting that he would be able to write them down later. They seemed to remain in his head and easily come to memory, so he decided to wait until after supper to write them down. Mr. Parsons, wherever he was now, was a really smart man. If Alex had gone back to his church, changing beverages and melting clouds, and telling everyone that is how to heal people, the people's attention would be focused on how silly or awesome or scary Alex was. Once again, God would appear in the form of love, and they would totally miss Him. No, it was better that Alex practice those lessons privately, and allow God's glory to take its course in his life, letting things manifest at their proper time. Mr. Parsons really understood that living as love, or becoming love living, was the key and Alex was learning it from him.

Alex arrived at home a few minutes later than usual and was quizzed by his mom, who wanted to make sure everything went right. From his back pocket, he took out an IOU that gave an acceptable explanation for the few minutes extra, without having to say much about it.

"You make sure you pay him now. You want us to drive back over there and do it tonight?" Mom asked.

"No. I want to do the route again next week if the weather is right. My legs need it for basketball, and it gives me time to think," he said without letting on what he was thinking. He wanted time to heal more clouds.

"Hi, Alex," Kaitlyn said, coming down the stairs.

Surprised, Alex had to ask, "What did you do to your hair?"

"Momma colored and cut it," she said as she gave it a flip up with one hand and made a slight bend at the knees like movie stars do on the red carpet.

"You like it, don't you, Alex?" Mom called from somewhere back in the kitchen.

"As long as you're not going to do mine," he replied, thankful that he and his dad had standing appointments every three weeks at Josh's Barber Shop.

"Alex, you need to set the table, Hon. as this is Kaitlyn's night for dishes. Dinner will be at least an hour still, but it would help me out if you set the table now."

Alex never minded helping in the kitchen, and setting the table was a breeze. They had adopted the process they had seen at camp, where everything that was needed for a table set–up for a meal was placed in a basket and left in the center of the table. Here at home, everything was set in a basket and left on the sideboard, ready to go to the table. It did make it easier with only the four of them. On nights when they had company, they just added more of what they needed, and then put the extra away afterwards.

"Can you peel these potatoes and carrots?" his mom asked as she was folding the top crust over a blackberry pie. She started using a fork to crimp the edges all around, and then she cut three slits into the top. Alex watched as she put the finishing touches on the pie, and thought about the many times he had helped Grandma with pies. When the pie went into the oven, she stood up and wiped her face, using one of the most colorful aprons Alex remembered his Grandma having when he and Grandma used to cook together.

"Now to dinner," she said, looking to see what progress Alex was making with the potatoes and carrots.

"Okay. Just keep going on those, Alex. You want boiled onions tonight?" he heard her say.

"Nah!" was the instant reply.

"Okay," she said, pointing to a crock–pot that she had started earlier, "then it is stew beef, mashed potatoes with stew beef gravy, and carrots."

"Yummy" Alex responded.

"Oh, and we need to make biscuits. You do the biscuits, Alex. I did the pie!" she said, knowing full well that his delicious, from scratch biscuits would be made without a recipe. "Now let me get pots on the stove for those," she said, pointing at the vegetables he was peeling.

With the biscuits done, Alex had the perfect excuse to get out of the house. He told Mom that it was just too hot in the kitchen and that someone needed to go tell his father that dinner was ready. Heading toward WCSS, he used those few minutes to again think through Mr. Parson's sayings about God and love, since he had yet to write them down. His brain was in overload with visions of teaching everyone what he had learned, yet still he remembered his instructions to teach no one yet.

When he got near the front of the store, thanks to Kaitlyn's call telling Dad dinner was ready, his Father was already outside, turning the key in the lock.

Alex looked at his dad out of the corner of his eye as they started the walk back toward home. Alex thought about how much Dad looked like Mr. Parsons, and how much he wished his dad had been there today. Someday, someday for sure, they would meet. Alex was sure of that.

Dinner was all Alex had hoped it would be. Thanks to God, as always, was the starter before the food was passed. Alex's delight was that it was Kaitlyn's night to do the dishes, and he could get up and leave when he asked to be dismissed. With his mind still in overload, rerunning the statements about love that he had heard earlier, he almost asked to be excused too soon. He was ready to open his mouth when his mother asked, "Alex, will you go get the ice cream out of the freezer so we can put it on the hot blackberry pie?"

Now that was worth keeping his mouth shut about! After pie and ice cream, Alex was eager to ask to be dismissed. With permission, he headed immediately to his bedroom and to his desk.

He took out some sheets of the same kind of lined white paper he had used for his previous lesson's notes. At the very top, he wrote "Love Living." Then, thinking back through his day, he wrote the following, which was not necessarily written in the order in which he had heard them spoken.

Love is all there is.
Love is what God is.
God is love.

Love never changes.
Love changes all things.
What love touches, love changes.
Live as love so that you are love living.
Instead of seeking love, know that you are love; so live love.
Give love to receive love.
Love heals all wounds.
Love heals all wounds: physical, emotional, and spiritual.
Love heals!

The last one on the page was the only one Alex put an explanation mark after. Truly, this day had been about love, but it was really all about using love to heal. Alex now knew and understood that love when applied to anyone or anything brings about a positive change, making that which love touches more of what love is because the presence of Creation is never not there. As he read the list several times trying to make sure he had written them all down, another memory came to mind as a statement about a lesson coming in the future. Alex turned the sheet over and on the back in nice bold writing wrote that expression.

I am an infinite being and only subject to what I hold in mind!

Several thoughts came to Alex as he sought to grasp the feelings that came from just seeing what Mr. Parsons had told him in writing. In his head he could hear Auntie Meg saying, "*You never get enough of what you don't want because you attract what you don't want.*" A time with his dad speaking quickly also came as he heard what some thought was only computer language, however Alex realized it was life as well, "*Garbage in … garbage out.*" After pondering a couple minutes longer, Alex decided to write one more statement near the bottom of that page.

Life is a mirror reflection of what is on the inside.

Alex figured that in order to hold something in mind, you had to have references within that allowed you that opportunity. For a bit, he held a repeated thought over and over, *what I hold in mind … what I hold in mind … what I hold in mind …* then along came another inquisitive thought, *I wonder what he meant when he said that I am called?*

He thought about writing notes, like a "how–to" on healing clouds and beverages, and then remembered that he still had five potential raspberry healing miracles in his closet. Taking another can down off the shelf, he headed back to the kitchen to get a glass. Although he totally believed it would change, there is still something to be said for being able to prove something to one's inner satisfaction, when one's practical nature still argues in favor of its impossibility.

Mother called out to Alex as he passed through the room, "You going to help Kaitlyn?" She was sitting in her now–favorite rocking chair that came from Grandma's parlor.

"No. I just need something to drink," was his swift reply. Glass in hand—he had filled it with water for now—Alex headed quickly back up the stairs to where he had left his unopened, fresh raspberry soda can on his desk. Popping the top, he poured what he judged to be half the can into the glass. He tasted the drink in the glass first, sort of hoping that it would taste like cream soda; however, as he should have expected, it tasted like raspberry. After Alex checked to make sure the beverage in the can tasted the same, he held the cup in two hands, and as he looked intently into the liquid, he pictured Jarman, Jon's dog, in the middle of the beverage. He also added the memory of what he felt and thought when the drink went flat. It did not take long this time before he realized that cream soda was what he'd created, just like he had at the stream. This time the beverage seemed to have gone an even paler shade of pink from the deep raspberry starting color.

He put the glass down and went to the window to look for a cloud. Although it was still daylight, there was not the slightest hint of a cloud in the sky. His mind wandered back to another time when he had sat on Grandma's wicker swing and stared at a cloud, only to have the cloud disappear. Had it disappeared, or had he just lost his focus and the cloud moved on? *Nope,* his mind told him, *you have melted clouds before.* With that feeling of accomplishment, he made plans to spend considerable time sitting once again on the WCSS front porch and to trust that the sky would fill with the most magnificent puffs. Surely, he would melt them all. He would learn how to teach the world to love, and he would help others to heal, one cloud at a time. In his mind's eye, he was already seeing clouds as some form of cancer tumor, ready to be dissolved, or as a cloud ready to be healed.

Looking around his room, he noticed that his mother had placed the latest issue of a basketball magazine on his bed. It caught his eye and motivated him to change into his pajamas and just lie on his bed reading stats and studying the pictures. Dad ordered the magazine for him when he made the junior varsity team, sort of as a reward. Later that night, while Alex was still reading the magazine, his dad stopped by and knocked on the door, asking, "Any idea when the last game of the season is, son?"

Alex told him he wasn't sure, because it depended upon if they made the championships and those dates, but he would find them all out on Monday. "With your schedule, your weekend biking, church, and so on, we might not get to go fishing at Lobster Lake?" Dad said it as if a question.

"I don't have to go biking next Saturday," Alex quickly replied, remembering that Mr. Parsons had definitely said, "I will find you." And he had never missed finding him yet.

"Okay. I'll talk to your mother. Tell you more tomorrow … Night, love."

*Wow!* a voice spoke out inside Alex's head. *Did you hear what he just called you? He said, 'Night, love!' He called me love. I heard it. It's working already.* Alex's active imagination was telling him that love living was already showing signs of working. Alex made his way to the bathroom to make final preparations for bed. This had been some day. The way it was going, it might just be some night.

As he turned the light out and pulled the covers up, he made a mental note to get to Chad's Repair Shop sometime this week to get a new bike tire. It was good to have a new tube, but he would feel more comfortable if he had a new tire as well. Furthermore—oh! He remembered that he needed to pay off the IOU for the tire tube! But what if they go fishing? He would just have to see what he could do about that. As Alex sought ways to solve all of his problems, he finally settled in for a peaceful night's rest. Tonight, no dreams would awaken him.

# Chapter

Sunday turned into a fun day just arriving at church. Alex, as usual, looked around everywhere for someone by the last name of Parsons, but he was nowhere in sight.

Robert Ackers had to tell Alex all about their new potato harvester. This had many more features than the last one. He said it would reduce the need for another picker on the line, as it would dig potatoes up and separate the tops, etc. in such a way that they never got deposited back onto the ground. The potatoes would go into a big bin truck and be taken directly to the cold, in–ground barns. He asked Alex if he could walk over on the trail through the woods next Saturday, but Alex's heart was set on the prospects of going fishing with his dad. He thought about asking whether Robert could come along, but then decided not to because those times with his dad didn't happen as often as they used to before the computer store opened.

"Here's my buddy," Jon Campo, his best school friend said, as he passed him heading to Sunday school. "You are coming? Save you a seat?"

"Yup, be right there."

Alex walked to the curb and looked in both directions, still hoping that Mr. Parsons would make today an exception and show up for church. Without being visible in any way, he crossed back over the grass and into the side door headed down to his high school Sunday school class.

Brian Thompson was filling in for his regular teacher today. His regular teacher had gone to be with her father, who was expected to die soon of cancer.

The class went well. He spoke about music in the Bible and showed great pictures of the different types of instruments they used. The kids could see that people back then would have been shocked by the sound of a symphony orchestra. The one Alex liked the most, and Mr. Thompson actually brought one to class, was called a shofar. It was a real ram's horn, normally blown in a synagogue on Rosh Hashanah and Yom Kippur. The sound it made when he blew it was quite impressive. The six of them in the class tried it, but couldn't figure out what to do to force a sound to come out the other end. The reason that he brought it was to teach about Joshua bringing a group of people together to blow shofars at the walls of Jericho, and when they did, the walls of the city came tumbling down. He read the whole passage to them, and then blew it one more time, only this time it brought Pastor in to find out what that noise was all about. He approved of the lesson, but asked that the decibel level be kept down.

That morning, as church was just about to start, the sound of a ram's horn was heard once more. Pastor McGregor had convinced Mr. Thompson that it would be appropriate to, as the joke was told, "Wake the dead in the pews back to life in time to hear the sermon." They all had a hearty laugh when he told the story a little later in the service. I don't think anyone slept through it either.

The sermon was truly interesting. The title, just as he had told Dad and Alex, was "What the Church Mouse Learned." He even worked in the new optical mouse Dad had donated when we returned his computer. The word *Church* was still showing in white on the bottom of the mouse.

The message was about a little mouse called Church Mouse. He did all the things he knew he should behind the scenes. He was someone everyone took for granted. No one seemed to care about him, but they never saw him, either. He heard everything, and knew all about everyone in the church. One day, Field Mouse, his best friend, came to help clean up the crumbs left behind after a church party, and asked his friend why he stayed in the church. He replied that he just wanted to be closer to God. He told Field Mouse that he had learned from the people that they come to church because that is where God is. Living outside, God doesn't make any difference in people's lives, and they can do whatever they want to. Then when they feel like they need God again, they just go to church. Well, at his friend's urging, the little Church Mouse agreed to make a trip into the outside world, and was somewhat surprised to find that God was out there, everywhere, in so many ways. What Church Mouse had heard was right; people did do whatever they felt like doing out there. They paid no attention to the fact that God was everywhere. However, there was no place that the two mice could go that God was not. Although Church Mouse felt really good when he lived at the church, he discovered that if he opened his heart to allow the feeling of the presence of God to be with him at all times, the Lord would never leave him nor forsake him in any way. After that, Church Mouse lived in his hole in the wall at the back of the church sanctuary only on weekends. He could still feel the excitement of the people as they came in with the expectancy of finding the presence of God in his church. What he discovered was different was that when he left his mouse hole, God's presence went outside with him, everywhere he could possibly go, and he was very careful to show that he knew it.

"Oh, something else you should know," Pastor said as he neared the close of the sermon. "Church Mouse left me a note one day, saying that since his ancestors came over on the ark, would I mind telling the story of Noah again sometime."

This really was an interesting Sunday. When the pastor stood at the door shaking everyone's hands as they left, he would look off somewhere, point, and say, "Look. There's God. Run and catch him now before the Church Mouse does!" People would smile and head down the steps with a second reminder that God is everywhere. After all, that's what the Church Mouse learned, and it changed his behavior and his life.

The kids sure enjoyed that sermon. After church, they congregated at the side of the parking lot and waited for Pastor to make his final wave, as was his custom. When he did, they sang a familiar melody to him that everyone seemed to know. The song had to do with a famous mouse called Mickey. The only difference was that they were singing new letters. The group of them sang out, "C–H–U; R–C–H; M–O–U–S–E." They goofed the ending a little, but everyone within earshot enjoyed the fun.

This Sunday was the rotation date for Alex's family to have the pastor over for Sunday lunch again. The women in the church kept a rotation schedule, for any who chose to participate, to host their widowed pastor for lunch each Sunday as well as on special holidays. Mom and Dad started toward the house the minute the benediction ended. They had gone out through the right side door nearest their house a block away, looking forward to discussing the sermon over lunch. Alex stayed behind to walk over with Pastor, and Kaitlyn was on her own somewhere, maybe even home already.

"So, did you like the church mouse, Alex?" Pastor said as he came out of his office to join him in the short walk.

"It was funny," Alex said. "I think you need to tell them next week that he left you another note saying that he also came over on the Mayflower."

Pastor laughed and said, "I guess you heard it all. That mouse of your dad's, or I guess I should say, your dad's Church Mouse, made a big hit. Those could be a big seller down at the store."

Alex laughed right along with Pastor, his mind picturing a sign in the front window of the shop: "Church Mouse for Sale." He wanted to remember to tell his dad that one.

Pastor beat him to it as they came through the door, remarking, "I'll bet you'll have a run on that new church mouse at your shop this week."

To which Alex added, "I can make a sign for the window that says, "Church Mouse for Sale." You can also offer a special Field Mouse for those with two computers at home."

Even Kaitlyn, who had beat them home, laughed at that one. The thought of Dad selling mice was too funny. The truth was, if he had real mice in his shop, she would never go there.

Lunch was a familiar meal of roast beef and made–from–scratch gravy, which was perfect over everything for added flavor. Mom added a variety of veggies, and warm yeast rolls that she popped right into the oven the moment she got home from church.

Mom had made up her mind that even though Pastor's so–called favorite desert of all times was Grandma's famous molasses cookies, she was not going to serve them this time. Because so many of the church women knew that was his favorite, she thought surely he'd had his fill by now. When it came time for dessert, she placed a hot pie, fresh out of the oven, in the middle of the table. It smelled absolutely wonderful, but no one knew what kind it was from just the delicious aroma. It looked a little like blackberry, smelled a little like blueberry, and yet? When she stood and cut the first warm piece, she said, "Mixed berry delight today!" and the faces around the table lit up when they saw blackberries, blueberries, raspberries, and strawberries all blending their flavors in one pie. They tasted the berry delight between the homemade butter crusts, and agreed that it was one of the most delicious blends of Maine wild berries. There were several distinct tastes, and yet one overall mouth–watering flavor that called for seconds.

Mom cut the pie in her usual way, in half and then across those slices again until there were eight portions for five people. Alex was hoping for seconds, and thought that maybe Mom and Dad would say they were full, making that desire possible. The way it worked out, there would be a piece for each of them tomorrow night as well, because Mom had made two pies. Mom would take a piece with her to work tomorrow for her friend Polly. Kaitlyn and Alex had picked the blueberries and blackberries that Mom put into the pies, but Polly contributed the raspberries and strawberries from the back of her family's farm. There was a good supply of wild blackberries and blueberries near Alex's house. They tried to pick and pack into the freezer as many of those as they could, with lots of them going on bowls of hot winter cereals, but Polly's raspberries and strawberries were a special treat.

When all were finished eating, Mom declared Alex the official dishwasher of the day. Pastor announced that he was going to be the kitchen assistant, like it or not. He told them all, "I have a cooking date I need to get set with Alex, and I think this would be as good a time as any to try to set it up." Alex didn't mind trying to arrange it, as long as it really meant Pastor was going to help wash dishes.

Before long, the sinks were full of hot water. One sink had soapy hot water for washing and scrubbing, the other hot water for rinsing. Pastor insisted that he was doing the scrubbing just like he often did to help out at church camp. Indeed, by the time they were done, he looked just like he did at church camp, with both sleeves so wet that you could almost wring them out.

By the time they made it into the living room, Mom had made another pot of coffee and was ready to pour that second cup for Pastor, who was now more than ready to receive it. He and Alex never did set a firm date for cooking class. They discussed what they would be needing, and made the decision that it could be done at either Pastor's or at Alex's. Pastor said he needed to make a firm decision when he had his planner in front of him.

Kaitlyn was up in her room working on her scrapbooks. She had found a neat way to take pictures with her new digital camera, print them on the computer, and make up storybooks she would send with Andreas, who was a missionary to Mexico. She really had gotten good at it. Earlier, she had shown Pastor her two latest creations. He'd told her they were good enough to be published.

Dad usually brought up a subject for discussion, and today asked Pastor whether he had ever studied pain as being something a person could move around.

"I can't say that I've even read anything about that," Pastor replied. "Are you studying something new I don't know about?"

Will told Pastor about the time he and Alex were sitting on the porch swing, and that they both had headaches that seemed to disappear when they focused on an object in the distance.

Pastor seemed intrigued, but didn't understand the implications of what Alex's dad was saying.

Will went on to tell him that he had even thought of a few memories that really bothered him, and that the pain accompanying them seemed to be healed in his thinking, the same way his headache had been healed.

"Well, we're all spiritual people having a human experience." Pastor said. "I don't totally understand why what you're doing works; however, I do know that energy can go where you apply your focus, and what you intend can create the end result. If your intention is to move pain, and your focus is somewhere outside of where that pain resides, then yes, I guess it makes sense that it would move, if it can. I just don't know."

It still seemed a little deep for Pastor. However, for Dad and his son, Alex, who was listening intently to every word, it was as easy as focusing and shooting the energy out in a new process that both had proven effective.

"I'll have to try that sometime," Pastor said, and then changed the subject. "Learn anything from the little mouse that roared today?"

"Impressive little guy," Dad responded.

Alex took over the conversation for a bit with a tough, right–on–the–head question aimed at Pastor McGregor: "Does love really heal?"

Alex's mom looked right at Alex and spoke real fast. "Why would you ask that?"

Alex responded, "I've been thinking about it, and I just want to know how love heals. The Bible says love never changes and love heals. I want to know how love heals."

"That's a good question, Alex" Pastor started. "From what I learned in seminary, *love* is a word with lots of power in it. It is a word that can change people's lives completely. It can heal a broken heart, mend a broken soul. However, can love heal? I would have to say yes, it can. But I don't think anybody really knows how it works."

"I do!" Alex responded, surprising his mother the most. They were all quite eager to hear the rest of what he had to say.

Alex continued, "God is love, and love is God, and if anyone needs to be healed, they just have to love what is wrong, and then what they get is God healing them."

"Wow! I think you have that very carefully thought out, young man. You're sure to become a preacher if you keep thinking up things like that," Pastor said.

"Of course that's true, son," his father remarked.

"Then why don't people love what is wrong with them?" Alex spouted out. "All I ever hear people say is how much they hate cancer, and how much they hate diabetes, and how much they hate everything they go to the doctor for. Why can't they just say, I love my cancer?"

"Okay, Alex. I think you have said enough for today," his mother interrupted, "Time for you to go find something to do."

The others were becoming uncomfortable with what Alex was saying as well. Even though there was truth to what he was saying, it was asking a lot for anyone to expect to love a disease. The ritual to follow was to beg God until he took it away or the person died. Everyone knew and practiced that already, but, to Alex, it did not work.

His dad broke in, "Your mother's right, son, it's time for you to go biking or something."

With that, Alex went up to his bedroom and changed his clothes to go biking. There wasn't much to the rest of the conversation that took place in the living room, but it sure didn't have anything to do with loving what needs to be healed. Pastor did not stay late, as he usually did. He excused himself, saying that he had a previous commitment, and took his leave soon after.

While riding partway around the second block, Alex was a little mad at himself for saying as much as he had, but this love healing thing was really on his mind. He wondered whether he was wrong—or was he right? Of course he was right! Mr. Parsons himself had taught him the power *in* and *of* love to heal. It had to include cancer and diabetes.

Rounding another turn, he noticed that the clouds were just the perfect size for metaphorical healing, and he knew he could use the practice. Making it as fast as he could to the wicker porch swing at the shop, he climbed the stairs in eager anticipation of proving to himself that he was right, Mr. Parsons was right, love heals all wounds, and that dis–ease, or disease, could be called a wound that needed love.

Picking his first cloud was simple, as it seemed to smile right at him, begging for him to just "love it to life." That was what cloud melting was like for Alex. He began doing it as he was taught by Mr. Parsons, and in no time it had turned gray in color, but didn't change any more than that. He kept watching it, and watching it, and finally realized that what he was doing was nothing more than that: just watching it. He went back to feeling the love inside and focusing that feeling of love on the cloud, and, *Poof!* The cloud melted away. There was a lesson in there as well.

He did his practice on cloud numbers two, three, four, five, and then finally allowed his mind to stop battling to prove what he knew to be right, to just be right and let it go. He learned another lesson as well. If you start loving something, what you're doing does not guarantee change immediately or instantly. You have to love it always and ever if you're going to love it to life, especially for such a real disease like cancer. You can't just say, "I love you," and feel yourself loving a tumor once, then leave it on its own to do its own thing again. Every time you think about it, you have to love it again. Otherwise, you may be thinking *it did not heal,* and stop the energy of healing. It is asking to be loved. It is love asking to return to itself. That is what Mr. Parsons said—love asking to become more of what love is.

Alex was finally ready to go back to riding, but he determined rather reluctantly that, at least for now, he would not say any more to anyone about using love to heal. If the Pastor did not understand him, why would anyone else? He would just have to become love living, and maybe from his life they might all learn the necessary lessons.

As life would have it, some of that framework was already laid. Alex had not gone far on his bike before Divine intervention made it possible for him to learn to participate in the healing process.

*Pop!* Not paying attention to where he was steering his bike, Alex nearly ran into a mailbox, and, swerving to avoid it, just clipped the mail deposit arm sticking out hitting right on the center middle of his forearm. That vaguely familiar sound was the sound of a bone breaking. The popping sound came from his right arm, and he began to feel a rush of heat coming from the site of the fracture in his radius bone. At first, he tried to act like nothing was wrong, but the swelling made his arm hurt almost immediately. It did not take long for him to admit to himself that he should ride straight home as quickly as possible.

Once in the house, Nurse Mary immediately took over, applying ice in a wet cloth, while Alex explained about hitting the sidewalk mailbox.

"Call Dr. Daniel," she told Will. "Tell him I'm taking Alex to get an X–ray at the clinic. And tell him for me that Alex's arm is broken."

Wanting to stabilize the arm, his mom grabbed two big, wooden serving spoons from the bowl on the counter and placed them on each side of the arm. Then she carefully wrapped a rolled elastic bandage from the supplies she had home from the church camp infirmary around the arm, making the spoon splints hold the bone in place, hoping to minimize the pain. "Alex, this is broken. I can tell you that right now."

"No, it's not broken," Alex refuted, not willing to admit that his basketball career may have ended for this year.

"Well, I think the X–ray will confirm it. These bones are out of alignment," she said. Then heading toward the doorway, she grabbed her purse and car keys.

Dad stayed behind with Kaitlyn on this one. He had seen enough pain in his days overseas. Mom was the nurse, and what better hands could Alex be in?

"Thanks for coming in," Mom said to tall, handsome Dr. Daniel as he walked through the door of the exam room. His six–foot–plus frame, broad shoulders, wavy brown hair, and contagious smile made his patients feel more at ease.

"Okay. What have we got here?" he said, walking straight to a wall where they were just posting three X–ray pictures of what would make Alex very unhappy.

"Ouch! What did you do that for, son?" Dr. Daniel said, looking back at Alex.

"It's not broken, right?" Alex responded.

"No question, son. It's broken. That's a good, clean, transverse fracture. You managed to break it straight across the bone. You hit something straight on with full impact, and really sharp."

"Right," his mom said. "A mailbox on the street corner down from our house."

"Man, how fast were you running?" Dr. Daniel said, now looking at Alex, surprised that he had somehow managed to hit a street mailbox hard enough to create such a clean break.

"I was on my bike," Alex answered back. Continuing, he demanded, "So just tell me how long I'll be out of playing basketball."

"Truth is, son, the radius—that's the bone you broke here—" he said, pointing to a sharp line across the bones showing in the nearest picture, "is the shorter of the two long bones in your forearm. It will be at least six weeks before your cast comes off. And I can't guarantee it will take just six weeks. It might take longer to knit the bones back together, but we'll probably take X–rays again. I'll cast this break to keep it together and ensure it heals right, but you won't find it easy to do many things for awhile."

"What?" Alex shot back as if not having expected any time out.

"Give it some time, son, and you'll start to find it comfortable—to dribble, I mean. However, as for playing on the team …" He just stood, shaking his head. "It will take some time for the swelling to go down, but we'll look at it again in about three weeks. However, you'd best set your mind to behaving like you should so that it will heal. Any type of pressure against it, even after I set it, won't be good."

Alex was not delighted to be given the latest in synthetic fiberglass casts, with some added materials to hold the arm more stable. When he asked if he could go fishing, Dr. Daniel did at least say that should be fine if he's careful because the cast was water–resistant. However, the padding underneath was not, so no swimming. He would use a waterproof liner when he recasts it in three weeks.

To use the expression "Alex was not a happy camper" was putting it mildly. When he got home, he told his father, "Dr. Daniel said I'm off the court for six weeks. But he said we could still go fishing."

"Six weeks!" Those two words kept repeating in his head as the medicine Dr. Daniel had given him for the pain and swelling began to take effect. He almost went to sleep sitting up. His parents helped make him as comfortable as possible before they left his room that night.

"No! No! No!" He mumbled these words as his parents walked quietly out of his room. His team needed him. His school needed him. And what about Dad? He had his heart set on Alex being on that team.

Just rolling over in bed was a chore nearly beyond his abilities. He drifted in and out of sleep, often feeling distressed by what he was dreaming. Weird bad dreams seemed to be a side effect of the pain medication. In one dream, he became the team mascot with a leash around his neck, and all the cheerleaders were taking him to center court for group cheers. Nothing seemed right in those dreams, as they drifted from one nonsensical theme to another. The good part was that they were not filled with images of horror, as might sometimes happen with pain medications. In another dream, while flying with butterfly–style wings, he found a secret place where information on all types of physical healing was stored. To his disgust, it was all written in a foreign language that he had no idea how to read. The walls, however, showed various scenes of people being very ill, and then healed. At least that was the way Alex made the interpretation. It was the feeling of spider webs that made him leave, as his sensitive wings did not like that feeling at all. The wings seemed to have voices that shouted, "Danger! Danger, Will Robinson! We've got to get out of here!" Alex understood that, and so he did. Because he could fly, he quickly found himself in a rainforest, looking for more secrets to healing. At one point more toward the earlier hours of the morning, Alex felt the urge to go to the bathroom. That experience reminded him, his bone is broken and some things would not be as easy as before. *No!* That word came into his mind again while looking at his cast. *Why did I have to go and do something so stupid?* his mind cried out in frustration.

When Alex got up again, looking into the bathroom mirror, he realized how much he did blame himself for something as stupid as hitting a mailbox. He was the only one who could be held to blame. He just had not been paying attention, and he had also still been a little mad because adults didn't seem to understand love like he needed them to. If they did, they would be willing to talk about it. Turning and heading back to bed, his inner voice said something that would prove to be a turning point for Alex: *I hate you.* He thought it casually, as though it were right and correct. Alex turned back to the mirror and looked right into the reflection of his own eyes. Inside, he said it again. *I hate you!* At first, he rationalized that it really wasn't himself he hated; it was only a part of himself that he hated. He hated his arm! *No. I hate you!* the voice said again, because the "you" inside was beginning to realize the full weight of responsibility for his injury.

When he finally lay back down, he remained wide awake for some time, thinking about the power in the words he had spoken to himself. They were right, and yet they were so wrong. He raged an inner war between the lessons Mr. Parsons had taught him about love, and the truth that he did actually hate his broken arm very much, and hated himself for having broken it. In his mind, he still heard the voice of Dr. Daniel—"Six weeks"—and imagined the reaction from his coach and teammates. Only Bert, a sophomore, would be pleased, because that would move him up into the starting lineup.

Trying in some way to get his mind off the pain now returning to his arm, and to find some solace in all of this, he thought back to the stream at Creek Bed and the meeting with Mr. Parsons. It became like a dialogue for Alex, where the two of them could talk and begin to work out what was really going on here.

"Aren't you really being just like them?" Mr. Parsons said, reminding Alex that he was saying, "I hate you," to something that needed love to heal.

"But this is different," Alex answered.

"In what way, Alex?" Mr. Parsons asked.

"Because this is *my* arm!" Alex fought back.

"Exactly, son. Your arm is not worthy of being loved because you're choosing not to love what is, believing that if you just deny it, it will go away. People deny their diseases, Alex; their diseases kill them."

There was a pause of silence in Alex mind. Alex wanted to control this conversation into another direction; however, it would not let him steer it.

"For you, it will go away, Alex, in six weeks, maybe more," he added. "Or?" he tagged the question.

Alex couldn't answer. It was like the lesson came alive again and his broken arm, as he looked at it, became first a beverage with a cast in it; then it disappeared and reappeared as a cloud in a cast. In his mind's eye, he just stared at it, loved it, and it healed. In his mind, he would repeat the healing process many times with his broken arm until his thoughts could only see it as healed with no cast on. Into the early hours of the morning, the after–effects of the pain medication were wearing off, and memories of working with pain would come forth to his thinking. Thinking of the beverages and the clouds that he had already changed, he rolled over onto his back and just stared at a spot up on the corner of the ceiling. He knew that his headache went when he stared at that bird. He had no doubt that the process he had used worked. Throughout the balance of the early morning hours, the pain in his arm would make him aware that it was not yet healed; however, he would just stare at that corner spot, and the pain would move out and away, and would lessen.

Sleep finally came peacefully for a while until Alex was ready to wake up. He awakened still facing the ceiling, with his blankets pulled up under both arms, which rested on top of the covers. He lay still for as long as he could. When he did start to move, his arm reminded him that it had not miraculously healed.

About the time he sat up, his favorite nurse came in with a pill in one hand and a glass of water in the other. "I know it hurts, love. Just take this, and it will help make the day easier," she said with a smile. Moving his arm had made Alex decide that the pill was not a bad idea. It would not knock him out, but it would allow him to feel more comfortable by not having to fight the pain.

"Mom," he spoke, "it will be all healed when I go back to the doctor in three weeks."

As natural as if this were an everyday conversation about things that are just truth, Mom responded. "Of course it will be, honey. Now, is there anything I need to do for you before you come downstairs for breakfast?"

Alex assured her that he could do all the things he needed to do, just like he did last night, and she left the room. Brushing his teeth did prove a little challenging because his left hand had never been trained to do the job. He chose a shirt with buttons, because trying to put his hands over his head to get into a T–shirt was certainly not appealing. His entire body felt as though it were in shock from yesterday's accident. He was soon downstairs, where Dad was already sitting and having a cup of coffee. "Hi son. How's it feeling this morning?" Dad asked.

"It will be all healed when I go back to the doctor in three weeks," Alex said, with confidence. "I am going to love it to life just like I told you yesterday."

Although both of his parents heard what was said, neither seemed to notice the importance of that statement. Life went on, with breakfast being served, and preparations for the day being made. Mom drove Kaitlyn to her school, and Dad drove Alex, since he would not be able to ride his bike for a while. It would be nearly two weeks before he even sat on the seat again.

His first stop at school that morning was the classroom his coach taught in. As he walked through the door, Coach Crooker was the first to speak. “Oh, Alex, looks like you got one of those boo boos even the best of the pros get.”

Just that statement made it a little easier on Alex as he walked toward his coach.

The coach continued to speak. “Tell me how you did it, Alex. Then we can talk about what you can still do to help your team.” After hearing it all, the coach had only one comment to make with a smile on his face. “Just don’t go and kick the mailbox prior to soccer season, okay?”

That statement alone made Alex feel a little better than he had a few minutes before. It also indicated that Coach Crooker must be considering the value of having Alex on the soccer team. Once that statement had sunk in, he felt even better.

They discussed things that Alex could do for six weeks, like becoming assistant score keeper, and similar rolls he might fill. As a result, he would continue to actively participate for the next six weeks’ games, and even be out there on the bench, just not in his game uniform. He would wear the sweat suit he wore for team warm–ups.

“Oh, I’ll be all healed in three weeks,” Alex assured his coach.

The coach said nothing more, having dealt with many kids’ injuries over the years. He knew it took at least six weeks and sometimes longer, for a broken bone to heal, but why argue with a kid?

The rest of Alex’s day went well. Some of the other students seemed to feel sorry for him, while others acted as though they couldn’t care less. Several asked to sign his cast, but Alex made the decision that for now he would prefer to keep it clean.

It was the next day in school when his fellow students first saw a big, red heart on the center portion of the cast, and inside the heart were the initials “A.W. luvs B.A.” That took them all by surprise and certainly started rumors. They tried to guess who B.A. was, but Alex had decided the night before that he would never give it away. As he was already learning, it was not what he said to other people that mattered, as much as the example he lived. He could just imagine the look on their faces if they found out that it means Alex Williams loves his Broken Arm.

Because the heart on his cast got so much attention, each time it was mentioned Alex would close his eyes as if showing that he did not intend to respond, but what he was doing was simply seeing his arm heal completely, as he just loved it to life like he said he would.

Friday night came and went. He found plenty to do to help the team. His whole family attended the game as usual, and no one complained that he was not a starter. Many of the fans stopped to talk to him, noticing that he was wearing only his sweats and that he sported a wonderfully colorful cast. One dad was so determined to know who B.A. was, as to go to Alex's father and ask outright. Will, still not knowing the whole story, replied, "It's a joke, and it's working beautifully, according to Alex." His dad never did demand any greater explanation than what Alex had already given them the first morning he painted it on before breakfast. "It's a joke, and it sure will give me lots of fun at school because no one will figure it out."

Whether at school or home, Alex continued what seemed like a ritual of seeing his arm healed and just loving it to life with a belief that there would be no recasting. He would practice looking inside and seeing only the most perfect bones. In fact, he did it enough so that he ultimately never did think of it as being broken anymore, and anytime he did think about it, it was healed.

# Chapter 8

Arriving home from the game, Dad made sure that Alex sprayed the grass with water the way he had been taught to do it, as tomorrow was Saturday and they would need worms for fishing. By agreement with a friend, his shop would be covered, and they would have the whole day to themselves. Fishing at Lobster Lake was a trip that took a whole day. It was a trip they had made many times before. When morning came, Alex was the first up. He had all the worms they would need before he snuck in to wake up his dad. Mom was startled at having someone in the room and, since she was now awake, asked whether she could get up and fix breakfast. Dad thanked her and said no, since part of the fishing ritual was a stop at Angela's Donut Shop for maple–frosted donuts. Dad didn't say it, but Alex later found out that today would be an exception when Dad told him that they would each get three maple–frosted donuts instead of just two. Two were for breakfast and one for the trip home. Dad cautioned Alex, "Mom shouldn't be told. She would never approve of that much sugar … and sometimes men can have secrets."

As they arrived at Angela's Donuts, they both expected to see the lady from the church choir who usually waits on them that hour of the morning, but they were told she was on vacation. That made it much easier for Dad, as he said, "We will have six maple–frosted donuts and two cups of coffee. Just make one of them about half coffee and half milk for my sidekick here." It wasn't long before two cups of coffee and four of the donuts were gone as they were driving right toward the sign at the T and made the last left turn onto the Kankamongus Highway.

Dad asked whether Alex's arm hurt, but this morning Alex seemed to be feeling nothing that he would call pain. He had managed to keep his cast clean up until now. The only marking on it was that big heart with "A.W. luvs B.A." Dad couldn't help but inquire, because up until now, Alex had not shown special interest in any one girl, and knew that it had to go beyond being a joke. "Okay, Alex … out with it. I want the rest of the story on this heart joke on your cast. We can keep this a man's secret."

Alex just beamed at his dad. It would not bother him now to tell his dad what it meant. "It means Alex Williams loved his Broken Arm, Dad! It reminds me to love my arm until it heals." The look from his father was a little strange, but it changed when Alex said. "Remember when I asked Pastor if love heals, and he said yes?"

"Yes."

"Well, I am going to prove *love works faster than any kind of medicine.* Every time I think of my arm or somebody says something about this heart," he said, pointing to his cast, "I just picture my arm as healed because I love it. It will be healed in two more weeks, before Dr. Daniel thinks he is going to cast it again. The X–ray will prove it."

"Are you sure he will take another X–ray?" Dad asked.

"He has to, or I will make him!" Alex quickly replied.

"Does your mom know you're doing this?"

"She knows I am going to heal it in three weeks, and I did tell her what the heart meant. She just smiled at me and shook her head like it was too funny for words, as though I'd just told her a joke. She said I would take a lot of ribbing from the kids, but I told her, just like I'm telling you, that it only makes me remember to love my bones to life. And it has worked very well as all my friends keep 'reminding' me."

Both just sat thinking for a bit as Dad hit the radio search button to bring up the local boonies radio station. He stopped pressing the button when a word caught his ear, something about the ministering work of angels. As they listened, the thing that struck Alex the most was that, according to the speaker, when angels minister to people, they generally are not even aware that their helpers are angels. When that radio show was over, Dad pressed the buttons again, but did not find any good music as he had hoped, and just turned the radio off. "I think this war has kept a lot of angels busy, son. You should hear all the stories the men tell of being out there in a smoke like fog or in the dead of night somewhere, wondering in which direction to go or who to turn to for help, when someone comes and provides the help. Later, they learn that, with no doubt, there was no one else out there. It can only be angels. One thing most people say is that they are generally big people. They're not in the least bit threatening; they are extremely loving and kind, just not small in stature."

Alex had to ask, "Do you think you have ever seen an angel, Dad?"

"I truly think I have, Alex. It was one time when we were all under fire while my bomb removal team was supposed to be clearing a wide path for tanks to pull through within hours. We were about three–quarters of the way through the minefield when heavy smoke came in. The wind blew so that the smoke came from the direction we had first started the clearing. However, there was no reason for it to be coming from that direction, and my radioman could not reach anyone to tell us why. I was ready to tell them to keep on crawling forward because we were on a schedule, when someone came up from behind, sent by the battalion chief because they had lost radio contact. In a commanding voice, he said. "Tell your team to freeze right where they are. Stay as low as you can, face down, until this smoke passes. We are on radio silence." Then he turned and walked back the way he had come. I gave the order to my men, and we held steady, lying face down, as flat and as we could, until further notice. Within fifteen minutes, we heard the sound of tanks coming from behind us, and could tell that they were not ours. As the sound of the tanks came closer, we realized that they were using the path we had already cleared. The smoke seemed to be the only reason they could not see us. When they stopped directly behind us, we could hear what was being spoken, although no one on my team understood the language. It seemed like an eternity before they began to move, and we were as thankful as we could be when they did. They turned to what was our left side from the direction we had been moving. From the sound, there appeared to be three tanks in their convoy. Two cleared the minefield edge completely. The third, somewhere near what we believe was the edge of the minefield, hit a mine that lit up the sky. The battalion chief behind us said that the smoke gave them enough cover to capture all of the survivors in the crippled tank. The other two tanks proceeded out of range at full speed. When we finished our job and our tanks had rolled through the pass as planned, I met with the battalion chief, specifically to thank him for sending the soldier up to warn us in advance. He told me that they had been cut off from us by the tanks before they even realized that the tanks were coming straight toward us down the path we had cleared. I did the best I could to describe the man in the smoke, who had come directly to me and definitely knew who I was. I couldn't change the battalion chief's mind; he had sent no such man. Shaking his head, the chief said, 'You and every man on your team had a divine appointment today. You should have taken pictures because today you met an angel of mercy who was shrouded in grace.' He believed that the smoke had confused the tanks, and that it caused them to turn slightly, believing that the path they were to follow was that way. He believed that if something had not confused them, they would never have veered. We even wondered if the angel was back there telling them where to go next in their language as a protection for us? Over one terrible tasting cup of coffee made with used coffee grounds, he told a couple of accounts of other angels in our midst. One man, still alive but bleeding profusely, was brought into camp by another soldier whom most say 'evaporated,' for lack of a better word. He was supposed to be on his way to the mess hall, but he never arrived. He was not a part of their battalion group, and no one saw him leave. He was never seen again."

Alex questioned. "And the other one?"

"It had to do with someone he knew who flew jets, and he claimed that he often had special help. He didn't go into details on these accounts, but said he has gotten used to flying with angels."

Dad pushed the radio button once more as they came within ten miles of the last leg of their trip, the dirt road that led to the parking lot at the lake. From there, they would walk the path to Lobster Lake. One of their favorite songs, the one about butterfly kisses, was just beginning as they reached the lot where one Jeep and a Hummer were already parked.

"Looks like we'll have to compete for fish today," Dad said as he parked and jumped out.

"Nah," Alex responded. "They all brought fancy hooks, and we brought the only thing real fish like: bait!" he said, holding up a silver tin with air holes along the sides and full of night crawlers.

It was true; many anglers seen in these parts had flown great distances and purchased the most expensive gear, only to come talk to Alex and his dad, hoping to learn how they caught so many fish. It all boiled down to the simple things in life, like having what the fish liked: real worms. Alex was always amazed at the imitations people would use. It was hard to believe that people don't think fish know the difference between rubber, plastic, and real live, excellent tasting, squirming worms.

They generally had one particular spot on a small peninsula that they liked to fish the most. One thing certain, they would not be going swimming. Alex's cast would prevent him, even though Dad said he could tie it off with a garbage bag he had in his pack. Alex didn't mind passing up swimming. The season was still colder; short sleeves were fine in full sun, but it was chilly in the shade. To think of going "skivvy–dipping," as they called their version, was out of the question today. Dad was wearing his usual fishing vest, but that came off once the fishing started. The big contest with them was always who would catch the first keeper. Alex had not only caught the first one on one of their trips, but it was also probably the biggest trout in the lake at 29 inches. This day, it was the older of the Williams who not only got the first fish, but also got the first keeper, at 11 inches. Before the day was over, they had added enough to their catch to allow them to make a fire and eat a keeper each, and still take twelve back home with them.

When they had been fishing for a while earlier, two boys who said they were driving the Jeep stopped to ask how they had caught so many keepers, just as had happened so many times before. Dad decided to just have some fun with them and tell them one of Alex's favorite fishing stories. He could see that look on his face as he glanced over at him, indicating that he was about to tell a whopper. He told them about the day he and his friend Cody had taken BBs, wrapped them in bread dough, and baked them in the oven. He actually convinced them that bread dough was the best fishing material because it didn't just dissolve in water, and it leaked a pheromone that drew the fish to the scent. He convinced them that what he and Cody did was throw the dough balls out into the water, and then wait three minutes for the fish to eat them all. Then they used a big, high–powered magnet on the end of a fishing line to catch the fish. For a few minutes, it seemed as though they really believed him. Alex nearly gave it away when he spoke up and said, "Tell them about worms!"

Without hesitating, as though Alex had been coached to say just that, Dad added, "The BBs, at least the ones that work best, are all laid by night crawlers. If you wet your grass at night, you can go out before the sun comes up and you'll see worms laying BBs." That was the first time Alex had heard Dad add that line, and he would never forget it. Dad had picked up right where Alex had left off, without missing a beat. Dad told the entire story with a straight face.

For the boys, that last edit did it. One boy looked at the other and began to laugh. Until then, Alex thought that they could have handed the boys a handful of dough balls and a magnet and they would have gone fishing with them. Maybe it was the fact that Dad had called them BBs from the beginning and not worm pellets. When they were about a hundred yards away, Dad hollered to them. "You're not allowed to use dynamite to fish here, either. It attracts too many bears. But I can tell you how good it works if you catch us again sometime. Just make sure to wash all the gunpowder off the fish so you don't end up backfiring all day." Alex could hear them laughing all around the turn onto another wooded path, as the boys headed north along the east edge of the lake planning to fish from the old wooden pier further up North.

Later that day, the boys were in the parking lot trying to get the burrs out of their clothes when Alex and his dad saw them again. They did get fish. One of them said that they had found worms by turning rocks over in the fields. They had to admit that worms work best for fishing.

Just as the walk in had been uneventful, they expected the same thing on the way out. The normally abundant berries, the ones that attracted bears, had been gone from the path for a while. The flowers that added so much color showed signs that at least one early morning frost had struck the area; shades of brown were becoming the dominant color over the new green that should be appearing. Soon all would be winter white. The walk out was different. They had not gone far from the lake before they heard the sound of a hunter's gunfire close enough to cause concern. Trained as they were, they both instantly dropped, crouching close to the ground. Staying low for a few seconds, they got a good chance to see a big bull moose cross the path just ahead about 200 yards, heading away from the sound. He may have been the target of the shot, but they were just thankful that he had not chosen them to be his target, as it is very difficult to outrun a charging bull moose. The area they were now in was more thicket than trees, and getting to a tree that would support them to get higher up would not have been easy.

Finally upright, the two had walked nearly to the parking lot when Dad put his hand up in a freeze position. Alex had learned that this signal meant not to move or say anything at all. The eyes and ears became the main tools for quickly learning about possible or impending danger. They were grateful that the wind was blowing in their faces, bringing scents toward them. Up ahead, where the trail made the next to the last curve into the parking lot, they saw the backside of a big, brown grizzly bear moving quickly away from them, running on all fours. Because of the timing, their first thought was that this must have been the target of the hunter; however, the bear was not sticking around for them to ask. The two boys Alex and Dad had met earlier told them that they had seen the bear coming from the back corner of the lot and quickly got into their Jeep, burrs and all. The bear never stopped. He growled twice at them but kept running on up the side of the roadbed and down into a ravine. One of them said that the bear was only after their dough balls, to which Alex said, "And you didn't throw dynamite?"

With everything loaded in the truck, Alex and his dad were soon heading toward the nearest town. Dad needed fresh coffee, and Alex was not waiting to eat his maple–frosted donut. It was gulp, gulp, gone. The day's events, with Alex's broken arm, and a great day of fishing which ended with moose and bear runs, had taken its toll on Alex. He barely made it to the end of the four–mile dirt road and the turn toward home before he fell deeply asleep. His dad did stop in the first small town they entered for coffee to go with his donut. The hot coffee was comfortably warming in the evening chill. The owner of the store had asked Dad where he was coming from, and then asked whether he had heard any gunshots. When Dad told him what he had seen and heard, he immediately got on his CB radio with the warden, because there were suspected out–of–state bear poachers in the area. Dad said that they had not parked in our favorite parking lot; however, there were other places farther up past the turn off on the logging road they take where they might be. One thing for sure, they were going to catch the poachers this time; there was no way out of that road now without passing a game warden roadblock. Warden Sinclair was thankful that there was only one way in and only one way out. He would wait, however long it took, unless he heard they used a seaplane and put out a dispatch to check and see if that might be the case.

Dad did not awaken Alex, even for coffee, until they were coming into their own driveway. It was now dark, and Dad told Alex that he would clean the fish by himself in the backyard. Alex insisted on helping, though, and together they completed the task quickly. Looking back towards his now closed computer store, Dad said, "Don't you wish Grandma were coming over to get a couple of fish?" Alex just nodded and picked up the big basin filled with the fish. Tonight, all of it would go into the freezer because Mom had left them plates of dinner warming in the oven; she was tired and not up to cooking fish tonight. Alex never did spring to full alert status. He went to bed not long after he had eaten his supper and washed the fish smell off with a warm shower.

Mom commented to Dad, "If he's going to heal that arm in three weeks, he's going to require plenty of sleep." There was no further discussion on the subject that night.

# Chapter 9

It would be about the middle of the second week before Alex would decide that it would be okay for other people to sign his cast. His friend Jon was the first. He wrote, "My hero!" in truth, wishing that he were the one getting all the attention, but without the broken arm. Someone else on the team wrote, "Good for 3 Points." The one girl from church who Alex would not admit to having any feelings for, but who somehow knew he did, wrote, "D.A., not B.A.," at which Alex laughed. When he got home, he privately showed it to his dad. Robert drew a potato with two eyes. Maria, one of the junior varsity cheerleaders, wrote all the way around the top edge so that he had to roll his arm to read "You go, Alex Goat," as they had cheered for him in past games. Many times, Alex had been accused of ramming the other team players. His friend, Jon, said, "If the name fits, wear it." Now it was sort of cast in stone, as the saying goes, on his arm. Alex was beginning to understand that extra attention goes along with problems like his broken arm. Illness and injury often bring people together in a way that provides the attention they may have been seeking. Because of the attention he got from having a cast, he decided to be observant to learn how others used their ailments to draw attention to themselves. What would amaze him most were the people who would stay sick because healing would mean a loss of attention and they could not stand to miss the secondary gain of attention.

By the end of the third week, all Alex desired was to play basketball. There was no doubt in his mind as to what Dr. Daniel would find when he went in for his so–called cast replacement. Finally, the day came. Dr. Daniel was already there working at the clinic when they arrived. Their appointment was a day earlier than three weeks, due to Dr. Daniel's schedule. Alex did not mind. He knew that one more day would make no difference. Walking into the clinic room, Alex grew uneasy when he saw the materials being prepared to redo the cast, complete with a waterproof liner. He stood just past the doorway and shook his head as if indicating that this was not right.

"It's okay Alex. I just need to cut your old cast off before we get the X–rays taken, and then we …"

That was all Alex wanted to hear. The rest of what Dr. Daniel said didn't even matter to him. The X–ray would confirm what he already knew. The X–ray would provide proof positive. Soon, he and his mom sat waiting to see the newly developed proofs of what still needed to be done. She still believed with her medical background that he would be recast.

"That's amazing," Dr. Daniel said, once again showing that wide smile that melted old ladies' hearts. "Look at this," he said, pointing to the X–ray. "That bone is as good as new! It is actually as strong as it will ever get, and even stronger than it was before. Here look at these X–rays. Say Alex, let me have a look at that arm," he said, and began taking the arm through a range of motion exercises. "Alex, that is excellent. I don't think we need to put a thing back on that arm." He spoke again, grinning. "I have seen babies with broken bones heal in three weeks, but you're not growing like babies do. I think we need to call this one a miracle." That was just what Alex needed to hear, and he flashed his biggest smile at his mother. "Call this one a miracle," she heard the doctor say. Alex knew what did it. He believed it had healed by the end of the second week, and now it was probably stronger just because it was healed. He would never doubt that love heals; he would be the living proof. All the people he knew could hate whatever they wanted taking place in their bodies. He would learn to be love living and, as such, change his world. He would teach them that *love works faster to heal than any kind of medicine,* by being an example of the possibility.

He still didn't say much about it when he went back to school. If anyone asked, he just told him that he didn't need a cast anymore because it had healed. No one seemed to make much of it. No one seemed to care like they did when he had the cast on. Once again, Alex was finding humans extremely interesting to study, just as his friend Mr. Parsons did. People seemed to bond by how they were alike, however pay attention to how they were different.

He did show Coach Crooker, his basketball coach, his "permission to play active sports slip" signed by his friend Dr. Daniel. He told Alex that he would check him out at the next practice to see if he was ready to go back to a starting lineup position. He thought it would be okay to tell his coach that his arm had healed as strong as it could possibly be in just three weeks. The only response he got was, "Good, that kind of healing will give you the strong arm needed for the volleyball team." It seemed that it was now no big deal that Alex's arm had healed in less than half the expected time!

Practice the following day went well. The coach told Alex that he did not think he was ready to be a starter yet, but when the starting lineup was announced at the game Friday night, Alex's name was on the list. I think his dad was more excited than he was. Even though Alex did get twelve points in the game, his team still lost 72 to 48. By the end of the third quarter, the people in the stands showed they felt it was over. All the excitement died down and the look on their faces told the story.

"The fans' lack of interest sure didn't help motivate any of us," Alex told his father later that night.

"You don't win because of the spectators, Alex; you win because of what's inside each of you," Dad responded. "And you can tell that to all the players. When the other team got a sixteen–point lead on you in the third quarter, it was as though you all gave up, so yes, we joined you. It is not so much what happens that matters, son; what is more important is what you do with what happens. Tonight, we all chose to quit by the end of the third quarter. And, your right, we all showed it."

# Chapter 10

Alex never stopped studying anything he could get his hands on about energetic therapies as he continued to live his life in the model Mr. Parsons had given him; love living. As the summer came and moved on, northern Maine went through the traditional changes that made for signs of the harvesting of the potatoes, and everyone's favorite: the changing of the leaves into the colors of fall. For the locals, it meant it was tourist season, for they came to see a beauty not available in most areas of the country. Mom said, "It is the time when God adorns his creation with a rainbow of his glory." It could be spectacular to go for a half–day drive and marvel at the wisdom of God to produce such glorious changes in the trees. Nothing beats looking into the deep blue color of a local lake or stream and seeing the colorful reflection of nature's most brilliant array all along the edge. It all seemed to happen so fast, like God breathed a breath of fresh frost as the canvas keeps changing colors.

Another month passed before the beginning season of white blanketed everything the eyes could see. Later in the season, snow plows cleared the roads once more. By the time Christmas had come and gone, the heavy–duty commercial snow blowers came out. The blowers created banks up to ten feet in height along the roadsides. It always fascinated the kids to ride in a school bus and not be able to see over the tops of the banks on either side of the road. It looked like something out of a movie; to look down a street with no houses and no driveways, just a long, white tunnel. The road tunnels were a little like the scene in *The Ten Commandments* where the waters of the Red Sea parted, only this time it was a frozen sea. Occasionally, there would be a spot where kids had spent most of a day tunneling all the way through a bank. When the plows and blowers layered back a snow mound fifteen feet in depth from the road, it was safe to build a complete channel of tunnels and "private," kids–only places to meet. Unless there was a fresh falling of new snow, no plow would be closing the entrance. Plows couldn't move that much snow at one time. If the contour of the banks had to be changed for safety, it took a bucket loader and other heavy equipment to complete the job. Otherwise, it was Mother Nature that took her time to make the changes to the form through wind, sleet, and a sun that rarely warmed anything much this time of year.

Only the tops of trees would be visible in a Maine winter, the trunks buried in snow. The damage ice and snow did to the lower branches would not be evident until spring. It was common for people to snowshoe into the local lake areas to clear off camp roofs to prevent them from collapsing under the weight of snow and ice. Shoveling snow, for those who had the back for it, paid good money, and was one of the ways people who mowed lawns in summer earned money in winter. Even though small snow blowers were convenient, a shovel was necessary to get to the point where a blower could be effective. At the shop, Dad had Mr. Ackers, Robert's dad, come with a plow that is attached to the front end of his bucket loader tractor after any snow of more than 4 inches. This setup worked very well. When Mr. Ackers was not available, the job went to ... no, not

Kaitlyn! She did sometimes clear the stairs at home and at the store, and throw the sand and salt mixture on them. That was always after much protest—until the day Kaitlyn said that it was something no woman in her right mind would do. That did it! That day, Mom took her out and showed her that it was something she could do, and told her that she would do it from now on, or else. Alex didn't think he had ever seen Mom as mad as she was when she said, "Young lady, grab your coat. You're coming with me.... Now!" Alex was looking at Dad when she said it, and saw Dad turn his face away from them so Kaitlyn would not see his smile.

One of the best things the town did for the kids was to take one central park area, clear it, and flood it, with the fire department's help, to make a giant ice rink. This gave the kids a free ice rink every year. They also dragged in a logging shack as a place for them to change into their skates. It served as the only means of getting warm again when the temperatures went way below freezing, as they often did. The same shack was used each year, as evidenced by the floors that had been chewed up by the ice skate blades. Alex always wondered what they did with it the rest of the year, because he never saw it anywhere else. Robert was the one to be the hero on skates—not figure skates, hockey skates. He was a guard on the hockey team that always captured the ice for the first forty–five minutes immediately after school each day. After that, anyone could skate until 9:00 p.m., when the automatic timer box on the light poles went *Boom!* leaving the area in complete darkness. Many a night, people would try to continue skating using car headlights, but most people were so cold by then that they couldn't wait to go home to warm up. An announcement was made through the sound system fifteen minutes before lights out, and each additional five minutes thereafter, right up until lights out. When the electricity was shut off, the lights in the changing shack went off, also. Whoever was taking care of the cabin put the remaining shoes and boots into a wooden storage box outside the building's front door, locked it up, and went home. Kaitlyn got new pink skates for Christmas that year, and she hated to leave the rink unless she was really freezing in the bitter cold. Alex used a pair of Bobby Hull hockey skates Jon had had before his feet jumped from a size ten to a size twelve. Although they were good Canadian skates, they did not help because Alex didn't have the ankle strength to lean out and down on all those sharp edged turns the way Jon Campo and Robert did. If he ever wanted lessons, however, Robert would be the one to ask. He was a wizard on blades and could cut turns on a dime. His favorite trick was jumping sideways with both feet while charging forward at full speed, thus spraying ice shavings all over. No one else could do it like that, so the other kids would pelt him with snowballs. Even when they played dodge ball with snowballs, Robert never lost. Robert was also an expert broomball player, which was much like hockey except that it was played in sneakers, with a worn out house broom as the stick. The rubber ball was one filled with air that easily fit your hand. Teams from neighboring towns would come to compete, and Robert nearly always scored the winning points. Alex's team would wear green lines on their faces to go with the "Wicked Whackers" name they chose. Their best competition came from the Maple Leaf team, aptly named since they were from Mapleton. They had two fearless women whose competitive streak did not tolerate losing. One of the women lost a front tooth, and the other broke her broom twice in one game. Those two were definitely the powerhouses of the Maple Leaf team. "Thank God for duck tape!" you would hear her say as she reenters the playing ice from her team side.

Although "official" sticks, which resembled worn–out brooms, could be purchased, they all agreed to an official rule prohibiting "official sticks," allowing the use of house brooms only. If for some reason there was no worn out brooms available, they would purchase a corn broom at Rich's Grocery and burn the first half of the bristles off. This made for a nice solid bottom pressing to the ice. Since Rich was good at broomball, he often brought extra brooms to sell with him. One thing they could count on, he would have plenty in stock just in case. Alex's team told them that if they wanted to know how to beat a team named Wicked Whackers, they had better know how to make things fly with a broom. Although it was all in fun, to Robert it was competitive.

When the winter carnival came around, the town was sure to be filled with magnificent sculptured things made of snow and ice. This year's theme for the ice carvings was Toyland. When the four–hour public judging period began, the sun was directly above each sculpture, providing special lighting. No one was surprised that the dragon won first place. Second place went to a line of dancers, toy soldiers named Rockettes, facing a cannon that looked liked it had shot them. That was the biggest sculpture. The people who usually won did a castle that went up into a tree branch. That garnered third place. A cart on the corner sold snacks and hot beverages. That was also where the spectator judging ballots could be picked up. Judging the sculptures was the real beginning of one of the most fun events of the year as long as the weather held true to bless them. At night, colored lights were placed around the sculptures, lending a beauty that could raise goose bumps, as if the cold weren't enough to do that already.

The kids got a full day off from school allowing them to participate in all types of skiing, skating, bobsledding, snow shoeing, and even snow machine races, or snowmobile races, as some called them. The kids age four and under got to participate in snow angel contests, as well as a snowball–throwing contest, throwing snowballs at people they might or might not even know. This year, there were many candidates to be targets, including church pastors, the town librarian, a barber, two hair stylists who specialized in children's hair, a Girl Scout leader and three retail store owners or clerks. The most likely candidates to be hit, however, were the fire chief and the police chief, because they showed up in full uniform and just seemed to stand out as the biggest and best targets. The police chief had on swat gear, which slowed him up. The fire chief had on a full fire protection suit, and that did the same for him. The children were given a plastic quart bucket from a local chicken restaurant, which they were to fill with snowballs that they would make from a mound of snow piled specially for them. The rules said to aim at the legs. Har!

Good thing they all wore some type of eye protection. It was easy for the kids to catch the targets off guard because the candidates all stayed in a temporary corral while the kids could throw at them from anywhere around the outside. The hardest part was keeping score. Each child was allowed only one bucket of snowballs to throw, and it was up to the parents to keep score. When all was said and done, five was the high number in a tie for first place. No one took accurate count, but the people handing out the buckets said they went through a case of fifty before the ninety–minute free throw was over. Some of the buckets were said to be used more than once.

A parade through town the second day gave everyone the chance to gather and shiver together. As always seemed the case, the sun was out nice and bright the morning of the parade. The first band rounded the corner as the first snow flurries began to fall. By the time the parade ended, there was a fresh inch of powder on the ground and a tremendous excitement in the air because new powder made for the best cross–country races. Snow piles up fast when the flakes are that big and the humidity is dry enough to not start packing it down.

The town required that all of the children who participated in the winter games be registered in the local schools or the local home school district. Still, that generally took in a 20–mile radius from the center of town and included kids from many other towns because of how the school system was organized. There was no rivalry between other towns or schools at these events. The colored pictorial section of the newspaper the next weekend would look like a who's who of local kids. The only pictures of the Williams family would be Kaitlyn on the ice all lined up for a 200 meter dash, and Alex headed into the final turns of the men's cross country. He came in sixth, which for him was a far better result than his thirty–fourth finish last year. He figured he still had more years to go and one of those would serve as his crowning achievement in going for the gold.

Another thing Alex thought he might like to win was Winter King. The only thing he did not like about it was that the king did not get to choose the queen, and he felt that with his luck, he would be embarrassed by whoever she was. Someone from the church with the initials D.A., who shall remain nameless, was sure hoping she would be queen, regardless of who was king. The royal couple presided over the Winter Wonderland Ball and was present when all of the big final trophies were awarded at the town square. Alex knew both of this year's winners, high school seniors, as was required. To his disappointment, they acted as though they did not know him.

Dad had both of the kids help him make a snowman in front of the shop. They used shovels to make a mammoth mound before they started to cut in to make the shape. When they were done, it looked more like a jumbo white snow woman. She stood all of ten feet tall when she was completed. She had the typical carrot nose; black coal eyes; a rainbow–striped scarf; and a few extra accessories for added detail. The kids got a surprise the following day when they found that Dad and Mom had carved a good–sized tunnel hole near the bottom of the snow woman. She was now holding a stick with a sign attached that read in big letters, "Home of the Church Mouse." A piece of fuzzy red yarn went down from the sign, into the tunnel hole, and up the back to connect to the back side of the sign. They said it went all the way through to discourage anyone from just pulling it back out. It was meant to be more like a red directional line from the sign to where the church mouse lived. Alex got smart and found enough pieces of rock he had collected to use with a Lionel train set he had to make the tunnel look a lot more like a home with a rock–trimmed edge and thus stand out a little more. With the rock, people did tend to notice it more. Lighting the hole from behind also helped, because the light shone through the hole as well providing backlighting for the whole white mass. Kaitlyn was determined they should go to the pet store and buy a rubber mouse but mom and dad vetoed it, saying that it would disappear in one night. Alex suggested freezing it inside a container of water; but Dad said it would still disappear, as many animals are scavenging the snow for morsels. More than once, people commented on the Church Mouse at the shop. Someone even bought one and asked Dad to label it appropriately. To Dad's surprise, a picture made it into the church section of the local paper, quoting Pastor McGregor as saying that his Church Mouse had gone on sabbatical to the Holy Land and would not be attending the winter carnival. Although it was in jest, the picture was perfect, and Dad framed a copy and hung it on the shop wall, along with the two pictures of his kids in their events. Kaitlyn made a small label and put it above the snowman in the picture so that it now read, "Snowman Visits Holy Land." Pastor McGregor happened to drop by and notice the label himself. Everyone laughed when he said, "Oh my. Does that means they'll soon be selling snowman holy water in the Holy Land?"

The Thursday after the carnival, Pastor called and asked Alex if it would be possible for him to teach the third and fourth grade Sunday school class this week. He was told that nothing fancy was required; he could just keep it simple and tell them a story. He might have as many as twelve students. Alex said yes. When Sunday came, Alex not only had his story ready, he had props that would help the kids learn the lesson in the story. There were seven kids in the class that day. *It will work out perfectly,* he thought, as he gave each kid a small piece of paper drawn to look like a healing wound. He sat them all in two rows facing him and then began the story.

"My name for the rest of this class is Naman. Today, you are going to help me tell my story. I work as the captain of the army for a king named Aram. The problem is that I'm sick. I have, in this true story, a disease called leprosy. Now I want each of you to come up one at a time and stick your piece of paper somewhere on my skin. That is what leprosy looks like, sores on the body." One by one, they each came up and, with help getting some tape from Alex, or Naman, each stuck their wound somewhere on bare skin. By the time they got about half done, they figured out that they could use more than just his arms, and Naman now had wounds on his neck, cheek, and forehead. He made the perfect specimen of a sick captain, with no cameras around to capture the event, just children's minds that would never forget it.

Alex began to speak, "My king, the king of Aram, has sent ten talents of silver, six thousand shekels of gold, and ten changes of clothes to the king of Israel, asking him to see that I am healed. The king of Israel got so frustrated at the request that he tore his clothes and said, 'Am I God?' Now, Elisha, a man of God, heard the king of Israel had torn his clothes and sent word for him to send Naman to him. He could tell him how to be healed. They called me and I went to his house in my chariot. He didn't even come out to talk to me. He sent a messenger who said to me, 'Go and wash in the Jordan River seven times, and your flesh will be restored to you, and you will be clean.'"

"Now, let me tell you, the river Jordan is one cold, dirty, muddy, brown river, so I can tell you that's not something I wanted to do. I mean, the rivers in Damascus, they flowed nice and clean. Why did I have to dunk my head in the river Jordan? Would any of you want to go hold your nose and dunk your head in that dirty river Jordan?"

"No!" was the immediate response.

"Okay. Then let me tell you, today's lesson is about doing what God wants you to do to heal, so I need you to help me on this one, okay?"

In unison, they said, "Okay!" because he had indeed captured their attention with his paper leprosy sores. "I'm going to go down to the river Jordan, and you're going to come with me, and every time I point at you, you're going to say, 'Because God told you,' And that's because God told me through Elisha, the man of God, to wash seven times. Okay. Now let's practice this. One, two, three," and he pointed at seven little kids who were immersed in the story and certainly had no trouble saying, "Because God told you."

Alex traveled around the room in his imaginary chariot twice and then told them that the Jordan River was just over there behind their chairs. They turned in their chairs as they watched him remove only his sandals. He said the water was so cold that he was not wearing just a bathing suit, and they laughed out loud. He stuck his foot in and gave them a freezing look like he could not believe how cold and muddy the water was.

"Oh yuck," Naman said. "I can't do this. Why should I do this?" And he pointed at the kids. Nearly in unison, some of them forgetting it was a cue, they said, "Because God told you."

"Okay, okay," Naman said. "I'm going in, but I am not dunking under the water." He carried out all the actions of going all the way up to his shoulders and then came back out of the water only to show the kids that he was still covered with scabs. "They're not gone yet," he said to the kids. "I was supposed to do that seven times, and I am supposed to hold my nose and go under." With that, he had all seven kids stand up so that he could use them to count each of his seven times going under the water. He proceeded back into the water and ducked one, two, three, four, five, six, and quickly came back out shivering and complaining while six of the kids in his class got to sit back down. When he asked the kids what went wrong because he still had his sores, it was little Peter, still standing, who said, "You only did it six times. God told you to do it seven."

Naman proceeded back into the water again, only this time he hesitated when he held his nose, asking, "Why should I do this again?" Now they were definitely in unison: "Because God told you!" And he quickly went under and managed the greatest of moves, removing all pieces of paper before he stood back up and walked out of the water, his back facing the kids. When he turned around, it was little Peter who once again spoke, "I told you to do it again."

With that, Naman asked the kids why it worked and pointed to them all. "Because God told you," was the immediate response. As the response rang out, Pastor McGregor poked his head in the door, having noticed that it had gotten a little loud in there. Alex was quick to seize the opportunity to have the kids teach the lesson. "Why do we do the things the Bible tells us to do about healing?" he said and pointed at the kids, who didn't miss the cue and said, "Because God told you."

"I think we need you to teach more often, Alex," Pastor said, smiled, and closed the door.

Since time allowed, Alex talked to them a bit more about being obedient to what God asks them to do. He told them that there was a price people paid called disease for not doing what they know is right. It is our act of disobedience or things we know that we did wrong, that causes us to feel separation or a part from God and bring dis ease to our bodies. Then he told them briefly how his arm had healed because he believed that God as Love flowed through him to help him participate in his healing, and it healed in half the time.

# Chapter 11

When spring took hold, the ground became visible around the forest trees. The deepest shades of evergreen in the trees prevailed throughout the harsh winter season; however, when the snow melted to where the ground was visible, the deepest greens became so many shades it would take a book just to show them all. Although you knew that everything froze solid, buds began to form on pussy willow trees, and the magic called spring unfolded. To visitors, it became clear that in spring, all the possible shades of green appeared like a patchwork quilt covering the forested hillsides as new growth broke forth into praise of life.

One year, when Alex and Kaitlyn were young children, Grandma played a game with them. They were told to pick only the freshest of pussy willows which started to come out just before Easter, and place them behind her potbellied, cast–iron stove. What they were lead to believe was that if the right branches were left there long enough, a kitten would come out. Sure enough, one day there was a little jet black kitten with the slightest white spot right next to his nose. Grandma named that kitten "Spot" because of the white mark.

Before Spot was a year old, feline leukemia came into the area, and Spot became a victim. After that, Grandma didn't want the children to bring any more pussy willows to her house. Alex and his sister eventually outgrew that fable, but every year the pussy willows always reminded them of little Spot, despite the short time he was with them.

It had been years since Mom's sister Margaret, better known as Meg, had come to visit. Today Mom announced that Aunt Meg was coming again, arriving on Tuesday. The last Alex had heard of Aunt Meg, she was in school studying alternative therapies. Alex figured he was ten years old when Meg was there before. Two weeks after Easter, Alex celebrated his fifteenth birthday. She would certainly find him very grown–up for his age, and a very deep thinker, even about subjects for which she herself had searched for answers. It was Kaitlyn and Mom who went to Presque Isle to pick Meg up at the airport. When they returned, Alex found that his aunt had not changed much. She was wearing a two–piece suit with a colored blouse under the jacket. Her short, brown hair showed not one hair out of place. She had learned to do makeup like they do on television actresses; her eyebrows looked as though they had been moved or changed in some way to make different lines on her face. Her lipstick was appropriate, for those who liked that sort of thing. It was her fingernails that excited Kaitlyn.

"Alex, Auntie Meg has acrylic nails! They're not even real!" she told her brother.

The only people Alex could think looked anything like Meg now were television lawyers, or maybe TV doctors. He was pleased when the first thing Meg did was change into a baggy pair of casual pants, and a sweatshirt that read "Cape Cod," before coming back downstairs, saying, "Oh, I finally feel like I'm home." In just a few minutes, she had transformed from a professional with a briefcase, to someone who might be seen out running. Seeing the look on the kids' faces after her transformation, she remarked, "Oh, really.

Believe me when I tell you I only dress like that," pointing up the stairs, "because I'm a woman. It's all about my image back at work."

There would be no serious conversation that first night. Dad and Mom brought out a special bottle of wine they kept in the closet. The three of them had a very casual and relaxing evening as the bottle went to empty. Alex and Kaitlyn were invited into the group when both had their homework finished, right about the time the marble cake was served. Kaitlyn had helped Mom make it on Sunday afternoon, knowing that Auntie was coming.

The next day, Wednesday, Meg spent a good deal of the morning discussing what features she'd like to have on a laptop Dad was going to set–up to be ready when she turned it on. There were a couple of things that he was going to design in that would help in her business. Mom had gone into work, but had managed to have all day Friday off, giving her and Meg a good early start to a longer weekend before Meg had to go home on Sunday.

Auntie Meg picked Kaitlyn up at school on Thursday and took her shopping. Dad didn't seem thrilled when she came home with plastic stick–on fingernails, but he decided to remain silent for now. He may have figured that the fire engine red would give her all the attention she wanted and that she would grow out of this stage, or at least lose the fake nails.

Mom came home with a bag of Chinese food that she had earlier talked to Dad about. All that the kids were told ahead of time was that she was bringing supper, and that they were to set the table with everything but food. This was going to be quite a treat, because the only time Mom brought home Chinese food was when they had company and Mom worked all day. Mom prided herself on her home cooking, but she did not like to keep people waiting for supper. After dinner, and after everyone had helped to clean it all up, Alex found Auntie Meg sitting alone in the living room and was finally able to ask her his first serious question.

"When you studied alternative therapies, were you taught much about memories?"

"Memories? In what way do you mean, Alex?" Auntie responded.

"I mean, how people store them, use them, and how to change them and make them better."

Meg smiled and said, "Your Dad told me that you've developed a fascination with, and maybe even a gift for understanding a lot about memories. The one thing we know for sure is that we all have them."

Alex laughed and asked, "But aren't they all just energy that we store somewhere inside?"

"Yes, they are energy, energy that we give our attention to, and the way they get stored relates to which representational system in the body we were using at the time we focus that attention. For example, I could name a smell and you could find a memory, like molasses and sugar."

"I know those cookies," Alex was quick to respond.

"What about autumn smoke?"

"Leaves burning?" Alex answered, as if questioning whether it were the answer she was seeking.

"Well, consider that autumn smoke could also have been a fire you observed one autumn, or a burn at the town dump, depending on where you were at the time you registered that smell you now refer to as autumn smoke."

Alex decided to test Auntie. "What if I said autumn smoke in the spring?"

"Grass fire?" she answered back, not sure now what he was looking for.

"So you changed it because I added another couple of words?"

"Yes, that's how memories work. It takes only a minute amount of any one thing to create change. If you add a lot of things, it can become something totally different."

Alex spoke next. "I've learned that if a person will think of a bad memory that really bothers them, and I give them words that can be used to change the memory as it was stored, the stingers will be removed, or I should say, the pain is gone."

"Your father said something about that. I think it's great. We'll have to talk more about that if we have the time. He said you have a process you use, a way of rewriting a memory, which seems to work the same way he rewrites computer programs. It appears that what fascinates you, Alex, is more about what memories do. Remember that memories are only what you have given your attention to. How they continue to produce a response in your life is based on what parts you continue to pay attention to. Let me just take one thing. Have you ever had a cavity or a chip in a tooth?"

"Who hasn't?" he said.

"Remember how your tongue just could not leave that spot alone until it was fixed? Remember how after that, the sensors on your tongue just seemed to forget all about it?"

"Yup."

"Well, memories are very much like that. The ones that you absolutely love tend to get stored away so that they're really not thought about very much, until, of course, you decide to pay attention to them again or something happens that triggers them back into your remembrance. Those bad memories that bother you tend to get more thinking time because they still bother you. You pay attention to them, and they remain bad, or even seem to get worse."

"Unless you change them," he added.

"Yes, Alex, since energy goes where you focus your attention, what you put your attention on expands in consciousness as energy, and because of that energy, people tend to attract more of what they don't want until the bad memories heal. Let me put it another way. Right now, I want you to *not* think about the number one. Don't see the number one at all, don't spell the number one, don't say the number one inside your head, do not think one. Tell me, Alex, what are you thinking about?"

"One," he replied, a chuckle in his voice.

"So, if what you were thinking about was the one thing that you did not want in your life, you would find that you would actually attract more of whatever it is because it is what you are thinking energetically, and thinking attracts. Does that make sense?"

"Yes, we practice making basketball shots using only our minds. In our thoughts, or mind's eye, as the coach calls it, the ball goes through the hoop with only a swoosh sound."

Meg asked, "And does doing that help you?"

Alex replied, "The coach says we improved our shooting by 21 percent."

Meg said, "So you thought about what you wanted and got the desired result?"

"Yes."

"Now, Alex, consider all the people whose thoughts focus on what they don't want, and yet they attract exactly that. From studying people as we do, we know that there are those who know exactly what they don't want in their lives. The problem is, as much as they don't want to, they expend time and energy thinking, trying to prevent that thing from happening. Because it's what they are thinking about, it is what they attract. Most of these people are afraid, for example, of making a mistake because they believe the price they would have to pay is worse. The world around them, in the mean time, becomes for them, one mistake after another in order to meet their needs energetically to prevent them. Alex, you can not prevent something you are energetically attaching to. Since energy expands in consciousness all around you, it still is there to be attracting more of what they don't want. These people have a cavity in their memory system; they never stop paying attention to it, and soon the cavity is much bigger and much worse, and then more cavities appear. The worse it gets, the more they seek to protect themselves from what they don't want. That memory energy expands in consciousness, and it only gets worse."

"So how do you rewrite their program?" Alex asked, using the computer analogy.

"In some cases, you have to take them out of the environment that produces the results they keep getting. But regardless, the point is that they think about what *was,* and that only serves to attract more of the same. What they must learn to do is pay attention to what they desire, and not what they seek to avoid."

"And you know how to do that?" Alex asked.

"Well, that is something that has been studied for years. It is just one part of what we seek to understand more about, and we certainly don't have all the answers. Many people, Alex, don't even realize they only search for the worst in everything. The problem is that they find it, which makes it even tougher to ever see the good. They come to believe that there is no good out there to be found. Then they get to where they don't even love themselves. They do this because when they find no good outside, which they see as a reflection of whom they are, they then believe that there is no good inside."

Alex then made a statement as his dad and mom walked in to join them. "Love is the one thing that heals people. Because love never changes, love changes whatever it comes in contact with."

"I am not sure exactly what you mean by that." Meg answered.

"Love," Alex responded.

"That's right, Meg," his dad broke in. "Alex seems to be on a path these days to study the power of love to heal. Did he tell you his broken arm healed in half the time necessary?"

Alex broke in, "All I did was love my bones to life; every time I thought about my broken arm, I remembered that it was me in there," he said, pointing at his arm, "and it healed completely in three weeks. I guess if I had thought about how much it couldn't heal, it would have taken longer than six weeks like sick people do?"

"I wish it were really that easy," Meg responded, as if it weren't really the answer at all.

Alex wanted to talk more, but his parents wanted to serve dessert and not make Auntie Meg talk about her work anymore. She was supposed to be relaxing and on vacation. As the night wore on and more general conversation took over, Alex's mind remained on what Auntie Meg had said about people focusing their attention on what they don't want, and getting even more of it. Because that was memory energy the way he perceived it, he couldn't help but wonder what would happen if, instead of hating something and producing more of it, they loved it. If they loved it, would it change? Would it cause something else to happen? Love never changes; however, love changes everything it comes in contact with. The question would be, how do you get people to love what they hate, and to understand that when they do, it would have no choice but to change? One thing he had already learned was that when you love a good memory, it made it feel even better; when you love a bad memory, it changes. He also knew that love changes the process and structure of healing. He had physical proof of that. Alex hoped he might have the opportunity to sit with Meg on the front porch swing at the shop and have a porch chat. There, he could teach her about love changing things like a drink, a cloud, or even people's bodies, just as it had his broken arm. He felt sure that she would understand.

On Friday morning, Mom and Meg were up and out of there so fast, hardly anyone had time to say a word. Mom said it was a girls' day out, and that those staying home would be lucky if we saw the whites of their eyes before dark. She told Dad he was on for taking care of dinner because she had made no arrangements. Dad and Kaitlyn made French toast for breakfast, and then they were off, Dad driving Kaitlyn to school while Alex rode his bike.

Kaitlyn would be thirteen in less than a month and was already acting the part of a teenager. If you asked her, she was closer to sixteen. Dad liked having his little girl grow up. Mom, on the other hand, spent many nights in private conversation with Kaitlyn, making sure she became a lady, and talking about issues she needed to be made aware of. One time, Alex asked if Mom had given her the birds and bees lesson yet. She acted dumb like she had no idea, so Alex said, "Touch a bird, it flies away. Touch a bee it stings you!" and left it at that.

Early that evening, Dad drove Alex and Kaitlyn to a restaurant where the servers wore roller skates, and told the kids that they could order whatever they wanted to eat. Mindful of what the evening yet beheld, Dad advised Alex to be sure to drink a milk shake and eat something really greasy to slow him down. This night brought a special rivalry game at school to determine who won the annual Milk Bucket Award. Although basketball season was over, this was a game the participants anticipated. This was one of those events that they would not be selling tickets to. It was the dads against the lads. Any dad with a student in high school could be on that team, while any student with basketball skills could be on the lads' team and get play–in on the rotations. That included any varsity players. All things considered, this was not the most exciting game of the year. This game was in addition to the one for the Potato Head Award, also kept in the school's trophy cabinet, a competition between the varsity basketball team and any of the teachers in the district. That one was much earlier in the year and drew a bigger crowd.

The number of spectators was light tonight because of the first soccer game of the season the following day. Bearing in mind that the other side of the bleachers was held for the opposing team, everyone local sat on the home side. Kaitlyn was in the stands in their usual location. You could see that she was trying to hold two seats for Mom and Auntie Meg. It was obvious whose families and friends were there by the sounds that came from the bleachers. Even Kaitlyn could be heard screaming for her father to win. Occasionally the proverbial cow bell was heard to be banged by Lisa the Town Librarians who never seemed to be absent from a game. She and her best friend Melissa made the best adult cheer leading squad in town, regardless of the game. A former college basketball coach was on the dads' team so that he could give them pointers during play. The boys didn't think the dads had a chance, but with a few judging violations overlooked by the referees, whose buddies were playing as dads, the lads only won by a small margin. The final score was 47 to 39. One thing the dads were good at was blocking plays without getting a foul called. The lads played hard because the last thing they wanted to see was the Dads' team name with this year's game date engraved on the trophy. When the game was over, Jon and Alex both said, "Race you to the showers, Dad," to which Dad instantly replied, "We're going home now! See you in the truck." He was exhausted and sweaty, and only wanted to crawl directly from the shower to his bed.

Alex's best friend Jon got eleven points in the game, not playing nearly as well as in varsity games during the season. John remained quiet on the ride home, perhaps lamenting his less than impressive performance on the court. When Dad said that it had been a great game, and that he thought both boys played hard and well, Jon still didn't perk up.

# Chapter 12

Saturday began slowly, no one eager to jump out of bed. The smell of coffee was what got Dad up. Mom got up and started the coffee, only to climb back into bed and fall immediately back to sleep. Dad assumed Mom was up, and had not even noticed her beside him as he crawled painfully out of bed and made his way out of the bedroom and down the stairs. Dad was hurting just about everywhere from his over–zealous play in last night's basketball game. Once he made it to the kitchen for coffee, discovering that Mom was not there, Dad stayed up because it was easier than going back upstairs to bed. By the time Kaitlyn and Alex finally made it downstairs, Auntie Meg was enjoying an English muffin and a cup of coffee with Dad in the family room.

"Fend for yourself," Dad said.

They did just fine. The only thing off limits was the remains of the chocolate cake. Kaitlyn chose an instant whole grain cereal, while Alex had an oversized bowl of apple and cinnamon oatmeal, his breakfast of champions. Alex started his usual Saturday biking exercise right after breakfast. Coach Crooker handled it well when Alex did not try out for his soccer team as Alex liked biking more than another team sport for now. Alex explained that he would be there for baseball, just not soccer this year. He had not done the full triangle route since the time he went to pay the man at the gas station for the IOU, and discovered that they had no idea who Alex's tow truck driver was. He knew he had the right shop. He was told that they never used IOUs, ever, and had no idea who the man was. Alex put the money in the missions offering the next day, after remembering that the man who had helped Alex suggested that he do just that. It felt strange to realize, as Mr. Parsons had told him, that "Angels do that." Mr. Parsons had also said that Alex might never see him again, although at the time he was sure he would, because he had an IOU that he had to repay.

Today, with company around and Alex hoping to talk a bit more, he just stayed in the neighborhood. He called Jon to ask whether he wanted to ride, but he said he really did not feel much like doing anything. He wasn't even going to the soccer game. But then, neither was Alex or any of his family.

Later in the day, Auntie Meg got up from a nap and asked whether Alex wanted to pick up where they had left off. What he wanted to do was go over to the shop and show her how to melt clouds; however, there was not a puff to behold. He was out of raspberry soda, so even that would have to wait. She asked whether Alex would mind if they took a cup of coffee over to his dad. He, of course, had no problem with that, but wished even more that there had been clouds. Maybe they would come. Meg made two big cups of coffee, and Alex poured a glass of milk. When they arrived at the shop, she talked to William for a bit, making sure that the new laptop he was nearly finished with would do everything she needed. Alex waited out on the swing, and finally, she came out to the porch.

Meg spoke first, "Alex, I thought if you would like me to, I might tell you some of the things about human behavior that we find most interesting."

"Should I take notes?" Alex asked, realizing that she was smart, but was a resource who would be heading back home on Sunday afternoon.

"You can if you want to, but I think you'll understand all of what I can teach you today. If not, ask good questions." Then Meg dove right into the details of her planned discussion with Alex on human behavior.

"Everyone lives in their own little, unique model of the world, Alex. Just as a street map is not the actual streets themselves, we make internal representations of everything that happens to us, using pictures, sounds, feelings, smells, tastes, and words. Two people experiencing the same event can describe it almost as two totally different events because of the two different representational systems they used to store the memory. A good example would be two kids at a baseball game; one comes home with the impression that it is a place you go to get a cold drink and a good hotdog. For the other kid, it is where you go hoping to catch a fly ball. They both attended the same game, but what they stored as the experience is not the same. The way each kid stores the game is called their personal internal representation."

"Because of the way we each store information individually and differently, we do not act or respond directly on what is happening around us. Instead, we act on our perceptions from the internal representations we have already created, which relate to what is going on around us. I guess the easier way to say it is that it is not the outside world that we see; it is what we perceive it to be, based on internal representations that we already created. I guess I could best say it this way: the outside world is a mirror reflection of what is on the inside. That's the way it is for all of us, Alex. No matter what is outside of ourselves, we only have the representations which we have stored within to use to create something the way you believe it to be. The world is full of things you know nothing about however, once you hear about them, it will be what you already know that will help you put your belief together as to what it really is. Even then, you may not be right, in other people's beliefs. Because of that, Alex, people will make the best choices they can in life, based on what they have stored as perceptions of truth about what they are dealing with. In other words, they are doing the best they can with the resources they have, and we have to let them. They may be making mistakes, however it is their belief that they are right and it is not our job to change that. At times, I sure wish they would let me just be me as well. I am sure you feel the same way."

Alex nodded and chuckled as if her statement was certainly true. Then Meg began to speak again. "Because everything comes from inside, like we've been talking about, people have everything they need to solve all of their problems. However, what most people do is look to the outside world for all the solutions, without realizing that the answers lie within. There is also always a desirable solution within to every problem. It is inside that we have the resources, and it is inside that the solution comes as a positive intent. Alex, because all people have their own internal representations, other people fail to realize that the response you are getting back from someone when you are talking to them is equal to the communications you are sharing. They are responding with the best of their ability according to their perceptions, based on the information you are sharing with them and what they have stored inside. You say baseball to one kid, it means hot dogs; to another, it means catching a ball."

Meg paused for a moment, trying to discern whether she was going in any direction that made sense. She had not had the opportunity to talk about things like this to anyone this young before, and did not want to be over his head. She continued. "Now let's add to that. Behind every thought or action there is always a positive intent. No matter what anyone does, although we may assume that it does *not* have a positive intent, for them, it *always* has a positive intent."

Aunt Meg thought back, noting that she had always made memories and meaning in life an inside job. Then she remembered back to what Alex's dad had said about Alex rewriting memories, and added, "Memory and imagination use the same neurological circuits, Alex, so they potentially have the same impact. That is why you are getting so good at changing memories, according to your Dad. You're using imagination to rewrite a bad program, and it works as though it is a new memory being stored. For that, I commend you. It sounds like you're onto something really good there."

Coming out to the porch from the shop, Dad announced, "Ready if you are."

Meg got up and followed him back through the door to see his latest creation for her. Alex followed right on her heels. He wanted to make sure she got a church mouse to go with her laptop. Although Alex brought up the subject of a new mouse, Meg seemed to feel that she had something at home that would work just fine. She just had not brought it with her.

Alex wished he had taken notes on what Meg had said. He knew that she was validating what he had learned and that it did work. Meg would be leaving for the airport after church the next day, so Alex was glad he'd had the opportunity to sit and have this discussion time with her.

Sunday came, and church was as much fun as ever. Alex saw Jon when he'd first arrived with his mom, but before they even made it into church, she felt his forehead and said, "I'm taking you home." Jon looked a ghastly white, and Alex could see that he didn't feel well. Alex would check on his friend later on, but it looked like Jon was coming down with something.

It was fun being a family of five for church, with Auntie Meg sitting between Kaitlyn and Alex. When they were taking the offering, Auntie Meg whispered to both kids that she would consider coming back at Christmas. She hadn't told them what it would take to get her back, but Alex planned to ask her after church because he wanted her back; he was loaded with questions. Pastor gave one short sermon that day, ending by asking three members to give special testimonies of what church camp had meant to them. The season for church camp was fast approaching. He also said that the testimonies had to be really good because at the end of the service, they would be taking a special second offering to help defray costs for those needing assistance with the camp fees, and half of the money that came in would be going to the maintenance fund to get the camp ready.

Mom was one of the three who spoke, claiming that she had

actually attended more church camp weeks than anyone else at church that day, since Mabel Kitchen, the cook, was not present. Mabel was really having trouble with her back from a fall on winter's ice. Her injury might even require that she be replaced as head cook this year. Mom talked about the joys of being bug–eaten, causing much scratching to break out throughout the church. She also talked about attending to the needs of the kids with poison oak. Bees and wasps also made their visits, attacking kids whether they were allergic or not. She rarely had need to send campers home, and she found great comfort in being able to help them and keep them all still at camp. The reason she talked about all the bugs is that there was so much screening that needed to be repaired on doors and windows, with no money to do it.

Mom described the latest additions to the new restroom buildings last year, and then reminded them of the good old days way back, when the only bathroom was an outhouse at the end of the longest path into the back woods. The paths were long in order to keep the obvious away from the tents and cabins. There was a sign at the entrance that read, "Burma Road." Girls and boys each had their own long, private path and the same sign. The most polite way a child had of asking to be excused was to say, "I need to go to Burma." It was polite, and everyone accepted it. There was no other mention of it, but there sure was a stench that hit fifteen feet from the building. People would always put off going to Burma as long as possible.

Now, as calm and collected as a church audience can be, snickers started before she even got to give the punch line, as there were several there who remembered what happened one August night. It was what they called Missionary Revival Night, patterned after those old–time tent revivals. It was the night of the biggest gathering in the wooden building they called the meeting hall. That was before they built the combination dining hall and meeting center, now known as the Cafatorium. Mom estimated that there were as many as two hundred fifty people there, including those from all around the area, to hear the guest missionary speaker. His introduction included his impeccable credentials, having come from a missionary family and having served four full missionary terms overseas himself. After he was introduced as the speaker, they sang one more song to give the night the tone of the old camp meetings and revivals. The song was "Victory in Jesus." When all of the verses had been sung, everyone sat down, eager to hear what this missionary would share. Dressed in some of the most colorful clothing imaginable, which represented his last missionary term in Tibet, he came to the podium. As his opening sentence, he said, "Tonight's message is about my missionary father. It is titled: 'Why Paul Spent Seven Years in Burma.'"

"Well, needless to say, the kids lost it first," Mom tried to say over the roar of laughter that was now running full pitch. When it calmed enough for her to speak, she said, "The missionary thought he had said something out of order, thus it took some time for the director of the camp to bring back enough order for things to continue. Even then, and you know what I mean, the snickers would start every time that word came up in his sermon, as people found it hard to contain humor so contagious. The missionary heard a lot of apologies afterward; however, he told the people that they had given him a new sermon lesson he could teach overseas as well."

As Pastor came to the podium to make the next introduction, he said, "That was worth $100," pointing at Mom who was about to sit back down in the pew. "Now, do I hear $125?" In his usual style of quick wit, he made everyone laugh. Pastor then introduced the next speaker, a local college student from the University of Maine who was now a senior camp counselor.

Auntie Meg took out a ten–dollar bill from her pocket book and handed it to Alex, saying, "Here. You put this in the offering plate. I'm just glad I was at camp that night!" He didn't realize that bill she handed him looked funny until he was putting it in the plate and noticed that it read 100 on the corner, and not 10. Mom saw it sitting there as the plate passed her and just looked at her sister in surprise. "You deserved it," she said to Mom. "I haven't laughed that hard in years. Your story made me remember that night as though we were there together again."

As soon as church ended, Mom and Kaitlyn went running to the house to get into the car. Auntie Meg's suitcases were already in the trunk. Meg ran up to Dad and Alex and gave each of them a quick hug. Alex could tell from experience that she had not been trained by Grandma. It was only minutes after church ended before Auntie Meg joined Kaitlyn and Mom in the car and headed back to the airport. Alex hoped she would return for Christmas, but he never had a chance to ask her what it would take to get her to come back.

After Dad and Alex made the decision as to where they would have lunch, Dad told him that Auntie Meg would find Mr. Church Mouse in her suitcase when she gets home. Without giving Alex the chance to ask, he said that he had painted the words "Church Mouse" on the bottom. Dad said he put it in when he loaded her suitcases into the trunk after breakfast. Her new laptop was complete, with a wonderful leather case she would hand carry onto the plane. Dad had found a padded, slim line case that looked like a pocketbook that a businesswoman in a suit might carry over her shoulder.

When Mom got back from the airport run, she said, "We're going out to dinner, and I don't care where. I like having a sister, but I still feel like I have to take care of her when she's here. I don't know about you, but I am worn out!" The local family–owned steakhouse Wilson's Ponderosa helped improve her mood considerably.

Although Alex talked about Jon looking sick and going home before church that morning, no one knew how sick he was until Tuesday after his appointment with the doctor. Jon's mother called Alex's mom to make sure Alex was feeling okay. The blood work that the doctor had done confirmed that Jon had infectious mononucleosis. Mom knew all she needed to know about mono to be of help to Rebecca. She also volunteered to see to it that those who may have symptoms that should be checked in their circle of friends were notified that they might be at risk.

# Chapter 13

Jon Campo was not only sick with mono, but his mom said that whatever he tried to eat didn't agree with him. When Rebecca called to report that he had gotten worse and not better, she asked whether Alex had time to walk Jarman, as Jon could barely make it out of bed, let alone walk his dog. Rebecca had her hands full just taking care of Jon while working full–time. Alex said that he would love to walk Jarman, and, in fact, would be happy to come and stay with Jon at times if he cleared it with his folks. All were in agreement. Mom did have Alex's blood checked just because she knew mono was one of those things that could sneak up on a person. The test was perfect. Nothing about Alex health was in question in any way. No one else at church had shown any symptoms, and no one in school had been reported sick yet, so it was unknown where Jon had caught it. Kids from school said it was called "the kissing disease" and tried spreading a rumor that it was from cheerleaders in a rival town. However, those with common sense knew that would not be true of Jon. Rebecca was his girl and she was one of the healthiest cheerleaders ever.

On the first trip Alex made to Jon's, he found Jon really too sick for company. He told Alex to try to come earlier in the day because by afternoon he didn't seem to have much energy left. Alex took Jarman for a combination walk and run using his bike to get the maximum distance out of Jarman and his 20–foot leash. When they came back home, Jarman headed straight for Jon, who was now able to sit up in bed. Jon implored Alex to first wash the drool off Jarman's face. Jarman was still a little hyperactive, and Jon was too weak to satisfy his dog's love of attention, so Alex held him back for a little grooming and calming attention. After Jarman had calmed down, Alex prepared to leave, promising to come back just after breakfast in two days. Jon liked that idea and promised he would rest a lot until then.

Jon kept his promise to rest, and two days later when Alex returned, he actually got up and walked out into the yard to sit in one of the over–sized green Adirondack chairs. Alex had considered talking with Jon about his illness. Because of the strength of their friendship, he felt that it would be okay to tell Jon "the more" about how his broken arm had healed so quickly. Alex started by saying, "Remember when I broke my arm, and it healed in three weeks instead of six, stronger than ever?"

"Yes," Jon replied.

"Did you ever wonder what I did that made it heal in half the time?" Alex asked.

"No," Jon spoke. "I never realized it healed in half the time, I just knew it healed."

Alex continued, hoping that what he had to say might help Jon to heal faster. "Dr. Daniel said it healed in half the time and was stronger than it was before the break."

Jon responded, "Okay. So?"

"So, I know the secret to what made it heal in half the time."

"Yeah, sure … protein shakes, right?" Jon guessed, with little enthusiasm since he and food were not the best of friends again yet.

"Nope. Let me show you something I learned how to do that I had never seen before. I haven't shown it to anyone, not even my dad. You have to promise not to tell anyone for now, or I'm not going to show you."

Without waiting for a reply, Alex took a can of raspberry soda and a clear plastic cup out of his backpack, and went through the whole process of loving a beverage to life. He explained to Jon in complete detail all he was going to do before he did it. He made sure Jon understood that his intention was simply to love someone inside that beverage, just like he had loved his arm, and in so doing, it would produce a healing effect. Alex was so sure of the process that he didn't taste the beverage beforehand; he only had Jon taste it. He told Jon in advance that the beverage would totally change. He would have Jon do the loving, however he felt Jon was not up to it yet, having never learned the lesson and would need to really experience Alex doing it first. When he was done, Jon didn't hesitate to agree with Alex that the soda did change—so much so, that it tasted like cream soda, as though it hadn't even come out of that can.

Then Alex explained that love was what did it. He told Jon, "God is love. Love never changes. Whatever love touches, love changes. That's the secret to healing my arm: love." The look on Jon's face showed that this was a healing exercise that he would need to do himself, like perhaps a trick was being played on him because he was sick and weak. Needless to say, that looked changed when Alex got out the next can and cup and repeated the exercise, only this time with Jon doing the loving. Alex had to open the can because Jon was too tired to pop the top, but he was more than able to love Jarman inside the beverage now that he knew more about the process. The results that time were equal to those produced when Alex was doing the loving.

Jon and Alex talked for a bit about all the changes that took place with the beverages, and then Alex started to change the subject a little. "You know how when people pray for someone who's sick they're always asking God to take it from them, right?"

Jon said, "Yes."

"Well, I'll bet you've heard some of those sick people say that they hate what is wrong with them, right?"

Jon said, "Right."

Alex wondered whether Jon hated what was wrong with him and just had to ask, "Do you hate your mono?"

"Oh, do I ever! You've got that right!" Jon flashed back.

"Well, maybe that's why you're getting worse, Jon. I mean, what I found out is that when you love what is wrong, it changes. When you hate what is wrong, it gets worse. Remember, God is love, so when we love something, we are applying God as love to whatever we are changing. Since the Bible tells us that love never changes, then whatever love touches, love changes. Does that make sense?"

"Sort of?" Jon replied in a slightly questioning tone.

"Well, rather than saying I hate something, and expecting God to take it away, I figured out that God wants us to participate in our healing so that it will all happen faster, like it did with the raspberry drink, and like it did with my broken arm."

"You mean I have to love my mono?" Jon asked almost as though that was still unthinkable.

"Why not?" Alex was quick to reply. "I loved my arm, and it healed in half the time."

There was silence for a couple of minutes as Jon digested all that they had experienced and discussed. Then he found his answer: "Wow! Do you feel that? That's creepy, like something is happening inside of me."

"You're healing, Jon," Alex smiled and said.

Before their time together today was over, they both agreed that this knowledge was not something they could just go share with anybody. Alex taught Jon how to focus on his mono and to know and understand the reactions of his hating or loving feelings about it. He then instructed Jon to think about a time when he had experienced healing before; to find and identify the feelings that he gets when he is healed, and give himself those feelings over the mono feelings that once came. The one thing Alex did not do was get Jon to paint a heart on his body with initials inside. He did, however, finally tell Jon what the initials on his arm cast had meant. Jon was so surprised that he laughed until he started a coughing spell.

Alex went on, "I want you to love your mono, and I want to help." To show Jon that he knew he had the ability to help, Alex melted a cloud. It only took one cloud for Jon to accept the fact that something was truly going on here that related to real love working miracles. He needed one. He was losing weight and strength too fast. They made a pact for Alex to truly love Jon's mono to life, while Jon agreed with Alex that he would use his every waking thought about mono as a reminder to love both himself and his illness. Alex told him that if he got stuck in any way with what to do, he should call his house and ask him to come over. He preferred not to tell Jon what to do over the phone because it helped to see his face when he talked to him. Alex was becoming good at reading people by their facial expressions.

When the boys headed back into the house, Alex could tell that Jon was already better than when they had first gone outside. Alex stayed on and took Jarman for a good run after helping Jon settle back into bed. When he got back to the house, Jon was already sleeping peacefully. When Jon's mom came home that night, he told her that he was feeling better, but said not a word about what he had learned from Alex that day.

It was Friday, two days later, when Alex biked over to Jon's to check on his progress and take the dog for a run. Looking forward to Alex's visit, Jon got dressed and was waiting for him in the yard. Alex could see that the color was returning to Jon's face, and, expecting nothing less, Alex shouted, "Yes!" and gave Jon a high five. The look on Jon's face spoke volumes. They each assured the other that their secret was safe. It was exciting to have such a new understanding of the power *in* and *of* love. They no longer held the old belief that God was someone out there who was expected to just come and take a disease away if they prayed hard enough, without them even participating in the healing. Alex was once again privileged to participate in the healing process. The first time, the healing of his arm, used a process similar to that of healing the beverage. The second time, working with Jon's illness, he employed the same process as when he melted the cloud from a distance. He loved what he was finding love could do. It was one loving time!

Jon had an appointment to have blood work done the following Wednesday. When he went, two weeks after making his pact with Alex, the doctor said that Jon's was a most unusual case. "Considering how bad you had it, son, you should consider yourself very lucky to have healed this much so fast. I've never seen anyone, with as bad a case of mono as you had, make such rapid progress. When you first came in here, you were one sick dude! I almost put you in the hospital."

When Jon was telling Alex, his mom said, "When he couldn't keep food down after the first week of this, the doctor gave him twenty–four hours to improve, or I'd have to take him in for fluids. That was when I called to see if you could help with Jarman. It was right about then that the miracle took place. Praise God. Thank you, Jesus." With this being his senior year, the only thing Jon wanted to do was graduate.

Months later, the best of friends parted for awhile as Jon left to go to the University of Maine, with all of his tuition covered by a full basketball scholarship. He was staying with an uncle a short walk from the school. It seemed things had really worked out well. One note Jon wrote to Alex right after he moved, told Alex that he should not look for much news about him in the papers because it seemed like they had overstaffed the potential team. It came as no surprise to Alex when the caption below the full–colored picture in the Sunday sports section of the Bangor Daily News read, "Jon Campo dunks to up–set win over University of Massachusetts." The picture was taken in such a way it looked like Jon had jumped over the net and was almost looking back down seeing the ball going through. That page got cut out and put in the locker room at school by our new Coach Thurston. "Aim high, boys," was all he would say to us when we next created a team.

In truth, the picture reminded him of afternoons when he and Jon would jump rope until their legs felt like they would burst or when they had jumping contests. Alex's trouble was he usually had his bike there and still had to pedal home after that. Jon would set a light out as far as the cords would reach from inside the garage, and they would take turns marking the bottom of the shadows they would cast on the side of the garage as they jumped up to get a ball through the net. If your ball didn't go in, your mark didn't count. Maybe the reason he made it into the school was because of the height he could jump. No, that was not it. He made it because he could jump and he could get the ball in!

# Chapter 14

Alex and Kaitlyn had each received a certificate for a new bike on Christmas. They were given just a certificate because with so much snow and ice, they would have no place to ride until spring had cleaned the ice off the roads. Although his father's car tires had special studs put in by Butch at the tire store, their new bikes lacked this feature and would require roads free of snow and ice.

It was a Thursday night in March, about the time daylight savings time would soon begin, that Dad, Kaitlyn, and Alex went to Josh Warren's Hardware Store to pick up the bikes he had called ahead to make sure were in. Considering how much Alex liked to ride, he was gifted with a bright blue 21–speed GMC Denali. It was one magnificent bike, with the lightest of aluminum frames, guaranteed to improve every aspect of biking. One of the things his mother insisted on was that it had an alloy water bottle cage so there would be no more strapping a bottle on. Although Alex got to see a picture of it in his Christmas card, it was now even more than he expected.

He had been riding a 10–speed for what seemed like ages. This bike looked like it could last a lifetime. Kaitlyn was pleased that she was not being offered his old bike with one of the center cross poles cut out and re–welded to look like a girl's bike. Her friend Susan had received such a gift and refused to ride it because of its appearance. Although Kaitlyn had ridden it, she hated to even get on Susan's bike because it was made for a man, not a woman. Her new bike was a Huffy Beach Cruiser. It was made so that the rider would feel comfortable sitting straight up. To Kaitlyn, the greatest thing about it was not the whitewall tires, but the hot pink fenders and frame. She would look like a teen straight out of a movie when she rode it. Their old bikes were destined to go to Salvation Army, where they would be renewed in a special program for underprivileged kids.

Since Kaitlyn's bike was the easiest to put together, and Dad had told Alex that he would be required to help, Kaitlyn made it to the streets first. When she was finished riding, she would park it in the garage at the store on a newly purchased floor rack specially made for the two new bikes.

When at last Alex's bike had been put together, with all the gears, wires, and cables working to perfection, he took his first spin. Indeed, it was more than he had ever hoped for in a bike. He had never ridden anything like it, and was not expecting the new ease for speed. In the back of his mind, he wondered whether this was going to hold up his driver's license in any way. He had already saved nearly $800 from money earned mowing lawns and clearing snow. He was adding money much faster now, since beginning to tutor in math and reading. The kids he taught loved him, and since the parents were willing to pay minimum wage, why not? Dad had agreed to put up a sign at the shop after Alex started with his first two pupils. He got two more within two months.

It was still getting dark a little earlier than Alex would have liked, considering a new bike was in his life. He knew that he had just a few minutes to ride that night. Afterward, he parked his racer in the new rack right beside Kaitlyn's pink one. He would dream that night of racing around the country earning trophies enough to fill a cabinet.

When it came time to go to school the next day, both took their new bikes, along with locks and plastic–sealed cable, and safely secured them in the school parking lot. Kaitlyn would ride hers back home after school, but Alex had a baseball game to play that night, so his bike would remain in the lot until the game was over, and then they would load it into the back of the truck. Each of the kids had received quite a few comments on their new rides. The girls talked about how hot pink Kaitlyn's bike was, while Alex's friends talked about the advantages of 21–speeds. For girls it was frills and for boys it was thrills.

When baseball season started that spring, Alex was a starter, playing shortstop on the varsity team. He was treated like a star because he could be counted on for guaranteed hits at bat. Alex and his dad had spent many hours of batting practice in the field behind the office. He got a base hit all but one time at bat in tonight's game. His speed at running also allowed him to catch many a fly ball. Alex played well, and his dad would tell him that he was proud of him, despite the fact that they lost by three runs to their fiercest rival. Alex knew that there hadn't been a thing he could have done differently to change the outcome of the game. He was never in a position to hit one that could have brought in the winning run. When Alex's game ended, he got his bike out of the lot and padlocked it into the back of the truck. When they got home, he rode his bike in the dark to the storage garage where he stood it in the rack. Tomorrow would be his first day to take his new bike on a distance ride, and he definitely had plans in his mind. In some ways, he found it hard to believe that he had now had the bike for two days, but had only ridden less than a few miles.

The next morning, Alex awoke to the sound of plows going by. Rushing to the window, he saw before him the magnificence of another coating of unexpected white. Sometime during the night, the winds had shifted, bringing the necessary moisture and cold from Canada to produce this new snowfall. Neither Alex nor Kaitlyn would make it out on a bike that weekend. Even with some good, strong sun, the wetness on the road would only make for a dirty wet streak that they would not want to wear up their backs. Aside from the obvious discomfort, that shiny, black spot up ahead could be a treacherous patch of black ice.

Mom knew how disappointed they both were, so she made it her responsibility to make something meaningful out of their day. With Easter only two weeks away, she announced that they were going to go shopping, with two goals in mind. The first was getting new clothes for church. Alex was in charge of helping to pick out something for Dad, because his day would be spent tending the store. He had a program he was writing and a repair that had to be finished by afternoon. He believed in, and taught, that commitments to others must be met. The second project was the creation of two gigantic Easter baskets for them to deliver on the Saturday night before Easter to the local children's home for orphans. They had done that for the last few years, and Mom had told the home they could count on them again this year. Each child would get a chocolate bunny with his or her name written on the package. There would also be goodie bags for each, containing jellybeans and marshmallow fluff Peeps. Last year, Kaitlyn got upset when Mom said no to adding Kisses to each goodie bag. Kaitlyn won in the end, so this year the children would all get Kisses along with a note from the Easter Bunny telling them that they had to give at least one kiss to someone on the home staff who helped them. Last year, Mom and the kids had the bags all filled and tied up, with the children's names on them, before they remembered the note with the kissing instructions. This year they would plan a little better.

The shopping went well. The Easter baskets, delivered on schedule by Mom, Alex, and Kaitlyn, were accepted with the appreciation of the home's staff. Several other people had brought in bags of goodies; however, no one else had provided anything like this that went directly to each individual child. Whenever they went there, Alex and his family were always grateful to be able to provide for the children, and it made them want to do more.

Easter Sunday began with a very cold sunrise service in the field across from the church. Even though they had hoped to host strangers, there was no one there who didn't know at least one person in their small group. The wind came the long way across the field and blew right into their faces. Pastor McGregor stood facing west, so that everyone would see the sun when it rose. He spoke on the power in the resurrection, but it was so cold that people may have had to make an extra effort to focus their attention on his message. As Pastor preached on the promise of a new tomorrow based on the resurrection, he said, "the promise of a new tomorrow," just as the sun's rays touched the congregants for the first time that chilly Easter morning. He couldn't have timed it better. They clapped in outdoor church! Pastor's message could have ended right there and they would have felt that the Lord had provided all the sermon they needed. In all, the service was only about forty minutes long as it was.

Immediately after the service, a pancake and scrambled egg breakfast was served by six men of the church. Dad prepared the hot beverages, and the others scrambled eggs, mixed pancake batter, and set up tables. There was a lot of food left over, so covered trays were made and sent out to several places where an Easter breakfast might be appreciated.

Between breakfast and the regular morning service, Alex decided to take a quick spin around town on his 21–speed. When he opened the garage door to get his bike out, he heard a creaking sound. He had heard sounds like that in the old garage many times before. Right after Grandma died, they had put a lot of her belongings up in the rafters, and Dad said that even though they held, that wood certainly was stressed. As Alex was backing out his bike, another big gust of wind blew in through the open front door and against the wall on the left side of the garage where the bikes were kept. Apparently that was the straw that broke the camel's back. Alex grew uneasy as the creaking grew louder, and then he heard a sound similar to a gunshot. From directly overhead, one of the cross beams bearing a little more weight than it should snapped, crashed down and hitting Alex. Even though he was aware that he was bleeding,

Alex was greatly relieved that the beam had only caught him on the side of his face and knocked him down, while the heavy contents of the beam fell down all around him. Had it hit him directly on the head, it may have caused life–threatening injuries because of the amount of weight on the beam. Gingerly touching his face, he felt a C–shaped tear on his cheek starting to bleed, and could tell he'd be feeling some deep bruising on his front shoulder area.

Before heading over to church to inform his mother that he needed medical attention again, he thought about what he had learned from healing his arm. He decided to get creative on this accident as well. He grabbed a white towel from a box near the corner and held it against his face, allowing his mind to remember the processes of change he had used in healing himself and others. The first one he decided to use was the one that took him outside the garage in his mind's eye to where the director of a new movie was auditioning him for a stuntman position. A big wooden (foam) beam would appear to fall and catch him on the head. He would be wounded, but still be able to carry on. As Alex was about to open the garage door in his mind's eye, he heard the director say, "Take one." He carried out his instructions for the scene with the realization that fake blood was being used for special effect. "Cut," he heard next. "Okay, let's do that one again. Take two." He continued until he heard the director say, "That's a wrap," and had no idea how many times he had performed his audition for the stuntman position.

Next, he moved to a monitor in his mind's eye, where he was allowed to see all of the takes and present his case as to which one he thought looked best. He especially liked how close the foam came and yet did not really hit him on the head. What he was hoping was that his body would forget some of what had happened and take the trauma out of the injury in the process of restoring the memory. It seemed to feel less traumatic already.

Next, he closed his eyes and looked directly in front of himself to where he could find an image of his once–broken arm, now totally healed, and knew that it possessed the knowledge of what it took to heal. It was to the right and a little up from center in his mental image. In reading some of the material on the Web about studies underway in healing, one thing researchers seemed to like to use as a tool was a time when a person had healed. It was often referred to as remembered wellness. Recalling this, Alex created a mental picture of his face and that gash he had already seen in the broken mirror on the wall. That picture was directly in front of him. Because the healed memory was off–center in his mental image, he took his hand and moved the picture of his cut face directly over the picture he had found of his healed broken arm. Keeping the image of his face in the exact location where the healed arm was, he watched his face go to completely healed, without the slightest imperfection. Upon completion of the process, Alex looked in the mirror again and discovered that healing had not taken place; in fact, he would need stitches for sure. He decided this would be a process which he would use repeatedly until there were no signs of a scar left. Every time he saw his face, he would find the picture of it and move it to the one where his arm was healed. He would watch his face heal in this way; not only heal, but heal without a scar. He believed this would work.

Finally arriving at the church, it was Kaitlyn who saw him first, and then immediately went and found her mother. She told Kaitlyn to find her dad, and to tell him that she was headed home now and would be taking Alex to see about stitches.

As gentle as a mom can be, and as thorough as a nurse can be, Mom cleaned the big C gash and applied bandages. There was no question in her mind that he needed stitches. The tear went nearly all the way through his cheek. She phoned the clinic and told them they were coming in. His shoulder was bruised and abraded, but nothing was broken. The beam apparently had first hit Alex's face, the front of his shoulder next, and then fell to the floor, in front of him. Dad decided that he was going to go with them this time, arranging for Kaitlyn to stay at church with her friend's family. Seeing Alex, his dad was reminded of the many facial wounds he saw during his time at war, but this time it was his son.

At the clinic, Dr. Daniel was once again the attending physician on call. "I see we have our miracle healer here again. What did you do this time, Alex, have a sword fight?" Alex very much enjoyed hearing the doctor use the word "miracle" and replied, "Got hit by a fake beam in a movie audition," without even realizing how easily it came out of his mouth as the memory he had now stored of what had happened.

Dr. Daniel seemed to like that one. "They keep making auditions tougher lately, Alex. It looks like they want you to have real stitches before the next take. Here, let's see if we can get more of this fake blood cleaned off." When Alex heard that, he smiled as best he could against the pain, and went immediately to the process he had taught himself where he changed the healing structure of the wound. Quickly, he was able to watch the cheek heal once more as he overlaid the pictures using the healed arm space. He liked the feeling it gave him of being healed already. Just that, each time he did it, reduced the pain.

Dr. Daniel applied lidocaine next, which helped keep Alex from feeling what he was doing as he sutured the inside of the wound, and then applied sixteen more sutures to the outside. As he did, Alex noticed that the skin in the edges where the lidocaine was not fully working itched. Remembering back to having had cuts and gashes on his arms and legs that healed, he remembered how much they itched once they really started healing. That gave him enough fuel to begin to not only see his face in his mind's eye as healed, but he would feel it itching until it could be called healed and only baby soft skin remained, with no signs of a scar. The stitches were scheduled to come out in eight days so that they could be removed in Dr. Daniel's office during regular hours rather than at the clinic. Alex determined that by then his face would look as smooth as a baby's. All the rest of that next week, he reran his mental audition tape, moved the picture of his face to its healed location in the image, and certainly managed to make it itch more than he would have liked.

Mom sought to change the bandages on the second day, and again on the fifth, and remarked, "Wow! This is looking really good." Alex managed to make it to a mirror after the second day's bandage change, and peeled away the bandages for a closer look at himself. Indeed, it was looking good, and now that new, healing image would be the one he would use to place over the picture of his healed arm. He would also see the new picture in his mind as being the one that itched from healing. After the fifth day's bandage change, he converted that new image in the mirror to the one he would use. He could not help but recognize that what he was doing was working, and working very well. He had had bad cuts before, and remembered how long it took for them to heal. Cuts healing gave him another picture to use, as he pictured them as healed. Thinking of them in only the totally healed state, he moved his face recollections to the location where he saw the cuts healed and there watched the baby skin come into being as well.

When the day came to have the stitches out, Dr. Daniel once again got the biggest surprise, as he was positive Alex would have a railroad track scar, probably for the rest of his life. There were only the slightest signs of the wound remaining after the stitches were removed. Had anyone not known of the injury, they would not even notice that his skin had ever been torn. By the time he had his summer tan, his baby soft skin was fully healed. Alex would have to take his finger and trace the outline of where the wound had been in order to remember it. Even then, he would close his eyes and move the pictures with a promise to himself that no scar would ever show.

Alex had learned well that life is all about the process. Everything that happens to us gets stored as a memory, using a process of identification based on a representational system for recall. Not only had he learned that it was all about the process, but Alex now had more friends than ever in school. The reason was very simple. Alex learned to become love living, and people wanted him to be their friend. They wanted to be around him. The younger ones wanted to be like him. The older ones trusted him and talked to him about things they would never have told others. Seniors in school seemed to forget he was one grade below them. The big question was, what he would grow up to be. For sure, it would have something to do with human behavior and healing.

# Chapter 15

By the end of junior year, Alex's popularity increased when he was named captain of the varsity basketball team. His biking had paid off by strengthening his legs and increasing his running speed and endurance. To Alex, he had thought about becoming a bike racer, but he was not willing to dedicate the hours he knew it would take to do that. He wanted to be like Mr. Parsons and study people.

Late in the spring, he overheard his mother talking with Mrs. Burns, who lived next door to the shop. Mrs. Burns told Mom that her daughter, Beverly, now twenty–seven, would be coming home to stay for a while because she had breast cancer. Her husband had left her just before Christmas last year, so Beverly would be bringing her two young children with her. Mrs. Burns had contacted Mom because she was hoping that Kaitlyn might help with childcare occasionally when Beverly moved back home. Alex wondered whether a porch chat with Beverly could be arranged.

The night Beverly first talked to Alex she had been home for a few days and was set to begin a treatment schedule in just over two weeks. Alex had not really known her growing up, as she was ten years older. From what she had heard about Alex, he was someone everyone wanted to know, and it did not bother her to open up and tell him the truth. For now, she was on a plan to die, and she knew it.

"I have cancer, Alex," she openly spoke, placing her hand right over the spot, indicating that she knew right where it was.

Ever since Alex first heard that Beverly was coming home, he had hoped for the opportunity to speak with her. Even so, he was a little taken aback by her frankness. Alex's reply was indeed strange. "So how are you *cancering* yourself?" he asked.

Without missing a beat, Beverly answered, "That's about the funniest way I have ever heard anyone ask about my cancer. I love it! That does not offend me at all, Alex. I love it! You certainly cut right to the chase on that one. Now let me see if I can honestly find an answer." She paused and then continued.

"Yes, of course I can find your answer. I once was married; now I am not. I am a woman with two small children who were neglected by a husband who was spending more time with his secretary than he was at home with us. I think that about does it. I guess you could call it rejection!"

Inside Alex's head, there was an analysis of what was being said, as he realized this meant she had memories he could help her with, if she would let him. Also significant, she used that big word—rejection—that kept coming up in his research on disease, and especially on cancer.

"Cancer is rejection, according to the studies I have been looking at online," he replied. "I don't know everything about cancer, but I do know you probably have the right answer already."

Beverly responded, "Well, that about sums up the crap in my life, and I don't mind saying I hate it! Having cancer is the pits, and Alex, if it weren't for my kids and my mom, I would have given up already. I hate it! My kids are my reason to fight, and to be honest with you, and with myself, I'm not going to make it; cancer causes death."

Alex seemed to speak again without even thinking about what came out of his mouth. "Does that mean that everyone who has beaten cancer shouldn't have lived?" Beverly looked shocked, so he continued, "I mean, the real question to think about is not what causes death but what causes life and health. People have lived! The way I would think of it is how can facing death now cause you to live as other people have?"

Growing upset, Beverly said, "You really can't know what it feels like to have this inside. I'm sure you've heard this before, so I'm just going to say it. Life sucks, and what I have growing in me …" She stopped and just shook her head no, as if checking inside to make sure she really felt what she was about to say, then added, "I hate it; anybody would."

To Alex, that was like an open door, and there was no way he would pass up that opportunity. He asked, "Can I ask you a question about life?"

"Sure. Ask away, Alex. I think you're one of the most refreshing acquaintances I've had lately. Everyone else is so doom and gloom that I just want them to go away and let me live as I am. I don't know why, Alex, but just talking to you really does make me feel better for some reason."

Alex looked right into her eyes and asked Beverly, "If you had to choose only one of two friends to keep for the rest of your life, and the choice was between one who loves you and one who hates you, which person would you choose?"

She was quick to ask, "Is that a trick question?"

"No. Seriously, which one? You can only pick one. Which one would you choose?"

"Well, I'm not stupid enough to choose the one who hates me—been there, done that. Next!" she said, almost laughing at the ridiculousness of it all.

"So, are you saying that you would choose the one who loves you?"

"Of course I would," Beverly replied.

"Why?" Alex had to ask.

"Why not?" she replied. "Who isn't looking for someone to love them? Isn't finding love what life is all about?"

"I only asked," Alex responded, "because I wanted to make sure you know that love is what you're looking for."

Then he continued, "So if I took you down to Dr. Daniel at the clinic, and he did a scan of your body, he would tell you that you have an energy field that the machine can read that goes like twelve feet or more out from your body, and that everything recorded in that scan is totally you. That is what the machine does, reads your field."

"So?"

"Well, since everything in there is totally you, do you think there is any part of you inside of you that is not you?"

"That is not funny, Alex. Why would I have a part of me inside of me that is not me?"

"So you agree that everything in your energy field is you?"

"Yes, of course! Like I said, I'm not stupid!" she insisted.

Alex continued. "Well, if everything inside of you is you, and you told me yourself that the thing you are looking for in life is to be loved, I was just wondering what would happen if ... " Alex paused, waiting to see if she caught it yet. "If your cancer—since we know it is you—is only looking to be loved as well? I mean, what would happen if ... ?"

Beverly sat staring off into the distance. It took some time, her thoughts a jigsaw puzzle with the pieces falling into a perfect fit, before she looked back at Alex and said, "Why did you say that? It seems right, and yet so strange to think of loving what is wrong in here," she said, again placing her hand over where the tumor was growing.

Alex told her about his arm and how it had healed in half the time expected. He told her about the C shaped gash on his face, and that it had also healed in half the time, showing her where the wound had been. Until he rubbed his finger over the hairline mark that remained, she had not noticed it. He spoke of teaching Jon and others what they could do to help themselves heal, and of the excellent results that were achieved. He did not say a word about healing a beverage or a cloud.

Beverly recognized the wisdom in what Alex was saying. They sat staring at each other for what seemed like an eternity. Beverly finally spoke again, breaking the tension. "I think I'm through with birthdays until you grow up and can marry me!" she said, a beautiful smile lighting up her face.

They both laughed, and Alex began telling Beverly a little bit about what he had learned and used with others about making painful memories stop hurting. She was fascinated by every word he spoke, and so agreed to meet the following day when he would use his lesson page to help her with her memories. He told her that she would not be telling him anything about the memories. She would only be making the changes that he would guide her to make, and she would be the one making the decisions throughout the process. Being in charge of her own life and thoughts was an exciting prospect to her.

The following day, having had more time to think about Beverly's situation, Alex was certain that changing a raspberry beverage was the next right step for Beverly. She needed to experience the power of love to heal. She needed to learn to love her cancer to life. He could hardly wait to get together with her on the porch swing at the shop for their next porch chat.

When he told his mom he was helping Beverly with her cancer and she wanted him to teach her what he had learned, his mom grabbed him and hugged him heart–to–heart. "You're 'called,' son, and don't you ever forget it." Alex said not a word about the fact that she was going to learn to change a beverage. He would tell Beverly that it was their secret learning tool, and trust her to keep it to herself because of its value to her learning process.

By the time Beverly met with Alex, she had already started to use some of the processes Alex had described in healing his arm and face. She had to admit that it was not easy to love her cancer, but since it was her, she was determined to see it through and mandate the healing, if that was possible.

Alex worked her through several memories that she felt needed healing, and she was amazed with the changes, compared to what she originally recalled. Alex told her to rate her worst memories on a scale from one to ten, and to think of the "tens" before he started the lesson page. After they were finished, he asked her to rate them again. All of them went down to a one or a two.

By the time Beverly changed the raspberry beverage, using her tumor to love, of all things, in the beverage to change it, she developed a solid belief that healing would occur; healing could not be prevented.

Over the course of the next two weeks, prior to the start of scheduled medical treatment, Alex did not see Beverly. When she left her doctor's office on the day she was scheduled to begin the treatment, however, she and her mother went straight to Alex's home.

With his parents both present, Beverly gave them all the good news. "They can't find a hint of the tumor, Alex, and they can't find any markers in my blood that say I even had cancer. I am healed!"

Mom cried. She cried because the news of Beverly's healing could not have been better. She grabbed Beverly and gave her an excited hug. Then she hugged her mom. William and Mary offered beverages and urged Beverly and her mom to stay for a bit and talk. They both wanted to hear of all she had learned from Alex, as well as what she actually did that led to her healing. Was it anything specific? They had known too many people who had died of cancer, and were eager to know all that she could share of her experience. She agreed, saying that they had nowhere to go. Dad got out a pad and wrote notes as she talked. They all laughed when she told them about Alex asking her how she was cancering herself, adding that it was probably the most refreshing thing to hear at the time. She said that it left her with no questions as to why she had had the tumor, and recommended to Alex that he never stop asking that question. Beverly recognized that converting a person's disease into a verb by asking how they are "diseasing" themselves, puts the responsibility of participating in their own healing squarely on their own shoulders.

She talked about the way Alex had described the processes he had used to heal his broken arm and his facial wound, and described using the same processes with different pictures. There was no question in her mind that what Alex had told her and taught her had made the difference. Before that, she had believed what the doctor had told her, and had even believed that her mother would be left with the responsibility of raising her two children. She did not mention that she had changed memories using Alex's lessons. What she did say was, "It was when he made me change the flavor in that can of soda that I realized my cancer was in a cell filled with water inside my body and that my tumor had no choice. It would respond to love and it would heal."

Dad looked at Alex with an expression of curiosity that said, "You haven't taught me that one yet." Mom seemed to accept it as just something Alex would do. Alex said that he learned that if he could move pain by staring outward, he could also move love inward and change the soda by staring into it, loving it like he did his arm to help it heal. "I'll show you both sometime," Alex offered.

No one would be surprised two years later when the man Beverly was dating, the owner of Rich's Grocery Store, got to meet her at the end of the aisle at the church. She would set the wedding day so that Alex could be one of the groomsmen.

# Chapter 16

Alex never stopped studying human behavior. With each person he helped, his desire to help others only grew stronger. This year, he was a junior. He had made no decision as to where he was going to go to college but he certainly was giving much time and thought to already researching the possibilities. Regardless of which school he would attend, he trusted that it would be on a full scholarship. Academically, his grades were near perfect. Although uncommon for high school juniors, Alex's grades and recommendation letters got him into interviews with representatives from several different schools. These interviews provided him with opportunities to gather information on what each school had to offer that would help him in the areas of understanding people and the emotional structure of helping people heal. He believed that the field he wanted to major in would be psychoneuroimmuniology. He believed that if he started there, he would study evidence of behavior–neural–endocrine–immune interactions, to which he could add a minor that would help him with his more conversational type of healing therapies. It would take some time for him to decide on which path to take that would best enable him to achieve his goals. He was hoping that Mr. Parsons would show up again so that he might get his opinion.

In doing his research on healing, Alex held two thoughts in mind. The first was, *It is all a process.* He knew that it was not what one did; it was how one did it that mattered. The second was, *It is all about love.* That one was sometimes difficult to bring into his thinking because his research findings were so concrete, compared to the more abstract quality of love. It was as though the people doing the research could take it only so far, but when they were unsuccessful in making a double–blind study out of it, the work stopped. He discovered that there was rarely any consideration given to the fact that life as we know it is all energy, a spiritual energy, in and of you. Ultimately, he would discover that what most would call love as spiritual energy was not a part of medicine. Still, his mind would continue to look at every possible process he could find or create. His intention was set on being love living and changing his world through love.

His parents had often found him drawing diagrams using words, lines, and pictures of things he was beginning to understand on a deeper level. He told them it was called mind mapping. He did this even more so after he read that a mind once stretched by a new idea never regains its original dimensions. He knew at the living level of his heart that it was not the words that mattered, as powerful as those words were. He knew that it was all about the process we use within for thinking, and what words did to interact in that process. His mind mapping drawings were often done using words that were opposites. What Alex was searching for, were the processes that he could use to help people do what they truly desired to do, when it was obvious that they actually did just the opposite.

Out of curiosity one day, while looking at all of his notes, he decided to choose just one set of words as a frame of reference for his research. He chose the words motivated and unmotivated. To choose a time when he was motivated, Alex thought about all the hours he and Jon had spent shooting baskets, and how the end results of that effort were greatly increased skills. On the other hand, the annual winter carnival cross–country ski race was a perfect example of what Alex was able to accomplish without adequate motivation. Although he was fairly good at skiing, it was not something that he put much time and effort into, as cold temperatures were not his favorites. Last year's sixth place had been his highest finish ever. Alex decided that this year's race would be his test to see what being motivated would do to his performance, since he naturally lacked motivation to train in the cold. Alex looked at the diagram on his process sheet and then closed his eyes. Somewhere out in front, in the field of vision of his mind, he saw a movie of all the training that he and Jon had undergone to bring him to where he had been this year on his basketball team. It all seemed to be seen straight out in the middle area of his mind's vision, just a little bit above the midline. When he thought about the training, or lack of training, that he put into the big ski race, he found that the mental movie played downward on the left of his mind's screen. Going back to the motivated event in front center, he noticed everything he could about that movie. It was as though the lesson sheet notes had come to life, and he found his energy levels building as he discovered all that he could about his process of storing that memory in that location.

When he was finished, he raised his hand as though it were possible to manually move his skiing movie right up to where the basketball movie was located. He made the picture the same size, distance, and all the other things he knew from his lesson notes. He then created a new movie in which he trained to the best of his skiing ability, all the way through to the gold medallion around his neck. He made all of the feelings of this accomplishment as powerful as they had been with basketball. It was exciting, almost exhilarating, as he combined the memory energy. When he was done, he took a clean sheet of paper and started figuring out what type of schedule he could put himself on that would allow for maximum practice up to the time of the winter carnival. Due to the snow, his bike was in winter retirement, but he was heartened to know that skiing would be a good substitute for his legs' strength training.

No one said anything about Alex spending much more time than usual on his cross–country skiing. It seemed only natural to them. He was athletic, and they all knew he intended to win the winter carnival race—he had made no secret of that. When the weather was too cold or when he was too tired to want to train, he would replay his movie. He had played it so many times that now it would play in the right slot. With progressive changes that he added as his skills improved, he knew inside that he was doing what he truly wanted to do.

When the day of the race finally came, Alex didn't even think about the possibility of not winning. Those thoughts had been gone from his mind for so long, that they would come as a shock if they came back. The day was as bright as a winter day could be, at a brisk 38 degrees, and with only a slight breeze. The lineup consisted of forty–eight high school aged competitors. Robert Ackers was just down the line from Alex. Alex had asked him several times to train with him. Robert had always said it was too cold or that he just didn't feel like it. Although he was great on the hockey team, all that extra weight he was now gaining would not do him any favors in this race.

When the policeman shot the starter pistol, Alex left the starting line in a slow and steady pace, with no emphasis on speed, unlike most of the other racers. He knew from experience that it was a nice, steady pace that would keep him going, and would ensure that he would cross the finish line. Passing most of the others was easy, because they would run out of energy forcing them to slow down. Some even stopped for a breather. Robert Ackers never made it into a position where he had to pass him. It was in the last quarter that Alex learned who his competition would be. The ones he had passed were all strong athletes who were capable of winning the race. The one he had not thought much about was Jorge Kleist whose family had moved there from Denmark before the beginning of the school year. Jorge was a sophomore in school, according to the stories, skied to school regularly when he lived back home in Denmark. Indeed, it was Jorge who would prove to be Alex's strongest opponent. When the thought actually came into his mind that Jorge could win, especially since Alex was running out of steam, he ran his movie while searching for every ounce of additional strength from within.

The newspaper picture of Jorge, Alex, and Michael standing with their metals was captioned, "Awe–inspiring lead wins!" The reason it was awe–inspiring was because, from somewhere within, Alex managed to find strength to draw upon and took such a lead that neither of the other two were even in sight as he crossed the finish line. When he took off for the last push to victory, he never looked back or even asked himself where his opponents might be. He was going to win this race just like he had imagined it. Michael, a long and lanky senior, came in third, and Jorge, who was well ahead of Michael, easily took second.

The following week, Alex had lunch in the school cafeteria with Jorge. Jorge's first question was, "How did you do it?" Their lengthy talk a few days later probably ensured that Jorge would be the uncontested winner for the next two years. Alex told him of the inner tools he used in complete detail. At least Jorge certainly could beat Alex in his next and final year of cross–country skiing if he practiced. Emily Sperling, the captain of the woman's cross country team made it a point to ask Alex as well and realized that the help he presented would work for her in her track races as well. She said it made her whole team produce some consistent rock solid results.

# Chapter 17

Susan was one of Alex's friends whose situation had been the toughest he'd had to work with. She had been on the back of her boyfriend's motorcycle when he hit a cement barrier. She had been thrown clear and only sustained a concussion, but Elias hadn't come out of the hospital alive. It was a few months after his funeral that Alex got to talk to Susan, shortly before Susan's senior year had begun. Because she had listened and was interested in healing her memory of that tragedy, she seemed to come alive again after Alex used his lesson page with her.

Among others whom Alex had helped was Derrick, a classmate who was diagnosed with leukemia during his junior year. Even though he still had the disease, what Alex taught him had helped him through the worst of it. He believed that he would win the battle against his ailment, and was further encouraged because his blood work was looking better each time he went in for testing. He had become good at mentally moving the pictures of his healing the way Alex had taught him. Derrick loved his dog Daisy, and since it was his blood that was diseased, he would lay the hand he patted and sent the love to Daisy with over his opposite wrist and love all the blood that was flowing directly under his hand with the presence of love as energy.

Sometimes it just seemed so easy for Alex to help others, as if it were becoming normal and customary. Barbara, one of the girls who had a crush on him, would fall apart when she had to take a timed exam. Alex said to her, "Humor me, and close your eyes," one day while a group of them were sitting and eating lunch. With a math exam coming up in the next hour, Alex told her, "Now, with your eyes closed, watch yourself as though you're in a movie. See yourself take the exam, and then simply allow your mind to go beyond the successful completion of the exam so that you can stand up and look back at yourself with the test all done—and done correctly—with time to spare." He did not push the issue; he did it conversationally, as though it were normal to talk that way, and then left the subject alone.

With some of his classmates who talked about their problems, Alex would simply begin talking to them with one of his favorite statements: "I was just wondering, what would happen if … " and follow up with a type of command that gave them the option of changing their internal processes to get a result they would like. He would leave it all up to them. The key for Alex was that he knew he was learning how words worked, as well as how to talk to people in such a way they received help and were not even aware of it. Sometimes when they presented a problem, just asking them, what would happen if you did … or, what won't happen if you did … or, even what would happen if you didn't … or, what won't happen if you didn't … would give them accesses to all the internal resources they need to figure out what to do.

Before the day was over, Barbara passed him in the hall at school, and Alex casually asked how her math test went. "Oh, fine. I think I aced it! I was one of the first ones finished, too." She said it as though it was the outcome she expected. It all seemed so normal and natural, just the way Alex wanted it to become with all of his healing conversations. He knew that test anxiety had been a major problem that needed to be healed for some time. Alex replied, "It's all about the process," and kept right on walking to his last class.

When Coach Thurston's son broke his arm, Alex offered to teach him what he knew about healing; however, the coach's belief was that everything healed in due time and that nothing we might do mattered. It was all about what the doctors knew to do, and his son's job was to follow their instructions. Although Alex was becoming well known around school as someone who understood healing in a nearly miraculous way, Alex's offer to his coach went unheeded.

Alex would discover that most people were apt to reject his healing gift, especially the teachers he would meet at his future university. As his junior year came to an end, he felt confident that he would be attending a major university, as so many of them wanted to meet him. Now he had a year to consider all of their scholarship offers. That year would be filled with more research and greater learning by this called–to–serve young man named William Alexander Williams, III. His life would never return to what seemed normal to others. He had a definite pull in very specific directions.

For Alex, it was becoming clearer all the time that everything was energy and involved a process. He saw things from a perspective no one else seemed to discern. People all around were noticing that he was living up to his name as a protector and conqueror. His parents understood why Mr. Parsons had said he was called; it seemed obvious. Alex knew that when he looked at everything as love living, then it was energy he perceived as the life of whatever that thing was. Life was becoming physically spiritual the more he made the decision to be *Love Living*.

You are an infinite being and subject only to what you hold in mind.

—David Hawkins, M.D., Ph.D.

Coming soon: **Healing Alex: The Miracles Last**

—Advanced teachings by Gary Sinclair adding to your ability to live as Love Living; a spirit being having a human experience; learning to break free of destructive attachments in mind, body and spirit. Mr. Parsons does return several times more.

For more information on the work of Gary Sinclair and Celebrate Life, visit the web site at www.HealingAlex.com. Gary is available for private training as well as group speaking engagements. He resides in Southern California where he maintains a private practice.

Previously books published by Celebrate Life and Gary Sinclair:

*Your Empowering Spirit: Yes to Quantum Healing*
*Your Best Thoughts Got You to Here*
*Living in The Land Of La Lar Foo Fue*
*Success ???, I Need a Miracle*